Jill

by

AMY DILLWYN

With an introduction by
Kirsti Bohata

WELSH WOMEN'S CLASSICS

Published by Honno
'Ailsa Craig', Heol y Cawl, Dinas Powys,
South Glamorgan, Wales, CF64 4AH

1 2 3 4 5 6 7 8 9 10

First published in Great Britain by MacMillan and Co, 1884
First published by Honno in 2013

© Introduction Kirsti Bohata 2013

British Library Cataloguing in Publication Data
A catalogue record for this book is available from
the British Library.

ISBN 978-1-906784-94-2

Published with the financial support of the Welsh Books Council.

Cover image © SIK ISEA, 'Frau mit Dienstmagd beim Baden' by
Félix Edouard Vallotton
Text design: Elaine Sharples
Printed by

Contents

Introduction

KIRSTI BOHATA

Amy Dillwyn was scathing about the conventions of romance, "I abhor domestic novels" and books with "too much love" in them. Aged just 17 she imagined providing a different kind of book:

> I am sure I could write a very uncommon finale & I certainly would never write about marriage & 'everything come all right' at the end. I suppose a hero & heroine are necessary evils but why not have a brother & sister for the chief personages? (19 March 1863)

By the time she wrote *Jill*, twenty years later, Dillwyn had done away with heroes altogether opting for a single heroine, with two supporting women for her to admire. *Jill* is a feminist bildungsroman, a story of the moral development of a tomboyish and feisty young girl into an independent woman with a measure of self-knowledge. Dillwyn paints a compelling portrait; Jill is a convincing mixture of cynical disregard for convention and propriety alongside admirable qualities of self-reliance, courage and frankness in telling the story of her life. The sardonic humour and dry wit sustain a fairly improbable story, in which Jill runs away from home, disguises herself as a maid, falls in love with her mistress, and has all sorts of adventures and scrapes. And the novel ends without a potential husband in sight.

Contemporary reviewers identified Jill as "a woman of the period" and Dillwyn is an early example of a New Woman writer – a feminist who sought out new ways of writing about women's lives and predicaments. *Jill* was the fourth and most commercially successful of Dillwyn's novels. Published by Macmillan in two volumes in July 1884, it sold out quickly and was reprinted in September that year. A cheaper one-volume edition was published in December 1884, and in 1887 a one-volume edition was produced for Macmillan's Colonial Library Series.[1] Contemporary reviewers commented on the unusual heroine: "Is the solitary heroine a species known to the human naturalist?" asked the *Pall Mall Gazette*, while the *Academy* welcomed *Jill* as "a somewhat daring, but very successful, experiment in realistic fiction… What is most to be admired, and that is very greatly to be admired, is the direct simplicity of the narrative." The directness and humour of the narrative – the "amusing vein of quiet cynicism" (*PMG*) and the "dry, almost grim humour" (*Academy*) – seem remarkably fresh even today. And Jill as a character captivated the imagination, several reviewers urged Dillwyn to tell more of Jill's story: "'Sequels' are, as a rule, the greatest of all nuisances in fiction; but Miss Dillwyn's readers will certainly expect her to tell them one day of the future of Jill…" (*Academy*). Dillwyn eventually obliged, with *Jill and Jack* in 1887, and even then one reviewer called for a third novel and another for a dramatisation.

Setting
Jill is a slight departure from Dillwyn's earlier novels which were explicitly set in Wales. The home of the

Trecastles – Castle Manor, near Greenlea, outside Sparkton – could be anywhere in provincial Britain, the only hint that it might be in Wales is the name of the postmaster, Jones, from whom Jill purloins the telegram. Trecastle is the name of a place in Powys, and the family name is broadly suggestive of a Celtic west ("tre" means town in Welsh and Cornish), while "Sparkton" seems a fairly apt toponym for the industrial town of Swansea with its history of metal extraction. In *Jill*, Castle Manor is simply a place from which to escape – first to London and then an increasingly exotic and wild Europe. But in the sequel, *Jill and Jack*, the area is better described and there are several features, including a fatal quarry into which a woman falls whilst lost in a mist, that suggest Dillwyn was drawing on her knowledge of the landscape around her home at Hendrefoilan, near Swansea. The trip to Corsica which is vividly described in *Jill* is also based on her own experience; Dillwyn visited the island with her father in 1878.

Form & Motifs

Dillwyn experiments with form in her search for a way of telling a new story. *Jill* is a picaresque novel and the episodic structure allows its author to indulge in a series of sketches of eccentric and absurd characters reminiscent of Dickens – from a lady obsessed with invasive germs, to the individual characters of the six dogs which are, at one point, in Jill's care, to the solicitors whose essence is expressed in their name, Messrs Fox and Snail. Children's rhymes and fairytales also lend coherence to the story. Jill's name is linked to the nursery rhyme, "Jack and Jill", which is supposed to refer to the beheading, during the French Revolution, of Louis XVI and his wife Marie Antoinette. Certainly the nickname is used to suggest a rebellious disregard for convention in this novel and Jill's disapproving mother objects to it as evoking "republican ideas, such as carrying pails of water, rough tumbles and cracked crowns" (p.13). The archetypal fairytale Cinderella, with its evil stepmother and selfish stepsisters, underpins the depiction of the new Lady Trecastle, and her daughters, who banishes Jill to the schoolroom. In a feminist rewriting of the tale, Jill decides to "act the fairy godmother for myself". (p.45) Having no interest in a prince, however, she takes herself off to London, like Dick Whittington, to seek if not her fortune, then an independent living. Most important of all, perhaps, is Dante's *La Vita Nuova* (1295), a medieval poem of courtly love which is both spiritual allegory – how earthly devotion prepares the soul for divine love – and an apparently semi-autobiographical account of Dante's love for Beatrice whom he encounters only twice, once when she is a young girl and later as an adult. Dante's representation of unrequited love particularly appealed to Dillwyn.

Autobiography

Jill is perhaps the most autobiographical of all Dillwyn's novels. Like her first novel, *The Rebecca Rioter* (1880), it is an attempt to play out in fiction Dillwyn's own desire for adventure and change, but in this book she can express her confidence in the resourcefulness of women and her belief that women could and should be given the chance to live independently, outside of marriage. Most of all, however, it is the story of Dillwyn's long, hidden love for another woman.

Aged about fifteen, a young Amy had fallen in love with Olive Talbot (1843–1894), a distant relation by marriage and the daughter of C L R Talbot of Margam and Penrice. Her diaries record the growing importance of her feelings for Olive over the next fifteen years: "I care for her romantically, passionately, foolishly, and try as I might, I cannot get over her." (27 July 1868) The two women were close friends, exchanging letters, visits, tokens of friendship and sitting up into the small hours in each others bedrooms holding long and intimate conversations; in later years they took trips together. But although Dillwyn eventually came to think of Olive as her "wife", it seems that Olive didn't fully return Amy's passion – "I can't make her love me as I love her". (16 July 1870) Small details, which recur in other novels, suggest that Dillwyn is deliberately using her relationship with Olive as a model in her fiction: Jill is the same age as Dillwyn when she feels her first powerful attraction to another woman, Kitty Mervyn, and, like Olive, Kitty is wealthy, distantly related and a little Jill's senior. And of course Kitty does not return Jill's feelings.

Unrequited love
Hidden, unrequited love is a major theme in *Jill*. Acknowledging the pain that goes with it, Dillwyn nevertheless focuses on the morally improving nature of same-sex desire even where the love is one-sided. In her diaries she wrote of Olive that:

> the thought of her seems like a good spirit to me sometimes... helping me on to the time when we may perhaps meet & know each other in Christ... Then perhaps she will know how she has helped me... whether consciously or unconsciously I do not know – but I do know that my love for her has led me always to be better & never to be worse. It has been the good influence of my life – even though I need to pray against it daily lest I

learn to love God's creature more than Himself. (2 March 1871)

And she believed that Olive was "the person who has influenced my character more strongly than any one else". (27 August 1871) Jill may be happy to lie, steal and forge as it suits her at the start of the novel, but this is ultimately the story of how she develops principles and strength of character through her admiration of other women: first the proud but plucky Kitty and then through her friendship with Sister Helena, a lady who has dedicated herself to healing the sick.

Comparing her diaries with her novel, there is further evidence that Dillwyn drew directly on her feelings for Olive in the portrait of Jill's love for Kitty. Dillwyn worked hard to quash her feelings for Olive in the beginning, but confided to her diary that:

> [R]eally it's absurd to myself how fond I am of her; I am perfectly infatuated about her... I know I'm a fool & can satisfactorily settle that I won't be any more when I'm away from her, but directly I see her again all my wisdom goes to the winds & I'm fascinated again... (7 January 1867)

The enduring power Kitty has for Jill is evoked in very similar terms when Jill sees her for the first time after a long absence: 'It was strange how the old charm which she had always had for me reasserted itself the instant I beheld her again. In her I seemed to recognise the sole human being in the world whose affections I would have taken trouble to obtain...' (p.283)

In depicting love between women, Dillwyn also drew, in her diaries and fiction, on wider ideas of love as a spiritual affinity that provided an imaginative or religious space for union with the beloved: "I knew that Olive would be at Church at Nicholaston [Gower] in the morning &... I wondered if I had a part in her Prayers – whether our souls met in the immaterial world." (3 March 1871) And again "Does my spirit, which is constantly seeking Olive & yearning for her, exercise any influence over hers or ever meet hers – so to speak – in that strange [immaterial] world?" (4 June 1872) The symbolic climax of Jill and Kitty's relationship includes a sublimated spiritual union when the two women find themselves imprisoned in pitch darkness in a mausoleum: "I realised that the common danger to which we were exposed was a link which united us so firmly that our separate identities were, for the time being, well nigh merged into one." (p.191) Jill's unseen 'link' with Kitty is further strengthened by her discovery of Kitty's own secret love for Captain Norroy which she has kept hidden from everyone else: "there yet existed between her and me the sort of half-bond which is involved in the possession of a mutual secret." (p.283)

Cross-class disguise
Jill and Kitty are of the same social order, but they are kept apart by Jill's cross-class disguise as a maid. Her assumed class allows her to serve and observe her mistress in ways Kitty doesn't understand, adding a voyeuristic frisson to their encounters. The very fact that her assumed class is only a disguise means that there is the constant possibility that Jill could come out at any time and declare herself and her feelings for Kitty, claiming their social station and distant family ties as a legitimate connection. She contemplates just this when threatened with dismissal: "for a moment I felt very much inclined to tell her who I was...I think I should inevitably

have yielded to the inclination, and imparted my history to her there and then, if there had been anything in her manner to make me believe that I had won a footing, however low down, in her affection – that she cared about me just one little bit." (p.239) A declaration of her true identity and class stands in here for a profession of love, which can only be risked if Kitty reciprocates Jill's feelings. Realising that there are no "softer feelings" motivating Kitty, Jill's "impulse to confide in her was frozen back". (p.239)

If supposed class difference keeps the women apart, then the crumbling of class barriers suggests a coming together. As already mentioned, Kitty and Jill are imprisoned in a mausoleum by some escaped convicts, and in this gothic villa of the dead their social differences fall away. To Jill's delight Kitty treats her "as if she had thought me her *equal*, as if the tomb had been a *leveller of ranks* to the living as well as to the dead, and as if in entering it *all social differences* between her and me had been *annihilated*." (p.187, my emphasis) In the immaterial world, as Dillwyn would have it, their regard for each other's welfare means they are "well nigh merged into one", while in the material world the two women lie down to sleep "pressing closely together for warmth". (p.191) Even the rope they fashion out of their clothes (those uniforms of rank and class) reinforces this merging of identities and pressing together of bodies, as the garments are twined and knotted together. It is not until they return to civilisation and back to their respective social roles that their intimacy is severed.

The difference in power and the potential for power struggles between mistress and maid, as well as the intimate services provided by maids, make the relationship particularly suitable for suggesting same-sex desire in literature. Indeed, nineteenth-century texts from conduct manuals, through fiction to pornography all engage with the erotic potential of mistress and servant. The novel exposes the potential power that a lady's maid may have over her mistress. Jill is party to family conversations and plans, but also eavesdrops, reads private correspondence and hides or reveals personal property to manipulate her mistress's feelings. However, Dillwyn was also committed to the model of chivalric devotion which could be transposed into the more mundane role of domestic servant. Identifying with the knight who loyally serves a superior "ladye love" whether or not his suit is hopeless, Dillwyn wrote, as a very young woman, "I should like to have been a knight in the old days of chivalry & whether she cared for me or not I would never have deserted my ladye love while I lived." (17 January 1864) And later, in 1871, she still found sustenance in the idea of serving her love, despite Olive's detachment: "My mind is taken with one line out of [Tennyson's] Guinevere – 'And worship her with years of noble deeds' – which represents how a knight should win his ladye love. That's just what I should like to do for Olive – how can I make my deeds noble to worship her with them?" (25 July 1871)

Class

In a novel about a lady who adopts a cross-class disguise, it is not surprising that social hierarchy is a major theme. Dillwyn is sardonic in her depiction of the double standards imposed by the rich upon the poor: a servant must be prompt for an interview while a prospective employer turns up at her leisure, an hour late; servants must learn all the little foibles and eccentricities of those they serve while their employers barely see, let alone recognise the individuality of, their staff.

Told from the perspective of a servant, the utter disregard Jill displays for the wishes of some of her more eccentric employers, whilst apparently indulging them fully, is humorous and convincing. Not a glimmer of the devoted retainer is present in this tale of urban employment, where a maid may pick up and abandon employers as it suits her. Yet not everything goes her way. Young maids were sexually vulnerable and Jill finds herself preyed upon not by the master or sons of the house, but by the master's valet, Perkins.

Perkins is rendered offensive through traits which appeal to class prejudice – he thinks a great deal of himself because he fancies he can imitate gentlemanly ways but the result is a grotesque mockery. His advances to Jill are repulsed with characteristic force, and her disgust at his overtures is expressed with explicit reference to the social order. Jill is "scandalised at the notion of a man-servant taking the liberty to raise his eyes to a lady", before she remembers that she is not a lady in his eyes: "I shuddered to think that I must endure being made love to by a valet: it was an odious and degrading idea." (p.116) Dillwyn uses class to articulate Jill's disgust, but there is a suggestion that it is in fact *men* she objects to: "I think it's a great pity that there are any men at all in the world" she thinks, adding only as an afterthought "or, anyhow, any except gentlemen." (p.117) Here, then, class difference operates as a way of articulating a profound and very strongly expressed sense of disgust that is at least in part linked to sex. Perkins's virility is represented by his enormous whiskers, which he caresses as he warns Jill he won't wait for her consent much longer. When he does force himself upon her, she defends herself by dashing a candle in his face and burning off, in a symbolic castration, this emblem of his manhood.

The ferocity of Jill's repulsion, "should I kill him on the spot, or should I expire from sheer disgust?" perhaps exaggerates Dillwyn's private response to the utterly unlooked for suit relentlessly pressed by the local vicar: "First thing after breakfast I had the felicity of receiving a long letter from Mr Bolney containing an offer in form! And after I had trusted Miss Buller's letter had quenched him! It was an aggravation & made me ferocious." (25 February 1870) It was not the last she would hear of him, and he would continue to press his suit for years to come.

In the opposite direction, class explains the natural affinity between Jill and Sister Helena, the woman in charge of the hospital to which she is admitted after a road accident and who is "unmistakably a lady by birth". (p.308) Jill is instantly attracted to her and tries to understand their growing intimacy in terms of class: "I do not know whether or not she had the same intuitive consciousness that I had of our both belonging to the same social order…" (p.309) In both cases, then, class is used as a means of representing repugnance and attraction for Jill and, as we have seen, cross-class disguise and the dissolution of class barriers are a central device for generating the erotic charge which underpins Jill's desire for Kitty.

Sisterhood
The portrait of Sister Helena is based on Dillwyn's own involvement, in her early twenties, with the Anglican Sisterhood, All Saints Sisters of the Poor, in Margaret Street, London. One Sunday in 1865, Dillwyn described the sisters bringing the orphans in their care to church:

> I think the smallest [child] of all could not do much more than walk & was led by the sister who had all the children in charge; she was a very tall and elegant looking person, with a grave yet very sweet face & it was pretty to

> see her holding the hand of this poor toddling
> tiny orphan. Sometimes it seems strange to
> see under the coarse ugly looking back veils
> worn by the sisters some graceful and well-
> bred looking face. (5 March 1865)

Jill's surprise that a refined lady could take on the role of
Sister draws on Dillwyn's own youthful prejudices and
she puts into Jill's mouth several statements that echo her
own feelings from this time, not least the conflict between
conscience and inclination. Struggling to find a purpose
in life and to deal with her own internal "storms",
Dillwyn seriously contemplated joining a sisterhood, and
in May 1867 went on a week's visit to All Saints Home
preparatory to making a decision to become a novice. Yet
for all her ardent desire to live "the highest life", to learn
self-denial in dutiful service to God, Dillwyn found it
hard to resign herself to a life of religious service: "I wish
I didn't like the world & pleasure & self pleasing so much
– or if so didn't think it right for me to give them up." (4
May 1867) In the end, Dillwyn did not pursue her plans
of entering a sisterhood. She kept up close ties with All
Saints for many years, including regularly visiting their
hospital for incurables, but by 1869 the fervid church-
going was at an end and by the early 1870s her faith was
less secure.

Cremation
Sister Helena is herself endowed with some of Dillwyn's
own beliefs. Dillwyn had some iconoclastic views on
death rituals and was a member of the Mourning Reform
Society. Jill's approving description of a Corsican
funeral, devoid of ostentation, making use of everyday
colourful clothing, yet solemn and dignified in its
simplicity, expresses the author's own values. Dillwyn

would attend her father's public funeral some years later, in 1892, in a colourful outfit as a protest against the convention of expensive mourning clothes that left poor families in debt and exploited seamstresses. She was also an early advocate of cremation. When Sister Helena meets an untimely end, her body is "burnt in a crematorium, in accordance with her own frequently expressed wishes on the subject":

> For it was horrible to her to think that her material part might possibly, after death, be the means of bringing death and sorrow to the fellow-creatures whom she loved so well, by poisoning the air they breathed or the water they drank; and, therefore, she had always been a steady upholder of cremation. (p.326)

Disposing of a body by cremation was a highly topical subject in 1884, the year *Jill* first appeared. In January of that year, Dr William Price of Llantrisant had been put on trial for his attempt to cremate the body of his infant son, Iesu Grist (Jesus Christ), and the reasons he gave for not wishing to bury the body were similar to those attributed to Sister Helena. The landmark ruling in the case of Regina v. Price established that cremation was not illegal. Nevertheless, the Home Secretary still refused to condone the practice and the Cremation Society of England-supported a Cremation Bill in parliament in May 1884 which they hoped would allow the licensing of purpose-built furnaces such as the one they had erected on a site in Woking in 1880 but not yet been able to use. The Bill was defeated and it was not until March 1885, eight months after Dillwyn published her novel, that the first official cremation took place in Woking. Dillwyn's claim in fiction that Sister Helena was cremated in

London in a novel published in 1884 is therefore an assertion of support for a practice only on the cusp of lawfulness.

Gender

Jill is one of a line of heroines who refuse to conform to "proper" feminine gender roles. Her early childhood experiences are important in the picture Dillwyn presents of Jill as an "unnatural" or at least unconventionally gendered woman. Jill revels in mess, abhors needlework, preferring mental exercises which she compares to solving problems in Algebra (a decidedly masculine pursuit according to contemporary thought). Most significant of all, her cold-heartedness is anathema to conventional femininity.

There is some autobiographical context for Jill's cold-heartedness; Dillwyn felt she came across as cold and unloving, although she knew she was really, in her own words, "hot-blooded":

> Have been speculating on some things in my own life lately & am not sure that it is quite a success. One leading idea I have always had is a hatred of sentimentality of all kind, sort, description, & and another idea of mine has always been that every one should be independent of everyone else. Well I'm not quite sure that these two Utopian ideas have been very successful practically. The result is that I seem to have no sympathetic bond with anyone else – I suspect an outsider, seeing my life in its relations to my own family, would say I am of iron – hard – & unloving. (13 June 1869)

Dillwyn was often lonely, as the passage above suggests. But in *Jill*, the rather more buoyant narrative turns the heroine's lack of feeling for anyone else into an asset, allowing the ardent adventurer to escape "the fetters formed from strong domestic attachments or other affection". (p.9) Jill declares that her "extraordinary cold-heartedness" is a trait she for which she is thankful, and since she is ordinarily devoid of filial love and respect, and lacking in all tenderness and sentimentality, her feelings for Kitty become all the more important. Significantly, Jill and Kitty – when they meet as children – reject the idea of commonplace sentimentality and a "romantic friendship", suggesting that Jill's interest in Kitty is something less conventional, something different, something more.

The rejection of conventional gender roles and the emphasis on "peculiarities of [Jill's] natural disposition" – she wonders if she is an "abnormal variety of the human species" and is described as "ill-made" by the hostile manservant whose advances she rejects – also suggests a more specific encoding of Jill as a mannish, or "odd" woman. The "odd woman" was the subject of gradually increasing scrutiny in the closing decades of the nineteenth century. The emerging field of sexology would come to define women who displayed conventionally masculine gender traits – such as an interest in logic and maths, assertiveness, a taste for smoking, an aversion to "feminine pursuits such as needlework", a lower voice, masculine dress – as sexual inverts. Dillwyn was writing before the major studies of inversion were published, but Jill and indeed Dillwyn herself, display many of the cultural and medicalised traits which came to be associated with lesbianism by the twentieth century. Dillwyn herself became famous for smoking a cigar – with many newspaper articles dedicated to this "extraordinary" habit – and she would have been well aware of the sexual ambiguity and scandal associated with other cigar-smoking women such as the French author George Sand and women's rights activist and founder of the Victoria Press, Emily Faithfull (whom she knew). In her sequel, *Jill and Jack*, Dillwyn plays with the idea of gender inversion even more explicitly, as the untidily but practically clad Jill is contrasted to the foolishly dressed dandy, Jack.

Meanwhile, the restrictive conventional clothes worn by Victorian women – the epitome of which was the corset – are used to symbolise emotional constraints and distress in *Jill*. Having just learned of Norroy's engagement to someone else, Kitty retires to her room where she can give vent to her distress in private. Blaming her indisposition on a headache, she tries to make light of her ailment to her aunt who has earlier pressed her to buy some extremely narrow Parisian stays: "The mere idea of such an enormity of tininess had so shocked her nerves, liver, lungs, brain and organs in general, that they had felt bound to make some forcible demonstration of disgust..." (p.232) This "nonsense" serves its purpose in distracting the prying aunt, but the image of a tightly laced lady recurs when Kitty's feelings are permanently cauterized in a loveless marriage and she has become of necessity or pride "incased... in impervious armour." (p.336)

Clothes are used to highlight restrictions on the physical activities as well as the emotions of girls and women. In a memorable scene, Jill, as a child, thinks to overcome her mother's prohibition of "mudlarking" and similar games by divesting herself of her clothes – as if gender could be shed at will – and plunging in to the stream, delighted that she has found a way to enjoy herself without upsetting anyone. Needless to say, her mother sees a half-naked nine-year-old girl playing in the mud in a very different light.

Amy and Olive: a Coda

In 1871, Amy Dillwyn wrote "Oh that I were a Dante to immortalise my Beatrice", noting "of course without in the smallest degree comparing myself to Dante". (10 July, 21 June) A feminist portrait of an irreverent, independent woman, who finally comes into her rightful inheritance, *Jill* is a coded story of Dillwyn's long, hidden, lonely and yet sustaining love for another woman. We do not know what eventually transpired between the two friends. Olive died in 1894, having lived out the last decades of her life in London, a wealthy philanthropist after the death of her father but also an invalid who was often in pain. Dillwyn's daily journal breaks off in 1875, at the height of her intense longing for Olive, and nine years before *Jill* was published. But the existence of the novel itself perhaps suggests that Jill's closing remark about Kitty at the end of the book holds true for Amy and Olive too, and that "the strange charm which she always had for me is not yet wholly dead." (p.335)

Acknowledgements
Quotations from Amy Dillwyn's journals courtesy of David Painting, who has also been a warmly supportive and uniquely informed friend during my research.

Kirsti Bohata is Associate Professor of English Literature and Director of CREW (Centre for Research into the English literature and Language of Wales) at Swansea University.

[1] *A Bibliographical Catalogue of Macmillan and Co's Publications from* 1843-1889 (London and New York: Macmillan and Co, 1891), pp. 451, 498, 605.

CHAPTER I

Jill Introduces Herself

I HAVE heard people say that men are more apt to be of an adventurous disposition than women; but that is an opinion from which I differ. I suppose it has arisen because timidity and sensitiveness are hostile to the spirit of enterprise, checking its growth and development, and not unfrequently proving altogether fatal to it; and as these qualities are especially characteristic of the weaker sex, it follows naturally that noted female adventurers are less common than male ones. But that seems only to show that an unfavourable soil has caused the plant to become blighted or smothered, and is no conclusive proof that the seed was never sown. It is my belief that the aforesaid spirit is distributed by nature impartially throughout the human race, and that she implants it as freely in the breast of the female as in that of the male. Once let it be implanted, and let it have fair play, untrammelled by nervous, hesitating, shrinking, home-clinging tendencies, and it will infallibly lead its possessor to some bold departure from the everyday routine of existence that satisfies mortals of a more humdrum temperament. A craving for continual change and excitement is a thing that is sure to assert itself vigorously and insist on being gratified, provided its possessor has also plenty of health and courage, and is unrestrained by the fetters formed from strong domestic attachments or other affection. Of people thus positively and negatively endowed it may be confidently predicted –

whether their gender be masculine or feminine – that
adventures will bestrew their road plentifully, meeting
them at every turn, and seeming to seek them out and be
attracted to them even as flies unto honey. I am myself an
instance of this, as I can see plainly enough in reviewing
my past career. At an earlier period I was less clear-sighted,
and failed to perceive the restless spirit that had taken
possession of me and become the constraining power of
my life; but the lapse of a few years is a wonderful aid to
discerning the true motives of former actions, and reminds
me in this way of the dark blue spectacles which the man in
charge of a smelting furnace puts on when he wants to see
what is going on in his furnace. Without them he can
distinguish nothing in the fiery interior; but the spectacles
have the effect of softening the fierce, blinding glare,
rendering visible what was before invisible, and enabling
him to watch the progress of the red-hot seething masses of
ore and metal undergoing fusion and transmutation under
his care. And in like manner does intervening time clear the
vision towards events, so that it is possible to estimate them
far more justly some while after they have taken place, than
it was at the moment of their occurrence. A retrospect,
therefore, gives me a more correct notion of myself than I
had before. I see how often, when I imagined myself to be
solely impelled by some purely external circumstance, I
was, in reality, also obeying the dictates of a longing for
adventure and impatience of sameness, which have always
had a very strong influence in determining my conduct. I
detect how love of variety manifested itself as the principal
cause of my actions, and made my course deviate widely
from that of other ladies in my rank of life, and furnishes a
reasonable explanation for behaviour which would else
seem unaccountable. To a person of this disposition,
monotony, dulness, and boredom in every shape are of
course absolutely intolerable; consequently I do not believe

that any position involving these drawbacks will ever content me for long, even though it may, in other respects, afford every advantage that the heart of man (or woman) can desire. And having supplied the reader with this much clue to a comprehension of the character of the individual whose story lies before him, I leave all further judgment upon me to be pronounced according to what is found in the pages of this veracious history, wherein I purpose faithfully to depict myself exactly as I appear in my own eyes, and as my life shows me to be.

A person's identity is materially affected (as regards both himself and others) by that of the immediate ancestors without whom he or she would not have existed at all; so the first step towards my self-introduction must obviously be to state my parentage.

My father, Sir Anthony Trecastle, a gentleman of small fortune serving in the Life Guards, was employed in London discharging the not very onerous duties expected from an officer of Heavies in time of peace, when he became acquainted and enamoured with a daughter of Lord Gilbert's. Sir Anthony's means were not sufficiently large for him to be reckoned anything of a matrimonial catch in that set of society to which both he and the young lady he admired belonged. He had enough to live upon, however, besides being a tenth baronet, rather good-looking, and the representative of a family whose name was to be found in the Domesday Book; therefore her relations and friends considered him to be a respectable though not brilliant match, made no attempt to interfere either for or against his suit, and left her perfectly free to please herself as to the answer it should receive. It was long before she could make up her mind in the matter; but, after considering it for more than a year, she at last determined to accept him. What may have moved her to do this of course I cannot say; but all I know of her character makes me think it more likely for the decision to have resulted from a reasonable and deliberate consideration of matrimonial pros and cons than from any love for her husband. Those who knew her well believed her to be so singularly cold and indifferent as never to have warmed into real love for any living creature during her whole life. And not only do my own recollections of her corroborate this opinion, but also I may say that I myself am a living argument to prove it true, inasmuch as I, too, am unusually exempt from the affectionate, tender emotions to which most men and women are liable; and it seems reasonable to suppose that this extraordinary cold-heartedness of mine must have been inherited from her.

I am sure it is an inheritance for which I have had much reason to be thankful; for I have no doubt it has saved me from many a folly that I should otherwise have committed. A warm hearted, soft, affectionate disposition is a possession which I have never coveted. It has generally seemed to me to be a cause of weakness rather than of strength to its owner; and besides, it is very apt to hinder and stunt the development of that source of delight – the spirit of enterprise.

This, however, is somewhat of a digression, as the extent to which my mother may have cared for my father does not much concern this narrative; at any rate she liked him sufficiently well to marry him, and that is all with which we need trouble ourselves here. He sold out of the army soon afterwards, and took his bride to reside at Castle Manor, as his country place was called; there I, their only child, was born. Had I been a boy it was intended to call me Gilbert, in honour of my maternal grandfather's title; as, however, I was a girl, and as my parents still wished to adhere as far as possible to their original intention of naming their first-born after the Gilbert peerage, the name was adapted to my sex by the addition of three letters, and thus I received at my christening the somewhat uncouth appellation of Gilbertina. As this was obviously too much of a mouthful to be convenient for common domestic use, an abbreviation was inevitable, and the first one bestowed upon me was Jill. But this did not find favour with my mother. She declared it was ugly, and objectionably suggestive of low, republican ideas, such as carrying pails of water, rough tumbles, and cracked crowns; therefore Jill was condemned and Ina substituted, as a more graceful and aristocratic manner of shortening my name.

Though I allude to this small matter, because Jill was the name to which I afterwards returned, yet I do not purpose to dwell long upon the history of my life up to the age of eighteen, at which period I launched out boldly upon an independent career. Still, however, the earlier stages cannot be left altogether unnoticed, as the events which took place then naturally have a bearing upon subsequent ones, and also may be thought interesting for the part they probably played in the moulding of my character.

Was I born destitute of the ordinary instincts of filial affection – in which case, be it observed, that it would be most unjust to blame me for what was simply a natural deficiency? Or is the fault of my defect in that way to be charged to my parents for having done nothing to develop the abovementioned instinct? Anyhow, whatever the cause may have been, certain it is that they and I were mutually indifferent, and never saw more of one another than we could possibly help. They went their way, and I went mine, and the less we came in contact the better was I pleased. I regarded my mother as a sort of stranger whom the accident of inhabiting the same house caused me to see oftener than any other stranger, and who had an authority over me and my affairs which was decidedly irksome, because our opinions as to what it was right and fitting that I should do or not do were always at variance with one another. She disliked untidiness, whereas I revelled in being in a mess. Consequently she aggravated me continually by insisting on my going off to wash my face and hands or have my clothes put tidy, when I thought they did very well as they were, and would have preferred staying where I was. Again, mud-larking, and many other of my favourite occupations which brought about a torn and dirty state of garments, were strictly forbidden by her, to my great annoyance. Imagining the restriction to be imposed solely in the interests of my clothes, I well remember how rejoiced I was one day when I thought I had hit upon a plan for enjoying myself after my own fashion without offending against her code, and how disappointed I was when my scheme proved a failure. I was about ten years old at the time, and was standing at the edge of a small stream, longing with my whole heart to go and paddle about in it, when it suddenly struck me that, as the edict against mud-larking and similar amusements was grounded upon the harm they did to my apparel, there could certainly be no objection to them provided nothing suffered except my own skin – that being an article which was surely of no consequence to anyone but myself. Inspired by this brilliant idea, I immediately took off my shoes, stockings, gloves, and drawers, turned my sleeves back to the shoulder, wound my petticoats round my waist, and plunged into the stream; there I waded about with the utmost satisfaction, constructing mud-docks and sailing bark-boats without in the least minding the cuts and bruises inflicted on my bare feet by stones, or the numerous scratches which my unprotected arms and legs received from overhanging bushes and brambles. What did that matter when I was having such a glorious mud-lark? And I enjoyed the fun all the more because I believed fondly that I had a prospect of plenty more of the same kind in the future, now that I had so cleverly discovered the way to get over the objection that had hitherto interfered with it. It must be clearly impossible for anyone to find fault with a proceeding which exposed nothing but my own flesh to risks of rents and dirt.

Alas! however, I was destined speedily to be undeceived. My mother, hearing how I had been engaged, gave me a tremendous scolding, declaring that she was quite shocked at me, and that if ever I did such a thing again I should be punished. For my part, I was perfectly amazed at this indignation, which seemed to me totally unreasonable, as I could not imagine what harm I had done. And the incident, like all others connected with her, strengthened the sulky injured feeling I had of being always wrong in her eyes. No matter what I might wish to do, she would forbid it, I thought.

I do not know that she was wilfully unkind to me, perhaps; but she certainly never was actively kind; and she stands out in my memory as a cold hard figure with which I could not come in contact without finding myself thwarted in some way or other, and being deprived of some pleasure. "Don't do that!" is a sentence odious in childish ears; and as that was the sentence that I heard oftener than any other from her lips, I naturally got into the habit of avoiding her company as much as possible – which was all the easier to manage because she had as little wish for my society as I had for hers, and only endured me with her at all, I think, out of regard to the *convenances* of English life. Never once do I remember her to have taken the trouble to supply me with any pleasures which she approved of to replace those which she prohibited; nor did she ever bestow upon me presents, indulgences, or marks of affection. Though she never attempted to teach me anything herself, yet she had me do lessons, and insisted on my learning needlework, which was my especial aversion; and I knew she was the source for the tasks I hated, even though she did not personally impose them on me.

Such being the terms on which she and I stood to one another, is it to be wondered at that I should have feared and disliked her?

I was about twelve years old when she died. As I had by that time read with great interest a large number of juvenile story-books of the exaggerated sentimental and goody kind, I was thoroughly well up in the behaviour to be expected from any girl-heroine on the occurrence of such an event. I knew that her father would at once become the great object of her life, and that she would devote herself utterly to the task of comforting him and endeavouring to replace Her (with a capital H) who was gone. Though the girl would of course be herself well-nigh crushed with grief, and indulge in paroxysms of sobs and tears whenever she was alone, yet she would heroically repress any public manifestation of distress, lest the knowledge and sight of it should increase that of her surviving parent. Her zeal on his behalf would know no bounds, and lead her to neglect the most ordinary precautions against illness for herself. This would appear in some absurd and wholly uncalled for act of self-devotion – such as sitting motionless for hours in a thorough draught and wet through, lest the sound of her moving might awake him as he slept in the next room, or something equally ridiculous; and by a few insane performances of the same kind the way would easily be paved for the invariably thrilling climax. A pillow bedewed nightly with tears; knife-like stabs of pain returning with increasing frequency; blood-spitting neglected and kept secret; pangs mental and bodily, concealed under a cheerful exterior; there could be but one conclusion to such symptoms as these. The overtaxed strength would collapse suddenly; consumption, decline, heart disease, or some other alarming illness, would ensue; and then there would be either a few harrowing deathbed scenes, or else a miraculous recovery and happy marriage of the heroine; in this last case her spouse would of course be some paragon young man, who should be in every respect ideally perfect, and thoroughly able to appreciate and do justice to the treasure whom he had been so fortunate as to win for a wife.

So invariably did this style of thing take place whenever the heroine lost her mother in the books which I had devoured greedily without perceiving how morbid and exaggerated they were, and without doubting their being faithful representations of human nature, that I had a sort of hazy impression of its being the inevitable accompaniment of that loss, whatever might have been the terms hitherto existing between the parties concerned. The folly of supposing that I could feel deep regret for a person whom I had always avoided as much as possible never occurred to me, and I was disposed to believe that what was described in the stories was an indispensable sequence of events that came after one another as naturally as spring follows winter, and summer follows spring. In that case, I too, must expect to undergo the regular course of emotions like everyone else. It would be a decidedly novel and mysterious experience, and one that I was by no means sure would be pleasant, and I looked out anxiously for the first indications of its approach as though it had been some kind of sickness with which I was threatened. A gush of poignant grief for my mother, an intense yearning over and pity for my father, sleepless nights and untasted meals, were, I knew, the correct preliminaries to the state of affairs that I was anticipating. Two or three days passed, however, and I found to my surprise that I had still no inability to sleep and eat as usual; no alteration in my former feelings about my parents, either living or deceased; nor any other reason to think I was about to behave in the same manner as those sentimental young ladies about whom I had read. Then I became perplexed as to the cause of this difference between me and them. I had taken it for granted that the stories showed exactly how human beings in general thought, felt, and acted; but how came it then that I, who was unquestionably a human being, should find my own experience of a great occasion of this kind so different from what the books depicted? The only way of accounting for it was by supposing either that they were not as true to nature as I had believed, or else that I must be unlike the rest of my fellow-creatures; and as it did not at all please me to consider myself an abnormal variety of the human species, I adopted the former theory as the probable explanation of what puzzled me. No one, thought I, ever dreams of judging fairy-tales by the standard of real life; and no doubt those stories that I fancied were true are in reality only fairy-tales in disguise. The characters are not real men and women, but only make-believe ones; and they are really just as impossible as if they were called ogres, gnomes, elves, magicians, or something of that kind.

It was a relief to me to arrive at this conclusion, and realise that there was no likelihood of my following in the steps of the afore-mentioned fictitious damsels; for, however attractive their experiences might be to read about, I had had very considerable misgivings as to whether I should find them equally pleasant to undergo in my own person. I may add that I am sure my incapacity for imitating them was a most fortunate circumstance for my father; he would, I am convinced, have been at his wits ends to know what to do with a daughter of the story-book stamp, and would have been unutterably taken aback and annoyed at any hysterical demonstrations of devotion or attachment on my part.

CHAPTER II

Foreign Travel

IT is time to say a few words as to what my father was like. Intensely selfish, and hating trouble, he was also extremely sociable, jovially disposed, easily amused, and endowed with an enviable facility for shaking off whatever was disagreeable. He seemed to consider everything unpleasant, dull, sad, or gloomy, as a sort of poisonous external application which must be got rid of promptly, lest it should get absorbed into the system. Consequently he never allowed anything to make a deeper impression on him than he could help. And in order to escape at once from the depressing influences of his wife's death he resolved to go abroad immediately after the funeral, and stay away for a good long time, wandering from place to place where his fancy took him, so as to distract his mind from all possibility of melancholy by a complete change of scene and life.

As he did not see the use of keeping up an establishment in England during his absence, he determined to let Castle Manor. Then came the question of what was to be done with me under these circumstances? His relations assured him that the best plan would be to send me to school somewhere till he should again be settled in his own home. After reflecting for a day on this suggestion, he considerably astonished those who had made it by announcing that he meant to take me abroad with him. Such a determination was certainly surprising on the part of one who could not endure trouble, and had no affection for me. But the fact was that since his marriage he had got so much accustomed to the feeling that there was someone belonging to him always within reach, that he did not now like to live quite alone again; and therefore he thought he might as well have me handy as a last resource to fall back upon for company when none other should be attainable. Wherever he went, therefore, there I went also; and for that reason we were supposed by many people to be wholly wrapped up in one another, and a touching example of parental and filial attachment. I accidentally overheard some remarks to that effect made one day by a couple of compatriots staying at the same hotel as ourselves at Naples; and, child as I was, I remember that I laughed cynically to think how wide of the truth they were, and what fools people were to be so ready to judge from appearances. For though he chose to have me living under the same roof as himself, yet he never had any wish for my society if he could pick up anyone else to talk to, and walk, ride, drive, or make expeditions with; and as his sociability and geniality made it easy to him to make acquaintance and fraternise with strangers, he was not often dependent upon me for companionship; so that I was left very much to myself, and spent the greater part of the time in solitude, or with my attendant who was a sort of cross between nursery-governess and maid.

We moved about from place to place for two or three years, rarely staying long anywhere, and not once returning to England. This roving existence had a great charm for me, notwithstanding its frequent loneliness, and was infinitely more to my taste than would have been the orthodox schoolroom routine that falls to the lot of most girls between the age of twelve and fifteen. Doubtless, too, it had a good deal of influence on the formation of my character; for the perpetual motion and change of scene in which I delighted could hardly fail to foster my inborn restlessness and love of adventure, as well as to develop whatever natural tendencies I possessed towards self-reliance, independence, and intolerance of restraint.

Meanwhile my education, as may be supposed, pursued a somewhat erratic course; and my standard of attainments would, I fear, have by no means been considered satisfactory by Mrs. Grundy. A life passed in hotels, *pensions,* and lodgings is unfavourable to regular studies; and, besides that, there was no one, after my mother's death, who cared sufficiently about my intellectual or moral progress to take the trouble of insisting on lessons being persevered with, whether I liked them or not. Consequently I learnt anything that took my fancy, and left alone everything else. On some out-of-the-way subjects I was better informed than the majority of my contemporaries; but then, on the other hand, I was ignorant of much that every schoolgirl is expected to know. My ideas, for instance, as to religious matters were extremely vague. I was but slightly acquainted with the contents of either the Bible or Prayer Book; never thought of religion as a thing with which I, personally, had to do; had not a notion of what constituted the differences between one form of religious belief and another; and never attended any place of worship except when some grand function was to come off. All I cared for in such a place was to listen to the music, and stare at the lights, vestments, decorations, ceremonial, and crowd; therefore I only went on great festivals, or when some especially prized relic was to be exhibited, or other unusual attraction offered; and, of course, I became more familiar with the interior of Roman Catholic churches and chapels than any other.

What accomplishments I possessed were such as would have qualified me well enough for a courier, and I think that I could have earned my livelihood in that line of business without much difficulty after I had been abroad for a while. I could speak several languages fluently, besides having a smattering of a few more, and of two or three *patois;* I was well up in the relative values of foreign coins, and capable of making a bargain even with such slippery individuals as drivers, jobmasters, *laquais-de-place,* or boatmen. Besides that, I was so thoroughly at home in railway stations that I could find my way about in any hitherto-unvisited one almost by instinct; I could usually tell, to within a few minutes, the exact time when any *rapide* or *grande-vitesse* was due to start from Paris for Spain, Germany, Italy, or the Mediterranean; when it ought to reach its destination; and at about what hour it would be at the more important towns on its route; and I had quite mastered the intricacies of the *English and Foreign Bradshaw, Livret-Chaix,* and works of a similarly perplexing kind, so as to be able to discover easily whatever information they could afford. My expertness in this way was chiefly owing to a happy thought that came into my head at Bayonne one day when I happened to be left alone for the afternoon with nothing to do, and no book whatever available except a railway guide. The prospect till night was not an exhilarating one, and I was disconsolately wondering how to get through the time, when it suddenly occurred to me that I would play at being about to start for St. Petersburg, or some other remote place, and obliged to look out the best and fastest way of getting there. I set to work accordingly with the railway guide, and became so engrossed in the game I had invented that I forgot all about the passage of time, and was quite astonished to find how quickly the afternoon slipped away whilst I was settling various journeys to my satisfaction. Such an easily-attainable means of amusement was a glorious discovery to me, and one which I commend to the notice of other travellers as a resource for wet weather and dull moments. Henceforth I had no dread of lacking amusement, provided I had a time-table; and many a long hour have I beguiled in planning skeleton tours to all kinds of places – poring over the times of arrival and departure of trains, diligences, steamers, and other public conveyances, and weighing in my own mind the prices and comparative merits of various routes with every bit as much care and attention as though the imaginary journey under consideration were a reality, and I were the sole person responsible to make arrangements for it. This employment had for me something of the same sort of fascination that working out a problem in algebra has for some people – indeed I do not think the two things are greatly unlike each other in their natures.

Besides the accomplishments I have mentioned, I had also some ideas as to foreign cookery, which I picked up here and there on our travels – chiefly on the rare occasions when we were in lodgings anywhere. I do not think I ever met any mistress of a lodging-house abroad who did not pride herself particularly upon her cooking of some one dish (sometimes more than that, but at least one), and who was not willing to initiate into its mysteries any lodger who evinced a proper appreciation of its excellence. There was an old woman at Genoa, I remember, at whose house we stayed for some weeks, who knew several delicious ways of dressing macaroni and vegetables, and who not only allowed me to watch her whilst she cooked, and gave me her favourite recipes, but even stretched her good nature so far as to let me try my own hand in the kitchen till I could join practice to theory, and produce a tolerably successful result for my labours. She was a kindly, motherly old soul, who was impressed with the notion that there was something peculiarly forlorn and provocative of pity in my condition; she generally called me *poverina* (to my amusement), and took me under her protection from an early stage of our acquaintance.

"See, *Signorina,*" she said to me on the second morning of our occupying her apartments, "you will no doubt wish to buy velvet here – as all the English do – and many other things also. But be guided by me, and go not to buy alone, or you will most certainly be cheated. No! when you see the thing that you desire, come to me – take me to where it is – point it out to me quietly. Then will I go forward as though to buy it for myself, and so shall you procure it at a reasonable price. You who understand not the modes of our merchants, would pay nearly, or perhaps even altogether – for there is no saying how far the folly of an English person may go! – the amount that they demand for their goods. But as for me! – ah! *I* know how to arrange these people, and you shall see what I will do! I dare to flatter myself that there is not a man or woman in the whole of Genoa who can get the better of me in a bargain!"

Experience soon showed me that this was no idle vaunt. Though – to her great disappointment – I declined to buy any velvet, yet I gladly availed myself of her services for other purchases, and never in my life, either before or since, have I met with anyone who was her match in bargaining. She never bought anything at a shop or stall without having taken a final farewell and departed from it at least twice, and then suffered herself to be brought back by the persuasions of the owner; I think she regarded this going away and returning as quite a necessary part of the negotiation, without which it could not possibly come to a proper conclusion. At all events

her efforts were invariably successful, and she forced
shopkeepers, market-people, and sellers of every sort
with whom she had dealings, to accept reductions of price
which seemed to me almost incredible. Meanwhile I, in
whose behalf she was exerting herself, used merely to
assist as a passive spectator, feeling that my knowledge of
mankind was being enlarged, and that I was gaining a
valuable insight into the amount of dishonesty and
cunning that was latent in human beings in general, and
Italians in particular. This was especially my feeling
when, as more than once happened, I perceived that my
friend herself was not altogether exempt from the failings
of her country-people; and that, relying on my knowledge
of Italian being less than it really was, she was making a
little profit at my expense out of the transaction she was
conducting for me. This was a fresh revelation of the
depravity of human nature, and impressed upon my
youthful mind the folly of trusting absolutely to any
professions of friendship, however genuine they might
appear. But, after all, it was not to be expected that she
would take a great deal of trouble for a stranger
gratuitously and out of pure love; besides that, she
allowed no one except herself to cheat me, so that in the
end my pocket was saved, notwithstanding the
commissions that she managed adroitly to retain for her
own benefit; and as, furthermore, I derived much
instruction from her in the art of bargaining, I saw that on
the whole I was a gainer by her help, and had nothing to
complain of. So I let her act for me as before, chuckling
inwardly at her vehement denunciations of the roguery
that surrounded us, and not telling her of what I had
discovered regarding her own.

I remember but little of most of the innumerable
people with whom my father was continually making
acquaintance; they seemed to me to come and go in

endless succession, having to do with us only for a few days or hours, and then vanishing into space, with about as much likelihood of our ever seeing them again as though we had all been so many dead leaves whirled away by gales from opposite directions. But there was one of these stray acquaintances who made more impression on me than the rest, and whom I mention here because of the relations which she and I were destined to have together in the future – little as we then suspected it.

Kitty Mervyn, the individual in question, was a girl of about a year older than myself, clever, vivacious, and agreeable, and promising to be very good-looking by the time she should be seventeen. She and I were cousins in some far-off degree, because her father, Lord Mervyn, was a cousin many times removed of my grandfather, Lord Gilbert. The cousinship, however, was so remote that we did not know of each other's existence; and my father and the Mervyns had never happened to meet until they arrived one evening at the hotel at which we were staying at Lugano. Then the distant connection served as an introduction between us; and as the next day was a dreary wet Sunday, the feeling of ennui and desire to kill time that was common to us all, led to our seeing more of one another than we should probably have done otherwise. Kitty and I paired off together naturally, as being nearly of the same age. As far as I can recollect, we spent most of the day in watching and laughing at the performances of some embryo bicyclists, who were too enthusiastic to be deterred by either rain or frequent tumbles, and who went on grinding perseveringly on their bicycles up and down a bit of road in sight of our windows which was their practice-ground. We did not find it very lively, certainly; but then there was nothing else to do, unless we had struck up a romantic friendship and exchanged sentimental confidences – as some girls thus situated would have done – and neither she nor I were at all disposed for that sort of thing. Our intercourse lasted only for that one day, as next morning the Mervyns departed south, whilst we went to Como. But in the short time I had been with Kitty she had somehow made a stronger impression than usual on my unimpressionable mind, and the recollection of her lingered in my memory longer than that of anyone else whom we met. Her good looks attracted me; her cleverness and liveliness made her very good company. Notwithstanding an incipient haughtiness about her, which might develop as she grew older, perhaps, she seemed at present to have a decided capacity for being what I called jolly; and, altogether, she had given me the idea of being remarkably likeable. I was sorry that the chances of travel made us separate so soon, and wondered if she was at all inclined to return the liking which I had taken to her. But she passed out of my head after a while; and it was only now and then that I recollected her existence, and thought how pleasant it would be if we happened to meet again some day.

CHAPTER III

A Widow's Manoeuvres

THE life of travelling companion to my father being very much to my taste, I was naturally disgusted at its coming to a conclusion. This happened when I was about fifteen, and was caused by an event to which I objected strongly, and which was destined to have a most important effect on my subsequent existence.

We were making a tour through Holland and Friesland, and, when at Amsterdam, happened to make acquaintance with a Mrs. Grove, a widow, accompanied by two daughters, who were respectively two and three years older than me. I did not take to her at all, and thought she seemed a flattering, lying, pushing, cringing, vulgar individual; but having carelessly thought that much of her, I dismissed her from my mind as a person with whom I had nothing to do, and whose character was quite immaterial to me – little thinking what a *bête noire* she was to prove to me afterwards!

She was on the look-out for a successor for the deceased Mr. Grove; and as my father appeared to her to be a very suitable person for the vacancy, she began at once to lay siege to his affections. She did not, however, wish to show her hand too plainly at first, by attaching herself to us so openly as to make it obvious that she meant to pursue us from place to place. Therefore, the plan she adopted was, to discover, by apparently careless questioning, whither Sir Anthony's wayward fancy was

likely to take him next; having done this, she would direct
her own course to the same district, go to some principal
town in it which we should be pretty sure to visit sooner
or later, wait for us there, and then pretend to be greatly
surprised when we arrived, and to consider the meeting a
purely accidental one. For instance, my father intended to
go from Friesland to Münster, which he considered would
be good headquarters whence to go to the neighbouring
town of Soest, where he wanted to see the *Wiesen Kirche,*
and other specimens of Gothic architecture. He had
spoken of this in Mrs. Grove's presence, so that she was
quite aware of his intentions in the matter. Consequently
there occurred what she called a curious coincidence, as
she also was moved by the self-same thirst for
archaeological studies at that particular time; and thus
when we reached Münster from Winschoten, we found
her already installed in the former city before us. At
Cassel and at Frankfort did we again fall in with her; and
on the very first night of our being at Heidelberg she and
her daughters joined us under the walls of the old castle,
as we sauntered about in the dark and admired the
brilliant fireflies.

Sir Anthony was too much a man of the world to
ascribe these perpetually recurring meetings entirely to
chance, and soon began to have a shrewd suspicion of the
widow's intentions. Then he took to amusing himself
with her, withholding information as to his movements
when she crossquestioned him about them, putting her on
a wrong scent, and otherwise baffling her curiosity. Once
or twice he joked about the matter with me (towards
whom she affected extreme friendliness), and asked me
whether I thought she wanted him as a match for herself
or for one of the daughters? This behaviour of his calmed
the state of perturbation into which I had been previously
thrown; for I was most indignant at the notion of her

wanting to marry him, and was in a terrible fright lest she should succeed. For one thing the mere idea of a stepmother was repugnant to me – be she who she might; and besides that, I had not the slightest confidence in the sincerity of Mrs. Grove's demonstrations of affection for me, which were, I felt sure, only assumed in order to ingratiate herself with my father; for I saw that she – like everyone else – was misled by appearances, and took it for granted that a man who insisted on taking his daughter with him wherever he went, must be so devoted to her as to be certain to entertain kindly feelings towards anyone who should appear fond of her. But my anxiety was relieved when I found that he was by no means blind to her designs, and was quite ready to laugh at them openly, and to take a mischievous pleasure in teasing her. That reassured me, and made me feel satisfied that her labours were in vain, and that I had nothing to apprehend from them.

This easy tranquillisation of my fears just showed my youth and inexperience. Had I been somewhat older I should have known what irresistible power over men almost all widows possess – which is the natural result of the insight into man's nature that they have acquired already, during their first matrimonial experiences. Mrs. Grove was no exception to the rule, and was as dangerous a widow as need be – having a thorough knowledge of the weaknesses of the male character and of the way to humour them, and understanding perfectly how to make herself agreeable to any lord of creation whom fortune might throw in her way.

It was no part of her tactics to leave Sir Anthony long in doubt that it was for herself, and not for either of her daughters, that she desired to captivate his affections. She was certainly vulgar; but as, also, she was a comely, well-preserved woman of little more than forty, who looked rather less than her age, it tickled his vanity pleasantly to find himself attractive to her; and notwithstanding his having ridiculed her for setting her cap at him, he did not, nevertheless, altogether dislike it in the bottom of his heart. It was true that he had not previously contemplated marrying again; but then that was only because he had not yet met any particular person to suggest the thought to him since my mother's death; and he had been sufficiently occupied and amused with his travels for the notion not to have occurred to him of itself. Now, however, that the idea was thus put into his head, he began to reflect upon the matter seriously; the more he considered it – being all the while insensibly influenced in its favour by the flattering attentions and blandishments of the widow – the more favourably did he regard it, and presently came to the conclusion that a wife was really almost indispensable to his comfort. He could forgive a little vulgarity provided she had money to gild it; and, feeling that Mrs. Grove's pecuniary circumstances had become suddenly interesting to him, he began putting out feelers on the subject when talking to her. He imagined himself to be going to work most diplomatically, and to have artfully concealed the true motive of his questions and remarks; but the widow was more than a match for him. She at once detected his curiosity, and guessed the reason for it; and managed cleverly to impress him with the idea that her jointure and settlements were considerably larger than was the actual case. Whether or not she would have accomplished her purpose without this stratagem, it is impossible to say; but, at any rate, it did what she intended it to do, and brought matters to a climax. The belief that a rich wife was to be had, and that it would be foolish of him to miss such an opportunity, put an end to his irresolution. He proposed, and was accepted; and within two months from the time that they were introduced to each other at Amsterdam, she succeeded in attaining what she desired, and became Lady Trecastle.

Her ladyship, being a thorough John Bull at heart, had no great fondness for foreign places and people. She had come to the continent because she believed it to be a likely hunting-ground whereon to find a husband; and as soon as she had secured her prey she did not care about staying abroad any longer. Another thing that made her wish to return to her native land was, that she was extremely proud of the newly-acquired handle to her name, and was burning to air it amongst those who would properly appreciate it; for what country is there in Europe, Asia, or Africa (about America I say nothing), where a title produces so much effect, and is so bowed down to and worshipped as in that abode of snobs – England? Therefore, as soon as she was engaged to Sir Anthony, she determined to endeavour to make him give up his nomadic existence, return home, and settle there. By way of paving the way in this direction she would reproach him, half in jest and half in earnest, for being an absentee, and having no proper patriotic spirit; or else she would deliver a harangue upon the roguery of most agents, and the folly of leaving property to be managed by them instead of looking after it in person; and with these and similar observations, she sought to bring him to wish himself to do the thing that she desired should be done. Finding him more inclined to listen to her than she had expected, she grew bolder, and passed from hints to a more direct expression of her desires. He was evidently not greatly averse to discontinue his foreign rambles, as I perceived with sorrow. The fact was that he had only gone abroad because my mother's death gave him gloomy and disagreeable associations with his house, and on that account he had taken a temporary dislike to it ; but his facility for getting rid of whatever was unpleasant had made him quite shake off that feeling of dislike by now. Before long Mrs. Grove had worked upon him so far that he began even to feel eager to return home, and to look forward with pleasurable anticipation to the idea of showing the place to its new mistress, and introducing her to the society of the neighbourhood.

I said what I could to oppose going back to England whenever I had an opportunity; but alas! what chance had I against the influence of the widow? Of course she carried her point without difficulty; and, to my great grief, notice to quit was sent to the tenants of Castle Manor. It so happened that there were accidental circumstances which made it convenient to the tenants to leave at once, without waiting for the expiration of the term of the notice, and thus the house was vacated at an unexpectedly early date. No sooner was this the case than Sir Anthony and Lady Trecastle returned home and established themselves there, accompanied by their joint families, which consisted of Margaret Grove, aged eighteen; Jane Grove, aged seventeen; and myself, aged rather more than fifteen.

CHAPTER IV

A Tight Curb

WHEN an indolent, easy-going, trouble-hating man, such as my father, marries an energetic, bustling, authority-loving woman, such as Mrs. Grove, it is not hard to foresee which of the two will bear rule in the establishment. A very brief acquaintance with Sir Anthony sufficed to show the widow that, with a little management on her part, she would be able to govern the household as she liked; that as long as he was kept amused he would not bother himself to interfere with her arrangements; and that all she need do in order to keep the reins entirely in her own hands, was to take care that her way and his were identical in whatever affected his personal comfort – she would then be free to please herself as far as all other things were concerned. She was not, at first, altogether easy in her mind as to how he would bear the discovery of what the real state of her money matters was; which discovery, as she knew, he must inevitably make soon, and might possibly cause him to be seriously angry with her. But she need not have feared this with a man of his disposition, who never worried himself about anything that could not be helped. Though he was, undoubtedly, much annoyed to find how much poorer she was than he had supposed, yet he reflected, with his usual philosophy, that it was no use making a fuss about it, now that he had married her, and that what could not be altered had better be made the best of. So he gulped down the disappointment with a wry face or two, and did not attempt to make her suffer for her deceitfulness as she deserved.

As soon as she was satisfied on this head, and felt that she was established in her seat securely, she turned her attention to me – who would infinitely have preferred being let alone. I had never trusted to the sincerity of the professions of affection she had lavished on me in the early stages of our acquaintance, when she had imagined me to be my father's especial pet; and it speedily became evident that this distrust of mine had been well founded. She thought it quite worthwhile taking trouble to keep the master of the house in good humour, and would study and humour his likes and dislikes in the most amiable manner possible. But she saw no reason for extending the same consideration to a mere insignificant nobody; and when she had discovered how little he cared for me, and that she might do as she pleased regarding me and my affairs without danger of interference from him, she proceeded to take my education in hand, and conduct it according to her own notions. As her ideas on the subject and mine were entirely different, and as the more she and I saw of one another the more we disliked each other, the result of this meddling of hers was fatal to my comfort. And the two or three years following my father's second marriage were so horribly dull and tedious to me that I cannot recall them without a shudder.

Everything seemed to go against me from the time of that wedding. In the first place, I resented having a stepmother, and finding myself forced suddenly into terms of intimacy with the three strangers (her and her two daughters) who had all at once become part of my family. Then came the termination of the foreign wanderings that I had found so pleasant. And now came the culminating misery of being under the commands of a selfish, vulgar, lying, bullying, stingy, pretentious, plausible, tyrannical woman, whom I could not endure, and who fully returned my dislike.

I had an unlucky knack of perpetually irritating her, and was always sure to be in the wrong in her eyes. Either I said or did something that was contrary to her notions of what I ought to have said or done; or I scandalised her by displaying grievous ignorance of some subject which she deemed an essential branch of knowledge; or else I shocked her prejudices in some other way. She was not the woman to put up quietly with offences of this kind in her own household, and proceeded without delay to attempt to remedy my deficiencies. Accordingly she informed my father that she considered my mental condition to have been neglected terribly; that I had been allowed to run wild till I was very nearly ruined; and that she saw no chance of my ever becoming a properly behaved young lady and decent member of society unless a governess were procured for me immediately, and I were kept strictly to the school room until such time as I should come out. Should she, therefore, engage a governess? My father, as usual, made no objection to a proposal which would in no way interfere with his own comfort. All he said was that she could do just as she thought best about it; that he did not himself see much to complain of in me, and had thought I was not at all bad company, considering my youth; but that he had no doubt she understood better than him what was necessary for girls, and that whatever she did was sure to be right.

Armed with this permission, she at once took steps to carry out her intention, and a few days afterwards announced to me the contemplated innovation.

"Your father and I have agreed, Ina," she said, "that it is high time to make a change in your present mode of life – you need to be put into harness for a bit and broken in.

Therefore, I have engaged a governess for you, and she will be here next week. What I wish to impress upon you now is, that when she comes you must do what she tells you, and that I shall expect you to pass your time with her. I do not approve of your fondness for sitting in your own room; nor yet of your habit of appearing continually amongst us elders when there are visitors here, just as if you were grown up and already introduced into society! The drawing-room is *not* the proper place for a girl of your age. Remember that in future you are to remain always in the schoolroom when indoors; and that, when not at lessons, you must employ yourself there in some quiet and ladylike pursuit – needlework perhaps, or something of that kind. And when you go out you will walk with your governess, and not go climbing trees, or digging out rabbits, or racing all over the place like a wild thing, as you generally do."

The idea of being thus hampered and restrained filled me with dismay; and in my despair I appealed to my father, in hopes that he would protect my cherished liberty of action.

"Why should I have a governess at all?" I exclaimed to him; "I'm sure I've got on very well without, for ever so long! But even if I *am* to have one, surely I may be free of the hateful thing out of lesson-time, mayn't I? Just think how *horrid* it would be to be obliged to be always with her – sitting in the room with her all day, and only going for stupid, straight-on-end grinds along the hard high road with her when I go out! Do say that I'm not to be condemned to that, at all events!"

No doubt I was a fool for my pains, and ought to have known better than to suppose that I could move him to oppose his wife on my behalf. So the event proved, for he declined to interfere in the matter; and the only effect produced by my appeal was to strengthen Lady

Trecastle's hands by increasing her conviction of the extreme unlikelihood of my father's ever paying attention to any complaint that I might make to him. From that time forth, therefore, she felt more secure than ever in her authority over me, and her tyranny increased accordingly. When the governess arrived I was kept immured in the school room the greater part of each day, and was surrounded by a variety of petty restraints and restrictions which were enough to have worried any girl, and were especially vexatious and irksome to one who had had the unusual amount of independence which I had been enjoying of recent years. I found myself deprived of freedom; always under *surveillance;* obliged to learn uninteresting lessons; bored; and constantly tacked on to the petticoats of an individual whose office of governess made her necessarily hateful in my eyes, however charming – even angelic – she might really be. Of course such an existence was perfectly odious to me, and I do not think that I could have anyhow managed to endure it as long as I did, if I had not fortunately hit upon a means whereby I could to some extent relieve its dreary monotony. This resource consisted in victimising, to the extent of my power, any rash female who had undertaken to instruct me, playing off upon her ill-natured pranks of all kinds, and leaving no stone unturned to make her life a burden to her till I had fairly driven her out of the house.

What a dreadful confession of unamiability! some reader may, perhaps, here exclaim. Well – I do not deny it. Be it remembered that the purpose of this narrative is, not to set forth an imaginary picture of virtue and excellence, but simply an accurate likeness of myself; and I should evidently fail of accomplishing that purpose if I were to conceal or gloss over those sentiments which I really entertained and acted upon. But even if my behaviour *does* lay me open to the charge of unamiability, I do not think that that need be wondered at, when the peculiarities of my natural disposition, of my bringing-up, and of my whole circumstances, are taken into consideration.

The occupation of bullying and annoying my governesses to the utmost possible extent had a double recommendation in my eyes. Not only did it supply an ample field for my ingenuity, and give me something amusing to think about in the dreary walks and long hours spent in the schoolroom, but also it afforded me the satisfaction of retaliation. I had a savage joy in knowing that I was able to pay off my companion for some of the vexations that she was the means of inflicting on me; and I relished the thought that even if I *did* have a rough time myself, yet at all events I did not suffer alone. Endless, therefore, were the tricks and practical jokes which I used to devise and execute for the aggravation of whatever unlucky individual happened to have taken charge of my education; and so skilful was I in my operations that it was but seldom any piece of mischief could be traced home to me, however greatly I might be suspected of its authorship. I was an adept, too, at the art of being extremely insulting and provoking without saying anything that would seem a just cause of irritation if repeated to a third person. I knew how to speak with an offensiveness of voice and manner which gave an injurious significance to words that were in themselves innocent; and by this method I have often succeeded in making a governess wildly angry, although I had given her nothing tangible that could be taken hold of and brought against me to substantiate a charge of rudeness. If she complained that I had been impertinent, I assumed an air of injured innocence, repeated exactly what I had said, asked what harm there was in that? and declared that it was very unfair to blame me because Miss so-and-so had chosen to fly into a passion about nothing. In fact I was aggravating enough to have provoked the patient Grizzel herself; and as governesses are not much apt to be patient Grizzels in their relations to their pupils (however gentle and long-suffering they may make themselves appear to the heads of the establishment), our school room was in a constant state of turmoil and ferment, and there was a remarkable difficulty in getting governesses to stay at Castle Manor. About a month or six weeks was generally enough to disgust them with the situation, and they rarely failed to give notice at the end of that time. This was an event that always gave me a sensation of unmixed satisfaction; as, for one thing, I then felt that I had scored a fresh victory and routed another enemy, and also, I knew that the arrival of her successor could not fail to bring some small amount of variety into the monotonous routine of existence of which I was so deadly tired.

But this constant change of governesses over which I rejoiced, and which was chiefly my doing, was by no means equally agreeable to Lady Trecastle. When an instructress went, it was she who had to procure a successor; and she did not find it at all amusing to be incessantly answering advertisements, writing for characters, and that sort of thing. And as, notwithstanding the difficulty of ever actually *proving* a misdemeanour against me, she had strong doubts of my innocence, therefore she considered me responsible for the bother she continually had about governesses, and regarded me with increased disfavour on that account. She had the sense to suspect that there would not be such endless storms in the school room if the pupil were not unusually unmanageable and turbulent; and, acting on that opinion, she made several efforts to induce me to be more tractable, in order that thereby she might be saved the trouble that my conduct entailed upon her.

At one time she tried the effect of addressing serious rebukes and admonitions to me; but I cared not one straw for them. Then she increased the strictness of my confinement, and ordained that every disturbance should always be followed by the loss of the next half-holiday or other pleasure of which I might have a chance; but still I remained unsubdued. Then a third method of overcoming me suddenly struck her, and she one day wound up a lengthy scolding by declaring that her patience was at an end, that she would *not* stand the perpetual commotions I caused any longer, and that the very next time one occurred I should be packed off to some school at once.

Now it was all very well for her to talk big of sending me to school; but in point of fact I felt pretty sure that she would do nothing of the kind, because it was very convenient to her to have a governess in the house on account of her own two daughters, for whom she did not want to go to the expense of masters, and who often needed assistance in the various accomplishments she wished them to acquire. This assistance they were in the habit of receiving from whoever happened to be in charge of me, though they were too old to be regularly in the schoolroom; and as my going to school would remove the ostensible reason for having a governess at Castle Manor, it was not at all likely that she meant to do what she said.

But though she knew the threat to be an empty one, that did not at all hinder her from uttering it. Being at her wits' end for something to hold over me *in terrorem,* it suddenly occurred to her that a girl who had always lived with her own belongings, as I had done, would probably dread the notion of being sent away alone amongst strangers, and that therefore the school project stood a very good chance of awing me into submission.

Instead of that, however, I evinced such delight at the prospect as took the wind out of her sails completely. I had not in reality the slightest objection to school, because it would be a change, and anything in the shape of a change would be welcome. And of course my manifestations of delight were all the more exaggerated as I perceived her annoyance at finding me look forward joyfully to the thing she hoped I should have feared. Thus she was thoroughly discomfited; and never again did I hear her say I was to go to school, though I several times returned to the subject of myself, asking to know when I was going, saying I hoped it would be soon, etc. etc. I must say that I greatly enjoyed having triumphed over her so completely; and I reflected with malicious pleasure on the vexation and humiliation it must be to her to know that I had detected the emptiness of her threat, and could henceforth look down upon her with all the contempt which an utterer of such threats is sure to inspire.

But though I did what I could to procure a little change and excitement by making myself disagreeable, and plaguing my stepmother and teachers, yet the tedium of my life was so great as to be almost unendurable; and again and again did I consider the expediency of putting an end to it by running away from home, and trusting to my own resources for getting a livelihood. I used to meditate seriously on how the thing was to be done, arranging every detail, foreseeing and meeting probable obstacles, providing for possible contingencies, and working the whole scheme out from beginning to end in my own mind. It seemed to me quite feasible; and as I was not a bit afraid of failure, or of what might happen to me when cast upon the world by myself, I should certainly have put my idea into practice if there had not been one consideration which deterred me and kept me where I was. This was the thought that I was very nearly seventeen. At that age I was convinced that girls invariably came out, and therefore took it for granted that

I should do so also. And as the yoke under which I groaned would be broken before long in the natural course of events, it seemed better to resign myself for the short space during which I should still be subject to it, rather than to anticipate the day of emancipation by so desperate a measure as running away from home.

But in my calculations as to the time of my being brought out, I had quite omitted one most important factor, viz. what might be my stepmother's wishes in regard to that matter. These, as it happened, were diametrically opposed to mine. She had no fancy to go about with three young ladies in tow, nor did she feel inclined to risk spoiling the matrimonial chances of Margaret or Jane by leaving either of them at home, and taking me out with her instead. Therefore she intended to keep me back in a state of pupilage as long as possible, and to endeavour to get one or both of her own daughters married out of the way before I should make my appearance in society. In consequence of this private scheme of hers, the attainment of the age of seventeen, from which I had hoped such great things, produced no amelioration in my condition. I was astonished and disgusted to find that the days and weeks dragged heavily on at lessons as before, and brought no indications of the approach of that liberty to which I had looked forward confidently. Of course, I was not going to stand this without complaining, so I remonstrated with Lady Trecastle, declaring that I was being treated very unfairly, that every girl came out at seventeen, and that I ought now to be let to share equally with my step-sisters in whatever invitations for balls, dinners, or other gaieties might arrive at Castle Manor. My complaints were unheeded, however, and my grievance remained unredressed. I was not fit to go into society, she said; I was so untrained, stupid, disagreeable, and bad-tempered, that she would be ashamed to take me out, and I must positively remain in the schoolroom till my manners and temper should be improved. Chafing and fretting under repeated disappointments, I managed to get through another dreary year of monotony; but when my eighteenth birthday arrived and found me still a prisoner in the schoolroom, I resolved not to stand this treatment any longer. It became evident to me that her ladyship destined me to play the part of Cinderella. As I had no fancy for that *role,* and as I had not a fairy godmother to come to my assistance, I must take the matter into my own hands and act fairy godmother for myself. Therefore I determined to execute the plan which I had already reflected upon so often, and to run away from home and take my chance of what might afterwards befall me.

CHAPTER V

Breaking Loose

HAD running away from home been a brand new idea that had never before occurred to me, I daresay I should have had to postpone carrying it out till I had had time to mature the design and consider how it was to be accomplished. As it was, however, there was no need for delay on that account, for I had pondered on the subject often enough to be thoroughly familiar with it, and to have discovered a variety of methods for executing the project. In all these schemes there was one point which I had always kept steadily in view, and that was the importance of so arranging my flight as to secure myself a long start before my absence should be discovered. I had but little fear of managing to evade pursuit, if only I could get a good way ahead of it at first. I saw that the best means of ensuring this would be to have the coast clear of authorities when I took myself off. Therefore I determined to put off my departure for a few days longer, in order to avail myself of a particularly favourable opportunity which would then occur, as my father, step-mother, and two step-sisters would be going to stay away for a ball and other gaieties at a friend's house. When once they were out of the way, there would be no one to interfere with me except my governess, Miss Smith, and I thought it would be odd indeed if I could not manage to get rid of her also somehow or other. Several expedients whereby this might be effected soon suggested themselves to me, and after a little consideration I made up my mind to try to impose upon her with a sham telegram. She was a somewhat colourless individual, much given to writing letters and reading novels, nervous, easily fussed, sentimental, and possessing a sister named Alice who kept a school at Carlisle, and to whom it was evident that she was very much attached. Now I felt certain that if she believed this beloved sister to be in need of her, nothing would induce her to stay away, and that a telegraphic summons from Miss Alice Smith would cause my Miss Smith to rush off to Carlisle as fast as trains would take her there. Such a summons, therefore, I must contrive that she should receive. The only difficulty about forging the telegram I required for my purpose was that I had not the proper paper or envelope; the latter I might possibly contrive to do without, if necessary, but the former was absolutely indispensable, and if I could not get hold of a piece of it, I should have to relinquish the telegram scheme altogether and substitute some other.

In order to procure what I wanted I pretended to be in need of stamps, and upon that pretext went to the post-office at Greenlea, as our village was called. The post-office was also a telegraph-office and sort of general emporium, and was kept by an old man named Jones, who had been there for years, and was certain not to dream it possible that one of the ladies from Castle Manor should have nefarious designs upon any of the stores over which he presided. Having bought my stamps, and made one or two friendly remarks to the proprietor, I affected a sudden interest in the working of the telegraph, and was, as I expected, promptly invited behind the counter to inspect the machine more closely. The blank forms and envelopes requisite for sending out messages were lying close by amongst some other papers, and somehow I was awkward enough to upset the whole lot of papers together on the ground. "Oh how very stupid of me!" I exclaimed, penitently, kneeling down as I spoke, and beginning to collect the scattered papers; "I'll pick them up again in a moment, Jones; don't you trouble!" What with old age and rheumatism, Jones' joints were somewhat stiff, and he was not sorry to be saved from the necessity of stooping down in the rather confined space behind the counter.

"Well, indeed, 'tis a shame for you to be doing that, Miss, and me looking on idle," he replied; "but I'm much obliged to you, too, and I won't say no to a good offer. We old folks ben't quite so flippant to move ourselves up and down as you young 'uns be; and it be a bit narrer in here atween the wall and the counter, you see." So he complacently received the papers from me and restored them to their places as I handed them up in instalments; and he never missed the telegraph form and envelope which I slipped swiftly into my pocket whilst his eyes were turned in another direction. I left his shop in triumph, having thus supplied myself with the means to which I trusted for removing Miss Smith off the premises; and I was now all ready to commence operations as soon as my stepmother and her husband and daughters should take themselves off upon their intended visit.

The eventful day arrived, and I stood looking at them drive away from the house with a curious mixture of feelings – partly gloomy and partly cheerful. There went these people who constituted my family, and I meant never to set eyes on them again if I could help it. They were going to lark about, dance, be jolly, and amuse themselves in all kinds of ways, and it was a horrid shame that I was not going too. I should have been, only that Lady Trecastle would not let me have fair play, and had chosen to spite me and to treat me like a child when I was not one. I considered that she had behaved infamously to me. Other young people of my age and position could go to balls, enjoy themselves, have lots of fun, and frolic to their heart's content, and it was grossly unjust to debar me from doing the same. I was an oppressed and harshly-treated victim. I was being defrauded of my rights and ousted from my proper place through the enmity of a malevolent stepmother and the negligence of a father, who was too selfish and indolent to care what became of me, or anyone else, as long as he was himself happy.

As I stood at the window watching the departing carriage, and meditating on the wrongs that had rankled long in my breast, and had now at last reached their culminating point, I felt a single burning tear gather slowly in each eye and brim over on the cheek beneath. Weeping is not a weakness to which I am given, for I am, as a rule, one of the least tearful of mortals. But that tear was an exceptional one, and was drawn from me solely by a feeling of bitter resentment for past injuries, not by any foolish regrets or sentimentality relating to my approaching separation from both home and family.

Mingled with these disagreeable thoughts, however, there was also present in my mind an exhilarating idea, which soon dispelled the unpleasant ones even as the sun disperses cloud. How could I mind anything now that liberty was so close at hand? What did it matter that Lady Trecastle had been able to convert my home into a hateful prison, now that I was about to break my bonds and cut myself adrift from it? Those people whose departure I had just watched should find a little surprise awaiting them on their return, in the shape of my disappearance! Freedom, novelty, and adventures lay before me. Without these things life was not worth having, and I was on the brink of enjoying them. Hurrah! The wide world was going to be open to me, and I was about to enter on an unknown future, wherein everything would be different from the past. The thought of all this made my pulses throb with excitement, and filled me with wild eagerness for the first taste of the anticipated joys.

I did not mean to deliver the forged telegram to Miss Smith till it should be nearly time for the train, by which I expected that she would go to Carlisle, to leave Sparkton – that being the name of our nearest town. As that train did not start till past four o'clock in the afternoon, and as Sir Anthony and Lady Trecastle and her daughters had left home in the morning, I had to control my impatience for some hours longer. Part of this time I employed in preparing the telegram. Upon the blank form I scrawled in a feigned hand as follows – "Alice Smith, Carlisle, to Miss Smith, Castle Manor, Greenlea, Sparkton. *Come without losing a moment I need your help immediately.*"

Having enclosed this in the proper envelope of thin yellow paper, and directed it to Miss Smith, I did not neglect also to fill in the blank spaces on the outside with the requisite information as to the time when the message was sent out, when handed in, etc. I knew that she would probably be far too much perturbed by the telegram to notice any little irregularity about its appearance, but, for all that, I meant to be on the safe side, and to have everything in order, so that there might be no possible ground for suspicion.

When the due time had arrived for me to spring the mine that I had prepared for her I betook myself to the schoolroom, where she was engaged as usual in inditing epistles to some of her numerous correspondents. The precious telegram was in my hand, and I proceeded to deliver it to her, and also to account for the unusual circumstance of its being brought by me instead of by a servant, according to the ordinary course of things.

"Here's something for you," I said; "I went out to pick

some flowers just now, and as I was coming back towards the house I overtook a child from Greenlea with this in its hand. Of course I saw at a glance that it was a telegram – one can't mistake the appearance of the article – and I asked which of the household it was for. It's for you; and as I was coming straight in then I thought I would bring it myself, and save the child having to come any farther."

The mere sight of the telegram sufficed to flutter Miss Smith's nerves, and her fingers shook visibly as she opened it. The instant she had perused its contents she jumped up in a tremendous state of agitation, and exclaimed: "Good gracious! it's from my sister Alice! She wants me immediately, but doesn't say what's the matter. What *can* have happened? Perhaps she's ill! I must go to her at once. What trains are there? Isn't there a *Bradshaw* somewhere? *That's* not it, nor *that,* nor *that*!"

As she spoke she hurriedly took up one after another of the books lying near, and examined their titles to see if either of them was a *Bradshaw,* although there was nothing in the room that bore any resemblance whatever to the well-known work. But she was a great deal too much upset to notice that. I, however, needed no *Bradshaw* to enable me to give her the information she wanted, as I had already ascertained exactly the starting-time of the next train that would suit her, and had it at the tip of my tongue.

"The last train to the North from Sparkton starts at 4.20 in the afternoon, I know," I answered; "that's the one for you to go by, and if you go at once you'll just have time to catch it. Better go and get ready as fast as you can, and I'll order the carriage to take you to the station."

"Yes, yes, that'll be the way; thank you so much," she returned, beginning to hasten towards the door. Before she had quite reached it a sudden thought struck her, and she turned round with a look of consternation,

exclaiming, "Oh dear! I quite forgot that you'll be all
alone! I'm afraid Lady Trecastle won't like it. How
unlucky for her just to have gone away! But really what
can I do? Read the telegram yourself, Ina; you'll see it's
absolutely *imperative* I should go at once. My poor, dear
Alice! I'm sure something quite *dreadful* must have
happened to make her send for me like this. It can't be
any *trifle,* I know, for she is one of the calmest, least
excitable mortals on the face of the earth!"

She's not much like you, then, was my inward
reflection, as I looked at the spectacle of pitiable
nervousness presented by my governess, with her fingers
twitching aimlessly to and fro, and her face expressing
feeble and helpless apprehension of evil. Indeed, I was
not altogether free from a feeling of compunction for
being the means of throwing her into such a state of
distress, which must continue, as I knew, till she should
reach Carlisle, and discover that the telegram had been a
sham. But then she had to be got out of the way somehow
or other, and it would never do for a young woman who
meant to make her own way in the world, as I did, to be
squeamish about inflicting pain on other people if
necessary; and after all it was partly her own fault for
having become the governess of a person who did not
want one at all. Besides that, the more miserable she was
now, the greater would be her joy and relief when she
should learn that her fears were unfounded. Really the
bliss of that moment would be so exquisite that I quite
looked forward to it on her account!

·When she handed me the telegram I of course affected
to have no previous knowledge of its contents, and even
made believe to have a difficulty in making out one or
two of the words. Having read it through, I said, "Oh
certainly, you're bound to go at once; there can't be a
doubt of that. Don't bother yourself about Lady Trecastle;

I'll tell her exactly how the matter was. You know she and my father will be back in a couple of days, and I shall be all right till their return. But you'll lose your train if you don't look sharp now."

Reassured by this speech, she hurried off to get ready, whilst I rang the bell to order the carriage. It was an object to me to have her out of the room when I did this, as her absence enabled me at the same time that I ordered the carriage to send word to the cook that no dinner would be wanted that night. Miss Smith, I said, had been called away suddenly, and I meant to travel with her a short distance, to the house of one of my aunt's, with whom I should stay until Sir Anthony and Lady Trecastle returned. There was nothing unlikely about my paying a visit to my aunt when left alone unexpectedly; and I made this announcement to prevent the servants from becoming alarmed at my disappearance, and bringing about a premature discovery of my flight by communicating at once with my father.

I next went to Miss Smith to tell her that I was coming with her as far as the station to see her off; I said that I knew my father wanted to have some things mended at a shop in Sparkton, and that I thought I might as well avail myself of this opportunity of taking them to the town, now that the carriage was going there with her. Of course the discrepancy between this statement and the one which I had just made for the benefit of the household would become apparent, and put me into an awkward position, if she and the servants should happen to compare notes as to what I had been saying. But I felt I could reckon confidently that no such comparison would take place; as, for one thing, my governess was a deal too much flurried and taken up with her own affairs to think of anything else; and, for another thing, my precaution of not delivering the telegram till there was only just time to catch the train, prevented her from having time for idle conversation, even if she *had* happened to feel disposed for such a thing.

I had had considerable difficulty in making up my mind what to do about luggage. If I did not take any, that would look odd to the servants, who believed me to be going to stay with my aunt; but then Miss Smith, on the other hand, who fancied that I was merely going to drive into Sparkton to see her off, would be astonished at any appearance of boxes, bags, or portmanteaux that indicated an intended absence from home. Besides that, it would not suit my plan of action to be encumbered with anything that I could not manage easily to carry through the streets with my own hands.

I had considered this knotty point for some time before I could determine how to settle it. What I finally resolved upon was to take a small hand-bag which was just large enough to hold sufficient wearing apparel for a two night's visit (so as to impose upon the servants), and which was yet not too large for me to be able to carry about easily. Then, if my governess should make any remarks about its presence in the carriage, and wonder what I wanted it for, I could tell her that it contained the things for my father that were going to be mended. Into this hand-bag I had already packed all the jewellery I possessed, and as many clothes and other articles likely to come useful as there was room for. Thus all my preparations were completed, and I was ready for a start.

I did not wish to go away without bidding adieu to Lady Trecastle, so I had written her a farewell letter; and whilst Miss Smith was putting on her things, I placed it where my stepmother would be certain to find it on her return. It ran thus –

"LADY TRECASTLE – In my opinion it is high time for me to see the world and enjoy myself like other people, and as you seem resolved that I shall do nothing of the kind, I am going to settle the matter without asking your leave. I have timed my departure to suit the sailing of a vessel which is going where I wish to go, and by the time you receive this I shall be out of England and far away. You and I have hit it off together so badly, that I have no doubt you will regard my leaving as a subject for sincere congratulations – which permit me to offer to you. I fear that you will not receive them from anyone else, on account of the hypocritical appearance of grief under which you are sure to think it necessary to conceal your real joy. I foresee also that you will affect the utmost anxiety to recover me; this will, of course, involve a considerable amount of expense, since you will find it difficult to satisfy Mrs. Grundy of the sincerity of your protestations, unless you employ detectives, and send out far and wide in search of me. I reflect on all this with pleasure, for I know well how you will grudge every penny that is spent on so unworthy an object as myself; and as I have no fear of being found, I am sure that the money will be spent in vain. Think of that, Lady Trecastle, you who hate waste – think of all that you'll have to throw away on *my* account! Sincerely trusting that you and I may never meet again, and that Margaret and Jane may be able to continue their studies without the assistance which they have hitherto received from the governesses who were supposed to be engaged for my sole benefit – Believe me to remain, yours in no sense at all, INA TRECASTLE."

It is not to be supposed from this letter that I had any idea of going straight abroad; on the contrary, I had made up my mind to get to London as quickly as possible, and there to hide myself, and be lost to pursuit by the time that my flight should be known. But I put in the bit about leaving England on the chance of Lady Trecastle's believing it to be my real intention, and being thereby thrown on the wrong track, and caused extra worry and expense. She being my especial enemy, I wanted to annoy her as much as I could; and as my father always managed to slip out of whatever was troublesome, I knew that all the bother of the search after me would certainly fall upon her shoulders, and that the more troublesome and costly it was, the more my longing for revenge would be gratified.

It cost me nothing to leave my father. Since his second marriage he and I had seen but little of each other – I having been kept closely in the schoolroom, and he not having troubled himself to alter whatever arrangements his wife thought fit to make. Whether I were at home or not would make no difference to him I knew. I cared for no one, and no one cared for me, exactly describes the condition in which I was on that afternoon when I drove off from Castle Manor with my tearful and apprehensive governess, to catch the 4.20 train at Sparkton. I was leaving a home wherein was no person or thing that was dear to me, where there was nothing for me to regret, to which I was bound by no sweet or tender associations, and which had no kind of hold over me. And I was about to exchange dulness and dreary monotony for action, adventures, excitement, and an unknown state of existence, where I must be always on the alert, ready for everything, and trust to no one except myself. To all this I looked forward with a delight that was not marred by the faintest tinge of timidity, anxiety, or fear of failing in what I had set myself to accomplish. No wonder that I was radiant with joy, and found some difficulty in preserving my usual demeanour sufficiently not to arouse Miss Smith's suspicions.

CHAPTER VI

A Photograph

THERE are two railway stations in Sparkton, which is a town of sufficient size and importance to have two different railway companies competing for its patronage; and this circumstance rendered it all the easier for me to escape without leaving traces for any pursuers to follow. The train by which I intended to go to London would not leave until about two hours later than Miss Smith's train to the north, and did not start from the same station. What, therefore, I meant to do was to dismiss the coachman, John, and send him home under the impression that I had gone away with my governess, according to the announcement of my plans which I had made to our Castle Manor household. Then, as soon as I had seen Miss Smith safely off, I intended to take my bag in my hand, and proceed on foot to the other station, there to await the departure of the London train.

It would, of course, never do for Miss Smith to see the carriage, which she imagined was going to take me home again, drive straight away directly that it had deposited us at the station; so, when we got out, I told John to wait a minute, and then accompanied her to the ticket-office. Some other travellers who had arrived before us were blocking up the entrance, and she had to wait her turn to take her ticket. This delay greatly increased her nervousness, and she began to be in a desperate fidget lest she should be too late. I showed her, by the station-clock overhead, that she had fully ten minutes to spare, but she was too much upset to be calmed by reason. Pulling out her purse she commenced fumbling at it hurriedly, and was dismayed to find that she could not open it. "Oh, Ina!" she exclaimed, helplessly, "what *am* I to do? Something has happened to my purse, and I can't get it open! Dear! Dear! I *know* I shall be too late! Can you lend me some money?"

The purse would not open for the very excellent reason that she was tugging at the hinges instead of at the clasp; I doubt whether she would ever have found this out for herself in the condition in which she then was; but I quickly saw what was the matter, and rectified it for her. As soon as I had done so, I said, "By the by, there's a parcel to be called for at a shop in the next street, which John will have plenty of time to go and fetch whilst I'm waiting to see you off. I forgot to tell him of it before I left the carriage, so I'm just going to send him there. I won't be a minute, and shall be back before you've got your ticket."

The poor woman looked at me with a bewildered air at first, as though she had hardly understood what I said to her, and felt only alarmed at the idea of being left alone in the crowded station. Then, seeming to realise the position of affairs all of a sudden, she answered quickly, "Oh, but I forgot, hadn't you better go and do your shopping at once without waiting for me to start? I'm afraid if the horses were to catch cold or anything, Lady Trecastle would be very much vexed; and, perhaps, she might think it was my fault. Not that I want to lose your help, only I shouldn't like to make her angry. If these people in front will only be quick, I *may* still be able to catch the train perhaps!"

"Don't be afraid – you've heaps of time," I returned; "and I'm sure there's no chance of the horses taking cold;

besides, they'll be kept moving by going on this errand that I'm going to send them off for. I mean to stay and see the last of you, put you comfortably into your carriage, get you some papers to amuse yourself with on the journey, and see that you don't forget anything at the last moment."

In her then condition of mental disorganisation on account of her anxiety about her sister, she was really hardly capable of looking after herself. She seemed to be vaguely aware of this, and to regard me as a sort of tower of strength which she could rely upon, and her face brightened perceptibly at the assurance that she would have the benefit of my protecting presence until she was fairly under weigh.

"Thank you, dear Ina," she said, gratefully. "I'm so *much* obliged. I can't tell you how kind and good I think it of you to give yourself so much trouble about me."

"Oh, it's no trouble," I replied, repressing with difficulty an inclination to laugh at the thoroughness with which she was being humbugged. So saying I left her, and hurried away to give John his instructions. Though the situation struck me as being ludicrous, yet I had an uncomfortable sense of being in a false position, and did not feel particularly anxious to listen to her expressions of earnest gratitude. I had, for my own purposes, deliberately thrown her into a state of serious distress caused by what was absolutely false, and was now staying with her merely because it suited me to do so, and not at all out of regard to her necessities; considering all this, it did seem a little strong for me to be posing in the character of her especial friend, and receiving thanks as though I were remaining to see her off out of pure good nature! Yet, after all, I could not help acting as I had done. I was bound to clear the course for myself somehow or other; and if the process of being swept aside happened to be unpleasant to any obstacle, why, that was unfortunate for the obstacle, but no reason why the sweeping aside should be given up.

Having told John that he need not wait any longer, I watched him drive away, and then returned to my governess, who was, by that time, again in need of assistance. She had paid for her ticket with a £5 note, and received a considerable amount of change, which she had managed to let slip through her trembling fingers as she was transferring it to her purse, and it had rolled hither and thither on the floor. Firmly convinced that the train was on the very point of starting, she was, when I arrived, just about to hurry off and take her seat, and abandon the money to its fate, though she could but ill have afforded to lose it. Luckily I was in time to stop this folly, and persuaded her to stay and join me in picking up the scattered coins, which we soon accomplished. Whilst thus employed, I could not help reflecting on how differently she and I were constituted, and on how much the most fit I was to look after myself.

It must be a queer sensation, thought I, to care for anyone to such a pitch as she does. Fancy being in such a state of mind as she is at the mere idea of some other person's being ill, or in trouble of some kind or other! Well, I thank my stars I am somewhat tougher than that, and not *quite* such a softy. Precious little chance I should have, else, of shifting for myself, and fighting my own way in the world, as I mean to do!

It was with a sense of pity, wherein (as is often the case) there was a strong admixture of contempt, that I escorted her to the train, found her the right carriage, established her in it with such travelling comforts as were to be had, repeated over and over the names of the places where she would have to change before reaching Carlisle, for fear of her forgetting them, and paid her whatever other little attentions I could think of. She, poor woman, was quite overwhelmed at such thoughtful politeness on my part, and received it with the utmost gratitude, without dreaming for an instant of the desire to make some kind of amends for the anxiety I had brought upon her, which was the real motive of my unwontedly civil behaviour.

I tried hard to raise her spirits, and when the train began to move I walked beside it for a step or two saying cheerful parting words to her. Faster and faster did the long line of carriages slip along by the platform, and I stood still, watching her wave me a farewell with her tear-besprinkled handkerchief. In a minute more she had passed out of sight, and I felt, that now the last link of my chain was indeed broken, that I had got rid of all the authorities whom I detested, and that I was in very truth my own mistress.

The first thing for me to do now was to make my way to the other station, and there await the starting of my train for London. In order to avoid the risk of being recognised by anyone in traversing the town, I had, before leaving home, put into my pocket a thick veil; this I now donned, and then, with my bag in my hand, issued out into the streets. Here I soon had cause to congratulate myself on having taken the precaution to wear a veil, for, on turning a corner, I suddenly found myself confronted by our own carriage, with John on the box, drawn up close to the pavement. John was profiting by the absence of his master's family to do some shopping on his own account, and also to enjoy the society of a female acquaintance, who was perched up on the seat beside him, displaying manifold and gaudy ribbons from that point of vantage with an air of immense complacency. Though he glanced at me as I passed, he did not recognise me through my thick veil, and I reached my destination in safety, without meeting anyone else whom I knew.

The train by which I was going was not due to start for some time to come, and I could not take a ticket for it yet. As I was anxious not to attract observation by being seen hanging about the station, I withdrew into the waiting-room with a book in my hand, and settled myself there quietly, as if to pass the time in reading. I was, in truth, too much excited to fix my attention on my book, but I wished to *appear* to be engrossed in it all the same; and as it is obviously impossible to read much through a thick veil, I threw mine back when I began to pretend to study the volume which I held.

I was undisturbed in my seclusion for a considerable while; but just as I was beginning to think that it was getting near time for the train to start, and that the ticket-office would soon be open, two ladies entered the room, attended by a footman laden with their rugs, bags, and etceteras. These he deposited on the table and then retired, touching his hat respectfully, and saying that the tickets would not be given out for another five minutes.

The lady nearest me was a middle-aged person. I saw at a glance, as she entered the room, that she was a complete stranger to me, and I looked at her carelessly, without at first noticing her younger companion. I had, for the moment, forgotten that my veil was up; but then, suddenly remembering it, and also the expediency of con-cealing my face before going to take my ticket, I was just about to lower the odious stifling mass of thick gauze, when the younger lady moved towards the table to take something out of her travelling-bag. She looked at me in passing, and as our eyes met I felt a thrill of alarm, and a conviction that she was someone I had met before, though I could not recollect where or how, or what her name was. Luckily she had evidently no recollection of me, but passed on without a gleam of recognition in her face, got what she wanted out of the bag, and returned to her seat.

None the less, I was perfectly certain I knew her, and all at once it flashed across me who she was. She must be Kitty Mervyn, the girl whom I had met and taken a strong fancy to at Lugano four years ago. Since then we had both of us grown and altered considerably in appearance, and she had developed into a tall, handsome, stately-looking young woman. But it was so uncommon an event for anyone to make any great impression on me, that I was not likely to forget whoever had been able to work that miracle, and I felt positive that I could not now be mistaken as to Kitty's identity. I perceived, also, that she had no idea whatever of who I was, which was most fortunate for me, as it would have greatly interfered with my plans to be seen there by anyone who knew me. I was quite aware of this, and rejoiced at my good luck; and yet – strange creatures that we are! – even whilst I rejoiced, I suffered a pang of keen mortification. Hardly ever in my life had I felt disposed to honour one of my fellow-creatures with any especial degree of liking or approval; and when, for once, I had been moved to do so, it seemed as if the individual thus distinguished ought certainly to have felt some corresponding amount of inclination for me. Yet this had not been the case, since Kitty Mervyn had forgotten me, though I had not forgotten her. And therefore I had a sense of annoyance and humiliation at this forgetfulness, notwithstanding its opportuneness, and the inconvenience that it would have been to me to be recognised just then, when it was my great object to leave no trace that could show what had become of me after the time that I had parted from Miss Smith.

As soon as the ticket-office was open, the footman returned to inform the ladies of that fact; then they left the waiting-room attended by the man carrying their *impedimenta* for them as before. Having stayed a minute longer to let them get out of the way, I was on the point of following them, when I noticed a small article lying under the table, and picked it up. It was one of those purses that are purse and pocket-book combined, and I guessed that it had probably fallen out of Miss Mervyn's bag when she had opened it just now to take out something else. What should I do with the purse? I had little doubt of who the rightful owner was, and could easily restore it to her if I chose. Only the question was whether I *did* choose, for there was no one near to see me find it, and I was free to do as I pleased. At some other time I might, perhaps, have followed the dictates of honesty, but at the present moment I was out of charity with Kitty. I had not forgiven her for the wound which she had unconsciously inflicted on my self-esteem, and was much more inclined to spite her, if I had a chance, than to do her a good turn; therefore, after hesitating for a few moments, I pocketed what I had found, postponing the examination of its contents to the first opportunity when I should be at leisure and unobserved.

Now that I was going to trust to my own resources for a livelihood, money was a most important object to me, and as I had no intention of wasting it in needless luxury, I contented myself with a humble third-class ticket. Having secured this, I took my seat in the London train, and was, in due course of time, whirled away from Sparkton towards the metropolis, where I meant to seek my fortune. At starting there were two or three other passengers in the carriage with me, but they got out at the first few stations where we stopped, and when I found myself alone I thought I might as well take that opportunity of seeing what Miss Mervyn's purse contained.

I was glad to find in it several pounds in gold and silver. Some extra cash would be extremely handy to me in present circumstances, and would no doubt be far more

useful to me than to her, I thought. Then I turned to the
pocket-book half of the purse, and began to explore that
also. Here there were some postage stamps, a set of
directions for some kind of fancy-work that was just then
all the fashion, and a letter addressed to the Hon.
Katherine Mervyn – which last was a conclusive proof
that my conjecture as to the ownership of the purse was
right. I took the liberty of unfolding and reading the letter,
which was a heavy bill for gloves and fans. The largeness
of the amount caused me a surprise, which was soon
changed into envy as I reflected that I, too, might have
been in a state to require a similar profusion of these
articles, if my step-mother had not unjustly shut me off
from the privileges of my age and rank in life. It was
strange how the perusal of that bill, and the thought that it
had been incurred by a girl no older than myself, irritated
me afresh against Lady Trecastle, and increased my
former sense of being a much injured and aggrieved
mortal!

The bill, stamps, and work directions appeared at first
sight to comprise the whole contents of the pocket-book;
I was about to shut it up under that impression, when I
bethought me that I was in want of a new purse, as mine
was a good deal worn, and that if Kitty's was in good
condition I had better substitute it for my own. This idea
made me take up again the one I had found, and look it
over carefully. The close inspection revealed an inner
pocket underneath the flap of the other, and ingeniously
contrived so as not to attract notice. Within this sly
hiding-place was a piece of cardboard wrapped in silver
paper, which, on being opened, disclosed the photograph
of a very good-looking young man in military uniform.
My curiosity was aroused as to who the original might be,
and I turned it round and round in hopes of discovering
some name or initial; there was, however, nothing of the

kind except the name of the photographer to be found, and so my curiosity remained unsatisfied.

Whoever could that young man be? I wondered, and why was he so interesting to Kitty that she carried his picture about with her, done up and concealed with such care? It was not a brother, as I knew that she had none. Was she engaged to be married, and was it the likeness of her future husband? Only in that case the portrait would be more likely to be carried openly than to be thus hidden away in the inmost recess of her purse, as if it were a thing to be ashamed of.

As I mused over it, and over the desire for secrecy that seemed to be conveyed by the place where I had found it, the thought crossed my mind whether it could be some unacknowledged lover, whose addresses were being paid against the wishes of her parents. Yet somehow I could hardly fancy that to be very probable either. There was a stateliness and haughtiness about her that gave the impression of a person who would be most unlikely ever to condescend to anything so mean and underhand as a clandestine love affair; she would have too much self-respect and sense of dignity. Well! be the young man who he might, I had no clue to his identity or to his connection with her, and it was no use my bothering myself with vain speculations on the subject. At all events, she would have to get a new copy of his photograph, as I had no intention of returning the one that had fallen into my hands. And with that reflection I dismissed the matter from my mind, and applied myself to the more practical consideration of what my immediate future was to be.

CHAPTER VII

A Few London Prices

I HAVE not, as yet, said anything about what I meant to do on reaching London, and how I intended to support myself; but it must not, therefore, be supposed that I had not carefully considered, and fully made up my mind upon that important matter. Various ways by which a young woman in my position might earn her livelihood had suggested themselves to me; and, after mature deliberation, I had selected the avocations of daily-governess, shop-assistant, or travelling-maid, as being those in which I was most likely to succeed.

This reduced the limits of my choice to three. For awhile I remained uncertain to which of the three I should give the preference, but finally came to the conclusion that the latter was the one for which I was best fitted by my gifts – both natural and acquired. Lack of training would, of course, make it foolish for me to think of under-taking the place of an ordinary stay-at-home lady's-maid; but that training was by no means so essential for a travelling Abigail. What would be chiefly wanted for such a situation was, a knowledge of languages, a good head, a capacity for looking after luggage, and such abilities as would enable the maid to supply the place of courier whenever necessary; and in all these respects I had little fear of being capable of giving satisfaction to any employer. As far as needlework was concerned, I could do plain sewing well enough; and though I did not

know how to make dresses, yet I anticipated no difficulty
on that score, because, as it would evidently be unreasonable to expect a servant to have cultivated both
brains and fingers alike, therefore proficiency in all
inferior art, like dressmaking, was not to be looked for in
a person who had studied the far higher branch of
knowledge – languages. And, besides that, people did not
generally want to have clothes made when they were on
their travels.

There was another part of a lady's-maid's business
which was much more likely to be required, and of
which, also, I was at present ignorant; and that was
hairdressing. But that was a deficiency which could easily
be remedied by some lessons from a good hairdresser;
and the first thing that I meant to do in London was to
inquire for an artist of this kind, and become his pupil
until I had learnt from him enough of the art to fit me for
a maid's place. Of course, paying for the lessons, and
finding myself meanwhile in board and lodging, would
cost money – and expense was a consideration that was
on no account to be overlooked. But I was prepared to
practice strict economy; and, what with the contents of
Kitty Mervyn's purse and my own, I had enough to live
upon for some weeks at least, and did not doubt that my
resources would hold out till I should have learnt
sufficient hairdressing for my purpose. Altogether I
believed that I should make a capital travelling-maid; and
it was an occupation especially attractive to me, because
well adapted to gratify my taste for much change and
amusement.

One thing which I did during the journey to London
was to effect a considerable change in my appearance.
The more I could make myself look unlike what I had
been when I left home, the greater would be my security
against pursuit, and I did not neglect the opportunity for

doing this which was afforded by the solitude of the railway carriage. I had not got the materials for a complete disguise, but a good deal may be done with a different neck-wrap and pair of gloves, and a brush, comb, needle and thread. These things I had stowed away in my bag, and by their aid I soon contrived sufficiently to alter my exterior to make it unlikely that I should be identified as corresponding to any description that might be given of the Gilbertina Trecastle who had seen off her governess at Sparkton Station.

By the time we reached London night had set in. As we steamed slowly into the spacious and brilliantly lit-up terminus, the bustling, animated scene which I beheld gave me a thrill of delight, and a pleasant sense of having undoubtedly got away from the tranquil duck-pond where I had been vegetating, and having entered the rushing stream of life – a stream which tolerates none of the slimy scum and weed that are apt to accumulate on the surface of stagnation, but speedily washes away every vestige of them.

I saw railway officials of various grades hurrying to and fro, and all intent on some business or other. Loud shouts for hansoms and fourwheelers began to echo through the glazed walls of the great station even before the train had stopped. Porters swarmed at the windows of carriages still in motion, jumped on to the steps, opened the doors, commenced taking out hand-bags, wraps, umbrellas, and similar small articles, reiterated eager exclamations of "Cab, sir? Cab, mum? Any luggage? Where from?" etc., and vied with one another in pressing their services upon all passengers from whom a tip was likely to be expected. Under this head the occupants of third-class carriages were evidently not included, and not one of the offers of assistance that were being lavished so freely in other directions fell to my share, as I emerged from my compartment with the bag that contained all my goods in my hand. It was a neglect, however, which I certainly did not wish altered under the circumstances, as the less notice I attracted, the better was my chance of evading any enquiries that might subsequently be made about me.

It was too late that night to set about hunting for a lodging, but as hotels are usually to be found in close proximity to railway stations, I had no fear of having to go far for a bed. I was not mistaken in this confidence. No sooner had I got into the street than I saw just before me an immense building with the words RAILWAY HOTEL flaring in large coloured letters upon a gas transparency over the door; and underneath this inscription was another, in smaller sized letters, stating that within this magnificent hotel travellers of all classes were supplied with every comfort and luxury at extremely moderate prices.

Turning my steps thither, I entered through the open doors into a large, softly-carpeted, handsomely furnished hall, where a porter in a gorgeous livery and sundry waiters were lounging about and talking. To one of these I addressed myself, requesting to be shown a room for the night, and adding that I wished it to be as inexpensive a one as possible. My request was referred to the presiding genius in the hall, who was an elegantly attired young lady, with the most nonchalant expression of countenance that it was ever my fortune to behold. She was deeply engaged in a book; but on being spoken to she put it down, glanced at a list of rooms, rang a bell, uttered oracularly the single word "18," then resumed her volume, and at once became as deeply absorbed in it again as though her studies had never been interrupted at all.

Meanwhile, one of her satellites conducted me up innumerable stairs to the chamber assigned to me –

lowness of price and of situation being in the usual inverse proportions. At last we arrived at No. 18, which proved to be a room small enough to have done duty as a convent cell, and scantily furnished with a table, a chair, a cracked and fly-spotted little looking-glass, a washing-stand, a tiny chest of drawers, and a short narrow bedstead, whereon was an abominably hard and fusty-smelling mattress.

The charge for one night's occupation of this palatial apartment was 5s., and for that sum one would have supposed that a little civility from the hotel servants might well have been thrown into the bargain, without there being any danger of the visitor's receiving an unfair amount of return for the money spent. Such, however, was by no means the opinion of the waiters and chamber-maids, who were at no pains to hide the supreme scorn with which they were inspired by the spectacle of a traveller attempting to combine hotel life with economy. To their minds the two things evidently were, and ought to be, absolutely incompatible; and I am inclined to think that they deemed it one of the objects for which they had been put into the world, to make that incompatibility as plainly apparent as possible.

Fortunately for me, I was as little affected by their contempt as I was by the indifferent quality of the accommodation provided. Neither the nasty smell of my couch nor its hardness, nor yet the sense of being an object of scorn to a pack of waiters and chambermaids, had power to interfere with my repose; for I slept soundly all night, and awoke in the morning as much refreshed as though I had tenanted the most luxurious room imagin-able. Observing a tariff of hotel prices hanging up over the washing-stand, I proceeded to read it as soon as I was dressed. From this document I learnt that a single cup of tea or coffee was to be had for 6d. (would that include milk and sugar? I wondered), and that the cost of a breakfast, consisting of tea or coffee and bread and butter, was 1s. 6d. Not bad that, thought I, for a place which professes to supply every comfort and luxury at extremely moderate prices! I should rather like to know what is the landlord's idea of *im*moderate ones.

Paying for food at this rate was not exactly consistent with the rigid economy which my circumstances imposed upon me, so I sallied forth to procure breakfast elsewhere. This was not difficult to accomplish, as there was a tidy little restaurant only two doors off, where, for the sum of 6d., I was supplied with coffee, a good-sized roll, and a pat of butter – all of excellent quality. The small round table on which the food was served was destitute of a cloth, but quite clean; and I ate my meal with as hearty a relish, and enjoyed it every bit as much, as though it had cost 150 per cent more, and been consumed in the sumptuous coffee-room of the hotel.

The proprietor of the restaurant was an Italian. I was, just then, his sole customer, and, as he did not seem particularly busy, I spoke to him in his own language when I went to the counter to pay for my breakfast, and asked him if he happened to know of anyone who gave lessons in hairdressing. The chance of a conversation in his native tongue appeared to please him; for he became so communicative that I think it would have needed but little encouragement on my part to draw from him, there and then, the whole history of his life. With some difficulty, however, I managed to check his confidences, and to keep him to the point on which I required information.

Did he know anyone to teach hairdressing? He must consider a moment. Yes, to be sure! there was his friend, Monsieur Candot, a French *parrucchiére,* who could do hair, make frisettes, plaits, puffs, curls, wigs, everything.

He was not *certain* that Monsieur Candot gave lessons; but thought it highly probable.

Had Monsieur Candot much practice? I asked; because otherwise he would not suit me, as I wished only to learn of a really high-class and fashionable hairdresser. Then, seeing the Italian's face clouding over at the idea of my venturing to doubt the superior talent of a man whom he recommended and called his friend, I hastened to smooth down his ruffled feelings by adding that I felt sure he would excuse my asking the question, because – as he well knew – there were wigs and wigs, and the mere fact of making them did not necessarily imply that they were made well; that, in short, if it were permissible to take liberties with Giusti's epigram about bookmaking, one might say –

> "Il far' un' parrúcca è meno che niénte,
> Se parrúcca fatta non piace la gente."

This pacified the Italian's rising ire. There could be no possible doubt, he said, of his friend's wonderful talent. Monsieur Candot was a genuine artist, who never executed any work of art that was not first-rate, because, if it fell short of the perfection at which he aimed, he would destroy it unhesitatingly, and make another and more successful one in its place. His merit was appreciated everywhere; he was in request in the very highest circles, and made wigs *"anche per le duchesse."*

There was no resisting such a recommendation as this, so I procured Monsieur Candot's address, and set off to find him. He resided in a small street near Edgeware Road, and when I got to his abode I was fortunate enough to find him disengaged, and to be admitted without delay to his presence. I told him I was a maid who was anxious to learn hairdressing, and asked if he gave lessons in that art. He replied in the affirmative, saying also that he was constantly having applications like mine, and that he had no doubt of being able to make an expert *coiffeuse* of me in about a month – however ignorant of the matter I might now be. Was I going to take the lessons on my own account, or was it by the wish of my mistress?

At the time I could not conceive what was the motive of this question; but I subsequently discovered it to be, that his price for lessons given to a maid at her mistress's expense was nearly double what it was when the maid paid for them out of her own pocket. I, in my present state of life, highly approved of this practice; and, as my answer showed me to be entitled to the benefit of the lower rate of payment, our terms were soon arranged, and the interview came to a satisfactory termination.

So far, so good; and now to find myself a cheap habitation not far from Monsieur Candot's residence. After wandering about for some time in the neighbouring streets, I discovered a lodging that seemed likely to be suitable. The landlady, however – either because a long experience of lodgers had made her distrust them as a body, or else because there was something she objected to in my appearance – did not evince much eagerness to let her room. She hesitated and eyed me doubtfully, demanding what was my name and occupation, and whether I could pay a week in advance – *i.e.* fifteen shillings.

I had already determined that, whenever I should be asked for my name, I would adopt the abbreviation that had been bestowed upon me in my earliest years; so I replied that I was a lady's maid called Caroline Jill; that I had recently left a situation; and that I did not intend looking out for another until I had had some hairdressing lessons. And, as I spoke, I laid upon the table the rent in advance which she had asked for.

There was nothing at all improbable in my story, and the sight of the money gave her confidence, so she consented to receive me as a lodger. I then bethought me that she would be almost sure to expect a lady's-maid to be accompanied by at least one big box, and that her distrust might very likely be reawakened at sight of the extremely modest amount of luggage which I had to bring; so I mentioned, casually, that I had left almost all my goods at home in the country, and had only a very small bag with me, as it was so inconvenient to be moving about with a lot of heavy things. And having thus prepared her mind for the diminutive size of my bag, I set off to fetch it from the hotel.

The hairdressing lessons were not to take place till the evenings, or late in the afternoons, so that I should be idle during the greater part of each day; and, as I returned to the hotel, I began considering how to employ profitably all the spare time that I should have on my hands. Evidently the thing to suit me would be a temporary engagement as daily-governess, as I should then be adding to my slender stock of money even whilst paying for Candot's instructions. I would endeavour to get such an engagement as soon as possible; and, in order to lose no time about it, I would go straight to the hotel reading-room, where I should be sure to find the day's newspapers, wherein I might perhaps meet with some advertisements that it would be worth my while to answer.

On reaching the hotel, therefore, I turned along a passage over which was a notice to the effect that it led to the reading-room. A waiter outside stared at me with wrathful surprise, as if he thought that the luxuries of that apartment were unlawful for any one badly off for money, and that it was the height of presumption for so humble a person as myself to attempt to enjoy them. But I knew well that whoever stays at a hotel has a right to profit by its reading-room; so I walked calmly in, without heeding his indignant looks. Daily and weekly newspapers, journals, and periodicals of various kinds, were spread on the table, and I proceeded diligently to study the advertisements for daily governesses which they contained. It was not every such place which would do for me, as I wanted one situated in London, and where only morning work was required; therefore I had some difficulty in discovering an advertisement that was at all likely to suit. At last, however, I hit upon a couple in the *Morning Post* that seemed tolerably promising; and as it was too late to think of going to apply for them on that day, I copied the addresses for use on the morrow, and then left the room.

As I entered the hall on my way upstairs a gentleman who had come to call upon someone staying at the hotel was in the act of leaving his card. It was a strange coincidence that that particular individual should have happened to be there at the very moment when I was passing through; for I immediately saw that he was the original of the mysterious photograph which had been put away so snugly in Miss Mervyn's purse, and as to which I had felt inquisitive. Surely now I should be able to gratify my curiosity so far as to find out his name, I thought; and, so thinking, lingered in the hall in hopes of an opportunity for attaining that object.

Not far from the door there were a lot of pigeon-holes for the purpose of receiving any letters and cards that might arrive for visitors at the hotel; and in one of these receptacles the gentleman's card was deposited by the servant to whom he gave it. This afforded me the chance I wanted. Pretending that I thought there might be a letter for me, I went to the pigeon-holes and inspected the bit of pasteboard just placed there, and thus learnt that its owner's name was Edward Norroy, and that he was a captain in the Fusiliers.

Well, that was *something* to have discovered about him, certainly, but not very much; I had never heard the name before, and was still as far off as ever from knowing what he and Kitty had to do with one another, and why she should care to carry his picture about in her pocket. It was no business of mine, of course, as I very well knew. Yet the singular attractiveness which she had for me made me feel more interest in her concerns than in those of the generality of human-kind. It was strange, too, considering that I had seen her but twice in my life, and was by no means of an impressionable nature, nor yet particularly inquisitive. But that did not prevent me from speculating about her to an extent at which I myself was astonished; I had an idea that I should like to be able to observe her, and study her character.

Reflecting how queer it was to take so much interest in the affairs of a person with whom I had absolutely nothing to do, and wondering whether it did not show a tendency to reprehensible weak-mindedness, I left the hall, and climbed up to my bedroom. I had very little packing-up to get through, so I was soon ready to depart, and then I rang the bell and asked for my bill.

It might, not unreasonably, have been supposed that the 5s. which was the price of the room I had occupied would have fully paid for all that I had had from the hotel, and left a pretty fair margin for profit as well. Not so, however, was the opinion of the manager; for a tiny foot-tub and jug of water which I had used to wash myself in on rising were dignified in the bill by the name of "bath;" and for that, and for "attendance," an extra half-crown was tacked on to my expenses.

I had had quite enough experience of hotel bills to know that "attendance" was an inevitable item on them, and that it was no use grumbling at the charge. Still, I had found the article so unusually conspicuous by its absence in the present instance, that I could not resist the desire I felt to give a little bit of my mind on the subject to the chambermaid who had brought me the bill, and, was now waiting for its payment.

"What an odd thing it is," said I, gravely, "that *attendance* and *nothing* should be two words that have precisely the same meaning. Don't you think so?"

I spoke with the utmost seriousness, and I think that she imagined I was going to dispute the bill. "Do I think what?" she returned, pertly; "I don't know what you're talking about."

"Why," replied I, "if you look at this bill, you will see that *attendance* is charged just as if it were something extra which had really been supplied to me; that is not the case, as you are perfectly well aware, so the natural inference is that the word must mean nothing, you see. Otherwise one would be obliged to suppose that those three syllables had some special privilege attached to them to enable hotelkeepers to rob people openly and with impunity; for there certainly isn't any other article – such as dinner, wine, drawing-room, etc. – which a visitor can be made to pay for if he hasn't had it. I thought you might have been struck by the singularity of this circumstance, but probably you are too much accustomed to it to think it odd. Here's the money; I wish to have the receipt as soon as possible, if you please."

The woman coloured angrily, and looked as if she had an uncivil reply at the tip of her tongue. Just as I finished speaking, however, a bell rang which she was called to go and answer; so she was compelled to deny herself the pleasure of a retort. She hurried away, muttering something about having no time to waste in listening to all the rubbish that fools found time to talk; and the receipted bill was presently brought to me by another of the servants.

Taking my little bag in my hand, I descended the stairs and bade adieu to the grand Railway Hotel, without feeling the very slightest inclination ever again to make proof of the accommodation which it offered "at extremely moderate prices" to "travellers of all classes." Yet I myself told lies unhesitatingly whenever I found them convenient; so what right had I to complain of other people for doing the same?

CHAPTER VIII

A Street Incident

BEFORE going to bed that night I wished to arrange my plans for the next day, and to make up my mind which of the two daily-governess situations that I had in view I would apply for first. For this purpose I carefully compared the advertisements together to see if either one contained anything that made it seem likely to be preferable to the other. As, however, there did not appear to be a pin's point to choose between them, I left the selection to chance, and settled the question by tossing. The result of this appeal to hazard was to decide me to try first for the place of A. G., who required personal application to be made between noon and two o'clock in the afternoon, at a given address somewhere in the Bayswater district.

It was no use going there before the hour specified, and I did not feel in the humour to settle down to any steady occupation till it was time to start, so I spent most of the following morning in watching what went on in the street below my window, and making guesses as to the characters and employments of the various passers-by. Amongst these there was one to whom my attention was particularly attracted. This was a little girl of about nine or ten years old, with a basket containing some bunches of common flowers for sale. It was quite early in the morning when first I noticed her, and afterwards I saw her pass my window again and again; for though, at intervals, she made excursions into other neighbouring streets, yet after each of these excursions she returned to the one wherein my lodging was situated. At first she looked tolerably bright and smiling as she ran here and there, making assiduous efforts to dispose of her stock in trade. But she was not in luck's way, and failed to sell a single bunch; and she evidently took this ill-success greatly to heart, for all the smiles and cheerfulness gradually died away from her face, and she looked increasingly sad and melancholy each time that I saw her pass.

Presently a big coarse-looking woman, who was also selling flowers, came into the street. She and the child met, and stopped to talk, just opposite my window; and though I could not hear what they said, yet their looks and gestures enabled me to make a very fair guess at what they were talking about. The little girl, I could see, was timidly asking some favour which the woman refused. The child, though apparently much in awe of the other, yet seemed to screw up her courage to urge the petition; evidently she desired very much to have it granted, as I could see by the pitifully earnest wistfulness expressed in her countenance, as she looked up with quivering lips, and eyes brimful of tears. Whatever her request was, however, the woman had no mind to grant it; and, seeming to become impatient at the child's persistency, pushed her away roughly and left the street. For a minute or so after her departure the little girl stood sobbing, and looking a picture of disappointment and misery. Then, using the corner of her shawl as a pocket-handkerchief, she dried her eyes, blew her nose, and mournfully resumed her former occupation.

She did not again come in sight of my window, so I saw no more of her till it was time for me to start on my situation-hunting expedition.

I was walking down towards Oxford Street, with my

head full of my own affairs, when I heard a shrill, quavering, little voice pipe out close at my elbow: "Flowers, lady! bootifle fresh flowers. Won't you please buy a bunch?" Looking down, I saw beside me the same little girl whom I had previously been watching. The contents of her basket were still undiminished, and she was sitting wearily on a door-step, but now started up to offer me her wares, and try to induce me to become a customer. Though I could do very well without flowers, yet I liked them, and thought they would be a considerable improvement to my dingy little lodging; besides, I pitied the child for the bad luck she had hitherto had that morning; so altogether I had half a mind to buy of her. But then the warning voice of prudence interfered, saying that I had no money to waste on vanities like flowers, and that the more I departed from my strict rule of denying myself every superfluity, the more irksome it would be to keep to it at all. I thought prudence was perfectly right, so I followed her counsel, and replied to the little flower-seller; "No, thank you; I don't want any."

She, however, was unwilling to take a refusal, and exclaimed; "Oh, but do *please* 'ave some, dear lady. Sitch bootifle flowers, they be! Jest one bunch!"

I was not going to offend any inward monitor by disregarding her advice, so I merely shook my head, and walked on.

For a few steps the child trotted beside me, continuing her importunities, but desisted when she found I was not to be moved. I looked back to see what she was doing when I reached the corner of the street, and saw that she had buried her face in her shawl, and was crying bitterly.

I was provoked at such a very unpractical proceeding; and, thinking that at all events a word of good advice would cost me nothing to give, and that perhaps she might be the better for it, I returned to her, and said:

"Now, you know, its excessively silly of you to behave like that, and you'd much better dry your eyes. You're just as likely as not to be losing a chance of a customer while you're crying; and you don't want to do that, do you?"

"Oh, *indeed* but I can't 'elp crying," she replied, between her violent sobs; "its cos I'se so 'ungry – so dreffle 'ungry."

"What makes you so hungry?" said I. "Didn't you have enough breakfast?"

"I 'asn't 'ad none at all," she returned. "When mother sent me out this mornin', she said as I shouldn't 'ave no brexshus till I'd got the money for it with these 'ere flowers; and she telled me the same a bit ago, when I met 'er and axed 'er to let me 'ave a penny to buy suthun to eat, cos no one wouldn't buy none of the flowers, and I was jest starved. She sez as its all my fault for not sellin' of 'em, and that if I wasn't idle, I could get rid of 'em fast enuff. But that's not true, for I'se done my best – indeed I 'as!"

It really did seem a hard case. I knew, from personal observation, that the charge of idleness was undeserved; and it was very unfair to make the poor little thing suffer for a slackness of trade which she could not help. To keep a growing child running about all the morning in the open air without giving it a morsel of food to appease its hunger till nearly twelve o'clock, was a piece of barbarity that quite shocked me. For, however hard I may be by nature, and however apt to drive my own barrow through the world without troubling myself about the toes that happen to be in the way and to get pinched, yet I do not think I have ever been guilty of gratuitous cruelty to either man or beast; indeed, the mere sight of it always fills me with disgust.

The mention of breakfast gave me a sudden bright idea

of how to assist the child without laying myself open to the reproaches of prudence. Had I not saved a shilling the day before by breakfasting at the restaurant instead of at the hotel? and was not a penny saved a penny gained? I had never calculated on being able to begin gaining anything as yet, so that that shilling was an addition to my funds which I had not reckoned upon, and which I was clearly entitled to regard as an extra – a thing that I could throw away or do what I pleased with – an accidental item which need not be entered on my receipts at all, so that prudence had no right to expect to be consulted as to what was done with it. And, feeling quite certain of the soundness of this argument, I did not wait to hear whether prudence took the same view of the matter or not, but instantly presented the coin to the child, recommending her to spend part of it now in getting breakfast, and to reserve the remainder against some future emergency.

The sight and feel of the shilling checked her tears with surprising quickness, and her wan, melancholy, little physiognomy brightened up wonderfully. Holding her basket towards me, she offered either to let me pick out the best flowers for myself, or else to do it for me if I liked; adding, with a slight hesitation, that perhaps there *might* be one or two old flowers since yesterday that had got mixed among this morning's lot, and if so, she would be more likely to know the fresh ones than I should. The touch of confusion with which this was said, made me suspect that the contents of her basket were by no means so fresh as she professed them to be, and that she, being well aware of that fact, was moved by an impulse of gratitude to proffer her services as chooser in order that I might not be cheated.

Evidently it would be prudent to accept her offer if I wanted to have anything out of her basket. But that was just what I felt rather doubtful about doing. I had intended the shilling as a free gift, and had had no idea of receiving anything in return; besides that, it would be a nuisance to have a handful of flowers to carry about with me, and they would probably have begun to fade by the time I got home; so, altogether, I at first thought I would refuse them. On second thoughts, however, I changed my mind. The flowers would certainly brighten up my room, and I knew that I should like them if I could have them transported there without trouble; and, after all, it was just as well to have some value for one's money; and as she took it for granted that I should do so, there would be no disappointment to her in my having them. I said therefore, "Will you pick me out a couple of good, fresh bunches, take them to a house that is not far off, and leave them there, with a message that Miss Caroline Jill wishes to have them put in water till she comes back?"

"'Iss, lady," she answered; "I'll pick you the werry bestest and freshest as I 'as – and thank you kindly for what you've give me. What's the 'ouse as I'm to take 'em to?"

I gave her the address of my lodging, and then we separated; she disappearing into the nearest baker's shop, and I continuing my way to A. G. My experience of life had not given me enough confidence in human nature to make me think it very likely that a street child was to be relied upon to keep a promise; and consequently I thought it highly problematical that I should find any flowers awaiting me on my return. But yet I did not the least regret the shilling I had thrown away upon her. It was a satisfaction to think that her hunger was being appeased, at any rate; indeed, if I had not known that that had been done, I should have exposed myself to the risk of feeling uncomfortable whenever I thought of her ravenous condition all day. So I had evidently acted for my own interest as well as hers.

CHAPTER IX

A Nervous Lady

ONE of the numerous omnibuses running down Oxford Street deposited me pretty near where I wanted to go; and, after alighting, I had no difficulty in finding someone to direct me to the address I was in search of. This proved, to my surprise, to be a small greengrocer's shop, where one would certainly not expect that there would be any demand for a governess. However, it was unmistakably the address that had been given in the advertisement, so I edged my way in, past the piles of earthy baskets by which the entrance was almost choked, and spoke to the owner of the shop – a jolly-looking, burly, middle-aged man.

"Excuse my troubling you," said I, politely; "but I've called in consequence of an advertisement for a daily governess by A. G. in yesterday's *Morning Post.* Is this the right place?" And as I spoke it flashed across my mind whether perhaps the initials in the advertisement represented the words "a greengrocer."

As soon as the man heard the object of my visit, his face twinkled with amusement in a way that seemed to imply there must be some capital joke connected with the affair. "Oh yes, Miss," he answered, "this be the right place, sure enough! P'raps you b'ain't used to greengrocers as rekvires daily-guvnesses vere you comes from – be you now?"

The man looked so perfectly good-tempered that it was

impossible to take offence at his enjoyment of the unknown joke, and I laughed as I replied, "No, I can't say that we do often have that happen."

"Ah, well, so I thought," he returned, chuckling. "And that just brings us to the werry pint as 'as to be considered in this 'ere bizness. That is – no offence my askin' – but vere *do* you come from, Miss?"

I told him the address of my lodging.

"'Ealthy districk, Miss, is it?" he enquired.

"Yes, as far as I know," replied I, feeling rather astonished at the question, and reflecting that my assertion was a perfectly safe one, seeing that I knew nothing whatever about the matter.

"Any illness in the 'ouse, Miss?" he continued, holding up his fingers and checking off on them the name of each successive disease as he enumerated it; "any fivver, diptheery, coleera, measles, mumps, small-pox, chicking-pox, 'oopin'-corf, nettlerash – that's only nine; there's a tenth as I was to ax about, I knows; what the juice was it now? Oh yes! the one as is a flower and a colour – yaller-rose– rose-yaller! Dashed if I can say it right."

"Is roseola the word you want?" I suggested.

"That's it, Miss, thanky!" he exclaimed joyfully, but without venturing on a second attempt at pronouncing the word; "Now, be there any of these 'ere as I've mentioned at the 'ouse vere you're livin'? or any other infexshus complaint as I 'aven't mentioned, as p'raps may be some bran new invention of the doctors since the old list was made out?"

I had never thought of making any inquiries of the kind at my lodging, so I answered "no" boldly. Even if there were any illness, at all events I did not know of it, so my negative was obviously not to be considered as wilfully misleading, whatever the state of sanitary affairs might be. "Werry good," he returned; "then if you'll be so good as go round the corner of the street over the vay, you'll find yourself in Fairy Avenue, and at No. 114 you'll find A. G., that's to say, Mrs. Green. You see she's mortial afeard of what she calls jurms, and's allers thinking as strange people's sure to have 'em in their pockets or their clothes, or some-veres about 'em, ready to turn loose on whoever they meets. So when she advertizes for a guvness or a servant, she mostly axes me to let 'em come 'ere fust, that I may make sure as they don't come from no infexshus place afore they goes to 'er 'ouse. Did you ever 'ear of sitch a ridiklus fancy 'afore in all your born days? It makes me fit to split with larfin sometimes. But there! it ain't but werry little trouble to me, and I don't mind oblidgin' a good customer like 'er, as takes a sight of wedgebuttles and fruits and sitch things. 'I considers 'em pertickler 'olesome artikles of dite,' sez she to me often. 'So do I too, mum,' sez I back to 'er. And good reason vy I *should* inkcourage the notion, 'seein' as she buys 'em all from me!"

Thanking the man for his information, and feeling that I had gained an insight into Mrs. Green's character which might come useful to me in my dealings with her, I proceeded to 114 Fairy Avenue. On ringing the bell and saying that I had come about the governess' situation, I was requested to wait in the hall, whilst the servant went to see if Mrs. Green was disengaged.

It was very evident that that lady took care no one should enter her doors without undergoing some amount of fumigation, as in the middle of the hall there stood a sort of small brazier, wherein some kind of disinfecting compound was smouldering, and sending out light curls of smoke which impregnated the air with a sickly smell. By the odour of this smoke, combined with that of carbolic acid, the whole house was pervaded, as the floors were scrubbed with carbolic soap twice a week regularly, and carbolic acid was freely applied to whatever incoming thing could, by any stretch of imagination, be regarded as a possible medium for the introduction of those "germs of disease" which Mrs. Green held in horror. In the efficacy of any inodorous disinfectant she had no belief at all. How, she would say, could stuff that was not strong enough to be perceptible to the nose be strong enough to be relied on to purify the atmosphere, and affect any germs that might be floating about in it? Don't tell *her* to use a thing like Condy's fluid, that had not any smell at all! No, give her carbolic acid or chloride of lime, which made difference enough in the air for one's nose to take cognisance of – then there could be no mistake about their presence, and one could feel satisfied.

She did not admit me to her room till she had sent the servant back to inquire whether I had been to the greengrocer's and been forwarded to her by him. My answer being satisfactory, I was ushered into her sitting-room and invited to take a seat near the door, and a good way off from herself. We then proceeded to talk business, and I found that she wanted a governess to come every morning to instruct and take charge of her little girl of ten years old, and that the amount of knowledge necessary to satisfy her demands was not beyond the limits of my acquirements. Having discovered this much I lost no time in asking what salary she gave, for I did not want her to anticipate this question by asking me how much I expected to receive, as the fact was that I had not an idea of what daily governesses were generally paid, and feared exposing my ignorance. The terms she offered were so far beyond what I had thought likely, that I was delighted, and at once determined not to let slip the situation if I could help it. Consequently I became very anxious to ingratiate myself with her, and looked out for an opportunity of doing so by manifesting sympathy with the dread of infection which I knew to be a weak point of hers. For if people have any specially absurd craze, they are sure to regard an indication of the same mania on the part of another person as a strong recommendation and reason for thinking well of that person. I had not long to wait for the opportunity I desired, as she said; "There is one thing I must tell you, Miss Jill, and that is, that I insist upon every member of my establishment, without exception, conforming to the regulations I make in order to guard against the introduction of infection to the house. Should you be prepared to do this?"

"Most certainly," I replied; though in truth I had no intention of troubling my head about the matter more than I had done heretofore – that is to say, not at all. "I shall be only too glad to do so. For I must confess that on that point I am what some people call quite foolishly nervous."

"It is *impossible* to be too nervous about it," she returned, "and I am glad to find that you have a proper appreciation of the necessity of a carefulness which is a duty no less to society than to one's self and one's family. A fresh case of illness means the setting up of a fresh manufactory of horrible, insidious, deadly germs of disease, which, once set going in the world, cannot be recalled, and can only with difficulty be destroyed. How many deaths might not be caused by germs made in and issuing from this house, if we were to have some infectious illness here? And if the illness had been admitted through any negligence of mine, should not I be responsible for all of those deaths?"

"Quite true," answered I, gravely. "I never was struck by that before, but I see how unanswerably correct your reasoning is. How I wish that everyone else had an equally sensitive conscience!"

"Yes, it is indeed sad," she replied, sighing, "to see what an amount of culpable carelessness and foolhardiness exists in the world! I do my best to make these things appear in their true light, but it is not often that I can succeed in inspiring my own spirit of prudence into anyone else. I assure you that I have even heard of my precautions being laughed at and called ridiculous."

I kept my countenance heroically; and as she paused, as though expecting me to make some remark, I exclaimed, "It seems hardly credible!"

"So one would have thought," she returned sadly, "and especially in the face of the outbreak of scarlet fever which has recently occurred in so many parts of London, and which everyone must have read of in the papers. However, to return to business. Will you kindly let me have the address of your last situation? Should the answer to my inquiries there prove satisfactory, I shall be glad to engage you, as, from what I have seen of you, I have every reason to think you will suit me."

Now, of course, I had foreseen that no one would be likely to engage me without knowing (or supposing themselves to know, which would come to the same thing) something about who I was, and I foresaw also that it might be against me not to be able to give the name of anyone who could be inquired of about me, either personally or by letter. To meet this difficulty I had concocted a story which would, I hoped, be accepted as a sufficient explanation of the matter. But I had never dreamt of anyone's being so absurdly afraid of infection as Mrs. Green was; and the discovery of her foible inspired me with the brilliant idea of offering her a personal reference which she would be certain not to avail herself of.

I replied, therefore, that as I had been a little out of sorts I had been living quietly at home for the last six months, in order to regain my health, and that I had been previously teaching in the family of Mr. Thomson – mentioning the name of a clergyman in the east of London whose parish I remembered having read about not long before in a newspaper as being pretty nearly decimated by scarlet fever. This gentleman, I said, had been most kind to me, having not only given me a written testimonial to character, but also promised that he would at any time write to, or see, any person on my behalf. I only hoped, I put in parenthetically, that he was not overworking himself in the terrible visitation of scarlet fever that had lately come upon his parish; but he was such an excellent man, and so indefatigable in his labours amongst the poor, that I feared it was but too likely he would sacrifice himself to them. If anything should happen to him I should feel I had lost one of my best friends. But, however busy he might be, I felt sure he would keep his promise, and would certainly find time to answer any inquiries that Mrs. Green might wish to make about me, whether in person or by post.

She, however, would as soon have thought of walking into a blazing furnace as into Mr. Thomson's parish in its then condition, and, as I expected, thought epistolary communication with him was but little less perilous.

"Ahem!" she answered, "I am afraid Mr. Thomson is not a very easy person to refer to just at present, and I do not quite see how it is to be managed. I could not *think* of going to see him, and I am doubtful that it would be prudent to write to him either, especially since he is so devoted to his parishioners, as you say. Men of that kind are almost invariably careless about proper precautions. Perhaps he would write me an answer when actually in a sick-room; and then imagine how that letter, full of contagion, would be mixed in the post with other letters, impart to them its fatal properties, and thus scatter sickness and, perhaps, death far and wide! No, never will *I* wilfully run the risk of causing disasters in this way, whatever other people may do."

"I have the testimonial he wrote me at the time I discontinued teaching in his family, if you would think that sufficient, madam," I replied, beginning to fumble in my pocket as though in search of the document in question. Of course I had no such thing about me in reality, but I knew that I could easily pretend to have forgotten it, and then write a sham one and send it by post.

She raised her hand hastily to check my producing the paper. "Wait one moment," she cried, looking somewhat uneasy. "How long is it since the testimonial was written?"

"Just six months ago," answered I.

"Was there any fever or infectious illness in the parish at that time?" she inquired. "Not that I am aware of," I returned. "Still it might have been there without your knowledge, might it not?" she continued.

I allowed that this was not impossible, but added that I did not believe the district to have been at all unhealthy then.

"What makes me anxious for certainty about this," she said, "is, that supposing Mr. Thomson had visited some sick person just before writing your testimonial, he would have probably had germs of disease clinging to him; and those germs, being communicated to the writing-paper, would be lingering there still, and be a source of peril to whoever comes in contact with that piece of paper. Possibly, however, you have taken the precaution of disinfecting it by fumigation, or in some other way?"

"No, I have not," I answered; "I am ashamed to say that I did not think of it – a most reprehensible omission on my part!"

"Ah, well," she replied, with an air of indulgence, "it was an oversight, no doubt; but then you are still very young, and one can hardly expect young people to be as thoughtful as old ones. But we will remedy the omission at once. There is some disinfecting powder in that square box on the table beside you. I shall be obliged if you will sprinkle it thoroughly over the paper before giving it me to read."

I recommenced feeling in my pocket, and then exclaimed, "Oh how very stupid of me! I made sure that I had brought that testimonial with me, but I must have left it on my table, as I find I have not got it after all. Will you allow me to post it to you as soon as I get home? Should you think it satisfactory, and write me word when you wish me to commence my duties, I will come at whatever time you appoint."

The look of relief that came over her face on hearing that I had not got the testimonial showed me that she regarded it with considerable distrust, and was not greatly desirous of touching it.

"Yes, you can post it to me as you propose," she said; "and I will let you know my decision by letter also. Of course you will disinfect the paper carefully before sending it. I shall be glad if you will take some of this powder for the purpose, as it is a disinfectant on which I can rely thoroughly, and has so strong a smell that if you were to forget to use it, my nose would immediately inform me of that fact, and I should be thus warned against opening the paper. By the by, in the event of my engaging you, should you be likely to continue the engagement for any length of time? or to break it off again shortly? My reason for asking is, that I am most averse to constant changes in my establishment, because that means constant fresh risk of infection from strangers; and therefore I prefer not entering into an engagement with anyone who likes to be perpetually moving about from place to place."

It will be remembered that my intention was merely to take a governess's place temporarily, to eke out my means till I had learnt hairdressing and could get a travelling-maid's situation. But I really did not see that she had a right to expect me to confide all my private little schemes to her, so I said nothing about this, and only assured her that I had a horror of perpetual changes, and that a permanent situation was exactly what I was hoping to find.

"There is one thing more that I forgot to mention," she continued. "I should object to your making use of an omnibus or tram-car in coming to give my daughter her daily lessons. I consider public conveyances of that kind most unsafe, on account of their liability to contain germs of disease left by someone or other of the great variety of passengers who travel in them."

"I quite agree with you," I answered, "and hardly ever go in one of those conveyances on that account. I should hope to come here on foot as a rule; and if the weather should make that impossible, I should take a hansom, as being the least dangerous vehicle available."

I felt I was pretty safe in making this promise, though I meant to come by omnibus all the same. There was not much chance of her inspecting the passengers in the numerous omnibuses running down Oxford Street and the Bayswater Road; and they did not pass up Fairy Avenue, so I should have no choice about walking the last part of my journey. Thus she would see me arrive daily on foot; her mind would be at ease; I should be perfectly free to use the convenient omnibus as much as I chose; and so we should both be happy.

Everything being settled, I took leave of her, and had reached the door of the room to go, when she spoke again.

"On the whole, Miss Jill," she said, "I do not think I need trouble you to send me that testimonial. From what I have seen of you, I have very little doubt that we shall suit each other; and I feel satisfied to engage you at once, as the peculiar circumstances of the case render it impossible to hold any communication with the person who is your reference. Can you begin the lessons to-morrow morning at nine o'clock?"

"Certainly, madam," I replied; "you may depend upon my being here then, and I am much obliged to you."

Who would have thought that a letter six months old could have inspired her with so much fear as to induce her to dispense with every shadow of precaution about ascertaining the character of an individual to whose care she was willing to commit her child?

Marvelling greatly at her folly, and congratulating myself on my success, I returned to my lodging, where I found that the little girl of whom I had bought the flowers, had duly left them for me. It was more than I had expected her to do, certainly; and the only way I could account for such astonishing honesty was by supposing that no one else had wanted to buy them, so that there had been no temptation to her to break her promise and defraud me of my nosegay. But I believe I judged her with too much cynicism; for, long afterwards, she proved that she had been really grateful for the breakfast I had given her, and was anxious to show her gratitude in deeds.

CHAPTER X

Change of Situation

I WAS naturally rather curious to know how my family would take the discovery of my flight, and for some time afterwards I used to look in the newspapers with a half-expectation of seeing a paragraph headed "Mysterious disappearance of a young lady;" or else an offer of a reward for information concerning me; or else, perhaps (but this I considered as being merely *possible,* and not at all *likely),* an entreaty to me to return, and all should be forgiven. As nothing of the kind appeared, however, I perceived that my relatives had the good sense to understand the wisdom of washing their dirty clothes at home, and that they did not intend to draw a needless amount of attention to the fact that I had run away from them. It was inevitable that my having done so would be a nine day's wonder and topic of gossip in the immediate neighbourhood of Castle Manor; but it did not follow that our domestic want of harmony need be proclaimed to all the world and his wife also; and so the matter was not published in the papers.

Mrs. Green's little girl Fanny, to whom I was engaged to give instruction, was heavy and uninteresting enough to have driven well-nigh distracted any governess who cared about shoving on her pupils, and deriving credit from them; so it was lucky that I was less energetic and devoted to my work. As it was for only a very brief period that I meant to superintend Fanny's studies, it was perfectly immaterial to me whether she progressed in them or not; and I did not attempt to teach her anything beyond what was to be got into her head without much trouble – which limitation reduced our educational labours to a surprisingly small compass. Her stupidity did not prevent us from getting on together most harmoniously; for though I did not do much towards increasing her stock of knowledge, yet I atoned for that deficiency by opening her mind with an amount of general and varied entertainment with which no previous governess had ever provided her. Sometimes I told her any marvellous stories that I knew, adding touches, as I went on, to heighten the interest of whatever parts seemed to astonish her especially. Or else I would say or do something extravagantly absurd, just as gravely as though it were the most matter-of-fact speech or action possible, and amuse myself by watching the look of absolute bewilderment that would come over her face at first, and speculating on how long an interval would elapse before it would be followed by the succeeding grin which betokened that her slowly-working brain had at last awakened to the fact of there being a joke afoot. By such methods as these I contrived to find amusement for both myself and her, and I have very little doubt that she approved of me highly, and regarded me as being far and away the pleasantest teacher she had ever had to do with.

That portion of my time which was not occupied either in giving or receiving lessons I spent chiefly in attending to the necessities of my wardrobe, loafing about in the parks and streets, and doing whatever sight-seeing was to be had gratuitously. I did not indulge in any amusement costing money, except theatres, to which I allowed myself a few visits as a treat and reward for my self-denial in other respects – theatrical performances being a form of entertainment to which I have always been particularly partial.

Thus three or four weeks passed quickly away, and by the end of that time I had mastered the art of hairdressing sufficiently to enable me to undertake the duties of a lady's-maid; for I was far more industrious in the capacity of pupil than in that of teacher, and laboured a great deal more zealously to profit by M. Candot's instructions than I did to make Fanny Green profit by mine. It is wonderful how much easier it is to take trouble when one wishes to secure value for money spent, than it is when the object of one's exertions is merely to give an equivalent for money received!

Having qualified myself for the calling I meant to adopt, the next thing was to take steps to hear of a situation; and to that end I put an advertisement in the *Times, Morning Post,* and *Guardian,* offering C. J.'s services to any lady going abroad who required a thoroughly efficient maid, capable of acting as courier if necessary. This notice bore fruit speedily in the shape of a note addressed to C. J., which I found awaiting me on my return from Mrs. Green's one afternoon, and which ran as follows :—

"2000 EATON SQUARE, *Thursday.*
"Lady Mervyn writes in answer to C. J.'s advertisement, as she wishes to meet with a good travelling-maid. Lady Mervyn will be glad if C.J. will call at her house tomorrow evening at 5.30 *punctually.*"

How strange that my notice should happen to have been seen and answered by Lady Mervyn – a person between whom and myself there was a remote connection, and whom I had met years ago when I was a child! Would it be safe for me to enter her service? or should I be running too great a risk of recognition? No, I did not think I need be afraid. Kitty was the only one of the family who was at all likely to remember me, as I had been much more in her company than in theirs on the occasion of our previous meeting at Lugano. And that she had no recollection of me I had already proved at Sparkton Station; which forgetfulness on her part, by the by, I did not now feel the least bit inclined to resent, having quite got over the little soreness and irritation which it had caused me at the moment.

Yes; I believed I should be as safe from discovery at Lady Mervyn's as anywhere else, and determined that I would take the situation. I was pleased with the idea of being under the same roof as Kitty Mervyn, on account of the opportunities which I should then have of observing this girl, whose character had interested me and excited my curiosity. And then, too, I might reasonably look forward to discovering some explanation of her having chosen to keep Captain Edward Norroy's photograph hidden away in her purse as she had done. A *carte-de-visite* is ordinarily stuck into an album, and I wanted to know why she should have treated this particular *carte* differently to that of any other acquaintance.

These anticipations were checked by the sudden recollection that I was counting my chickens before they were hatched; that I had not yet got the place I was looking forward to; and that perhaps Lady Mervyn might not think fit to engage me after all. When did she say I was to go there? Looking again at the note I saw that it was dated the day before. Yesterday was Thursday, and to-day Friday, so I must wait upon her ladyship this very same afternoon, and had no time to lose in providing myself with that necessary article – a character.

About two months before there had died a certain Lady

Brown, who was rather a well-known person on account of her having lived much abroad and published a large number of books containing her experiences of the Riviera, the Dolomites, the Alps, the Rhine, and other foreign places. Her husband, Sir Bartholomew Brown, had gone to the East since her death, and was supposed to be wandering about somewhere in Persia at the present moment. As, therefore, no reference was possible to either the deceased Lady Brown or her husband, and as they had been childless, it occurred to me that if I asserted myself to have been her maid up to the time of her death, there was no one to disprove the statement. Accordingly, I indited a character purporting to be written by Sir Bartholomew, wherein it was set forth that Caroline Jill had been for two years in his late wife's service; had only left an account of that lady's death; had given entire satisfaction during the whole time of her service; was a first-rate traveller; and was a trustworthy, sober, steady, exemplary, and in-all-ways-to-be-recommended-maid.

I wasted several sheets of paper over this composition before I could please myself; and when I had succeeded in getting it to my mind I copied it out in a feigned hand – bold, rather scrawling, legible, and masculine-looking. Of course there was a danger of the forgery being detected, if Lady Mervyn should happen to be acquainted with Sir Bartholomew's handwriting. But then it was quite likely that she was *not;* and I would try to find out if she knew him before I produced the character; and, even if the worst came to the worst, the chances were that she would not take the trouble to prosecute me, and I should have just as good a prospect as before of obtaining a situation with someone else.

By the time my preparations were completed it was later than I thought, and as the underlining of the word "punctually" in the note made me think it important not to be late, I started off in such a hurry that I tumbled downstairs and bruised myself unpleasantly. However, I did not stay to doctor my hurts then, but hurried on, and arrived at my destination just as the Eaton Square Church clock was striking half-past five.

It then appeared that my fear of being late had been quite uncalled-for, and that I might have spared myself the bruises which my haste had caused me, for Lady Mervyn had not yet returned from driving. The fact was she had followed the usual plan of fashionable ladies and gentlemen, who, when they make an appointment with an inferior, take care that they themselves shall not be kept waiting, but do not the least object to inflicting that annoyance on the other party. No doubt such people consider that the time of a servant, tradesman, farmer, or poor person is much less valuable than their own, and a thing of so little importance that it may be wasted at pleasure.

On stating the object of my visit, and that Lady Mervyn had directed me to call at that time, I was told to sit down and wait till she came in. It was past 6 o'clock when she returned, and even then she did not send for me immediately, but delayed doing so till she had leisurely examined the cards that had been left for her whilst she was out, refreshed herself with a cup of tea, and written a couple of notes. Having accomplished these things, she at last gave orders for me to be shown into her presence.

She was about middle height, slightly made, and aristocratic looking. As she was rather shortsighted she wore a *pince-nez,* and this she put up, and coolly stared at me through, as soon as I entered the room. After a prolonged survey she dropped it, but had recourse to it again several times during the interview, always putting it up with an air of having suddenly bethought her of some feature, limb, or other part of me which she had hitherto omitted to study sufficiently, and at which she wanted to have another good look. I must say I thought that she used the *pince-nez* in a manner which would have been considered intolerably rude if it had been directed at any one in her own rank of life; but then she regarded a servant as being a different sort of animal from herself, and would have laughed at the idea of a maid's not liking to be stared at as if she were made of wood or stone, instead of flesh and blood.

She began by inquiring my name and age; to which I replied that I was called Caroline Jill and that I was just twenty-two. For, though my real age was eighteen, yet I thought that that seemed rather too young for a person representing herself as having been a lady's-maid for the last two years, and that therefore I had better give myself credit for a few more years than I was actually entitled to.

"Twenty-two!" she repeated; "you don't look your age. I should not have thought you so old as that. How long were you in your last situation? and what was the cause of your leaving ?"

"I was there two years, and I only left on account of the lady's death," I replied. "Did your ladyship know the late Lady Brown?"

She shook her head.

"Perhaps your ladyship may have heard of her," I continued; "she was the wife of Sir Bartholomew Brown, and used to write books sometimes?"

"Oh yes; I did not know her, but I know who you mean now," answered Lady Mervyn; "was hers your last place?"

" Yes," I replied, feeling that the ground was safe, and that I might produce my false testimonial. "Ever since her death, two months ago, Sir Bartholomew has been away from England; but, before going, he kindly gave me a character, for fear of my having any difficulty about getting another situation through there being no one from my last place for me to refer to. Here is what he wrote. He was good enough to tell me, when last I saw him, that he considered me to be the best maid his wife had ever had to travel with, and that I did just as well as a courier."

So saying I handed over my forgery to Lady Mervyn, who perused it carefully, and then returned it to me.

"I always prefer a personal reference if possible," she said; "but perhaps I might consent to dispense with it for once, in an exceptional case like this, where it evidently cannot be had. Certainly Sir Bartholomew speaks of you in very high terms. I do not want you for myself, but for one of my daughters, who is going abroad with my sister, Mrs. Rollin. You would have to attend partly on Mrs. Rollin also; but she will not want much done for her, as she does not care about a maid's assistance in most things. As they do not intend taking a courier, they must have a really efficient travelling-maid, who can see to their luggage, take tickets, and all that sort of thing. I suppose you have had plenty of experience in that way with Lady Brown? Can you talk French and German pretty easily?"

I replied in the affirmative, that I also knew Italian, Spanish, a little Dutch, and a few words of Greek, and that I could keep accounts in some foreign coins.

"En verité, vous ne vous vantez pas mal!" she returned, looking insultingly sceptical as to my accomplishments being as extensive as I claimed them to be. "Voyons d'abord pour le français." And she then continued the conversation in French, whilst I replied in the same tongue. The question of wages was propounded next. I had no intention of depreciating my value by demanding too little for my services, and I knew that courier-maids were always paid very high, so I said that I should not like to take less than what I had received from

Lady Brown, which was £35 and all found. That was very high Lady Mervyn said; still, she would not object to give it to a maid who was really worth it. After a few more questions she observed that my French was satisfactory, at all events; and that, as she was not herself a very good German scholar, she would get her eldest daughter to test my proficiency in that line. Ringing the bell she told the footman, who answered it, to request Miss Mervyn to come to her. When that young lady arrived her mother desired her to find out how I talked German. As I came triumphantly out of her examination, and also translated accurately an Italian quotation which happened to be in one of the newspapers lying on the table, Lady Mervyn's incredulity as to my accomplishments evidently diminished. I could see that she began to think my pretensions to knowledge were better founded than she had at first supposed them to be, and that she was now inclined to take upon trust the skill in foreign moneys, and in Spanish, Dutch, and Greek, to which I laid claim.

She hesitated, considered and reconsidered, and scrutinised me through the *pince-nez* for some time before she could make up her mind whether to engage me or not, and finally decided to do so. Mrs. Rollin and Miss Mervyn were going abroad in another ten days, she said, and as it would be well for them and me to have a few days at home in which to get used to one another before starting on our travels, she wished me to return to her house and begin my engagement on that day week. This I was quite ready to do, as I had no doubt of quickly getting free from Mrs. Green whenever I chose.

One thing which I had evolved during the conversation with Lady Mervyn was a grievous disappointment to me; and that was, that I was not – at all events for a while – to become a member of her own establishment. I had been confidently reckoning on being brought near Kitty; but it appeared that this was not to be my destiny after all, unless, by some piece of luck, she should chance to be the daughter who was to accompany Mrs. Rollin, and whose especial attendant I was to be. My mind was set at rest on this point before I left Lady Mervyn's room, for, just as I was about to depart, she exclaimed, "Wait a moment! I forgot that the young lady whom you will wait on may like to see you if she is at home. Perhaps, however, she is not, as she was to dine out early to-night before going to the theatre. Has Kitty started yet, do you know?" she continued, turning to the daughter who had been experimenting on my German.

"Yes," was the answer; "she went ten minutes ago, just before I came to you."

"Ah, never mind then, Jill; you can go now," returned Lady Mervyn. Whereupon I took myself off, mightly pleased at having discovered that the Miss Mervyn whom I was to serve was just the one whom I wanted it to be.

The next thing was to terminate my engagement with Mrs. Green, and I meant to make her do this herself. For this purpose I informed her morning that I was sorry to say that I found the daily walk to her house was more than I could manage, therefore I must ask her to permit me to come by omnibus in future.

She replied (as I had felt very sure she would do) that she could not on any account consent to expose herself and her household to such a risk of infection. Could I not change my residence, and come to live nearer her house? I answered that I did not wish to do that, as I was quite comfortable in my lodging, and should probably have a difficulty in finding another to suit me equally well.

She returned that it was most annoying, and that in that case there was no choice but to conclude our connection together. That would necessitate her looking out for another governess, which she greatly disliked doing because there was always *some* danger of infection from strangers coming to the premises, notwithstanding all the precautions she could take. She would never have engaged me if she had thought there was a chance of the engagement lasting so short a time; but I had seemed so anxious for a permanent place that she thought I was as averse to constant changes as she was herself. However, there was no help for it if I declined to change my abode, for it was out of the question for her to allow anyone coming daily to her house to make use of an omnibus.

Poor woman! I think she would have had a fit if she had known that I had done that very thing day after day since I had been teaching her child; and she was certainly an excellent illustration of the truth of the old proverb, "Where ignorance is bliss 'tis folly to be wise." Yet I don't think she was very singular in this after all. How many of us are there – especially of those who are heads of houses – whose peace of mind might not be con- siderably disturbed if we did but know the extent to which other people are in the habit of setting at nought and ignoring some particular pet prejudice of our own?

It amused me to affect deep sympathy with a piece of folly which I was laughing at in my sleeve all the time; so I replied that I fully recognised the truth of what she said, and that I was truly grieved to be the means of exposing her to fresh peril from germs of disease clinging to the clothes of applicants for my situation; but that since *she* objected to my coming by a 'bus, and *I* objected to leave my present lodging, there was unfortunately no option about my ceasing to instruct Fanny.

She sighed, and answered that she was afraid that was true. At the same time, she could not in justice omit to say that she considered me to have behaved very well in at once telling her honestly of my inability to continue to attend to my duties without travelling by that dangerous conveyance which she had expressly prohibited me from using. She feared there were some people who would have been less straightforward, and who would, in such a case, have slily disobeyed her, and endeavoured to conceal from her what they were doing. But then no one was likely to be guilty of such unprincipled conduct as that whose views were as sound as she knew mine to be on the subject of infection! Could I go on coming to her house as before for a few days longer? If so she would be very glad, as, perhaps, by then she might be able to hear of a successor for me. But if the walk was too far for me to manage, why, of course, the engagement must come to an end at once, as she could not consent to my coming by omnibus for even one single day.

To this I made answer, with perfect truth, that I should be most happy to go on coming in the same way as I had hitherto done till the following Thursday. After that, however, I could undertake it no longer, and supposed, therefore, that she would wish our engagement to conclude then. She assented to this, and we parted on the best of terms with one another.

Perhaps it may be thought odd that I did not pursue the ordinary method of simply giving notice, and taking myself off, when I wanted to go to another situation. Of course I could easily have done so if I had liked; but in that case I should have lost all the fun that I got out of the matter by the other plan. It amused me to make her act as I chose, and herself dismiss me when I wished her to do so; and I enjoyed feeling that her weak point rendered her in my hands an unsuspecting puppet, that would kick or not, according to how I chose to pull the strings. Be it remembered that love of fun has always been a much stronger element in my character than amiability.

CHAPTER XI

An Unwelcome Admirer

SO now I was going to be a lady's-maid. I knew that the customs, ideas, traditions, and general mode of thought prevailing in the rank of life I was about to enter, would be likely to differ in many ways from those to which I had hitherto been accustomed; and this knowledge naturally made me rather anxious as to how easy I might find it to adapt myself to my novel position, and to the people with whom I should have to associate. I felt that I was on the brink of a completely new experience, and looked forward with more trepidation than I had expected to my initiation therein on joining Lord Mervyn's household as a servant. Under these circumstances I laid down two rules for my guidance, to which I determined to adhere as far as possible: these were – first, carefully to avoid making enemies amongst my fellow-domestics; and secondly, to try and discover and conform to whatever unwritten laws of etiquette might be generally established amongst them. And in accordance with the second of these rules, I determined that on the day when I was due at 2000 Eaton Square, I would not make my appearance there till towards supper time; for I had often noticed at home that whenever a new servant was coming, he or she was sure not to turn up till as late in the day as possible; and from this I inferred that to arrive early at a new place was probably not considered the right thing.

It was, therefore, quite late in the evening when I drove

up to Lord Mervyn's door. The various articles I had had to purchase in order to equip myself properly, had caused my possessions to outgrow the modest little bag that had sufficed to contain them when I came to London a few weeks before; and so I was now accompanied by a box large enough to make a respectable show as it stood on the roof of the cab which brought me.

That cab, by the by, is always a sore recollection to me; for I cannot forget that it was the means, indirectly, of my vanity receiving a sharp blow. The way of it was this.

As I knew that Lady Mervyn would defray my expenses in getting to her house, of course I did not hesitate about coming in a cab; and of course also, in charging the fare to her, I put it down as being just double what I had really paid. When she came to settle her accounts with me she demurred to this item, saying that the charge was far beyond what it ought to have been for the distance from my lodging to Eaton Square. I replied innocently that I had thought it seemed a good deal, and had said so to the cabman at the time; but that as he had declared it was not a penny more than he was entitled to, and as I had supposed he must know the proper fare better than I did, I had given him what he asked.

Lady Mervyn accepted the explanation as satisfactory, and passed on to the next item without further question. But, when paying me, she remarked contemptuously that I must be uncommonly silly to let myself be cheated so easily, and that in future she advised me to remember that the word of a London cabman was not *always* to be relied on implicitly.

As if *I* needed any advice of that kind! Was it possible to hear myself credited, with such folly, and yet not refute the insulting accusation instantly? *I* to be considered such a greenhorn – I who considered myself on being anything but soft and easy to take in!

Stung to the quick by her scornful words, my self-esteem would hardly consent to submit to the affront in silence. It urged me to remind her of the fact that there could, in any case, be no question of my having let *myself* be cheated, since it was not *I* who was the person by whom the fare was eventually to be paid. But such a retort, though gratifying to my injured feelings, would have evidently been to the last degree unbecoming to my position as lady's-maid. Luckily my sense of this sufficed to keep me from answering her as I longed to do, and I managed to listen humbly to the unmerited reproach of gullibility, just as though I acquiesced in the justice of it. But it was only by a desperate effort that I could thus control myself, for I was wounded in a point where I was peculiarly sensitive. The thought of the slur that had been cast on my knowledge of the world and hard-headedness rankled in my breast for long afterwards, irritating me to such an extent that I could not help feeling that my dishonesty in overcharging Lady Mervyn was punished after all, and that I had only come off second best in the affair. For the amount of pecuniary profit I gained by it was absolutely insignificant, and certainly inadequate to counterbalance the mortification which it entailed upon my pride.

The thought of this annoyance has led me away from the proper course of my narrative. I apologise for the digression, and return to the evening when I and my chattels were deposited by the cab at 2000 Eaton Square.

The dignity of the post I was to fill exonerated me from having to join the common herd who supped in the servants' hall, and gave me standing in the higher and more select society occupying the housekeeper's room. Here we fared most sumptuously, for Lady Mervyn had had a small dinner-party that night, and on these occasions it was customary for the servants to finish up the relics of the feast if they cared to do so. Bearing this in mind, the cook never omitted to make the dishes of a liberal size, or to concoct a sufficient amount of whatever sauce was required for the various *entrées,* puddings, etc., to be able to keep back some of it when they were sent up to the diningroom. By this means it was easy afterwards to renovate most of them for downstairs use, even though the sauce might have been popular with the gentry, and wholly consumed upstairs – at least, as much of it as ever went there. Our meal, therefore, was little inferior to, and almost identical with, that which had been set before the guests overhead. It terminated with some capital ice pudding and dessert ices, of which there was an ample supply, in well frozen condition; – this was thanks to the care of the butler, who had helped the ladies and gentlemen with a very sparing hand, and then at once sent the remainder to be preserved for us in the refrigerator.

My companions seemed so well inclined to be civil and to welcome me amongst them, that I began to shake off my nervousness, and to think that I was going to get on swimmingly. It was evidently considered that in the presence of a newcomer like me, the first appropriate topic of conversation to bring forward was the character of our employers; and as everyone in the room delivered his or her opinion on the subject with perfect freedom, I soon picked up a good deal of highly interesting information.

Lady Mervyn was described as being "reg'lar out and out worldly, a good bit more of a Turk than you would think from the quiet looks of her; a bit mean, too, and one of those ladies who go poking their noses into a larder to see what's there pretty near every morning." I could see that the cook considered the last mentioned custom to be highly objectionable, and an amount of *surveillance* which was both uncalled for and aggravating.

The verdict on the eldest daughter was that she was "not much to look at, and a bit of a screw, but better tempered than Lady M."

The most popular member of the family was evidently Kitty, who was pronounced to be "'andsome, merry, spirity, and pleasant-spoken to both 'igh and low. For all that, though, you can see that she'll never be satisfied without being first fiddle, or pretty near it, wherever she is, and that in 'er 'art she likes 'igh folk and swells better than them as isn't. She don't show 'er pride on the outside, p'raps, so much as some do; but it's there all the same, and you won't often find an 'ortier young lady, go where you will. She's 'er ma's favourite, she is, and bound to marry a top-sawyer some day – she'd never be 'appy with anyone as wasn't."

I took the opportunity of enquiring whether there was supposed to be any particular individual in the wind, and I half expected that in the answer I should hear something about Captain Norroy. This, however, was not the case, nor was his name ever once mentioned during the whole conversation. I evolved that she had plenty of admirers, and was very gracious to them all, just as she was to everyone else; but that whenever any of them had been cheated by her amiable manner into the belief that he had a chance of becoming her husband, he had speedily been undeceived, and learnt, to his cost, that her readiness to be great friends with him was no indication of a disposition to be anything more. The most desirable of her many admirers was, in the opinion of my informants, a certain Lord Clement, who was clearly at her disposal if she chose to have him, but whose affection she showed no signs of reciprocating.

Her obduracy in this matter was quite inexplicable, I was told, he being a rich young earl not more than eight years her senior, of good family and irreproachable character, an excellent match in every respect, and whose wife's rank and position would be high enough to content any reasonable woman. There was no doubt that *her* family approved cordially of his suit, and that *his* relations, also, had no objection to it. One would have thought that any girl would have been glad to get such a husband, and more particularly a girl like her who set store on being a nob. Yet, for some reason or other, she seemed not to know he had any attractions at all to offer, and turned up her nose at him as if she didn't care a straw about such things. Not that she was what you could call uncivil to him – oh no, it was not her nature to be that to any one – but she certainly contrived to give him more cold shoulder than encouragement. Whether or not he had ever ventured to declare himself to her, in spite of this, was a matter as to which opinions varied. The housekeeper did not believe he *had* proposed; whereas the butler took a contrary view in consequence of what he had heard from a waiter friend of his who had had opportunities of observing his lordship and Miss Kitty together at several parties. But it was mere conjecture, and everyone agreed that there was no certainty about the matter either one way or other.

It can easily be imagined that gossip of this kind was extremely interesting to a person in my position, anxious to learn all I could regarding the lay of the land which I had come to inhabit. The communicativeness of my new associates, and the facility with which I was getting on with them at starting, reassured me greatly. I began to wonder at my former qualms, lest in descending to a lower social grade I should find things to put up with that were distasteful and unpleasant. Entering service was, after all, no such formidable ordeal as I had imagined; there was nothing that I should not quickly grow accustomed to in my unfamiliar surroundings; nothing to shock the prejudices or fastidiousness of any reasonable person; no reason whatever why I should not be able to fraternise, and make myself at home, just as well in that class of life as in any other. Alas for these *couleur de rose* anticipations of mine! They were destined to be of but very brief duration, and were soon ruthlessly destroyed by the following most vexatious occurrence.

As there is no accounting for tastes, and as even the ugliest of women need not despair of meeting with some man in whose eyes she will appear beautiful, or nice-looking at the very least, therefore I might obviously have foreseen the possibility of my encountering some male fellowservant or other who would consider me sufficiently attractive to flirt with. Of course, I ought to have taken this into my calculations when I was contemplating the various chances and events to which I should be liable on entering service. But it was a contingency which, somehow or other, never once occurred to me; I suppose I was too destitute of vanity about my own charms to think of it.

Now amongst my new companions was Lord Mervyn's valet, Perkins, a pale-faced, sandy-haired, thick-lipped, abominably-scented man, who wore flowing whiskers of inordinate length which he greatly cherished; who believed himself to be universally acceptable to the weaker sex, and who was conceited, cowardly, and revengeful. As bad luck would have it, I happened to take his fancy at first sight; and it all of a sudden dawned upon me, to my amazement and dismay, that he was actually making me the object of very marked and unmistakable attentions.

Scandalised at the notion of a man-servant taking the liberty to raise his eyes to a lady, I could hardly trust to the evidence of my own senses at first. But then the matter seemed less unlikely when I remembered that he had not a suspicion of there being any inequality of rank between him and me; and that, as far as that went, I was in his eyes just the same as any other maid in the house.

What he should find to admire in me, who had certainly done nothing to attract him, was beyond my power to imagine; but that did not alter the very unpleasant fact that he *did* regard me with favour, for he made it too plain for there to be a doubt about the matter. I shuddered to think that I must endure being made love to by a valet: it was an odious and degrading idea. Had I realised the possibility of it beforehand, I hardly knew whether I should ever have placed myself where I should be exposed to the risk of anything so disagreeable. Disgusted and angry at the admiration which I deemed an insult, and was yet powerless to resent, I endeavoured to nip it in the bud by energetic snubbing. Alas! he only thought that I was affecting coyness in order to draw him on, and persisted in his objectionable attentions all the more.

To add to my annoyance, I perceived that I was meanwhile incurring the bitter enmity of Lady Mervyn's maid, Robinson, to whom Perkins had, before my coming, devoted himself chiefly, and who strongly objected to any transfer of his affections. Too much blinded by jealousy to see how unwelcome his vulgar compliments were to me, she attributed the fickle conduct of her swain entirely to my wiles, and thought that I alone was to blame for his deserting her.

Unluckily the man had a smattering of French, and though his accent was as bad as a Corsican's (which is saying a *great* deal), he was immensely proud of his acquirements as a linguist, and aired them on every possible opportunity. Knowing that I, too, was supposed to be accomplished in this line, he kept on addressing me in the one foreign tongue which he believed himself to know, whenever he could recollect enough of it to translate any remark that he wanted to make. By this proceeding the flames of Robinson's wrath were constantly being fanned higher and higher; for she – understanding not a word of any language except her own – jumped to the conclusion that whatever French observation he addressed to me must necessarily be something of an extra-tender description, which would be unsuited to the ears of the general public.

I – anxious not to quarrel with her, and recoiling with horror from the idea that anyone could possibly suspect me of having the faintest approach to a private understanding with Perkins – invariably answered his speeches in English. But my efforts to undeceive her were in vain, and by the time we retired to bed she had begun to express her hostility in various unmistakable ways – such as darting angry glances in my direction, giving vent to frequent sniffs betokening great mental irritation, and making half-audible observations as to the rudeness of talking secrets in company, and the intense objection she had to meddlesome strangers who intruded and made mischief amongst friends.

A nice kettle of fish this is! thought I, in reviewing the events of the day before I went to sleep. I certainly do not see how I am to keep to my intention of not making enemies at this rate. And just when I was beginning to feel sure that everything was going to be so comfortable, too! Why could not that wretch Perkins have let me alone, I wonder? Faugh! The idea of supposing that I could be pleased with what *he* considers pretty speeches. I think it's a great pity that there are any men at all in the world – or, anyhow, any except gentlemen.

There was something worse than mere pretty speeches in store for me. On the day after my arrival I was going upstairs from dinner when I suddenly saw Perkins coming towards me. No one else was in sight, and he evidently thought it a good opportunity for prosecuting his courtship vigorously.

"Miss Jill, my dear," whispered he, leering at me detestably; "I'm *dying* for a kiss from them sweet lips of yours. Do give me one now there's no one to see."

I was too much taken aback to be able to think of any answer which would adequately express the intense horror and indignation with which his insolent speech inspired me, so I pretended not to have heard what he said. But I suspect that my face showed something of what I felt, for he was not deceived by my affectation of deafness, and continued, with a conceited snigger, whilst he stroked his beloved whiskers complacently:

"What – not just yet, my little partridge! *Tray biang!* This evening, or tomorrow, then, eh? Only I reelly *can't* wait long, mind; and if you go on being 'ard-'arted, I shall take that kiss without asking leave. That's just what you want, I dessay. Bless you! *I* know the way to please the ladies. You're all the same – longing to be courted and kissed, and yet making believe that you can't abide nothing of the kind, all the time."

I reached my room in a state of fury that was mixed with alarm, lest he should attempt to execute his threat. Being stronger than me, there was a chance that he might succeed in spite of all I could do to prevent it. And since it made me frantic merely to *think* of such a humiliation, what should I do supposing the monster actually did manage to profane my face with his lips? Should I kill him on the spot, or should I expire from sheer disgust? How unutterably horrible it was to have to associate with a creature who had such coarse, boorish ideas of what was the proper way for a man to make himself agreeable to a woman! This, verily, was a degradation for which I had not bargained. It was a comfort that I was going abroad so soon; if I could escape for a few days more, I should be out of reach of the danger. And with this reflection I consoled myself as well as I could, determining to be constantly on my guard as long as I was in that house, lest the dreaded and hateful salute should come upon me unawares, from some obscure corner or lurking place.

My apprehensions were but too well-founded, as I experienced on the following evening. It was after dark, and I was proceeding along the passage near the pantry, with a lighted candle in my hand, when my enemy suddenly sprung out from some recess where he had been lying in ambush. He endeavoured to throw his arms around me, exclaiming, as he did so: "Now's our time, my pet! I can't *possibly* wait no longer; and no one's looking, so you needn't purtend not to like it."

Moved by rage and fright to defend myself at all hazards, I had recourse to the only weapon available; and against the odious face and lips that were approaching mine I thrust the candle that I carried. He tried to avoid the impending peril by blowing out the light; but either he was too much confused, or else I was too quick for him, and he failed to extinguish it. In another instant there was a strong smell of burning hair, and one of his cherished whiskers was on fire. He let go of me with an oath, and an exclamation of pain and fear – for he was a shocking coward; and I passed on, quivering with excitement, and divided between exultation at my escape and self-hatred for having subjected myself to the disgrace of being thus forced into a sort of romping struggle with a valet.

When next I saw him he bore considerable traces of the contest. The hairy appendages to his face, in which he delighted, were gone; for the whisker I had set on fire had been so much destroyed that it had had to be shaved off, and then of course its companion had been obliged to follow suit. And besides this, there were on his lips and cheek sundry inflamed and angry-looking burns and blisters, which I regarded with vindictive satisfaction.

When the other servants commented on the change in his appearance, and inquired into the cause thereof, he accounted for it by a story which I did not trouble myself to contradict – about his having had an accident with an unusually explosive match, the head of which had flown off and burnt him. There was nothing so abominably dangerous, he said, with savage emphasis, as all ill-made thing like that, going off all of a sudden, and flaring and skipping about like mad, when it looked as safe and quiet as possible. Regular man traps, he considered them to be; and if he could have his way, they should be burnt, or got rid of somehow, every one of them.

As he spoke he cast a malignant glance at me, which convinced me that I had incurred his undying resentment, and that in his abuse of the imaginary match he was conveying his opinion about my deserts.

To that, however, I was indifferent; for in my eyes his hatred was infinitely preferable to his love; I did not at all suppose he could do me any harm, and only rejoiced to find what a wholesome effect my violence had produced. He could by no means forgive the loss of his whiskers and disfigurement which I had inflicted on him; and after the encounter above recorded he took no notice of me, except when he thought he saw an opening for saying or doing anything likely to annoy me – of which he always availed himself.

Some of the ways by which he tried to show his spite were highly ludicrous, and all the more so because they failed completely of having the effect he desired. For instance, in helping the vegetables he would omit to supply my wants in the proper order of precedence belonging to my position, and would serve some inferior domestic with potatoes before me. This, as I subsequently learnt, was intended as a mortal offence, which ought to have wounded my feelings desperately. But I was happily ignorant of it at the time, and had no suspicion of the intended insult. As long as I had enough potatoes, it was all the same to me whether I had them first or last; and when at dinner, he passed over me, and handed the dish to the second housemaid before me, I was all unconscious of the affront that was being offered, so that my peace of mind was in no wise affected by it.

But though, since he had given up making love to me, I was impervious to most of his methods of annoyance, none the less did I find the prevailing state of things uncomfortable in 2000 Eaton Square; and it was with sincere joy that I found myself at last fairly off from London, and accompanying Mrs. Rollin and Kitty to the Continent. I hoped that I had seen the last of Perkins; or that, at all events, if he and I should be destined to inhabit the same house again when I returned from abroad, he would have got over his present bad temper sufficiently to keep the peace with me. Certainly I never suspected the implacable enmity of which – as I was to find by experience – he was capable.

CHAPTER XII

The Photograph Again

WHEN fingers are set to work for the first time at dressing and undressing anyone else than their natural owner, they are apt to feel uncommonly as if they were all thumbs; such, at least, was the conclusion I came to at the outset of my career as lady's-maid. But a very little practice sufficed to make the awkward sensation wear off; and, after that, I was able easily to fulfill the duties of my post. To these duties I had no dislike, and much preferred being engaged in performing them to spending my time amongst other domestics; for I could wait on two ladies without shocking my self-respect in any way, whereas I felt ashamed and degraded at the mere idea of being liable to be persecuted by a man like Perkins. I tried hard to conquer this squeamishness, telling myself that it was ridiculous and inconsistent for a woman like me to be so particular, after having deliberately elected to knock about in the world, and take what came. But my endeavours to reason myself into a sensible view of the matter were in vain, and completely failed to uproot the feeling that to be taken liberties with by a man-servant was a humiliation not to be endured.

The Perkins incident having put me out of charity with the whole class – females and males alike – to which he belonged, it was a satisfaction to me that I was to be the sole attendant accompanying Mrs. Rollin and Kitty Mervyn abroad. This obviated all danger, at all events for the present, of my having to associate with obnoxious comrades. On the score of being dull for want of company I felt no uneasiness, for I knew by experience that I could amuse myself perfectly well when left to my own devices. Besides – had I not now the opportunity which I had desired for observing Kitty Mervyn, and trying to make out her character? I habitually regarded every one with indifference; but she had for me a strange fascination, which was strong enough to overcome that indifference, and I was quite astonished at the extent to which she interested me. Let me enumerate some of the attractions and qualities, both bodily and mental, of this young lady, who was at once my mistress, and also – though she would have been very greatly surprised to be told so – my connection.

In appearance she was tall, handsome, and imperial-looking, with a bright and open expression of countenance. Her disposition was upright, proud, honourable, and averse to everything mean. In conversation she was clever, quick-witted, lively, and pleasant. And as, furthermore, she was endowed with great social talent and a remarkable knack of pleasing all with whom she came in contact, she won hearts right and left, and was considered charming wherever she went. She was, however, far from faultless. The germ of worldliness, which inevitably creeps into an education amongst fashionable people, had begun to develop itself, and to taint her nature; and the conclave in her father's housekeeper's room had certainly not erred in attributing to her pride and ambition. So marked was her inclination to haughtiness that, when first I knew her, it sometimes puzzled me why she should take the trouble she did to make herself universally agreeable – even to people for whom she did not care, from whom there was nothing to be gained in return, and who were nobodies in her estimation. As, however, I came to understand her better, I discovered the key to this enigma, and perceived that she was actuated – whether consciously or only instinctively I do not know – by a strong desire for two things which seemed almost as indispensable to her as the air she breathed. These two things were popularity and power, and without them she was never really happy.

Her frank genial manner was well adapted to make people believe her to be an unreserved, easily read individual; but the more attentively I studied her, the less inclined did I feel to think that impression a correct one. I had doubts whether she ever showed much of her real self; whether there were not recesses, of unsuspected depth, hidden within her where no mortal eye could penetrate; and whether she did not often make use of unreserve as a mask to conceal its opposite. The possibility of this made her all the more attractive to me. Curiosity as to what might lie beneath the surface she presented to the world, served to increase the drawing towards her that I had always felt; and had I been so placed as to have a chance of making friends with her, I should certainly have tried to do so. But it was, as I well knew, hopeless to attempt such a thing in my present position; for she was not the sort of girl to condescend to familiar intercourse with social inferiors, and in her eyes I was simply a maid. Under the circumstances, it would obviously be ridiculous if I were to let myself become fond of her, and I resolved firmly not to be guilty of any sentimental folly of the kind. Yet, in spite of this prudent resolution, I must confess that I sometimes had hard work not to yield to the indefinable charm which she had for me; and had she vouchsafed me any special marks of favour, I am afraid I should inevitably have made a fool of myself, and become romantically devoted to her. As, however, I had no particular attraction for her, such as she had for me, that fact contributed greatly to restrain my liking within reasonable limits. To indulge in an unrequited attachment had always seemed to me decidedly weak and contemptible (notwithstanding that such a man as the author of the *Vita Nuova* had done it); and it would have discomposed me immensely to detect in myself any symptoms of being capable of that weakness.

In short, I was sufficiently smitten with Kitty to have cast prudence to the winds, and let my whole heart go out to her, *if* she had held up her finger to me. But that little word "if" made just all the difference. My sense of dignity might safely be reckoned on to assist reason and prudence in fighting against an infatuation for any person who did not care for me in return.

From London we proceeded to Paris; thence we travelled slowly across France, stopping at various places of interest, and presently reached Cannes, where my two ladies meant to make a stay of a week or so before journeying on into Italy.

So far, I had seen and heard nothing to confirm the gossip about Lord Clement's admiration for Kitty, which had been communicated to me by the servants. But I received ample proof of its truth on the day after our arrival at Cannes; and this happened in the following manner:–

I was engaged in brushing the dust off a dress which Kitty had been wearing, when I found in the pocket a letter which she had received that morning from England. I did not hesitate to read it. When letters have secrets in them, people do not leave them about, thought I; so, since Kitty has not troubled to take this one out of her pocket, of course there are no private matters in it, and there is no reason why I should not see if the contents are amusing.

The epistle was from Lady Mervyn, and the portion of it which most interested me ran thus:

"Lord Clement told me last week that he thought he should go yachting to the Riviera at once, and as I have little doubt what is the attraction that takes him there, I daresay you will see something of him before long. I do hope, dearest Kitty, that you will not set yourself against him, and that you will try and reconsider the answer you gave him before. I am, as you know, the *last* person to try to over-persuade you into a marriage against your own inclinations; but yet I cannot resist putting in a good word for him, for it touches me to see how truly he loves you, and how constant to you he is, in spite of your refusal. Besides that, he really is a man in a thousand, and one to whom any mother would trust her daughter joyfully. Not only has he the recommendations of rank and wealth, but moreover he is unusually amiable, high-minded, conscientious, steady, and superior to the temptations to folly and extravagance to which young men in his position are so peculiarly open. With the exception of yourself, I doubt there being a single girl in London – or in England either – who would not accept him gladly, if only he asked her. And I'm sure one can't wonder at his being so run-after as he is, when one remembers what his money and position are, what immense influence they give him, what an excellent character he bears, and how thoroughly good he is in every way. However, you know already how high he stands in my good graces, and I had better drop the subject for fear of boring you by going over the same old tale again. Only do remember, my darling, that it is only the earnest wish I have to secure your happiness which makes me so anxious for you not to dismiss him without well considering what you do. Otherwise you may, perhaps, some day find yourself repenting your past decision, and regretting that you were so persistent in rejecting one of the few men of whom it may truly be said, that he is all that a husband should be."

Not badly done, my lady, thought I, as I refolded the letter, and restored it to its place. You knew what a tempting bait power is to Kitty when you put in that bit about the influence which the young man's position gives him. And you understood who you were writing to when you reminded her of his attractiveness to other people – she's likely enough to value goods at the price the rest of the world put upon them. Evidently you, like the servants, are puzzled to account for her indisposition to receive the proposals of this rich, titled, desirable, and altogether delightful suitor. Well! it rather puzzles me too. Can it be that she prefers someone else? No one seems to suspect such a thing; but yet it might be true for all that. What if that photograph I found in her purse were the explanation of the mystery? There is no impossibility in the idea of a *tendresse* existing between her and Captain Norroy, which they have hitherto managed to conceal from other people. I wish I could see them together, and then I should have some chance of discovering whether this conjecture of mine is right or not.

Whilst speculating thus, a brilliant idea suddenly flashed into my mind. This was, that I might avail myself of the surreptitiously-obtained *carte-de-visite* (which I had carefully preserved), in order to find out what I wanted to know. I would produce it unexpectedly, when there was no chance of Kitty's being particularly on guard, and watch for any signs of emotion that she might show on seeing it.

Wrapped up exactly as it had been when in her purse, and even in the self-same bit of paper, I put it into a blank envelope, which I presented next time I went to wait on her.

"I picked this up on the floor, just outside," said I. "I was going to take it to the landlord; but then I thought perhaps it might be something of yours, as I found it close to the door of your room, so I had better ask you about it first."

The envelope was not fastened, as I had feared that if it were closed she would scruple to open it, which would be fatal to the success of my stratagem.

"Thank you," she answered, taking it from me carelessly. "I don't think it belongs to me, but I can soon see."

I was doing her hair at the time, and commanded an excellent view of her face reflected in the looking-glass opposite which she sat. Her expression of *insouciance* vanished like magic when she had undone the paper and seen what it contained. The colour rushed into her face, which softened for a moment in a way I had never before seen it do; then came a stern, rigid, haughty, resolute look, as though she would defy the whole world to discover whatever secret she chose to conceal.

She did not speak at first, but turned round the photograph again and again, examining both it and the paper in which it had been wrapped.

At last she said: "This certainly is my property; but I can't imagine how it came to be where you found it. I fully believed it to have been lost some time ago."

"Don't you think," I suggested, "that when you thought you had lost it, you had perhaps really only slipped it into your writing-case, or into some book or papers which you haven't happened to open since then until now? Then it fell out without your noticing it, and either you were at that time at the place where I picked it up, or else some one's dress may have swept it there from your room. It was very near to the door."

"That is *possible,* no doubt," she returned, thoughtfully. "Yet still, I can hardly believe it to have happened so. I felt as positive as one can be about anything, that it was not in an envelope at all, and that I had put it" – she hesitated a moment, and then finished, "somewhere else."

As she did not seem inclined to mention where she really had put it, I thought I had better pretend to suppose that its destination had been a photograph album.

"It would be very easy to be mistaken about what you had done with it, though," said I. "Probably when it was given you it was in an envelope, and then you were interrupted just as you were going to stick it into your book, and after that you forgot all about it, and it got mislaid."

"Well, you may be right," she replied. "Indeed I don't see any other way of accounting for the matter. But it is odd how I can have been so completely wrong in the impression I had as to what I had done with it."

The theory I had propounded seemed sufficiently plausible to content her, and she did not again allude to the affair. But I had little doubt that she thought about it a good deal for all that, because of a new look which I noticed in her face occasionally during the next day or two, and which was different from any other that I had seen there hitherto. A gleam of soft light would flash out from her eyes, accompanied by an expression of countenance which was curious, half-ashamed, tender, and wistful, and gave the impression rather of unhappiness than of the joy a girl would be likely to feel when thinking of her lover. This look of sadness would last perhaps for a minute, and then invariably be succeeded by one that was scornful, hard, and impenetrable.

It was beyond me to interpret these signs satisfactorily. That Captain Norroy had power to excite emotions of *some* kind in her breast I felt sure; but whether these emotions were pleasurable or the reverse, I was unable to make out.

CHAPTER XIII

Lord Clement

LADY MERVYN'S prediction regarding Lord Clement's movements proved to be correct. His yacht, *La Catalina,* arrived at Cannes two or three days after we did, and that event was speedily followed by the appearance of her noble owner at the hotel where we were staying.

The interest with which Kitty's affairs inspired me had led to my speculating a good deal on the subject of this young lord; and I had made up my mind that he was almost sure to have something or other disagreeable about him which would counterbalance his many charms, and afford some explanation of her unwillingness to accept him. No doubt, thought I, he is loutish, silly, ugly, untidy, bad mannered, eccentric, or in some other way objectionable. This anticipation, however, turned out to be wrong, and I soon perceived that he had none of the defects with which my lively imagination had credited him.

He was rather below middle height, dressed well and quietly, and could never by any accident be mistaken for anything but a gentleman – which, indeed, he certainly was in every respect. Neither handsome nor ugly, his face was amiable and mild, but possessed no other very marked expression of any kind. One would not suppose him to be powerful or weak, distinguished or insignificant, a genius or a fool. If there was nothing specially attractive about his appearance, neither was there the reverse.

His intellect was not in any way brilliant, but he had good sense and fair average abilities, was eminently painstaking, and would work as laboriously at whatever he thought it his duty to do as though his livelihood had depended on his exertions. In short, I think that the most appropriate description of him is mediocrity, in respect of everything except moral qualities; but where these were concerned he was by no means mediocre, being far more conscientious and anxious to do right than are the majority of rich young men who have the world at their feet.

The most trying thing about him was a tendency to make a fuss about trifles, and to attach a needless importance to all the minor proprieties of life, which was sometimes rather irritating. But, after all, fidgettiness and extra deference to Mrs. Grundy are only very small defects in the eyes of most people. I could understand that Kitty might occasionally be aggravated by these failings, yet they alone were not, in my opinion, sufficient to account for his being refused by a girl who was ambitious, and who had enough perspicacity and worldly wisdom to appreciate what an excellent match he was, and what an opening for ambition would be afforded by the position of his wife.

I was curious to know how Kitty treated him, and profited by every opportunity I had of watching them together. From these observations I came to the conclusion that he had inspired her neither with affection nor aversion, and that she was struggling to bring herself to accept him. I thought that her reason and judgment were pleading for him, and expatiating on his attractions, as her mother had done, and that she was lending a willing ear to these advocates, and doing all she could to let herself be convinced by their arguments. Yet I had a great idea, too, that the effort went against the grain with her, and that she often could not help keeping him at arm's length, even in spite of her own wish. It was as if she had been conscious of the grasp of an invisible hand, from which she could not wrench herself free, and which constantly drew her back when she strove to approach nearer to her suitor.

Is it Captain Norroy's hand that restrains her? I asked myself, as I pondered over this result of my observations. Yet, if so, it seems very odd that no one except me should have discovered their attachment for one another. From all that I have seen and heard I should have thought that a young couple in society would never have managed to become spoons to any serious degree without giving rise to some amount of suspicion as to the true state of affairs between them. However can these two have contrived to deceive the lynx eyes of gossip-loving servants, and to hoodwink the worldly and wide-awake Lady Mervyn whose heart is set on securing a brilliant match for her favourite daughter?

Lord Clement's behaviour towards Kitty after his arrival at Cannes seemed to me that of a man who felt himself to be on trial – was nervous lest she should think him over eager in his addresses, and objected to getting himself talked about with a girl who perhaps would not marry him after all. His first proceeding was to get introduced to Mrs. Rollin, who had till then been a stranger to him. The introduction was easily effected, and after that he had no lack of opportunities of meeting the object of his affections; for Mrs. Rollin responded cordially to his advances, inviting him to join in all the excursions to neighbouring lions which she and Kitty made, and letting it be apparent that he was most welcome whenever he chose to pay them a visit, and to accompany them anywhere.

I have no doubt that this civility of hers resulted, in the

first instance, from something said by Lady Mervyn as to his admiration for Kitty, and the desirability of encouraging him as much as possible. But though this may have been the original motive of the *empressement* with which Mrs. Rollin received him, there was no fear of her not welcoming him for his own sake when once she had made acquaintance with him and discovered what he was like. For she was a person who held that the most important matter in life was to stand well in the world's opinion, and consequently she was quite charmed with his scrupulous regard for *convenances* and extreme horror of doing anything that could shock Mrs. Grundy.

"There's nothing of more consequence," Mrs. Rollin would declare, "than to keep up appearances, because, provided one does that, one is quite safe to be thought perfect. And that's what everyone wishes to be thought, or, if they don't, they ought to. I call it quite wicked of anyone to pretend that it doesn't matter what the world's opinion about them is. Depend upon it, that whatever the whole world thinks *can't* be wrong; and that if a person is generally condemned or praised, there's always some good reason for the blame or the approval."

Keeping up appearances in the eyes of the world was, therefore, her standard of perfection; and she strove zealously never to fall short of that standard, and always to fulfill its requirements punctiliously. Nevertheless, it would be a mistake to deduce from this that she was such an abject slave of the world's opinion as to let herself be governed by it in things which it did not see. On the contrary, she drew a line between her public and private actions, and did not allow it to interfere at all with the latter. If she had tastes and inclinations to which it objected, she did not, on that account, sacrifice them, if it was possible that they could be indulged in secret. How she would act, under such circumstances, was illustrated

by her behaviour regarding French novels. These she preferred to any other kind of reading, and greedily devoured
as many as she could lay hold of. But as she knew that the
world sometimes thinks fit to frown at an indiscriminate
study of these books (who shall say whether that
disapprobation is real or feigned?), therefore she was
careful not to reveal her partiality for them. Yet she did
not rush to the opposite extreme and disclaim any
acquaintance whatsoever with that class of literature. She
had no idea of hiding her light under a bushel, and not
being duly credited with as many accomplishments as she
possessed, and therefore liked to have it known that she
understood a foreign language well enough to read and
enjoy works written in it. So what she did was, to profess
to read French novels solely with the laudable object of
keeping up her French; while, at the same time, she was
most cautious in talking about them in public, and never
betrayed the slightest knowledge of the contents of any
that were not fairly decorous and proper.

But *I* knew better than that. It was a matter in which
her maid could not be deceived as easily as the rest of the
world.

Bohemianism being an open setting-at-defiance of the
world's opinion, was quite detestable to her, with all that
savoured thereof; and the very correct Lord Clement was,
of course, a man after her own heart. There was, however,
a wide difference between the respective ways in which
he and she regarded Mrs. Grundy. For while the
gentleman had a genuine esteem for that great social
authority, and paid her homage in all sincerity, Mrs.
Rollin did it only in appearance, and was moved thereto
chiefly by fear.

The room in which I slept was immediately over Mrs.
Rollin's sitting-room; and by sitting at the open window
in my room I could hear – when the weather was calm –

most things that were said by people on the balcony beneath. Thus I overheard an interesting conversation as to plans which took place after we had been at Cannes for about as long a time as my two ladies intended to stay there. Where to go next, was the question they were debating. And as Lord Clement happened to call just then, Mrs. Rollin appealed to him to assist them with his advice in the matter.

His manner of complying with this request was eminently characteristic of him. Kitty's society was the object of his keenest desires at that moment, and he was averse to the idea of any movement that would involve his being separated from her. Under these circumstances, and considering the amount of encouragement he had received – especially from the young lady's *chaperone* – some men would have taken it for granted that their companionship was acceptable, and that it was a matter of course for them to accompany the two ladies to their next destination. Not so, however, would Lord Clement behave. Thus openly to attach himself to them as a travelling companion would inevitably give rise to gossip; and to do anything likely to be talked about as unusual was quite contrary to his ideas of propriety. Though the real object of his visit to the Mediterranean might have been Kitty, yet the ostensible reason had been yachting; and this pretext he had no intention of renouncing by leaving his vessel. In taking part in the discussion as to what our future movements were to be, he gave no indication of being personally interested in the matter in any way, and assumed the air of a strictly impartial adviser. At the same time, however, his opinion as to the desirability of places was in such remarkably exact proportion to their availability from the sea, that I listened with much amusement, and thought that the disinterestedness of his counsels might very fairly be doubted.

Various localities had been suggested and talked over without any determination being arrived at, when Kitty observed, "Now I've quite a new place to propose; and that's Corsica. I saw it looking just like a purple cloud resting on the sea the other day, and I have a great fancy to go and see it close. For one thing, there's no railway there yet; and I should like, for once in my life, to feel that I was in a land through which locomotives have never puffed. It would be an absolutely new sensation to me, and one which the present rate of civilisation will soon render unattainable, I expect; so I vote we experience it while we can. Besides, I'm sure it would be a good place for sketching. What do you say, Aunt Georgina? Don't you think it'll be pleasant to get away from this cockney old Riviera, and go a little bit out of the regular beaten track where *everyone* goes?"

"Kitty, Kitty!" remonstrated her aunt, "it quite distresses me to hear you talk like that! You really shouldn't speak contemptuously of the beaten track, and be so anxious to get away from it. Remember that the fact of its being worn by many feet is also a sure proof of its being smoother, pleasanter, and in every way preferable to other tracks."

"All right, aunty," laughed Kitty; "I won't abuse your favourite walk since it vexes you! But doesn't it strike you that I should appreciate its merits all the more if I were to see with my own eyes – just for once you know – how horrid some other route can be? And isn't that a good reason for going to Corsica? *Do* let's go there; I've quite set my heart on it."

Kitty rarely failed to get her own way with Mrs. Rollin, who was as susceptible as the rest of the world to the girl's powers of fascination. But the hesitating, reluctant tone in which the elder lady answered, showed me that she had no great fancy for this Corsican visit.

"Well, I hardly know what to say," she returned slowly; "to begin with, How does one get there? and in the next place, What's it like when one *is* there? I think I've heard you say you were there once, Lord Clement; do help me to make up my mind about this, and advise me whether or not to do what this rash niece of mine wishes."

Corsica naturally found favour in the young man's eyes as being convenient for yachting purposes. "Oh, if you ask me, I decidedly advise you to go," he replied; "it's really a pretty sort of country, besides being interesting as the birthplace of Napoleon. By the by you should read Boswell's tour if you go. As for getting there, you could go by steamer either from Marseilles to Ajaccio, or else from Leghorn or Genoa to Bastia. But I hope that you will allow me the pleasure of taking you over in *La Catalina,* which you'll find far more comfortable than either of the regular steamers – they're all nasty, dirty, uneasy little boats, I believe."

"I'm sure we are greatly obliged to you for so good an offer," answered Mrs. Rollin, "and I think we should gladly avail ourselves of it *if* we were to decide upon going. But I fancy I've heard it said that one can't get anything to eat there which wouldn't suit me at all. And then, too, there are the dangers from vendettas and banditti to be taken into consideration."

"Oh now, don't go being a perverse aunty, and making difficulties out of nothing!" exclaimed Kitty. "How could the natives exist if there wasn't something to eat? And a vendetta is a strictly private family affair, which doesn't affect strangers one atom. And as for banditti, it's not Corsica but Sicily that is full of them; my belief is that you've gone and mixed the two islands together in your head. The Corsicans are always supposed to be a particularly amiable and friendly set of people as far as ever *I* heard. Except, of course, when there's a vendetta to excite them, and that wouldn't matter to outsiders like you and me."

"I assure you that that is true, Mrs. Rollin," added Lord Clement, "and that you have really no cause of apprehension from robbers. The only danger of that kind which I ever heard mentioned during my stay there was from escaped convicts. Now and then a few manage to get out of the prison, I believe, and support themselves *à la brigand* on the mountains, till they are either retaken or else contrive to get across to Sardinia to join some of the banditti there. But that only happens so very seldom that it really is not worth taking into consideration."

"How about the hotels?" inquired Mrs. Rollin; "are there any good ones to be met with?"

"Oh, they are not at all bad at the two chief seaports – Ajaccio and Bastia," he replied, "and there would not be any necessity for you to sleep anywhere else. I could take you from the one town to the other in my yacht, and from those places you could make inland expeditions within the limits of a day, which would enable you to see a great deal of the country without having to rough it at all. I can't say much for the hotel accommodation anywhere except at the two chief towns, and shouldn't recommend you to go travelling about in the interior. But of course you would not care to visit the more wild and out-of-the-way parts."

"You mustn't be too sure of that," said Kitty, laughing. "Whatever a place may be, it's attractive to me if it's different from any other that I've ever seen before. And Aunt Georgina isn't *quite* so miserable when beyond reach of luxuries as you might think to hear her talk. I've even known her go without five o'clock tea and yet be happy! For my part I begin to feel an intense desire arising in my breast to hunt up an escaped convict and fraternise with him, or at least to go and inspect his lair.

What a novel subject for a sketch it would be! And I'm *sure* that you'll like to do whatever pleases me, aunty, for you always do. Now isn't that true?"

"Well, well, perhaps I do my dear, but only within reasonable limits, please to remember," returned her aunt, who was considerably influenced by Lord Clement's support of the Corsican scheme. "People of my age don't regard 'roughing it' with the same enthusiasm as some of the young ones, who don't really know what that process implies, and for whom it has all the charm of novelty. I should certainly draw the line a long way before the escaped convict you wish to meet. However, joking apart, from what Lord Clement says, there does not seem to be any reason against running over to the island and gratifying your whim to have a peep at it, though I quite agree with him as to its being undesirable to penetrate into any remote and inaccessible parts, where neither pleasure nor advantage are to be gained. I never can see the good of going to places where no one else goes. There's no one one knows there; and besides that, as no one knows anything about them, there's no chance of finding them necessary, or even useful, as topics of conversation in society. So that visiting such places is mere waste of time and money in *my* opinion!"

"Well, then we may consider Corsica to be our next destination anyhow," said Kitty triumphantly. "That's the first thing to settle, and there is no need to make up our minds as to anything further just yet. Time enough for that by and by, when we get there."

After a little more discussion it was decided that we should be conveyed to Ajaccio in *La Catalina;* which vessel, though not containing berths enough for us to have slept a night on board, was yet quite capable of accommodating us very comfortably for the time requisite to perform the passage between Cannes and

Ajaccio. What our plans should be after reaching the island was left quite uncertain; for though Mrs. Rollin was well inclined to stay only at the two chief towns and move from one to the other in the yacht, as Lord Clement had proposed, yet Kitty was not to be induced to commit herself to any definite approval of this scheme, and without her approval it was impossible to feel sure of its being carried out, for she generally got her own way about things she cared for. All she would say was, that perhaps it might be a good plan and perhaps not, and that there was not the least need to settle the matter positively yet.

Lord Clement was evidently happy to have had his offer of the yacht accepted – for the voyage across at all events. But I think that his satisfaction was somewhat marred by a dread of Kitty's taking the bit between her teeth when once she should be at Corsica, running away with her aunt all over the island, and getting out of his reach from the sea; if the whim to do it came to her, there was but small probability that she would not accomplish her purpose.

CHAPTER XIV

At Ajaccio

THE inevitable Mediterranean roll was in less force than usual when we crossed to Corsica, and as we were all pretty fair sailors we had a pleasant passage, notwithstanding the anticipations to the contrary of our especial waiter at the Cannes hotel. He was a brisk, cheery little fellow, with such a power of sympathising with other people that he always identified himself with those guests who were under his particular care, and took their affairs to heart almost as though they were his own. Going to sea and being sea-sick meant precisely the same thing to him; consequently, from the moment he heard of our contemplated trip he became full of compassion for the sufferings we must undergo, and was good-naturedly eager to think of, and suggest, every possible alleviation for the misery which he confidently predicted for us. As we departed from the hotel his final words were to impress upon my two ladies that, last thing before going to sea, one should always eat a hearty meal, because, "ça facilite – et sans ça, c'est si fatigante." I am sorry to have to add, however, that this well-intentioned speech was received in by no means as friendly a spirit as that in which it was offered. For it was quite contrary to Mrs. Rollin's notions of propriety that one who was a man, and an inferior, should presume publicly to give her advice as to the management of her interior; so, instead of making the amicable response that was evidently expected, she swept past him with a freezing look and an audible remark to Kitty about the atrocious vulgarity of foreign servants who had never been taught to know their place.

When we arrived at Ajaccio we separated from Lord Clement, he remaining on board *La Catalina,* whilst we proceeded to a hotel. During the voyage Kitty had been more civil to him than usual, perhaps as a reward for his assistance in persuading her aunt to come to Corsica, – and this favourable humour still continued on reaching *terra firma.* A question hazarded by him as we left the yacht, as to what should be done next day, was replied to by her with a graciousness which made it apparent that his company would be acceptable, if he chose to join her and her aunt in whatever they might be doing.

Accordingly, I was not surprised to see him appear at our hotel first thing next morning. Shortly afterwards they all three sallied forth to see the pictures at the *Collège* Fesch; then they ordered a basket to be packed with provisions, and, the weather being splendid, hired a carriage and drove off for a day's outing beyond Pisciatella. The special object of the two younger people was sketching, to which Kitty was greatly addicted, and for which she had a decided talent. Lord Clement, on the contrary, had no natural gift in that line; but, none the less, he strove laboriously to acquire the art, because he regarded drawing as a highly moral, elevating, correct, and unexceptionable amusement, and therefore one to be cultivated and encouraged as much as possible. As for Mrs. Rollin, she had a French novel in her pocket, and would be perfectly happy to bask in the sun and read whilst her companions sketched or flirted, as might seem good in their own eyes.

My employers being thus disposed of for the day, I was left alone with nothing particular to do. The streets were too filthy to be very inviting, so, being a good walker, I went for a stretch along the road towards the Isles Sanguinaires. It was a lovely day, and I thoroughly enjoyed the beauty of the walk, and the contrast between winter, represented by snow-covered Monte Oro in the distance, and summer, felt in the hot sunshine that warmed me through and through, and sparkled on the brilliant blue sea beside the road. And when I got beyond the limits of the town there were wild hillsides rising on my right, all covered with low bushes of some kind of cistus, which, though now brown and scrubby-looking, would be beautiful, I thought, when in full bloom.

But I must not expatiate on the scenery, as that has nothing to do with my story. What I saw in the course of that walk, to which I now wish particularly to call attention, is this: Near the outskirts of the town I came to a number of small houses standing pretty close together on one side of the road. Each was in the middle of a little plot of ground which was surrounded either by a wall, or else by strong iron railings; and this enclosure was only to be entered by a gate, whence a short drive led to the door of the house within. Some, but not all, had a family name stuck up at the entrance; and some of the plots of ground were merely turfed over, whilst others were nicely laid out in flower-beds and borders.

One would naturally have concluded these buildings to be villas, if it had not been for the curious fact of their being destitute of windows. This puzzled me; for I did not suppose that Corsicans could be different from the rest of the world in disliking to live in windowless habitations.

Whilst I was staring at these mysterious houses, and wondering what they were for, a funeral came along the main road, and turned into the gate of the outer enclosure of one of them. This excited my curiosity still more, so I addressed myself to a respectable looking passer-by, and asked him what those little villas were, and to whom they belonged. He replied that they were "chapelles mortuaires," or, in other words, private burial places, and that each one belonged to a different family. On questioning further, I learnt that these "chapelles mortuaires" were by no means peculiar to the neighbourhood of towns, but were found in remote parts of the island also, as the possession of them was quite customary amongst all Corsicans.

I thanked the man for his information, and continued my walk. I thought it seemed a quaint idea to build villa residences for the dead, and then dismissed the subject from my mind. Certainly it never entered my head that I myself was destined before long to make acquaintance with the interior of one.

That evening I discovered that Kitty had a new scheme in her head. What instigated her to it I cannot say. It may have been the spirit of perversity, or else a guide book which she had been studying diligently; or else, perhaps, that she was tired of being civil to Lord Clement, and wanted to escape from him for a while. But anyhow, for some reason or other, it had been borne in upon her that it would be the most delightful thing possible to make a fortnight's driving-tour through the island for the purpose of seeing the country and sketching. Knowing that she would probably have a difficulty in getting her aunt to consent to this scheme, she did not intend to propound it until she had first ascertained that it was really feasible, and also found out whatever information might be requisite for its execution.

Her first step, therefore, was to impart the project to me, telling me that she wished me to make inquiries as to various matters connected with it – such as what sort of inns were to be found at the small inland towns; whether the roads were in good condition for travelling on; whether they were likely to be blocked by snow in the mountainous districts; what it would cost to hire a carriage; who was the best jobmaster in Ajaccio, etc.

I was charmed at a plan which harmonised so well with my own love of change and adventure, and entered into it readily. Being curious to know whether she contemplated being accompanied by Lord Clement or not, I put a fishing question to that effect. "What sized carriage am I to ask about?" said I; "how many must it hold?"

"Why, my aunt and I, and you, *of course,*" she answered rather sharply, as if not well pleased at my having entertained a doubt on the subject. "I should have thought you might have known that yourself. We should only take a couple of carpet bags with us, and leave the heavy luggage behind, so as to travel as light as possible; therefore we shouldn't want at all a big carriage. It should be an open one, and have a hood to put up in case of rain."

Oh, thought I, on hearing this, evidently then my lord is meant to be left to himself; his fair weather has not lasted long after all. I suppose that she has been putting a strain on herself to be civil to him, that now comes the reaction, and that she is going to fly off at a tangent from the line of conduct which was dictated by worldly policy, and not by natural inclination. Well, it does not matter to me whether she marries him or not, so I do not want to interfere one way or other; I have only to look on at the play and be amused. I hope she will be able to carry out this driving-tour scheme anyhow; for it is just the sort of thing I should like myself.

I lost no time in performing her commission to the best of my ability. Entering into casual conversations with sundry natives – waiters, for instance, a couple of talkative shopkeepers, and the driver of a fiacre, who was sunning himself on the steps of his vehicle – I cautiously led up to the topics which I had been told to find out about, knowing that a stranger was more likely to arrive at an honest opinion in this indirect way than by blunt, straightforward inquiries. By means of questions that were apparently purposeless, I elicited a good deal of information as to the relative merits of different hostelries and individuals, which might very likely have been withheld if I had let it be seen that I had any especial reason for wishing to know. Thus I learnt too who was reputed the best *patron des voitures,* and how much would be the probable difference between what he would *ask* and what he would *take* for the hire of a carriage; this difference being a sum of from 8 to 12 francs a day, according to the opinion he happened to form of the hard-headedness and determination not to be cheated of whoever engaged him.

Having found out as much as I could, I passed it all on to Kitty, who, armed with this knowledge, took the opportunity of hair-brushing time that same evening to suggest the driving-tour to Mrs. Rollin. That lady at once pronounced the scheme wild and impracticable. On being asked why, she brought forward all the objections she could think of, every one of which was met and answered by Kitty with a readiness that quite staggered her aunt. Mrs. Rollin had been far too much engrossed in one of Zola's novels to notice the attention with which her niece had recently been perusing books of Corsican travel; and the unexpected and intimate acquaintance with the subject suddenly displayed by Kitty almost took away the aunt's breath. Evidently it had never occurred to her that there was a possibility of Kitty's thus making up her mind, and finding out all requisite particulars, without having given a single hint of what she was thinking of. Yet here was the plan, all cut and dried and ready, with every detail gone into.

Certainly the girl made the most of what she had read and heard; and no one, to hear her talk, would have believed that this was her first visit to the island. She discoursed learnedly about where the best scenery was; what towns had good accommodation; what were the names of the various inns; and what the cost of living and of the carriage would be. She had got up her subject thoroughly; had an answer ready for all difficulties that it was possible to suggest; made everything look *couleur-de-rose;* and quoted, as a precedent for what she wanted to do, which would have weight with her hearer, the example of an English lady of rank and fashion, who had been travelling about in Corsica a few years before, and of whom she had just happened to hear. Kitty's energy, skill in pleading her cause, and powers of persuasion, were more than her admiring and less strong-willed relative could resist. The scheme, as thus set forth, appeared quite delightful; Lord Clement was on board his yacht, beyond reach of being taken into consultation; and so the end of the matter was, that Mrs. Rollin assented to all that Kitty wished, and that I consequently received orders to go out the first thing next morning and arrange for hiring a carriage.

This I accordingly did; and as I passed through the streets towards the residence of the *patron des voitures,* I met Lord Clement on his way to the hotel, looking just as usual – that is to say, the essence of propriety, clean, well-dressed, placid, gentlemanlike, English, and (to my mind) uninteresting. I did not dislike him, but his intense love of respectability and correctness aggravated me; and I thought, maliciously, that his present placid satisfaction would be ruffled by the news of the contemplated expedition, and that I should like to see his face when he heard of it. For it could hardly be expected that a man who had brought the object of his affections to a place where he hoped to be able to be with her daily, would relish the sudden discovery that she was going to leave him in the lurch, and take herself off out of his reach for a fortnight at least, if not longer.

CHAPTER XV

A Driving Expedition in Corsica

MY position as a servant gave me no opportunity of knowing whether or not Lord Clement made any attempt to oppose the projected driving-tour. If he did, however, his interference certainly produced no effect; for the orders I had received were not countermanded, and on the following day we three unprotected females departed from Ajaccio, and set out upon our travels into the interior of the island. Our conveyance was a light open carriage, with a head that could be raised or lowered at pleasure. As the trap only held two people comfortably inside, I sat on the box by the driver; and the very moderate amount of luggage that accompanied us was fastened securely at the back of the vehicle.

It was a beautiful morning, and everything seemed to promise well for our expedition. Driving in an open carriage was a thing which Mrs. Rollin greatly affectioned, and always declared it to be impossible for her ever to tire of; and as she was rendered additionally complacent by having been able to procure a sufficient stock of French novels to obviate all risk of dullness, she was in a happy and contented frame of mind, which Kitty and I – ourselves in the highest spirits, and ready to make the best of everything – were most anxious she should retain.

The scenery was much admired, especially the lovely views that were to be had, looking back over Ajaccio and the blue waters of its bay. The small, jet-black, silky-looking sheep were noticed and commented on; so were the vineyards which we passed; the chestnut, fig, almond, and olive trees; and, beyond everything, the arbutus bushes, which called forth many exclamations of admiration and delight. No wonder; for it really was a sight to see acres and acres of them growing wild in luxuriant profusion, and covered with magnificent luscious-looking fruit, whose size and brilliancy of colouring far exceeded that of any arbutus berries which I have ever seen elsewhere.

A drive of about three hours brought us to Cauro, where there was some idea that we should sleep that night, if the inn looked inviting; if not, we were to go on to St. Marie Sicché. Corsican inns are generally extremely clean, and the one at Cauro was no exception to the rule. But alas! it could supply neither milk nor butter, and nothing in the shape of meat except "merles."

I was not at all astonished at this, because I had already been told in Ajaccio that travellers in the island could not rely on finding meat everywhere, and that at the present time of winter butter and milk would certainly be un-attainable, except at one or two of the very largest towns. This piece of information had been duly communicated by me to Kitty; but somehow or other it had not reached the ears of her aunt, and that good lady was disagreeably surprised at a scarcity of luxuries for which Kitty and I were quite prepared. She at once voted for not sleeping at Cauro, but going on to St. Marie Sicché, where she had no doubt there would be a better stock of provisions. Of course Kitty and I were not equally sanguine as to this; but we did not tell her that fact, as she would find out the state of affairs quite soon enough for herself, and there was obviously no use in damping her spirits just at the outset of the expedition. Accordingly, we refreshed ourselves with coffee, eggs, bread, and fruit, and then continued our journey as soon as the horses were baited.

In crossing the Col de San Giorgio there were fine views over the surrounding country which excited Kitty's artistic instincts; so the carriage was stopped for her to make a sketch, and meanwhile Mrs. Rollin buried herself in one of her beloved novels, and I beguiled the time by talking to the driver, and drawing out his notions as to things in general connected with his country. I found that he was a pleasant, conversational individual, who avowed his mercenariness with unblushing frankness, and laughed at the idea of being expected to entertain any political opinions of his own. "Celui qui donne le pain à un Corse, c'est son père," said he; "that's one of our proverbs. I'm imperialist, royalist, republican, or anything else, according to who my employer is. Just now I'm whatever pleases your two ladies, as it is they who pay me." Perceiving that he carried pistols, I asked him if he did so because of a vendetta – thinking that in that case it might be a little awkward for us if he should happen to fall in with an enemy whilst he was in our service; and that it was as well to know what one had to expect. However, the unmistakable sincerity with which he disclaimed anything of the kind put me quite at my ease again. "A vendetta!" he exclaimed; "no indeed! neither I nor my family have a quarrel with any living creature. For all that, I never go unarmed on this sort of expedition because of the *penitenciers,* who manage to get out of prison now and then."

"Poor wretches," said I; "I should have thought that they'd be more afraid of you than you of them. Did they ever do you any harm?"

"No," he answered; "I've never had any trouble with them myself, but they *have* been known to attack carriages, and to be very awkward customers, too; and as

I like to be on the safe side, I always take arms with me, as you see."

"Why, one might think these escaped prisoners were regular banditti to hear you talk," I returned, rather scornfully; for I did not believe in there being any real ground for alarm on account of *penitenciers*.

"Well, and so they are," he replied; "there's plenty of room for any number of people to hide amongst the various kinds of bushes – *maquis* as we call them – which grow wild over the hills and large tracts of uninhabited waste land. They form almost impenetrable thickets, where a *penitencier* has little trouble in keeping out of the way; there he lives as best he can, subsisting chiefly on the quails and woodcocks, of which the *maquis* is full, and helping himself to the property of other people whenever he gets a chance. For he is sure to be a *vaurien.*"

I shrugged my shoulders, thinking it would be a long while before *I* should take the trouble to carry arms for fear of some Mrs. Harris of a *penitencier,* who probably had no existence save in the imaginations of the timid and the credulous. Our conversation ended there, as Kitty had completed her sketch, and we resumed our course. That evening I told her of the driver's absurd precautions, and found she was as much amused at the idea as I was, and we had a good laugh at the man's excessive prudence. It was, however, a joke which was not imparted to Mrs. Rollin, as she, being somewhat inclined to be nervous, might possibly not have regarded the matter in the same light that we did; and the knowledge of the driver's thinking it necessary to carry pistols would perhaps have put uncomfortable notions into her head. Of course anything likely to do that was to be avoided most carefully; as, if she became alarmed or disgusted in any way, she might insist on cutting short the expedition, and returning at once to more civilised places, which would have been a great bore. I was far more afraid of this happening than of any perils from *penitenciers;* and I eagerly seconded Kitty's efforts to make everything smooth and pleasant, and to keep her aunt contented.

I began to foresee, however, that there would be some difficulty in doing this for long; and I felt considerable misgivings as to whether Mrs. Rollin would be induced to carry out the driving tour programme in its entirety. The good humour in which she had started in the morning already showed signs of diminishing. In spite of the cleanliness of the inns, they were a good deal rougher than she liked; and though at the hostelry at St. Marie Sicché there was fortunately some meat, yet she was again obliged to put up with milkless coffee and butterless bread. It was the latter of these two grievances to which she especially objected.

"Though I like *café au lait* best myself," she said, "still I don't so much mind drinking black coffee, because that is quite correct, and a thing that numbers of people do – especially after dinner. But as for dry bread! – why, that's what paupers in the workhouse have to eat! I do hope, Kitty, that you won't mention to our friends at home that we had to put up with such mean food; I shouldn't like it to be said that I went travelling in places where the people were so poor or so stingy as not even to afford themselves butter!"

We both did what we could to pacify her; Kitty by promising inviolable secrecy, and I by making the landlord rummage out some *confitures,* which, though but indifferent, would at all events save her from the reproach of having had to breakfast on dry bread, whether she liked it or no. This appeased her partially; but still I saw that her wonted serenity was not altogether restored.

Up to this point we had been travelling along the

highroad used by the diligences, the *route nationale, royale,* or *imperiale,* as it is called, according to which party happens to be in power. But we turned off from it next day, on leaving St. Marie Sicché, and took to smaller and inferior roads by which we ascended to higher ground, until we reached the town of Zicavo, perched on the side of a steep hill and surrounded by chestnut trees.

Unluckily the picturesqueness of its situation did not suffice to reconcile Mrs. Rollin to its deficiency of milk and butter, or to the roughness of its inn, and she expressed much astonishment that a town of its importance did not provide better accommodation for travellers. Another thing that was beginning to annoy her was the republican equality and disregard for class distinctions which she found prevailing everywhere, and which were by no means to her taste. The Corsicans, though perfectly civil and well behaved, were no respecters of rank, and each one seemed to consider himself quite as good as anyone else. When the driver came in the evening to ask for his orders for next day, he sat down while talking to the ladies, as a matter of course; and the landlords of the inns took the same liberty in their presence, all of which was much to Mrs. Rollin's disgust. Then, too, she had to do without a private sitting-room, for the inns had only one room that was not a bedroom, and that one was a big public room, which served as sitting-room and dining room to all classes alike; so that she was obliged either to stay altogether in her sleeping apartment, or else to condescend to sit at the same table with the landlord, his family, the driver, me, and any *commis-voyageur*, shopkeeper, peasant, or other person who might happen to come in. Besides this, the inquisitiveness which is characteristic of Corsicans offended her. She could not bear the freedom with which people whom she considered inferiors would cross-examine herself and Kitty as to their age; whether they were married; if not, why not; what they did with themselves; what relatives they had; where they were going; and similar personal matters. And as I perceived her growing irritation at these various petty annoyances, I became more and more doubtful whether we should be able to reconcile her to them sufficiently to induce her to put up with them for a whole fortnight.

One of the reasons which had brought us to Zicavo was the fact that it was only five or six kilometers from the baths of Guitera, where there are warm sulphurous springs. Mrs. Rollin, who never willingly lost an opportunity of bathing in mineral waters, was very anxious to see what the Guitera baths were like; and if they proved satisfactory, we should probably remain for a few days at Zicavo, whence she could drive over and have a daily bathe. Accordingly, on the day after we got to Zicavo, she and Kitty went to inspect the bathing establishment at Guitera. However, they found it so wretched looking a little place, and of so uninviting an exterior, that she at once declared nothing would induce her to set foot inside it, and that, as there was nothing to stay for at Zicavo, we had better go on again immediately in hopes of finding better quarters elsewhere. It was decided, therefore, that we should next day proceed across the Serra Scopomeno to St. Lucia di Tallano. We must allow plenty of time for the journey, we were told, as the roads were heavy, and it was not impossible we might be hindered by snow. Consequently my mistresses determined to get off early in the morning, in order to have the whole day before them. And after giving directions to that effect, Mrs. Rollin secluded herself and Kitty in their own bedrooms, and remained there for the rest of the evening, beyond reach of contamination from the company in the public room.

I, however, was less particular, and sat there till I went to bed, fraternising with the landlord's wife, watching all that went on, and enjoying the opportunity of seeing a little of the manner of life of a foreign race. It was a novel experience, and that is a thing that I always like.

What made it still more interesting was that the landlord was also *maire* of the commune, and as he used the public room as his *bureau* in which to carry on official transactions, I heard all that went on between him and the different people who came to see him on business. He seemed to be a good sort of fellow enough, only with rather an excessive estimate of his own importance and omniscience. Just as one of the visitors was going away, he suddenly bethought him of something that had hitherto slipped his memory, and turned back at the door.

" By the by," said he to the *maire,* "someone said yesterday that they heard there were one or two escaped *penitenciers* about again somewhere or other. Have you heard anything about it, and do you suppose it's true?"

"True," repeated the *maire;* "of course not! People are always setting about some foolish report in order to have something to talk about, and so pretend that they know more than others! No – *I've* not heard of it, because it's well known that I make it a rule to pay no attention to absurd tales unsupported by reliable evidence, and that makes the tattlers somewhat shy of bringing their stories to *me.* A pretty state the country would come to if the important officials were to believe all they're told, and go disturbing themselves about every idle rumour!"

I was amused at the *maire's* evident annoyance at someone else's having heard this piece of gossip a whole day sooner than he had. Otherwise I paid no attention to the matter, as I was not in the least degree apprehensive of *penitenciers.* When a danger occurs but rarely, the chances are so great against its occurring to any given person that one is apt to regard it as non-existent.

Before going to bed that night I repeated the orders that had been given to have breakfast, our bill, and the carriage, in readiness for an early start next day, and took care to make sure that they had been thoroughly understood. Consequently I was provoked to find, when I left my room in the morning, that the whole household had overslept itself, and there was no sign of preparation for our departure.

It was not to be endured that I should incur the stigma of being a neglectful or incompetent travelling maid – I, who prided myself on my talents as a courier! so I instantly set to work to arouse the establishment from its sloth. Hunting about till I discovered where a servant slept, I dragged her forcibly out of bed, and set her to light the kitchen fire and prepare food. Then I woke the driver, and insisted on his beginning at once to get ready the horses and carriage. In short, I flew hither and thither, helping, hustling, and exclaiming "Dépêche!" with such vigour that I managed fairly to startle the leisurely Corsicans into a little activity, and to procure breakfast for the two ladies, and get under weigh only half an hour later than had been originally intended. The poor driver was quite alarmed at my unexpected display of energy; he did not even venture to wait to break his fast before starting, but hastily crammed some food into his pocket for consumption on the road. I am sure it was a relief to him to find that my severity relaxed when once we were off, and that in order for him to eat his breakfast in comfort, I was even willing to take the reins and drive, as I sat beside him on the box.

The weather was still propitious. Enough snow had fallen in the night to whiten the tops of the hills surrounding Zicavo, but now the sun was shining, and warming the keen, delicious mountain air as we drove down the valley.

We had not gone far before we met a funeral, which was so perfectly simple, matter-of-fact, and devoid of anything ostentatious or needless, that I thought it a model worthy of imitation in less primitive places. Two mules drew a rough cart, in which lay the corpse, uncoffined, and covered over with a gaudy-coloured shawl, which allowed the outlines of the human form beneath to be plainly visible. After the cart walked a dozen or so of people, betraying no emotion, but looking serious and stolid. No vestige of black was to be seen. They were dressed in their ordinary everyday garments, carrying the bright-hued umbrellas which are popular in the island, and the men having the customary wine-gourds slung round their bodies. About the whole thing there was an absence of fuss, ceremony, and demonstrativeness, combined with perfect gravity and propriety of demeanour, which made me wish that all arrangers of funerals would come and take a lesson at Zicavo.

The only stop we made during the morning was at a tiny little village, where we waited a few minutes for the horses to be watered. Whilst this was done, the two ladies and I did not get out of the carriage, but sat where we were, drawn up outside a miserable tumble-down sort of hovel that did duty as an inn. The loungers of the hamlet soon gathered round to stare at us, and were joined by two men who issued from the house. They both had guns, as I saw; but there was nothing in the least remarkable about that, because a Corsican almost always carries a gun *or* an umbrella, and sometimes both, so that their being armed did not at all astonish me. Nor did I think it in any way peculiar when I heard them ask our driver who we were, and where we were going. For I had by this time seen enough of Corsican inquisitiveness to regard such inquiries as a mere matter of course, and demonstrations of curiosity seemed to me more natural than their absence.

The two men left the inn almost immediately after their questions had been answered. I saw them leave the village, and a little way farther on I caught a glimpse of them again turning off the road, and plunging into the thick bushes on either side. I concluded that they were a couple of "chasseurs," such as one sees perpetually in Corsica, and then thought no more about them.

Our course at this period of the journey was very tortuous and indirect, in consequence of numerous narrow valleys which were too steep for anything on wheels to cross in a straight line. Therefore the road often had to go round for miles, in order to get from one side to another of a valley which was, perhaps, not a mile broad; and the distance from point to point that had to be traversed by whoever kept to the road was generally many times more than it would have been to the proverbial crow. Hence it evidently followed that a pedestrian, climbing straight up and down the precipitous hillsides would be able to get over the ground as quickly as a carriage could do. And if this is borne in mind, it will assist the reader in comprehending the events which I have now to relate.

CHAPTER XVI

Escaped Penitenciers

THE horses were to be taken out of the carriage to have a thorough rest, once in the course of the day, so we halted for that purpose between twelve and one o'clock. We were then exactly at the head of one of the long narrow valleys I have already mentioned. It was a wild desolate spot, where not a habitation was to be seen, nor any human being except ourselves. The view before us consisted of the sky overhead, and of two steep hillsides – at some places appearing to be barely a gunshot apart – which converged from the entrance of the valley to the point where we were. These were clothed from top to bottom with a dense mass of trees and *maquis*, whose sobre green tints, were only broken by a sharply-cut, thin, yellowish line, which marked, on one hand, the road we had just traversed, and, on the other, that by which we should presently continue the journey. The sun had quite sufficient power to make shade acceptable, so we seated ourselves under an *ilex* by the side of a clear bubbling spring of water, and ate the lunch that we had brought with us from Zicavo.

We were not long over the meal, and as soon as it was finished the driver was asked when he would be ready to resume the journey. He answered that the horses ought to have more than an hour longer of rest, and that then they would go on quite fresh to the end of the day. On hearing this Mrs. Rollin sent me to the carriage to fetch a couple of cushions, with which she established herself comfortably on the ground, and then opened one of Xavier de Montepin's novels. Meanwhile Kitty had got out her drawing materials.

"I think that I'll walk on, and see if I can't find a sketch somewhere," she said. "As there's only one road, I can't possibly lose my way; then you can pick me up when you overtake me in the carriage." But her aunt was not prepared to assent readily to this proposal.

"Oh, you'd better not go on all by yourself, my dear," she said uneasily. "Do try and find something to draw near here – a cloud or a tree, or a bit of the road, or something. It's not the thing for a girl of your age to be seen walking about the roads alone, you know."

"I don't think that need trouble us in these solitudes," answered Kitty laughing. "There's nothing except kites and crows to see what I do, and I don't imagine that *they* will be much shocked at my proceedings."

"Don't you be too sure of there being only kites and crows," returned Mrs. Rollin; "people often turn up so unexpectedly! There *might* be some acquaintance of ours travelling here now; and if so, he or she would be sure to meet us just when we didn't want to be met, and then go home and say that I let you go about alone just as you pleased, and that I took no care whatever of you! Besides, supposing your sketching were to take you off the road, perhaps we should not see where you were, and go past without knowing it. I should be in such a fidget for fear of that happening, that I know I shouldn't enjoy the drive *a bit* till I had you all safe with me again."

"You needn't be uneasy on that score," said Kitty, looking at her watch; "the jingling of the horses' bells could hardly fail to inform me of your approach; but I won't trust only to that. I'll keep an eye on the time, and as I can reckon certainly on your not leaving here for another hour, I can calculate when to return to the road if I *should* turn off it anywhere. I assure you I haven't the least intention of doing anything so silly as to let myself be left behind, so you can drive along with a perfectly tranquil mind, and an absolute certainty that I am somewhere on ahead, until you see me waiting for you."

Here I took the liberty of joining in their conversation. Having been sitting still and cramped up on the box for some time, I felt much disposed to stretch my legs; so I said,

"I shall be very glad to accompany Miss Mervyn if she has no objection. Then I could stay on the road near where she is, if she happens to leave it; and that would make it quite impossible for the carriage to go past her by mistake."

"Of *course,* that's the way to manage it," exclaimed Mrs. Rollin; "how stupid of me not to have thought of it at first! Yes, Kitty – you take Jill with you; it will look so much better than for you to be wandering on by yourself; and then my mind will be quite easy about not passing you by accident."

"Very well," returned Kitty; "I'm afraid it'll be rather dull for her dawdling about at my heels – only I daresay it won't be very lively to stay here with nothing to do either; so she may as well come. We'll start at once, Jill, please; for I want to have as much time as possible for sketching before the carriage overtakes us."

Accordingly she and I walked off briskly along the road which led towards our destination, leaving Mrs. Rollin, the driver, and carriage, to follow in course of time when the horses should be sufficiently refreshed. We must have tramped, I should think, about two miles before Kitty came to a place which inspired her with a desire to make a sketch. Of course the next thing to be done was to discover the most satisfactory point of view from which the sketch was to be taken. After a little reconnoitring she found a spot that was to her mind. It was a short distance below the road, and in order to get to it we had to scramble down through a mass of arbutus, and of an immense kind of heath, growing taller than our heads – which two shrubs constituted the chief part of the scrub (or *maquis*) at that place.

Having accompanied Kitty to the spot she had selected, and seen her comfortably settled down to her drawing, I looked at my watch. This showed me that there was still a long while to elapse before the carriage would be in motion again, and that, therefore, there was no need for me to be in a hurry about getting back to the road yet. Watching Kitty sketch was not particularly amusing, so I left her and wandered off through the bushes. About fifty yards from where she was I came to a bit of broken rocky ground, somewhat resembling a tiny quarry, and completely overgrown by arbutus. Here I tucked myself away snugly into a corner under one of these bushes, and lay lazily contemplating its splendid red and yellow berries, which were as big as good-sized plums. They looked most delicious; and as I knew the arbutus is not poisonous, I gathered a berry to ascertain whether the taste at all corresponded to the appearance; I was disappointed to find, however, that this was not the case, as the flavour, though rather sweet, was insipid, watery, and vapid.

My curiosity respecting arbutus fruit being thus satisfied, and I having nothing particular to do, I next began amusing myself by endeavouring to work out a rule-of-three sum in my head. But before my calculations had advanced far they were interrupted by a crackling rustling noise that issued from the bushes growing above, between me and the road. It sounded as if some heavy body were making its way through them; and the noise approached nearer and nearer, till it reached quite close to the recess in which I was ensconced. Then the crackling ceased, and I heard a male voice speaking in low and cautious tones. A bit of rock, on which grew the bush under which I was seated, intervened between me and the speaker, so that I could not see him; but he was near enough for every one of his words to be distinctly audible to me. He spoke in Italian – that being the language which the people of the country almost always use amongst themselves when they do not talk Corsican, though French is the official tongue, and the one generally employed in communications with foreigners.

"But where are they, César?" said the voice, with a somewhat impatient accent. "You say that from the top of the hill you plainly saw two of them who left the carriage to repose itself, and went on alone. Is it not droll how those English always desire to walk? In that case they ought to be somewhere about here now, yet we have looked both up and down the road, and they are not there. What then has become of them? May be that they have turned and gone back again."

"*Diavolo!* that would be too provoking," answered Cesar. "It was unlucky that I lost sight of them as I descended the hill, but it could not possibly be helped, for the bushes were too thick to see through."

"Well, there is sure to be fine spoil to be had out of these rich English," said the first speaker, "and we must try to get hold of it somehow. If we fail to find these two by themselves, I suppose we must do what we thought of at first – manage to upset the carriage at that sharp corner of the road further on, and attack when all is in confusion."

"But what if the carriage should not upset after all?" objected César; "or what if the driver should carry arms and show fight? Then perhaps we should be wounded, captured, and shut up again in prison. Bah! I hate that prison! Have we not been used like dogs there, and compelled to beat the *maquis* near Chiavari for *sangliers,* when some English milord wanted a *chasse?* And is it not an altogether detestable place? Truly I have no fancy to go there again, and I much prefer this second plan to the first one that we thought of. We shall have no danger to fear in dealing with only two women. Let us on no account be foolhardy, Napoleon."

"Certainly not," answered Napoleon; "I have no more wish than you have either to go back to prison or to encounter needless peril! Still, it will be a pity if we cannot secure the golden prize that destiny throws in our way. Those two *must* be somewhere not far off at this very moment, unless by bad luck they should have turned back just after you first saw them. Do you think they can have gone off from the road?" "It is possible," returned Cesar; "anyhow, it is too soon yet to despair of finding them. Do you, Napoleon, go and watch on the road, whilst I search the *maquis* on each side, first below and then above. Whichever of us discovers them can summon the other by a whistle."

"Good," replied Napoleon. And with that the two men separated and went off in different directions, as I knew by the rustling of the bushes.

Here, then, were two villains in search of Kitty and me, with evil intentions towards us, and we were quite defenceless. Truly, a pleasant predicament to be in! What was I to do now?

Had I been able to reason out at leisure what course a person ought to pursue in such a situation, I feel sure that my answer to the above question would have been: Take care of your own safety, keep out of the men's clutches the best way you can, and do not bother yourself about anyone else. But when the situation actually occurred, I acted on the impulse of the moment, because there was no time to think the matter over carefully, and take counsel with reason. And the consequence of being in such a hurry was, that I did not behave with that prudent regard to my own interests which was generally characteristic of me. I was frightened I must candidly confess, and I desired ardently to be anywhere in security, and to avoid meeting either Napoleon or César. Yet, strange to say, I was influenced at that moment by something else than care for myself. My predominant anxiety – the one object on which my mind was fixed – was, to get to Kitty as quickly as possible, to warn her of the danger, to stand by her, to try to save her. It was certainly very unlike me to have felt like that, and I do not know what occasioned so extraordinary a departure from my usual sentiments. However, there the feeling was, and *"c'était plus fort que moi."* Consequently, I only waited where I was till the men were far enough off for me to leave my hiding-place without danger of being dis-covered, and then instantly set out to rejoin her. Taking the utmost pains to move quietly, lest the shaking of the bushes should betray my presence, I crept through the *maquis.* Meanwhile I mentally reviewed the situation, and considered how we could extricate ourselves from it.

I inferred, from what the men had said, that they were not particularly brave, and would probably not venture to attack the carriage if they found its occupants prepared to receive them. Therefore, if we could get safely back to our driver and put him on his guard, there would not be much to fear from the rascals. But then the question was, *could* we get back safely? could we, by crawling through bushes, dodging behind trees, and keeping out of sight as much as possible, retrace our steps to the carriage unperceived? On the whole, I thought it was to be managed – provided, of course, that I could reach Kitty and get her away before either of our enemies had found her. As they did not know that they were detected, they would expect to meet us going about carelessly and openly, without the least attempt at concealment. This was all in our favour, as it would prevent them from looking for us as closely as they would otherwise have done. Besides, if they did not find us in that immediate neighbourhood, they would discontinue the search, under the impression that we must have returned to the carriage almost directly after leaving it. Therefore it would be only necessary for us to keep in hiding till we had got some distance from where we then were; after that, we could leave the *maquis,* and take to the road, where we should be able to run along at full speed, without troubling to keep out of sight.

As I thought of all this, it seemed to me that we had a very reasonable prospect of escape – unless, by bad luck, I should fail to get to Kitty before one of the men had found her – everything appeared to me to depend upon that.

I had left her on a small open space which jutted out a little from the hillside, so as to form a sort of diminutive plateau. Great was my relief, when I came to the edge of this place, to see her still sketching happily, and evidently without a suspicion of danger. She glanced towards me for an instant, and then at once resumed her work, thinking that I was come to fetch her away, and that she must make the most of every remaining moment. Thus her eyes were upon the drawing, and so she did not see the gesture which I made to her to be silent, lest an enemy should be within hearing.

"Is it time to go, already?" she said, speaking out loud, as it was natural she should do. "Isn't your watch—"

By that time I was within reach of her, and stopped further utterance forcibly by covering her mouth with my hand. Looking up in surprise and wrath at so unceremonious a proceeding on the part of her maid, she saw by my face that there was something seriously amiss.

I began to tell her in a whisper, as fast as I could, what was the state of affairs.

Unluckily the few words she had spoken had wrought the mischief I feared, and showed our whereabouts to one of the villains who were hunting for us. Consequently, I had hardly commenced my hurried communication in her ear, when a low whistle sounded close by, and next moment a man with a gun in his hand stepped out of the bushes, and on to the little plateau where we were. This, then, was no doubt the rogue named César, whom I had heard undertake to explore the *maquis* for us. As I looked at him, I recognised him to be one of the two men whom I had noticed inquiring about us two or three hours before, at the inn where the horses had been watered. That at once made the whole matter clear to me.

I have already mentioned that the nature of the ground was such as to enable a pedestrian to travel from point to point as fast as a carriage could do. Knowing this, César and his companion must have made up their minds to hurry on in front, and lie in wait for us at some spot which we had not yet reached, and which they deemed especially favourable for an attack on the carriage. But on their way to the place that they had chosen for an ambush, they had evidently caught sight of Kitty and me leaving the carriage, and been diverted from their first scheme by the hope of securing the coveted booty in a less hazardous manner than the one they had originally contemplated. It was all as plain as a pike-staff to me now.

César accosted us in French, saying, in the regular beggar's whine, "Will the ladies have the goodness to give something to a poor man?"

Though I had not had time fully to explain things to Kitty, she had picked up enough to know that we were in danger from two escaped *penitenciers,* and when she saw César she guessed that he was one of them.

This sudden confronting with peril, however, produced in her no trepidation, sign of cowardice, or inclination to quail. She was too proud for that. Her compressed lips, flashing eyes, and hard, resolute, disdainful, undaunted expression, showed a nature that would set its back to the wall (not that there was one handy on the present occasion, however), and fight to the last gasp, but would never flinch an atom, come what might.

"I have nothing for you," she replied, speaking as haughtily as though we had been in no way in the man's power.

"But I feel sure that Madame deceives herself," insisted César, who apparently did not wish to proceed to extremities till the arrival of his comrade Napoleon; "if she will have the complaisance to seek, she will without doubt discover money, a watch, rings, brooches, chains, or some such little thing that would keep a poor man from dying of hunger."

At this point in the conversation, it occurred to me that a good loud scream for help might be introduced with singular appropriateness; and I proceeded to put my idea into execution. César, however, was of a different opinion, and evidently considered the interruption an untimely one; for no sooner did I uplift my voice, than he aimed his gun at me, exclaiming savagely, "Silence at once, or I'll kill you!"

I had no option about obeying this order, because just at that moment, Napoleon – who was hastening up in obedience to his companion's summons – came through the bushes behind where I stood, and clapped his hands roughly over my mouth.

César grinned mockingly when he saw me thus reduced to silence, and lowered his gun again.

"That was an atrocious noise!" he remarked. "Permit me to inform you, madame – first, that screams cannot assist you, since there is no one but us within hearing; secondly, that my friend and myself have inconceivably tender hearts and sensitive nerves. Consequently we cannot endure the least sound of distress; and if you should utter another cry in our presence, we should be compelled, most reluctantly, to cut your throat in order to spare the exquisite sensibility of our natures. And having given you this caution, let us return to the more pleasing subject of the little *souvenirs* which you generous ladies are going to bestow upon us. Will you like us to save you trouble by helping ourselves to them?"

Kitty was as composed as though she had been seated in her father's drawing-room in Eaton Square, and now said to me in English: "I'm afraid he's right about there being no one in hearing to help us, Jill, so it's no good screaming. As resistance is useless, we may as well give up our purses and trinkets quietly." Then she continued in French, replying to what the man had said last: "No – you need not help yourselves. We will hand over to you all we have."

Accordingly we pulled out our money, and took off the few things of any value we happened to be wearing – such as watches, chains, and collar and sleeve studs. These, however, were worth but little, all put together. People do not take valuable jewellery with them on a rough driving-tour; and as Mrs. Rollin was our treasurer, Kitty and I had barely ten francs between us in our purses. The two robbers, therefore, who had been reckoning confidently on making a large haul, were greatly dissatisfied and disappointed at the insignificance of the booty they had secured.

"This won't do *at all*," grumbled César; "the idea of capturing a couple of the rich English, and then not getting more than *this* out of them! It is ridiculous! Let us see what is to be done – only first they must be kept from running away."

And then, after making fast our hands and feet, they drew a few steps aside, and proceeded to confer together in a low voice.

Though they had spoken to us in French, yet in their communications to one another they used Italian. Noticing this, it occurred to me that if they were to suppose us both to be ignorant of that tongue, they would probably talk more freely before us than they would do if they thought we understood what was said; in this way we might, perhaps, pick up valuable information; or at least *I* might – for Kitty's knowledge of Italian was very limited. I at once imparted my idea to her, and suggested we should pretend that we understood only French. I expected she would assent to this as a matter of course; but, to my surprise, she hesitated, and her face showed that the proposition was distasteful to her.

"Well – I don't know," she replied, after a minute's consideration, "I can't allow a couple of scamps to make me degrade myself by telling a lie. If they ask me whether I understand them or not, I shall most certainly tell them the truth."

I was dismayed at this clinging to principles of scrupulous honour in dealing with the two rogues who had us in their power. Her sentiments were very chivalrous and noble, no doubt; but they appeared to me both uncalled-for and out of place at the present moment, and I endeavoured to combat them. "Surely," I said, "you don't deny the truth of the old saying that all is fair in love and war?"

Her lip curled scornfully as she replied, "That has nothing to do with it. To my mind a lie would be none the less *mean* because it might be *fair.* I should lose my self-respect if I were to tell one."

Even whilst smarting at the reproof which was thus conveyed to me for having advocated lying, I could not help admiring the indomitable pride which was unaffected by considerations of expediency, and would under no circumstances consent to do what was contrary to its sense of dignity. The hankering after her good opinion which I always felt made me wonder uneasily what she would think of me if she knew how many untruths *my* self-respect had managed to put up with during my existence. And then I felt half-disgusted with my past conduct, and it flashed upon me that I had a great mind to turn over a new leaf in the matter in future, and behave more according to the principles which she approved of and practised. That, however, should be reserved for further consideration, as the present was obviously not a favourable occasion for inaugurating any reform of the kind. Having arrived at which conclusion, I silently resolved to carry out my plan for deceiving our captors, if possible, in spite of her objection. Consequently, when one of them, speaking in Italian, asked which of us two ladies was the most important one, I affected to be utterly unconscious of having been addressed. Kitty, fortunately, was seated farther off from the man than I was, and did not hear what he said, or discover that he was not still continuing the conversation with his comrade.

The man repeated his question a second time in Italian. Finding that we both remained mute, he asked in French how long it would be before he had an answer. I hastened to reply to this, speaking quickly and in a low tone, lest Kitty should hear what I said, and be prompted by her inconveniently high-flown sentiments to contradict me flatly. I made believe to be quite astonished to find he had been speaking to us, and most anxious to deprecate his wrath – assuring him that we neither of us understood Italian, and begging him to excuse us, therefore, for the involuntary rudeness of which we had been guilty in not responding to his question. Luckily my precaution of speaking indistinctly, and the fact of Kitty's being a few yards off, prevented her from catching what passed between me and my interlocutor. The two men then came and stood in front of us, and Napoleon said in French, "We want to know which of you two ladies is of the most importance – the chief one?"

"I am," answered Kitty.

"Good," he returned; "then it is to you that I will speak. We know that you cannot be travelling about with no more money than 10 francs, and that you English are always rolling in gold. It follows, therefore, that your riches must be in the keeping of that other lady who stayed with the carriage. Now, those riches we must and will have, and we propose that you shall earn your liberty by helping us to get them. Will you do this?"

"Tell me what you want me to do, first," answered Kitty; "then I will tell you, whether I will do it or not."

"Very reasonable!" replied Napoleon. "Our plan is this. You must write to your friend in the carriage such a note as will induce her to follow the bearer at once, in order to join you. The note will be entirely in French, and contain not a word of English, so as to make sure that you say nothing in it that we do not approve of. One of us will take it to her; then he will conduct her to a safe spot, and relieve her of the money and trinkets that she has. Should the worth of these be sufficient to satisfy our just expectations, you will none of you be detained any longer."

"And supposing the spoil is less than you anticipate," inquired Kitty, "what then?"

"Ah – but that cannot be, I feel sure!" he returned; "our expectations are most moderate; it cannot be that three ladies would travel about so far from their own country without having with them as much money as would satisfy us!"

"Still – I repeat my question," she said; "what would you do if *not?* And, in any case, what certainty have I that you would keep your word and release us afterwards?"

"If madame will not rely on our word of honour," answered he, smiling disagreeably, "I fear she will have to content herself without that certainty which she desires. *She* is hardly in the position to enforce any other guarantee of good faith; and *we* shall not insult ourselves by assuming such a thing to be necessary. And as for the quite unlikely event of your friend's purse being insufficient to meet our wants – why – ahem! when the case arises, it will be then ample time to settle what is to be done. Here are paper and a pencil. There is no time to lose. Will madame be so good as to write?"

Kitty looked at him steadily, without attempting to take the writing materials he proffered. "And do you suppose, then," she said, "that I shall consent to bait a trap to bring my aunt to be robbed? If so, you are very greatly mistaken. And what inducement have you to offer that should make me do so vile a thing? The mere chance that your thirst for plunder might then be satiated, and that you might think fit to set us free! I do not trust to your honour, nor will I do what you wish. I believe that the plan is merely a *ruse* to enable you to secure a fresh victim, and that if you could get my aunt also into your hands, you would keep us all three prisoners."

This accusation was met with vehement denials; and our captors again endeavoured to persuade her to assist them by assuring her it would be to her advantage to do so, and threatening her with evil consequences if she persisted in her refusal. Finding, however, that she remained unmoved by whatever they said, they bethought them that perhaps *I* might be made to write such a letter as they required, and applied to me accordingly. Kitty, on this, gave me peremptory orders that I was on no account to comply with their request; and I obeyed her in the matter all the more willingly because I had very little doubt that her surmise was correct as to the treachery which the scoundrels had in contemplation.

But however much Mrs. Rollin might benefit from our refusal to lend ourselves to their designs, it certainly did not help *us* in any way. The two men had made up their minds that they were going to get enormous spoils out of "these rich English," and had no idea of resigning their hopes merely because Kitty and I would not aid them to execute their first scheme. Therefore, when they saw they had no chance of carrying their point about that, they determined to adopt another line of action, which was announced to us by César.

People so unaccommodating and perverse as we were, he said angrily, deserved to be got rid of altogether; and in such a case as this, most gentlemen of the road would not be troubled with us any longer, but cut our throats without ceremony, and so make an end of the business at once. He and his friend, however, being of so gentle a disposition as never to resort to violence *if it could be helped,* would give us a chance of escape. It was their intention to communicate with our friends, and offer to restore us uninjured on payment of a specified sum, which would have to be handed over with such precautions as would ensure the safety of the recipients. Till that was received we should reside under their care in the hills. "But," added the ruffian menacingly, and addressing himself especially to Kitty, "we cannot wait for ever for the answer, you know; so we shall tell your friends that if the ransom is not forthcoming pretty quickly, we shall try to hasten its arrival by sending some little reminder, such as an ear, a nose, a hand, or a foot; and of course these *souvenirs* would, in the first place, be furnished by you, since you are of more

Manchester City Library
Arcadia Library: 0161 227 3725
Renewals: 0161 254 7777

Customer ID: *2256

Items that you have issued

Title: Jill
ID: C000000202232503
Due: 04 January 2023
Messages:

Title: Smile
ID: C000000202007419
Due: 04 January 2023
Messages:

Title: Winter
ID: C000000202228833
Due: 04 January 2023
Messages:

Total items: 3
Account balance: £0.00
13/12/2022 09:17
Issued: 6
Overdue: 0
Hold requests: 0
Ready for collection: 0

www.manchester.gov.uk/libraries

consequence than your companion. Hers would come later."

When I heard this I could not repress a shudder at the peril awaiting my cherished members – though, as those of Kitty were destined to be sacrificed first, the danger to mine was only a reversionary one. She, however, who was more immediately threatened than I was, neither trembled, changed colour, nor gave any other indication of emotion, but remained as unmoved and haughtily composed as before.

I did not forget that she had been affected by some feeling too strong to be concealed when I had suddenly showed her the photograph of Captain Norroy. And the difference between her demeanour then and now made me wonder more than ever what the feeling could have been which had had power to upset the self-command of a person so high-couraged, strong, and proudly imperturbable as she most certainly was.

CHAPTER XVII

A Chapelle Mortuaire

IMMEDIATE preparations were made for our departure from the spot where we were. A couple of coarse handkerchiefs were tied across the lower part of our faces, so as to stifle our voices if we should uplift them on the remote chance of any one being in hearing who would assist us. Next our feet were untied to enable us to walk. We were warned that if we attempted to escape or to call out, we should be instantly stabbed. And in order to convince us that this was no empty threat, a wicked-looking, dagger-like article, known in Corsica as a vendetta-knife, was flashed before our eyes, and we were shown that each of our captors had one of these knives stowed away in a little inside coat-pocket, where it was ready to hand at a moment's notice.

Then we moved off in single file. Napoleon went in front, with Kitty close at his heels; I came third, and César brought up the rear.

The robbers naturally selected to travel through the *maquis* rather than along the open road; and we two captives, whose hands were bound, sorely missed the assistance of those members to push aside the numerous boughs and twigs by which our progress was impeded. Now and then the man in front stopped to hold back obstacles in some very thick place, where we should otherwise have probably altogether stuck fast; but such an attention was exceptional, and, as a rule, we were left to make our way unaided as best we could, regardless of the scratches and bruises which we continually received, and whereby the discomfort and fatigue of the journey was greatly increased. Napoleon led us first down to the mouth of the valley; then branched off in a direction away from that which the carriage and Mrs. Rollin would take; then climbed a steep hill, and proceeded along the ridge of it for some distance; then descended abruptly into another valley, and we were kept trudging over hill and dale alternately in this way during the whole afternoon. Many of the places we passed were such as might have roused a lover of fine scenery to enthusiasm; but neither Kitty nor I were in a humour to appreciate that sort of thing just then, and the beauties of the landscape were quite wasted upon us, as we toiled wearily along obscure and seldom-used tracks, through desolate wild districts, without ever once approaching a human dwelling.

My having made the men believe that neither of us understood Italian caused them to converse together in that language as unreservedly as if they had been alone, and, thanks to this, I was able to discover what were their intentions for disposing of us for the present. I learnt that we were being taken to a cave up in the hills, which had been their headquarters since their escape from prison. Here we were to be left under care of one of the robbers, whilst the other descended to the lower lands to seek out Mrs. Rollin, and open negotiations with her on the important subject of the ransom.

This cave of theirs, wherever it might be, was evidently an unpleasantly long way off from the scene of our capture. On and on we went without ever pausing for a moment; and I grew so tired that I could hardly drag myself along, and began to speculate on the chances of having to be carried before the appointed resting-place would be reached. A slackening of speed or a halt would have been a most welcome relief to me; but of that there was no hope, as our progress was already too slow to satisfy the robbers, who kept constantly urging us to hurry on faster, lest we should all be benighted on the way. As daylight diminished, so did their impatience increase, and many were the angry oaths they uttered at the distance still to be traversed before attaining the cave.

Suddenly Napoleon stood still, and looked back at his comrade joyfully. "César," cried he, "I have a good idea! At the rate we go now, we shall not get home till midnight; whereas if you and I were alone, and not hampered by these women, we should arrive in half the time. Is not that so?"

"Obviously," grumbled César; "but what's the use of stopping to tell me what I know already?"

"Why this," returned the other; "that I propose we should disembarrass ourselves of them at once."

"Stupid!" rejoined César, irritably; "don't you see that the only way of doing that is to kill them, or else to let them go; and that in either of those cases we should be throwing away all chance of deriving further gain from them?"

"Ah, but I have thought of another method of getting rid of them," answered Napoleon – "a method which will enable us to keep them alive, and in our power too. I did a good deal of business in this part of the country formerly, and learnt to know it well; thus I came to know of a place near here, which I've only just recollected, and which will be most convenient to us at this moment. It is not exactly such a place as I would myself care to stay at, but it will do admirably for shutting up these two women in, and when we have disposed of them there, you and I can travel home as fast as we please. A famous safe prison it is, where there will be no need for one of us to stay and keep guard over them, as there would be if they were housed in the cave. Thus we shall be free to go together and see about the business with the ransom – which will, of course, be a great advantage, since two heads are better than one, you know."

César seemed still incredulous. "I believe you are talking nonsense," said he; "I cannot think of any possible prison about here to answer to your description."

"Nonsense, indeed!" retorted his companion; "no, in truth! A short distance from here, on the side of a hill, far from any inhabited house or public road, I remember that there is an old mortuary chapel. Years ago the family to whom it belonged left their country-house and went to live in Ajaccio; and since then it has never been used. This is the place in which I propose to imprison our captives. There will be no chance of their being heard, however much noise they may make; for the walls are thick, and there is nothing to bring anyone into the vicinity. And as they will certainly not be able to get out unaided, we shall have no need to trouble ourselves more about them, except to supply them with food."

"A deserted mortuary chapel!" said César, reflectively; "'tis a good idea, no doubt. Only it is getting late; and – well, to say the truth, I am not at any time over-fond of the company of the dead, and like it least of all by night. Still – it would be very convenient to do what you propose – the light is not gone yet – the chapel is close by, you say. Yes! there will be time to shut up the women, and remove ourselves to a pleasanter neighbourhood before dark. Go on, then, and let us get the job over as soon as possible."

Our course was resumed accordingly. The thought of the grim kind of hotel that Napoleon had found for us reminded me forcibly of Schubert's song *Das Wirthshaus,* and I seemed to hear its wild plaintive melody sounding in my ears as we hurried over the broken ground through the fast-increasing dusk. Horrible as was the idea of being immured alive in a tomb, yet I shrank from it less then than I should have done ordinarily. And for these two reasons: First, because the long march had reduced me to such a state of exhaustion that the prospect of rest was welcome anywhere – even in a *chapelle mortuaire.* Secondly, because it seemed safer and in every way preferable to be with the dead than with the two ruffians who had us in their power, and whom I regarded with the most profound distrust.

The chapel being near at hand, we reached it while there was still sufficient light to show something of the exterior of our prison.

We came first to a high wall, with no other opening in it than an iron gate, which was wide enough to admit a carriage. The bolt by which the gate was fastened was forced back without difficulty, and then a short straight bit of road brought us to the door of the chapel itself. This door was situated exactly opposite to the gate in the outer wall, and was secured by a great iron bar across the outside, and also by a chain and rusty padlock. With the help of a stone the men easily broke open the padlock, and then they lifted the ponderous external bar off its supports. There was now no further obstacle to opening the door before which we stood, but our captors – being not insensible to superstitious fears – did not wish to keep the entrance to the charnel-house open longer than was absolutely necessary, and therefore postponed unclosing it till the last moment.

They set our hands at liberty, and delivered to us such provisions as they had with them – consisting of a morsel of sausage, a slice of rye-bread, a good-sized piece of extremely strong-smelling cheese, a couple of onions and apples, and a gourd half-full of wine. Having thus provided us against famine, César made us a profound bow of mocking deference, and said in French: "Adieu for the present, ladies. You see our desire to treat you with distinguished consideration induces us to place you here, with a good roof and strong walls to shelter you, rather than to take you to the rough cave which serves *us* for a habitation. We do not intend remaining to share this splendid dwelling with you, lest we should intrude on your privacy; therefore we shall now, however unwillingly, tear ourselves away; but first thing tomorrow morning we will return with a supply of food, before departing to seek out and communicate with the other lady." Then, addressing himself to his comrade, he said: "Look sharp, Napoleon; open a bit of the door, and in with them!"

The door, which only opened outwards, was pulled just far enough apart to admit a human body. The men, without adventuring their own persons an inch within the building, thrust Kitty and me roughly in, and at once closed the entrance behind us again. Then came a scraping, grating noise, which told that the great iron bar was being replaced on its supports outside, and immediately afterwards we heard the steps of César and Napoleon hurrying away at full speed from the uncanny neighbourhood of the tomb to which they had consigned us.

At first we stood without moving from the spot to which we had been pushed, just inside the door, waiting to see if we should be able to distinguish anything when our eyes had become accustomed to the darkness; for the interior of the building was perfectly dark. Meanwhile we profited by the liberty that had been restored to our hands to remove the handkerchiefs across our mouths, which had hitherto prevented us from speaking.

Kitty's knowledge of Italian being limited, she had not comprehended what the men had been saying to one another; consequently she did not now know the nature of our abode, as I discovered from the first words she uttered when her mouth was free of its gag:

"I wonder what sort of place this is," she said; "don't you? It's a bore to have no light; however, I'm going on a bit further, to explore without it, as we can't possibly have it."

I laid my hand upon her arm, and checked her as she was about to advance.

"You had better be careful how you move," I said; "we are shut up in a *chapelle mortuaire*."

"A *chapelle mortuaire*" she echoed, interrogatively; "let me see – what is that? Oh I remember! Wasn't that the name of those buildings which you told me you had seen near Ajaccio, and which you called 'villa residences for the dead?'"

"Yes," I replied, doing my best to speak unconcernedly and carelessly, and to conceal from her the feeling of disgust and aversion with which the place inspired me, and which was growing stronger every moment; "rather an appropriate place for me too, I think, seeing that I'm nearly dead with fatigue. I haven't the least wish to move about, and intend to sit down just where I am now. The door will make a capital back to lean against."

I was not sure but what the knowledge of where she was might perhaps prove a shock to Kitty's nerves. But there was no trace of discomposure to be detected in her voice or manner as she answered me. "So it will," she said, "and I vote that we have dinner at once. Those wretches never offered us any five o'clock tea; and what with that and the long walk, I'm quite ravenous! You've no idea what a relief to my mind it was to find that they didn't intend to leave us all night without food."

Of course we both wanted to seem as happy and as much at our ease as possible, in order thus to help to keep up each other's spirits. I, however, was not very successful in the effort; for though I was perfectly free from any dread of the supernatural, yet there were material horrors attached to the position which I could not forget. I thought of the sights that would be revealed if there were light; of the grinning skulls, mouldering bodies, crumbling coffins, and ghastly relics of mortality, which might be expected in a tomb; and I remembered that these things must be so close to me that I might perhaps at any moment strike my hand against them. There was a gruesomeness and eeriness about the place, to which my state of bodily exhaustion rendered me unwontedly susceptible, and I felt more nervous and creepy than I had ever done in my life before.

"I don't think that I *can* eat in this terrible place," I said, with an involuntary shiver, in response to Kitty's suggestion of dinner.

Whether or not she was at all inclined to be affected by our dismal surroundings, as I was, I do not know; at all events she did not show it, and redoubled her efforts to raise my spirits when she perceived how much disposed I was to break down.

"Oh yes – you'll not think of where you are in a few minutes more, when you've got used to it," she returned, seating herself beside me, and proceeding to distribute the food. "What a funny idea to have a picnic in the dark – quite novel, too; I daresay no one ever did it before. Where is the bread? Oh you've got it. As for the cheese, there's no need to ask where *that* is, because one's nose may safely be trusted to supply the requisite information. I must say a knife would be rather handy; but I'm afraid we must do the best we can without, for I left my pocket-knife where I was sketching, and Messieurs César and Napoleon have omitted to provide for our wants in that respect. How lucky that my aunt is not with us, and obliged to dine in this primitive fashion, without any proper appurtenances! If she were, I verily believe she'd be unhappy lest any acquaintance should behold her in the act of committing such an enormity – even though the fact of the spectator would involve light to see by, and a chance of assistance; both of which *I* should consider to be most desirable things at this moment."

Thus she ran on, joking, laughing, making light of every discomfort, and chatting to me as if she had thought me her equal, as if the tomb had been a leveller of ranks to the living as well as to the dead, and as if in entering it all social differences between her and me had been annihilated. She could have devised nothing better adapted to accomplish her object, and help me to shake off the gloomy influences that oppressed me. Her example of bright good humour and courage was irresistible, and before our unilluminated repast had progressed far I became myself again, and eager to show a spirit as brave as her own. To this desirable result, too, the creature comforts of which I partook tended not a little to contribute. Though the victuals were hardly to be called choice, and the wine had acquired a nasty flavour from the gourd in which it was contained, nevertheless they revived me as well as the most sumptuous cates could have done; and when dinner was at an end I was a different creature from what I had been before. Kitty made no comment on the change in me, but I have little doubt that she perceived it, all the same, as she now, for the first time, turned the conversation seriously to the predicament in which we found ourselves.

"It seems to me, Jill," she said, "that you and I are having to do penance, with a vengeance, for our disbelief in escaped *penitenciers!* We must give our minds now to what we are to do next; but before entering on that subject I want to tell you how *very* sorry I am to have been the means of bringing you into this scrape. I can't help feeling that it is all my doing, and that if I had not gone on to sketch, or had not taken you with me, you, at all events, would be in safety at this moment."

Proud as she might be, pride had not yet taken enough hold of her to crush the naturally generous disposition which was more distressed at being the cause of another person's sufferings than at having to suffer itself. I was touched at the thoughtfulness on my account evinced by her last speech; and as I did not wish her to blame herself unfairly, I assured her that I had accompanied her quite as much for my own pleasure as hers. And in order to prove that we should not in any case have got off scot-free, I repeated to her the conversation I had overheard before we were captured, from which it appeared that the carriage would have been attacked if she and I had not separated from it and walked on alone.

"Thank you," she said, when I had completed my tale. "I can't tell you what a comfort it is to me to know all that, and to think that I am not the sole cause of this bother! And now to consider our next proceedings. The two things chiefly borne in upon my mind at this moment are – first, that it's no use blinking the fact of our being in an extremely awkward position; and second, that it won't do to be afraid, because fear, as Solomon says, 'is nothing else but a betraying of the succours which reason offereth.'"

This was no doubt true. But, unluckily, no amount of calmness and courage would show us any reasonable prospect of escape – look at the situation in what way we would.

It was no use to hope that our friends would rescue us, since it was manifestly impossible for them to have an idea where we were. When Mrs. Rollin continued her journey from the place where we had left her, she would, we knew, have reckoned on my remaining on the road, whether Kitty did or not. Consequently she would have gone on driving contentedly towards St. Lucie di Tallano without the least fear of leaving us behind; and there was no saying how long it might have been before either she or the driver became uneasy at not overtaking us. Then, when they *did* take alarm – as they must have done, sooner or later – there was nothing to make them suspect what had really happened. They would probably suppose we had simultaneously expired, tumbled over cliffs, sprained our ankles, or fallen victims to some other likely or unlikely catastrophe; and then they would have begun hunting about vaguely for us, without the slightest clue to where we were. Thus it was in vain to trust to external aid reaching us, and the question was, Could we anyhow manage to escape by our own unassisted exertions? Alas! the prospect was no better in that direction either. The door through which we had entered was the only outlet apparent; and that was, as we knew, fastened on the outside by a great heavy bar, which rendered exit in that way impossible. Shouting was of no avail, because the place was so solitary that we might have screamed till we were hoarse without a chance of producing any other effect.

Altogether, therefore, we saw no possible means of getting away from our prison, and came reluctantly to the conclusion that we had no alternative but to resign ourselves to stay where we were, and await the course of events patiently. This was by no means a satisfactory termination of our deliberations, and, having arrived at it, we sat in melancholy silence for a minute. The silence was broken by Kitty who said cheerily: "I'm sure we shall both be the better for some rest, so let us lie down and go to sleep."

"Lie down!" repeated I; "surely that won't be safe, will

it? It's too dark to see, and there might be – well – things that one wouldn't care to touch, knocking about in a place of this kind, you know. I should think we'd best try and go to sleep without changing our present position."

"No; we shouldn't rest nearly as well sitting upright, as we should lying down," answered Kitty; "and it won't do for us to play tricks with our strength in any way, or to risk losing an atom of it that is to be had. Very likely there may be nothing disagreeable up the middle of the floor, or, at all events, nothing that we cannot easily clear away. Let us stoop down and feel our way straight before us till we have a space to lie down in."

There seemed a tacit agreement between us that the ghastly objects by which we knew we must surely be surrounded were not to be defined in words, but to be kept strictly to ourselves, lest the imagination of one should supply some additional detail which had not occurred to that of the other, by which means the horrors of the situation might have been considerably increased. I am sure this was a wise precaution. As it was, I know I found my imagination vivid enough to picture a good deal more than was at all agreeable to think of; and it would, no doubt, have been still more troublesome if supplemented by that of Kitty also.

I did not by any means relish her proposal that we should clear sufficient space to lie down on; for I could not help shuddering at the thought of the things one might expect to come in contact with when groping about without light in a *chapelle mortuaire*. Still, I was not going to have her despise me as a fool or a coward, so I made no objection, and set to work heroically to perform my share of the unpleasant task.

The only suspicious thing which I met with in the course of my explorations was some small sized object, whose substance was cold and clammy, and whose identity I could not at all determine by touch. An exclamation of disgust rose to my lips when my fingers came against this unknown horror; but I managed to restrain any outward manifestation of emotion, and merely pushed the obstruction aside quietly, without letting Kitty know that I had found anything unpleasant.

As I made this effort to spare her feelings, I was struck by the quaint probability of her being at the same instant engaged in a similar endeavour to spare mine; and I realised that the common danger to which we were exposed was a link which united us so firmly that our separate identities were, for the time being, well-nigh merged into one. Whatever affected the condition of one of us must necessarily affect that of the other also; whence it followed that the bodily and mental welfare of both was a matter of mutually vital consequence, and that each was as anxious to shield the other as herself from any annoyance or shock that could possibly be avoided. Truly a queer sort of selfish unselfishness!

It did not take us long to make sure that we had room to lie down without fear of coming against any repulsive relics of mortality; then we extended ourselves upon the ground, pressing closely together for warmth, as the night was cold. Hard and rough as was the couch, and perilous as was our situation, we were too tired to be kept waking by either discomfort or anxiety, and were speedily asleep.

CHAPTER XVIII

A New Use for a Bier

AS I had no means of knowing the time, I cannot say exactly how long my slumbers lasted, but, as near as I can guess, it must have been about a couple of hours before I awoke. On opening my eyes I saw, with much surprise, that the moon had found its way into the tomb, as there was a patch of yellow light shining upon the opposite wall, and relieving the profound obscurity that reigned elsewhere. This was a most cheering and hope-inspiring spectacle; for, as the door was still closed as before, the moonlight certainly could not be entering in that way; and the obvious deduction was, that the chapel walls must have some second opening which we had not yet discovered. Whatever it was, might we not escape through it?

I aroused the still sleeping Kitty to point out to her the pleasant sight, and we got upon our feet to examine into the matter more nearly. The light was evidently admitted through some aperture situated in the gable of the roof just above the doorway, and the shadows by which the patch of light was traversed proved that the aperture was defended by bars. What the object of the opening may have been I know not, – perhaps ornament, perhaps ventilation, perhaps some whim of the architect's. Anyhow, there it was; and though darkness had prevented our seeing it on our first arrival at the chapel, yet now the friendly moon had come to our assistance, and was indicating it as a possible means of regaining liberty.

Never in my life had I felt such a sincere admiration for the moon, and such a conviction of its utility to the world, as I did then.

We were at that time standing where we had lain down, close to the door, and the aperture was too immediately over our heads for us to see it very well, so we advanced cautiously a few steps farther towards the middle of the floor, in order to obtain a better view. On looking up from this new point of observation, we saw that though the hole was small, it nevertheless appeared to be large enough for an ordinary sized person to be able to squeeze through, provided the bars were out of the way. This was encouraging. But it remained to be proved, first, whether we could get up so high without having any ladder or other means of raising ourselves; and secondly, whether, if we surmounted that difficulty, we should be able to remove the obstructing bars without having tools to assist us.

It was very certain that the window was too high up for us to get at it from the ground, since it was above the door, and I, who was taller than Kitty, could only just touch the top of the door with my fingertips when I stretched out my arm to its fullest extent. How on earth, then, were we to elevate ourselves to the height of the window? The first suggestion was, that if one of us was lifted up, perhaps she might be able to reach the desired niche, and we at once put the idea into execution. I, being the strongest and heaviest of the two, was naturally appointed to be the lifter; so I took hold of Kitty round the knees, and raised her up as far as I could. My utmost efforts, however, failed to get her to the required height, and I had to set her down again without having advanced an atom towards the accomplishment of our purpose.

"I'm sure I wasn't far short of touching the ledge of the window," she said, whilst I stood panting after my exertions; "if only I could get hold of that, and you were to help me by shoving, I expect I could pull myself right up, and manage to hitch on somehow to examine the bars. What we want is some kind of elevation for you to stand on when you lift me. Do try and invent some hoisting contrivance or other; it would be too provoking not to get up to the window now we've found it."

For a while we racked our brains vainly without discovering any solution of the problem. At last an idea flashed across my mind. No! – I would not mention such a thing – it was too horrible. Yet what I had thought of was a method whereby we might perhaps supply such an elevation as we wanted. And the unpleasantness of that method was no sufficient reason for being silent about it, when the urgent peril in which we were made it absurd to allow mere sentimental considerations to stand in the way of any possible chance of escape. Therefore I conquered my repugnance for the idea that had occurred to me, and said: "There must be coffins in this place. Very likely they are all more or less fallen to pieces, for Napoleon said that it had not been used for a long time; but yet some of the wood may still be sound, and perhaps if we grope about we may be able to collect enough boards to make a stage that would serve our purpose."

Kitty did not answer immediately. I daresay that she recoiled from the idea at first, as I had done. But if so, no doubt second thoughts showed her, as they had me, the imperative necessity of regarding matters from an exclusively practical, stern, and unimaginative point of view, and of absolutely ignoring any fanciful objections to whatever promised to aid our flight. She replied, after a short pause:

"Well, it is not a very attractive plan, certainly; but as there doesn't seem to be any other, I suppose we had better try it, and endeavour to forget its unpleasantness by looking forward to the delights of liberty if it succeeds.

So now let's go to work. It's a pity neither of us was ever inside a *chapelle mortuaire* before, isn't it? because then we should have some notion of how such places are generally arranged, which would be a great assistance to us just now in this pitchy darkness. As it is, however, I suppose we must imagine what the plan of the interior is *likely* to be like, and then proceed according to that idea. If I were an undertaker I think I should first deposit the coffins in a row along the wall, then pile them up, two or three deep perhaps, and only take up the middle of the floor when the sides were all occupied. Therefore I recommend our exploring the sides first, as likely to afford the largest supply of wood. Do you go to the right, whilst I take the left – unless you have anything better to suggest?"

I had not; so we separated, and went off to the right and left respectively, as she wished. But I had hardly got a yard away from the door when she exclaimed, "Come here, Jill; I want you!"

"Yes; what is it?" inquired I, as I crossed over to her.

"I've found something that seems to me promising," she replied eagerly. "I struck my hand against it directly I had got beyond the doorway. What it is I don't know; but it's pretty big anyhow, and it's not part of a coffin, and it's made of wood. I want you to help me feel it over, and see if we can make it out."

We began carefully investigating the unknown object with our fingers, and endeavouring to recognise by touch its shape and construction. For a while it puzzled us; then suddenly Kitty had an idea and said:

"Do you think it's a bier? I never handled one before, but I daresay it would feel something like this does. And it's not unlikely that it might have been left here and forgotten after the last funeral, is it?"

"No; that's it, depend upon it!" cried I; "and it's a

grand discovery, for a bier will help to raise us capitally, if only it's not got rotten, lying here so long."

To ascertain its condition was our first anxiety. Accordingly we took hold of the handles, lifted it off the ground, and gave it a smart shake, though not without considerable misgivings lest it should come to pieces in our hands. Fortunately it stood the test tolerably well, and did not break down. At the same time, however, it quivered and cracked in a way that did not give the impression of its being in very first-rate order; and we decided that it would be imprudent to expose it to the trial of bearing both of us simultaneously. If it would support one at a time, we would make no further demands upon its powers of endurance; and consequently we must utilise it in some other way than by my standing on it and lifting Kitty up to the window, as was our first idea.

Instead of that we raised it lengthwise, and placed it so that the handles at one end rested on the ground, whilst those at the other were against the door. When thus erected the upper part of the body of the bier was, of course, a good deal elevated, and made a foothold whence the window could easily be attained. To mount to this foothold was now our intention; and Kitty, being the lightest, was selected to ascend first. The only question was, How was she to get her foot to the top of the bier, which was too high up for any legs of ordinary length to step up to from the ground. But this obstacle was quickly smoothed away by my stooping down and converting myself into a stepping-stone. Mounted on me, and steadying herself against the door, she put one foot cautiously on the edge of the bier, and began to press upon it. The heavier she leant on it, the more ominously did it crack and tremble; still it did not give way, even when she at last stood upon it altogether, and it had to bear the whole of her weight. Hurrah! now we should know what the window looked like at close quarters; and whether the bars were wooden or iron, loose or tight, removable or not.

Kitty's report was satisfactory. She said that the window had a ledge on the inside which was broad and deep enough for a person to sit on by crouching a good deal, and that the bars were only wooden.

"Are they breakable?" I asked anxiously.

"Don't know yet," she returned; "I shall be able to tell better if I get right up on the ledge. They don't *feel* very solid; but I'm afraid of trying them from here. You see I'm not very confident of the stability of my present foothold, and don't care to indulge in violent exertions till I get to a safer situation. Wrestling with the bars where I am now *might* lead to an upset. If you'll help me by pushing below, I will draw myself up on to the ledge."

By dint of our united efforts, the further ascent was accomplished successfully. The ledge did not afford a very comfortable resting-place, as she had to sit bent nearly double, with her feet hanging down against the wall. But the position, though cramped and inconvenient, was secure, and was a firm point of vantage from which to attack the bars. She took hold of one, and shook it. Being completely rotted through, it came in two in her hand at once. The next offered a more obstinate resistance; in this also, however, as well as in the others, decay had begun, and had gone too far for the wood to withstand her vigorous jerks, pushes, pulls, shakes, and blows. Therefore it was not very long before she announced triumphantly that there was now nothing to hinder our egress through the window, which was, as we had thought, big enough for us to pass through.

"There's one thing I don't quite see, though," she said, after poking out her head and reconnoitring the exterior; "that is, how we're to get down on the other side. It looks to me rather far for a drop. I should say it would be a toss up whether we did it safely, or whether we broke our legs. Of course we must risk it if there's nothing else to be done; but if there *is* any other way of descending – why, I think it would be better."

"Is there room for us both to be on the ledge at the same time?" I inquired, after a moment's reflection; "because if I were up there by you, I might break the fall considerably by reaching down and holding you up when you drop. And then when you are down, you may be able to find some way of breaking the fall for me. Even if not, it would not matter so much for me. I think I could drop the distance without hurting myself; for when I was a child I used to do a deal of jumping and climbing, and was always good at falling light."

"Well – we might try that, at all events," she answered, "if the ledge is large enough to hold us both at the same time. I'm doubtful whether it is – but we can soon see. Wait a moment and I'll make more room by turning round, and sitting with my feet out instead of in. There – now they're out of the way. Come and stand on the top of the bier, and see if you can stow yourself away up here by my side."

It now for the first time struck us that it was by no means sure whether I should be able to get to the top of the bier without having anyone to assist me from below as I had assisted Kitty. Yet if I failed to reach that point, I must give up the idea of reaching the window; and as that was equivalent to resigning my hopes of liberty, it was evidently of the utmost importance that I should accomplish the ascent.

Kitty was the first to suggest a way out of the difficulty.

"Can you alter the position of the bier," said she, "so as to make it slant, instead of standing almost upright as it does now? Because then you might manage to creep up it."

"I've no doubt I can, only I hadn't thought of it," replied I, proceeding to drag the two lower handles away from the door, till the steepness of the incline was much less than before. Then I grasped the upper edge of the bier, and tried, partly by pulling and partly by crawling, to bring my feet up to where my hands were. Alas! the woodwork that was firm enough to support Kitty, standing upon it quietly, had not strength to bear a person of my greater weight, scrambling up it as I was doing. Collapsing altogether, it brought me violently to the ground with a crash which alarmed Kitty, who, on her perch overhead, half in and half out, could not see what was happening in the darkness beneath.

"Oh, Jill!" she exclaimed, "what is it? Are you hurt?"

"No*,* " I answered, feeling ready to cry with vexation, as I rose, and cleared away the *débris* of broken wood with which I was covered. "I wasn't far enough off the ground for that. But the old bier has smashed all to pieces; and however I'm to get up to the window now, I'm *sure* I don't know!"

"Are you certain," she returned, "that there isn't any sound corner still holding together, which would do for you to stick up, and stand on? It's worthwhile for you to feel about on chance of such a thing, at all events."

This was true; and I explored carefully amongst the splintered fragments in hopes of discovering some solid bit. But my efforts were in vain.

"It's no use," said I, ruefully; "the thing is gone to pieces completely."

Neither of us spoke for a while after this. First I exhausted my ingenuity in vain endeavours to discover some means of raising myself to the window. Then, when I made up my mind that I was doomed to remain a captive, I began to reflect enviously on the superior good fortune of Kitty. The only thing between her and freedom was the trivial difficulty of getting down safely on the other side. Once that was overcome, she would be off, and leave me by myself in this abominable place. I did not at all like the idea of her going. For one thing, I preferred having a companion in misfortune to being solitary. And for another thing, her absence would greatly aggravate my danger, as the *penitenciers* would be sure to be rendered furious by her having given them the slip, and would vent their wrath upon me. Of course, if she were to fall in with efficient succour, and return before they did, it would be a different matter. But then the chance of that seemed too remote to be worth reckoning on; and I thought it was decidedly more to my interest that she should stay with me than that she should regain her liberty alone.

Why did she sit up there silently without saying anything about her departure? I wondered. Ah! probably she hadn't yet discovered a satisfactory method of managing the descent outside, which she seemed to think difficult. *I* could tell her how it was to be done, if I chose – but then I wasn't going to choose anything of the kind. If her own wits couldn't show her how to profit by her advantages, then let her stay where she was, and keep me company!

These were the thoughts that first crossed my mind, when I recognised the melancholy fact that I had no chance of escape. Yet, somehow or other, I did not eventually hold my tongue, as I had intended to do, about the means by which her descent might be accomplished. What induced me to change my mind about it I don't exactly know. Perhaps the fancy that I had for her may have been stronger than I realised, and have made it impossible for me to refrain from doing whatever I could to get her out of the power of two such ruffians as César and Napoleon. Or perhaps I may have been influenced by the obvious unreasonableness of allowing two people to be exposed to a danger from which one of them might escape. Anyhow, the upshot of it was that I said – though not without an effort:

"I've thought of a way for you to get down from the window without damaging yourself. We'll tie our dresses, jackets – petticoats too, if need be – into a rope which must be long enough to go through the window and dangle down outside, whilst I keep hold of one end in here. The outside end must have a loop for you to put your feet in; and with the help of that, I'm pretty sure we can make the drop safe. Then, if you should be lucky about falling in with respectable people soon, perhaps you may be able to come back and get me away before the *penitenciers* reappear in the morning."

As I believed her to be only staying there because she did not know how to get away, I took it for granted that she would be delighted at my suggestion, and be in a desperate hurry to avail herself of it. Instead of that, however, she only said coolly;

"Thank you, Jill; but I think it's perfectly impossible that I should find help and return in time to rescue you, so I don't at all contemplate going off alone, and leaving you to face the indignation of César and Napoleon at my departure. Goodness knows what they wouldn't do to you! No; I was the means of getting you into this scrape, and I don't seem to see leaving you to shift for yourself now. If there's no alternative between deserting you or taking up my abode again inside the chapel – why, I prefer the latter. But it's too soon to despair yet. Having got *one* of us up here is something; and it won't do to abandon that advantage until we're quite positive that we can't turn it to account. There's your first plan of trying to get enough wood to make a platform – why not take to that again?"

"For two reasons," said I, with a thrill of indescribable happiness and comfort at finding that she was too staunch and plucky for there to be a chance of her deserting me. "In the first place there isn't time, because I should only get on at half the pace by myself that we should have done working together. And besides that, I think that the rottenness of the bier and bars is a conclusive proof that there isn't likely to be any sound wood discoverable here."

"True," she returned. Immediately afterwards she added, exultingly, "What idiots we are! As the men hadn't a key, they can't possibly have locked us in, and there can't be any fastening except the bar across the outside of the door. We never thought of that! As soon as I get down and take away the bar, you can march out without trouble. Off with your dress, and let's make that rope you talked of to let me down with!"

It seems extraordinary that neither of us had remembered this simple solution of the difficulty sooner; yet so it was. Now that it had at last occurred to us, however, we lost no time in going to work. Our garments were instantly put into requisition, and twisted and knotted into as good an imitation of a rope as we could construct out of such materials. The end which had a loop to it was hung out of window, whilst I retained the other end in my hands, and Kitty, placing her feet in the loop, began to lower herself gently.

As long as she could keep hold of the window her weight was thrown partly on her hands; thus I had not the whole of it to support until during the last few seconds, when, taking her feet out of the loop, letting go of the window, and clinging only to the rope, she descended as near as she could to the ground. I held on to the rope with might and main, till the tension relaxed with a sudden jerk that threw me down, and informed me that she had regained *terra firma*.

"Sprained ankle, broken bones, or anything of that kind?" I asked, anxiously.

"No, not hurt a bit," was the welcome response. "I'll get the door open as quickly as I can; will you begin undoing the rope meanwhile?"

"All right!" I returned, commencing to restore it to its normal condition of clothes as fast as I could in the dark. As I worked I listened hopefully to the scratching and fumbling that went on outside, and expected every moment to hear the downfall of the bar. But the minutes passed on, and still the looked-for sound did not come. I could not understand what could be causing so much delay about so simple a matter as removing a bar from across a door, and I began to grow feverishly nervous lest any unforeseen obstacle should even now intervene, and deprive me of the freedom I had begun to anticipate confidently. My alarm was not unfounded, for, to my dismay, she called out:

"This bar is so dreadfully heavy that I can't raise it. I can only move one end at a time, and lift it up a very small way above the support it stands on; but not high enough for what I want."

Then it was all over with me, and I was fated to stay there alone to be cut to pieces, or murdered in any way that might seem good to those two ruffians! And when I had thought, too, that I was so sure of getting away! The bitterness of the disappointment seemed to choke me for a minute, so that I could not speak. However, when I could control my voice, I shouted to her:

"There's no help for it! You can't get back inside again now, even if you wish to. So you've no choice about going away. Goodbye!"

"I'm not at an end of my resources yet," she replied. "I've thought of something fresh. I'm going away for a few minutes, but I shall be back directly."

The sound of her steps gave me notice of her departure from and return to the chapel. Then ensued much scraping, scratching, and other noises, to which I listened with intense anxiety, longing to know what she was about, yet fearing to ask, lest, if I interrupted her with questions, I might perhaps hinder my deliverance.

Her operations meanwhile, as I afterwards learnt, were as follows: – First, she went to fetch a supply of stones of various sizes. Returning with these, she put her shoulder underneath one end of the bar, and exerting all her strength, raised it as high as she could above the broad projecting piece of iron on which it rested. Then, before removing her shoulder, she inserted between the iron support and the bar enough stones to maintain the latter at the place to which she had raised it. This performance many times repeated, at last elevated that end so far above the other that the bar was all slanting, and only needed one vigorous push to set it in motion, sliding downwards across the iron projection on which the opposite end was supported. Moving slowly at first, the massive bar went faster and faster every instant as its own weight gave it additional impetus, till it dashed on to the ground with a resounding clang that seemed to me the sweetest music that ever gladdened the ears of mortal man or woman. I immediately pushed against the door. It yielded slowly, and next minute I was emancipated from that horrible *chapelle mortuaire,* and standing beside Kitty, free in the open air once more.

To describe the rapture of that moment is beyond my powers. If anyone wants to know true bliss for once in their lives, I recommend them to go through a similar experience. Only they must take into account the possibility of *not* escaping after all; which is evidently a serious drawback, since a failure in that respect would be quite fatal to the object of the experiment.

CHAPTER XIX

Off from Corsica

WE had no means of knowing how far advanced the night might be, but we knew that our enemies intended to return early in the morning; we saw that the moon was waning, and we naturally wished to get away from the vicinity of the *chapelle mortuaire* with all possible expedition. Having been obliged to partially undress ourselves in order to find materials for the rope, we began hastily resuming such articles of attire as had been taken off; whilst thus engaged Kitty said:

"It seems to me rather a chance that we don't run straight into the arms of those two villains when we leave this place. I don't the least know which way to go; for, except that we're in Corsica, I have uncommonly little notion of where we are. Have you?"

"Well, only this much," I replied; "in coming here we travelled a good deal more uphill than down, so I expect we must be in rather high ground. And when our captors left us I heard them say they were going to a cave in the mountains, so they will be coming here from somewhere above. Therefore, I think, we must obviously guide ourselves by the rule of going always downhill, if we want to reach a safe district, and keep out of harm's way."

"Yes; there's sense in that," answered she. "Downhill shall be our rule, as you say. But first of all, here's this enclosing wall to be got out of. We shall have to find some way of climbing over it, unless we can open the gate."

Luckily, however, the gate had only been swung to, and not fastened; so we had no difficulty in passing through it. Outside there was a roughly made road, much overgrown in consequence of long disuse, and going in two opposite directions.

"Come along," said Kitty; "roads almost always lead *somewhere,* and it is to be hoped this one is no exception; then we shall find ourselves at some inhabited locality or other at last. The way to the right goes downwards, I think."

Off we set to the right, therefore, at full speed, and ran ourselves out of breath; then we walked till we had got enough fresh wind to begin running again; then ran till we were blown again; and so on, recommencing as before, and ever and anon listening anxiously for any sounds of pursuit. For though it was not yet the time when the robbers had announced they would return to us, yet our fears suggested the possibility of their having changed their minds, and gone back to the *chapelle* sooner than they had intended. Presently the moon set; and after that the unevenness of the track and the darkness combined caused us to stumble, slip, and fall several times. But we did not slacken pace on that account, and continued our headlong flight, till at last we came to a road which was so much broader and better than the one we had hitherto been following, that we had little doubt of its being the route *nationale.*

We had now a comfortable sensation of being once more within reach of protection; and shortly afterwards we were yet further cheered by a sound behind us of wheels, horses' feet, and jingling bells, which announced that some vehicle was approaching. We hailed it as soon as it came up to us; but found, to our disgust, that our shouts produced no effect; for no one paid the slightest attention to them, and the thing lumbered heavily past in the darkness, giving a general impression of length and bulk which made us guess it to be a diligence, though we could not see it clearly. Having no fancy to be thus ignored and left behind, we gave chase, and quickly overtook the slowly-moving conveyance as it crawled up a hill. Being one of the mail diligences it had a letterbox hanging at the back, just above a broad low step, which it was easy to mount and descend from whilst the vehicle was in motion; thus anyone with letters to post could jump up, consign them to the box, and get down again without causing any stoppage, so that the diligence was a sort of moving post office. This step was most convenient to us at this moment. There was room enough for us both to sit upon it, and we very soon established ourselves in this muddy but not uncomfortable situation, rejoicing greatly at the welcome rest and security which it afforded. None of the people inside the diligence attempted to dislodge us, or took any notice of us, so I imagine either that our proceeding must have been too ordinary a one to attract attention, or else that they were all fast asleep. On the horses trotted again when the top of the hill was reached; the mud splashes bespattered us freely, and we had to hold tight for fear of being shaken off by some severer jolt than usual; but we maintained our position till the carriage, after travelling some distance, came to a standstill, and someone began to get down. Then, fearing lest gratuitous conveyance might be objected to, we got off and stood aside to reconnoitre before showing ourselves.

It appeared that the reason of the halt was our having reached an inn at which someone in the diligence was going to alight. The house door stood wide open, which indicated, I suppose, that accommodation might be had within by anyone who could manage to awake one of the inhabitants; but otherwise there was no sign of readiness for guests; the premises were totally unlighted; there was no guardian – human or canine – to give notice of the arrival of either friend or foe, nor was there any bell or other means of summons.

The diligence having drawn up opposite to this primitive hotel, one of the passengers got out with a bag in his hand, and the *conducteur* descended from his perch bearing a lantern. Then they entered the house, and as they did so the lantern went out, and we heard them go stumbling and groping their way in the dark upstairs to the first floor. Here there was a fastened door, which prevented a further advance, and a considerable amount of knocking, kicking, and bawling ensued, till some inmate was at last aroused to come and see what was wanted. Up to this moment the *conducteur* had appeared to consider himself as to some extent bound to look after the passenger whom his vehicle had conveyed there; but the instant his ears had assured him of the fact of there being a living person in the inn, he evidently felt that *his* duty in the matter was at an end, and all responsibility for the traveller henceforth transferred to the landlord. No sooner, therefore, were the first sounds audible of someone stirring within than the *conducteur* left his charge to take care of himself, and came clattering downstairs and out into the road again, without troubling himself to wait for the inner door to be opened, in order to find out whether the newcomer could be accommodated, or whether, perhaps, the little hostelry might be already full – in which case the visitor would have had no option about passing the rest of the night in the street, unless he had preferred going on again in the diligence.

"Not much like English ideas of travelling and arriving at a hotel, is it?" whispered Kitty to me, with much truth.

As soon as the *conducteur* returned to the road, we stepped up to him, and Kitty asked if he would kindly tell us the name of this place, and also what was the destination of the diligence, as we were strangers who had got lost, and did not know where we were. He looked at us with no little surprise, and answered that our present situation was St. Marie Sicché, and that the diligence was on its way to Ajaccio.

This was a welcome piece of information. St. Marie Sicché was, it will be remembered, the village where we had slept on the first night of our driving-tour; consequently we were not in an altogether strange district, and knew that we were within three or four hours of Ajaccio, where the best part of our luggage was left, and where we were more at home than in any other part of the island. There could be no doubt that the best thing for us to do was to get there and make ourselves comfortable at the hotel as soon as possible; and then, when the telegraph offices should be open in the morning, we would find out where Mrs. Rollin was, and relieve her mind as to our safety. The only obstacle was that we had no money to pay for our conveyance to Ajaccio; for the *penitenciers* had carried off everything valuable that we possessed; and, therefore, unless we could get credit, we must evidently be involved in a good deal of bother and delay before we should be able to leave our present situation, or do anything that we wanted to do.

In this difficulty Kitty appealed to the *conducteur,* telling him that as we had been robbed, we were at that moment penniless; and asking him whether he would take us in his diligence to Ajaccio, and let us pay for our places after arriving there. She also told him the name of the hotel where our baggage was left, and assured him that we should have no difficulty in having our respectability guaranteed there. The man hesitated, hummed and hawed, looked suspiciously at us – muddy and untidy as we were – and did not seem much inclined to believe her story. But after some trouble, she persuaded him to consent to her request by promising to pay double the ordinary fare.

Haying thus settled the matter satisfactorily with him, we anticipated no further difficulty, and were about to enter the interior of the vehicle – both *coupé* and *banquette* being full – when we were unexpectedly opposed by one of the passengers already established there. The conversation had roused him from his slumbers; and when Kitty attempted to get in, he started forward and protested energetically against our admission. It was a shame to take up anyone else, he said, when he and his fellows were already *"pressés comme des anchois"*; they had been crowded to the very verge of possibility by the person who had just alighted; it was absurd to think of cramming us two individuals into the space that that one had occupied; he objected – he would complain to the authorities – it was disgraceful to treat travellers in that way. Another diligence was due in about ten or twelve hours, and we ought to wait, and take our chance of finding places in that.

The prospect of waiting at St. Marie Sicché for another ten or twelve hours was by no means to our mind, and we were alarmed to see that the *conducteur* seemed inclined to listen to the irate passenger. But Kitty showed herself equal to the emergency. Turning promptly to the *conducteur,* she whispered to him that she hardly supposed he was going to leave us for the benefit of any rival vehicle; and that as it was important to her to get to Ajaccio at once, she would give him treble the proper fare if he took us, instead of only double, as previously agreed. He was evidently quite alive to the fact that an extra high fare would give him the opportunity of pocketing a nice little profit, by only paying the diligence company a single fare and keeping the rest for himself;

and her increased offer put an end to his hesitation about introducing us into the already full conveyance. Therefore he turned a deaf ear to the other man's expostulations – thoroughly well-founded though they were – proceeded to make room somehow or other, and finally stowed us away without heeding the discontented sleepy grunts and growls of the victims whom we had forced to compress themselves into an unnaturally small space. Then he shut us all in, climbed back to his place, and the journey was resumed.

The interior of a hot, crowded, stuffy diligence, packed closely with garlic-eating Corsicans clad in strong-smelling garments, would not generally be deemed a very inviting haven of repose. Yet it seemed so to us just then; for we were tired enough to find rest anywhere delicious, and were too full of joy at having escaped from serious danger to grumble at such trifling annoyances as mere discomfort and unpleasant odours.

A couple of hours' jolting brought us to Cauro, where the horses were changed; thence we continued our course to Ajaccio, which was reached soon after seven in the morning. Stiff and fatigued as we were, we should have been glad of a *fiacre* to take us from the *diligence-bureau* to the hotel; but no *fiacre* was to be had at that early hour, so we set off walking, accompanied (I need hardly say) by an envoy sent by the *conducteur* to find out whether the account we had given of ourselves was a true one.

As we were going up the street I saw a couple of smart-looking sailors coming towards us. The sight of them suddenly reminded me that there was a chance of Lord Clement's being still at Ajaccio, which possibility I had till then forgotten. If he were within reach, would Kitty turn willingly to him as a protector and counsellor, I wondered?

"Those two look like sailors from a yacht," said I; "if

they should happen to belong to *La Catalina,* I suppose you will send word by them to Lord Clement that you have returned, won't you?"

" No! what would be the good of that?" she answered sharply, and not at all as if she was in any hurry to meet her noble admirer again. But second thoughts made her change her mind, for she added: "Well, yes; perhaps it would be as well to let him know we're back, if he *does* happen to be still here. Both you and I are dead tired; and he could go and see to telegraphing, and all that's got to be done, while we rest. Besides that, in spite of the principles of equality of these republicans, I strongly suspect that a person who is rich, a man, and an earl, stands a better chance of being attended to by the authorities than a mere commonplace woman. So, on the whole, I daresay he would be useful just now to act as agent for me."

When we were close to the sailors we saw that they were part of the crew of *La Catalina,* as her name was visible upon their hats and jerseys.

"Is Lord Clement on board *La Catalina?"* asked Kitty.

The two tars stopped and stared in evident surprise at being accosted in their own tongue in the streets of Ajaccio at that early hour in the morning.

"Ay, ay," answered one of them.

"Just go back to the yacht at once then," returned Kitty, "and tell him that Miss Mervyn has returned here, and has gone to the hotel where she was staying before, and will be glad to see him there as soon as possible."

The men, who did not in the least recognise us, stared more than ever at hearing themselves ordered about in this fashion by one of two strange women presenting the extraordinary appearance which Kitty and I did at that moment. For it must be remembered that we had been splashed with mud from head to foot as we sat on the step of the diligence; that our clothes were torn, rumpled, and put on anyhow; that our hair was horribly dishevelled; and that we were altogether as untidy-looking objects as could well be imagined.

Evidently the sailors did not know what to make of us, and were undecided, for a moment, whether to do what they were told, or to be impertinent. But Kitty bore the stamp of high birth and breeding marked too plainly for it to be concealed by disreputable externals; and she spoke with the calmly-commanding manner of a person who is accustomed to be obeyed. The sailors were not insensible to this influence, and could not help recognising her as a legitimate authority, notwithstanding the peculiarity of her appearance. When, therefore, she repeated what she had said before, and again told them to be off at once, they looked at one another sheepishly, touched their hats, and departed obediently in the direction of the harbour. And that they executed their commission faithfully was proved by the promptitude with which Lord Clement arrived at our hotel and asked for Miss Mervyn.

Poor young man! thought I, as I watched him going upstairs to her room. I do not suppose you will be very pleased at what you are going to hear; for your Mrs. Grundy-loving nature is sure to abhor eccentric adventures; and I do not expect you will enjoy that your lady-love should be known to have been the heroine of such an unusual experience as Kitty has just gone through! Judging by the annoyed and disturbed expression on his countenance when the interview with her was over, and he left the hotel, I imagine that my anticipations were not far wrong, and that his sense of propriety and of the fitness of things was greatly shocked at what had occurred to the young lady whom he desired to marry. His annoyance, however, did not prevent him from taking all trouble off her shoulders as far as possible; and he made himself useful by telegraphing to various places till he had discovered Mrs. Rollin; then informing her that we were safe at Ajaccio; and also giving notice to the police of the nefarious proceedings of César and Napoleon.

Our loss had thrown Mrs. Rollin into a state of anxiety, nervousness, and discomposure, which none of the French novels she had with her had sufficed to calm. She had gone on hourly exciting herself more and more against Corsica and all its people, until she had worked herself into an unreasoning aversion to it and them. Consequently, when she rejoined us at Ajaccio, which she did on the evening of the day that we had returned there, the one fixed idea in her mind was, that she would never know a moment's ease or happiness as long as she remained in the island, and that we must get away from it immediately.

On hearing our adventures she declared that what had happened was fearful, ghastly, and shocking, but yet no more than was to be expected in an out-of-the-way, uncivilised, poverty-stricken country where nobody went, where the inhabitants lived without milk and butter, and where everyone was a savage or thief, or both. She very deeply regretted having let herself be over-persuaded to come to this Corsica; but, at all events, no power on earth should induce her to stay in such a vile, odious, unsafe, abominable place any longer. Besides, though the two *penitenciers* would probably never be captured, yet still, supposing by any accident that they *were* caught, and Kitty was within reach, then the girl would be wanted to give evidence against them, and that was another reason for taking flight at once. Else there would be the risk of Kitty's having to appear in a police-court, take oaths, be cross-examined and badgered by vulgar lawyers, and all that sort of thing, which was quite unfit for a lady to undergo. And what depths the vulgarity of lawyers in a republican country might reach, she, Mrs. Rollin, was afraid to think! Of course she by no means expected that the robbers *would* be taken; but as there was a possibility of such a thing, it was her duty to provide for it.

When she stopped to take breath, Kitty inquired why she was so certain that the culprits would not be recaptured, and that set her off again. She had seen, she said, enough of Corsicans by this time to convince her that they were all rogues alike, and all in collusion with one another. In hopes of keeping us staying on and on, and spending money amongst them, they might perhaps talk big, and declare that the offenders would soon be under lock and key; but meanwhile they would be let to escape quietly; or, if caught, good care would be taken that they should not be convicted. But *she* wasn't going to be so silly as to be made a fool of by these Corsicans, and to play into their hands by remaining there longer. No, thank you! She had discovered that there would be a steamer to Marseilles on the following day, and by that steamer she intended to go. And besides everything else, there was yet another reason, she averred, why she must now begin to make her way homewards. She found, from letters she had just received, that matters of business made it necessary for her to return to England sooner than she had expected. She must positively have a week's shopping in Paris on the way back, and she would not have time for this unless she started at once. Therefore it was, in every respect, out of the question that we should prolong our visit to this detestable island.

Her mind was made up too firmly to be shaken, and on the next day we quitted Ajaccio in *La Catalina* – Lord Clement having again placed that vessel at my two ladies' disposal. I am afraid, however, that this act of civility did not bring him the satisfaction that he probably expected.

For Kitty, instead of making herself agreeable during the voyage, professed to be headachy, and remained alone in a cabin; and as soon as Marseilles was reached, she and her aunt said goodbye to him, and set off for Paris by the next *rapide*. Very possibly he would have liked to accompany them there. But then yachting was his ostensible occupation at the present time; and if he deserted his yacht to go to Paris, people would be sure to talk, shrug shoulders, and say that there certainly was something on between him and Kitty. Though all this would not matter supposing it to be followed promptly by the announcement that they were engaged, yet, under other circumstances, it would in his eyes be highly undesirable; therefore he stuck to *La Catalina*.

As for me, I was a good deal disappointed, for I had been looking forward with vindictive pleasure to the chance of bearing witness against Messrs. César and Napoleon, and I grudged the hasty departure from Corsica which deprived me of this chance. A few days later I saw in a newspaper that they had been caught, and relegated to their former quarters in prison at Chiavari. That was some comfort, no doubt; but nothing like as satisfactory as it would have been to have contributed, in my own person, to bring about their punishment.

CHAPTER XX

Captain Norroy Appears

I HAVE already said that the circumstances connected with the photograph which I had found in Kitty's purse had made me fancy that there was some secret reason for her regarding Captain Edward Norroy differently from the rest of mankind; and I have said, also, that I was hoping some day to see him and her together, on chance that I might then succeed in discovering a clue to a right comprehension of what the relations between them were. This opportunity which I desired came unexpectedly on the day after our arrival in Paris, and was brought about in the following manner.

Mrs. Rollin was determined that she and Kitty must be photographed by a Paris photographer named Raoul, who was at that time so much the rage amongst fashionable people that to be in his town and not profit by the opportunity of having her likeness done by him, would have been a sin of omission which would have lain heavy on her conscience for the rest of her existence – or, at all events, for as long as he continued to be the fashion. It was, of course, necessary in the first place to ascertain when it would suit the great man to take the photograph. For this purpose she had intended to go to his studio in person on the day after reaching Paris; but as she happened to be a little out of sorts on that day, she preferred to stay at home reading *Rocambole,* and send Kitty in her stead, under my escort, to make the requisite appointment. At the studio we found a polite assistant, who was quite in despair to think that the ladies should be obliged to wait; but as his *patron* was just then engaged, he feared it was inevitable that they should do so, unless their business was of a nature which he, the assistant, could transact for them. If so, he should be proud and honoured to receive their commands.

Now Mrs. Rollin, having been much exercised in her mind as to whether it would be more *chic* to be done in morning or evening attire, had particularly instructed Kitty to refer the matter to Raoul, and find out his opinion about it. Consequently she declined the assistant's offer of his services with thanks, and said that she would wait till Monsieur Raoul was disengaged. On this we were shown into the waiting-room, which was as dreary as the rest of its kind, and where we endeavoured to find amusement by inspecting the various specimens of the *patron's* art that were dispersed on the table.

We were thus employed, and I was standing with my back to the door, when it opened to admit someone; at the same instant I saw Kitty – who was looking that way – flush violently and suddenly, and, on turning round, I perceived that the newcomer was Captain Norroy.

I need hardly say that I was immediately all eyes and ears for what would take place; and that my subsequent inspection of photographs was a mere pretence, which I kept up in order that the young couple might not suspect how attentively I was studying them.

They shook hands, exchanged greetings, and then went on to talk of the weather, the state of the streets, the hotels at which they were staying, etc., just as any ordinary acquaintances would do. There was not the faintest trace of consciousness about Captain Norroy's manner; and he was so evidently free from any kind of special emotion connected with Kitty, that I doubted, for a moment, whether my surmises might after all have been wrong. But then, again, I felt confirmed in them by Kitty, who was certainly not as cool and unembarrassed as was the captain. The first flush caused by his entrance had nearly died out; but there still lingered a tinge of unwonted colour on her cheeks, and a more than commonly brilliant light in her eyes. In both her look and manner of speaking I could detect a shade of nervousness, of pleasure, of restraint, of something different to usual, which I was unable to interpret. It was a difference so slight as to have been, probably, imperceptible to anyone who did not know her well; but to me it was so plainly visible that I felt sure I was not mistaken about it.

As it happened, the conversation presently took a turn which supplied me with such a clue as I wanted in order to read the riddle which had been perplexing me, and to arrive at some idea of how matters stood between these two people, in whom my interest had been excited.

The captain, looking at his watch, observed that Raoul was not very punctual, as it was already twenty minutes past the time when he had said that he would be ready to photograph the captain.

"What! are you actually going to be photographed?" said Kitty, laughing. "I can hardly believe it possible when I remember the vehemence with which I have heard you declare that, having gone through the operation once, you never would again. You professed to think it an intolerable bore."

"Yes – so I did, and so I do still," he replied; "but I'm going to sacrifice myself nobly for the sake of other people. You see almost everyone, now-a-days, has a *carte-de-visite* book, which they are desirous of filling by hook or by crook. Consequently, one is constantly being entreated for a photo by even one's most casual acquaintances. One don't like to be always refusing to do what one's asked, because it makes one feel such an ill-natured brute; but at present I can't help saying no when I'm asked for a photo of myself, for the very excellent reason that I haven't such a thing to give."

"Why not?" inquired Kitty. "Haven't you the photos which were taken on the solitary occasion when you *were* done?"

"Ah! that attempt had no *chance,* as the French say," he answered. "My batch of copies fell into the fire directly they arrived, and were all burnt except four, which I managed to rescue, and of which I gave three to my mother and sisters, and the fourth to Lady Cantern, who was just then perfectly ravenous for photos, because she and her sister were in the midst of a race as to which could get her photo-book filled the quickest. Of course this left me destitute of *cartes,* so I at once ordered a fresh lot from the photographer; but the fates were evidently against me, for the original plate had been accidentally cracked, so that no more copies could be struck from it. Curiously enough, too, the bad luck which attended that photographic effort pursued even the copy I gave Lady Cantern. You remember that time you and I, and a lot of other people, were staying with her last winter for balls, don't you? What a pleasant visit it was! and especially that last *cotillion* you and I danced together – wasn't it delightful?"

As Kitty assented, I noticed that she looked down somewhat nervously, as if she wished to avoid all risk of having the recollections evoked by the mention of that visit read in her face.

"Well," he continued, "she says that she missed my photo out of her book on the very day after her guests departed; and as she is positive it was in its place just before, she declares some one of them must have taken a fancy to it and carried it off. At first she accused *me* of being the thief as if it was likely I should care to have such a caricature of myself as I considered it to be! I can't imagine how she *could* suppose that anyone would wish for such an unflattering presentment of himself as long as looking-glasses continue plentiful! However, I undeceived her on that point; and then she said that if it wasn't I who had appropriated the thing, it must have been someone else. My own idea is that she must have put it away somewhere, and forgotten what she'd done with it. But, anyhow, she hadn't discovered it when last I saw her, and I don't believe she will – that batch had no *chance,* as I said before. Ah! here comes Raoul to lead off his victim. I shall have a few moments of grace whilst you and he fix the date of your execution; and then—"

Raoul's entrance terminated this conversation, to which I – whilst making believe to be engrossed in the study of photographs – had listened with the greatest attention. It seemed to me to throw fresh light upon the matter that had been perplexing me hitherto.

Evidently Kitty possessed a photograph of Captain Norroy of which there were only four copies in existence. As neither of them had been given to her, she must have come by it surreptitiously; and her possession of it was, no doubt, to be explained by the mysterious disappearance of Lady Cantern's copy immediately after Kitty had been staying in her house.

But though I thought there could be no doubt as to Kitty's having been the person who purloined this precious carte-de-visite, I was sorely puzzled to conjecture what possible motive she could have had for doing so. After reflecting deeply on the problem, I could find no solution of it except one, which did not seem to me to be altogether likely. It was this. Had the handsome young captain perhaps touched her heart more deeply than was expedient? and could she have fallen in love with him? If so, that might explain the things that now puzzled me: her stealing the photograph; the care with which it was concealed; the emotion she had betrayed when I suddenly produced it; and also the nervousness and peculiarity of manner I had noticed in her when she met him at Raoul's.

But however probable this theory might have appeared in the case of some girls, it hardly seemed admissible when Kitty was the person concerned. For as it was quite plain that the captain's sentiments towards her were simply those of an ordinary acquaintance, it followed that to suppose her to have a fancy for him involved supposing that she cared for a man who did not return the compliment. And her pride seemed to make such an idea impossible. Kitty Mervyn to have an unrequited attachment, indeed! It was absurd even to think of such a thing.

Yet again, on the other hand, who could tell what caprice might not rule an article so notoriously wayward as a woman's heart? And if love overcomes bolts and bars, why should it not conquer the stiffest pride also? Clearly it was foolish of me to think I could be *sure* of how any person would act, when there was a possibility of a strange and unknown quantity like love manifesting itself, upsetting the best-founded calculations, and altering the whole aspect of affairs.

Still, I could scarcely bring myself to believe that Kitty would have bestowed her affections on anyone who did not seek them. Ah! but then there was the question – had she perhaps imagined that they *were* sought? This good-looking Captain Norroy was as pleasant in manner as he was in personal appearance; his voice was soft and caressing; he gave me the idea of being a lazy, good-humoured, susceptible man, who would enjoy popularity with women and take pains to be agreeable in their eyes;

and who would unintentionally put an appearance of earnestness into a mere passing flirtation, which would make it dangerous to the other party. And possibly he had admired Kitty, and flirted with her mildly, without meaning anything serious; and possibly she had been deceived by his attentions into supposing he was in love with her, and not discovered her error until her heart was already touched.

If that were so, I could not help pitying her; for I knew that the knowledge of her own weakness and folly must be terribly galling to her, and that she must be in a continual state of anxiety lest anyone should discover, or even suspect it. Yet I could imagine, too, that the bitterness would be mingled with sweetness, in that she would be always hoping he might some day return her love. It was a hope that it would be most natural for her to entertain; for she could not fail to know how generally attractive she was to his sex; and as he was but a man like other men, was it not reasonable to suppose that he too might be affected by charms which his fellows seemed to find irresistible? And then the recollection of the numerous admirers she had had, and for whom she cared nothing, took my thoughts for a moment into a fresh channel, as I wondered whether those victims would not have thought it a no more than just retribution for her to give her affections without return. For I was aware that some ill-natured people had been known to term her a regular flirt; and I had heard of rejected suitors of hers who had complained bitterly of the impartial amiability with which she behaved to everyone, and had declared that she did it with malicious intent to lead men on to propose, in order that she might have the pleasure of refusing them.

Assuming her to be in love with Captain Norroy, I thought I could form a pretty good guess as to what her feeling about Lord Clement would be. Her pride would be all in his favour; for pride would be up in arms at the idea of her waiting to see if the captain would condescend to throw his handkerchief to her, and would urge her to terminate so humiliating a situation by marrying someone else. And thus pride would be a powerful auxiliary to the soaring ambition and desire to be amongst the great ones of the earth, which were marked features of her character. All this would evidently prompt her to accept Lord Clement and the high rank and position he had to offer; and I could only account for her not having done so already, by supposing that the voice of natural inclination had made itself heard on the other side. Perhaps it had pleaded with her not to be in a hurry, and not rashly to render impossible a happiness that might still be hers if she would have the patience to wait a while longer. Perhaps the struggle between pride and love was going on within her now, and she had not yet determined which voice to listen to. If so, I could by no means hazard an opinion as to what the issue was likely to be; and it seemed to me an even chance which would gain the mastery.

How far were all these speculations and conjectures of mine right? That remained to be proved; and I felt as if fate had kindly assigned to me a good situation in the front row whence to watch the progress of a play which it amused me to look on at. Yet, as it must interfere with one's enjoyment of a play to get excited about its termination, I should certainly have preferred for some other than Kitty to be the chief performer. For I was half afraid that I might find I cared for her too much to remain an altogether indifferent spectator where her happiness was seriously concerned.

CHAPTER XXI

A Newspaper Paragraph

OF course Mrs. Rollin and Kitty had a deal of shopping to do in Paris; for to be in that town and not buy clothes is – to most feminine minds – an unpardonable sinning of one's mercies. The dressmaker whom they elected to give their orders to was a certain Madame Jarrot, much patronised by the fashionable world; and having made an appointment with her at her own residence, they proceeded thither to keep it one day soon after the visit to the photographer which was related in the last chapter.

Now I liked much better to sit in their drawing room than in the poky little garret which was my bedroom; and when they did not want the sitting room themselves, I never saw any reason why I should not avail myself of it. No sooner, therefore, were they safe off than I betook myself there, and proceeded to make myself comfortable, according to my usual practice, during their absence. Lying on the table were some English newspapers that had just arrived, and I began to read them. In a column devoted to fashionable intelligence, I presently came upon the following paragraph – to me most entirely unexpected.

"The Duke of Murkshire and his family, who are at present in the French metropolis, will probably return at an early date to their ancestral halls, in order to make preparations for the marriage of his Grace's eldest daughter, Lady Emma, to Captain Edward Norroy of the

Scots Fusilier Guards. The engagement of the young couple has just been announced, and the wedding is, we understand, to take place shortly."

When I had read this I laid down the paper, feeling perfectly dazed. Captain Norroy going to be married to this Lady Emma! In my speculations about Kitty and her love affairs I had – without being aware of it – invariably put aside as absurd the idea of its being possible that anyone whom she might honour with her preference *could* remain indifferent to her; and therefore I had all along been unconsciously taking it for granted that Captain Norroy must inevitably fall in love with her sooner or later; and that if she did not eventually become his wife, it would not be at any rate for want of the opportunity. I knew well enough that I myself should have been at her feet if she had but held up her little finger to me. And as one is apt to consider it a matter of course that attractions by which one is oneself fascinated must be equally irresistible to other people, it was consequently not much to be wondered at that I should now be utterly taken aback at finding the man whom I believed her to care for was going to marry someone else.

The thing seemed to me hardly credible. He must be blind – a dolt and fool – to have a prize like Kitty within his reach, and let it slip! Why, there was no one so attractive and charming as she was; she was (in my eyes) quite incomparable. And though I had never seen this Lady Emma, and knew nothing whatever about her, I was none the less firmly convinced that she could not hold a candle to Kitty in any single respect.

How would Kitty take the news, I wondered? Had she any expectation of it? Had the possibility of such a thing ever occurred to her? No; I had an intuitive conviction to the contrary. When she had met him at Raoul's her manner had shown not only shyness and nervousness, there had been something more – something indefinable, of pleasure and hope – which made me feel sure that she had believed him to be heart-whole, and not the property of any other girl, or about to become so. Had she been in England, she would no doubt have heard some of the gossip by which the engagements of people conspicuous in society are usually preceded; but her recent absence abroad had, of course, prevented any rumours of a flirtation between Captain Norroy and Lady Emma from reaching her ears; and she must now be totally unprepared to hear they were going to be married. Of course, it would not matter to her an atom if she were fancy-free about him, and if the romance I had constructed was a baseless one. But then I was almost positive that it was *not* baseless, and that the news would be a blow to her, though she would doubtless strain every nerve to conceal that fact.

My poor Kitty, thought I sorrowfully; and, immediately afterwards, laughed at my own folly. How could I be so silly as to prefix the possessive pronoun singular to the name of a person who was not mine at all? Though she had always been kind and courteous to me, yet her manner showed plainly that she regarded me as one of an inferior order, between whom and herself existed, naturally, an impassable barrier; and knowing this, why should I concern myself about her troubles, as if she and I had been on terms of equality and intimate friendship? It would be ridiculous to do anything of the kind. Had I not resolved before now that I would put a check upon the inclination to be fascinated by her, of which I was conscious? Certainly I had; and yet how was I keeping that resolution if I let myself take her affairs to heart, and feel sorry for her, and indignant with Captain Norroy, as I was inclined to be at that moment? Provoked to see in myself such a disposition to be weakly sentimental, I was glad when my common-sense and turn for ridicule bestirred themselves, and applied mentally a douche of cold water which cooled down my first absurd impulse to be her ardent partisan.

After all, her affairs were no business of mine, and it was mere folly to let myself be vexed about them in any way. It could do no possible good, and I should be simply making myself uncomfortable for nothing. Besides, if she could see into my mind, I might be very sure that she would not approve of her maid's presuming to take so much interest in her affairs, and would consider me impertinent and officious.

Sensible reflections of this kind effectually repressed my previous tendency to a foolish softheartedness; and I resumed my interrupted perusal of the newspaper, and amused myself placidly during the rest of the afternoon till nearly dinnertime, when my mistresses returned.

I went to dress Kitty, wondering whether or not she had yet heard of Captain Norroy's engagement. Anyhow, if she had, it had not troubled her at all, for she was evidently in excellent spirits; and in that respect presented a marked contrast to her aunt, who came into her room during toilette operations, and who – as it was easy to see – had something on her mind which disturbed her. At first, I took it into my head, from this uneasiness, that Mrs. Rollin must have some suspicion of her niece's being attached to Captain Norroy, and that, having heard of his engagement to Lady Emma, she must now be worrying herself as to how Kitty would take the news, and as to the unhappiness the girl might suffer on account of it. But, from what was said, I speedily discovered that Mrs. Rollin's disquietude arose from a very different cause – neither more nor less than a pair of stays.

"Do you know, Kitty," she said, "that I've been thinking, ever since we left Jarrot's, of your flat refusal to have anything to do with that pair of stays she wanted you to wear. I cannot feel satisfied that you decided wisely. It's still not too late to change your mind, you know. Are you *sure* you won't give them a trial, and see how you like them?"

Kitty laughed as if the scene at the dressmaker's was an amusing one to recollect.

"Yes, I'm quite positive I won't," she answered; "they were at least three inches too small for me, and I really *couldn't* consent to such a wholesale diminution of the circumference of my waist! I suppose you are moved to plead for them by the recollection of Jarrot's horror and distress when she found my objection to them was quite invincible. Really I don't wonder. Her look of shocked and surprised grief would have been pathetic if the cause hadn't made it comic; and I was quite sorry to have to wound her feelings so deeply."

"Oh no, my dear, of course, it isn't *that,*" returned Mrs. Rollin, somewhat pettishly; "what have I got to do with a dressmaker's feelings? But what I was thinking of was, her declaring that small waists are becoming so much the rage as to be almost indispensable; and that no lady who cares to be *bien mise* ever *thinks* of objecting to have her waist reduced to the smallest size possible. Jarrot is safe to be a good authority on the subject, because she is employed by quite the *crème de la crème* of society. I am afraid you think only of what you like; and forget that people who don't do the same as their fellows are sure to be rash, even if not wrong."

"Only, then, one must draw a line somewhere," replied Kitty; "and I draw it at having my internal arrangements shoved out of their places. Not even to possess a small waist will I endure that! Jarrot regarded it as a mere temporary inconvenience, to which I should soon get reconciled, because she thought that what is comfortable is simply whatever one was used to. But there I don't agree with her. It amused me to see how confidently she quoted *il faut souffrir pour être belle,* as if that must certainly settle the question. Somehow or other, even that argument failed to persuade me to make myself ill, though I am not a whit more deficient in vanity and care for my personal appearance than the rest of my sex."

Mrs. Rollin sighed. "If you won't, you won't, of course," she said; "still I should have thought you might have made the attempt to do as others do, just for a little bit, as she wanted you to."

"You see I'm too fond of my precious comfort," answered Kitty, merrily; "and, do you know, aunty, I've a great idea that I'm not the only person in the family with that weakness; and that you, too, sometimes like to go your own way, even if it isn't exactly the cut-and-dried path followed by everyone else."

"Kitty, Kitty, you shouldn't say things like that," expostulated her aunt; "you know that I consider being different from other people to be a proof of an ill-regulated mind; and that, therefore, to accuse me of eccentric tastes is equivalent to saying I deserve blame. Please remember that I *strongly* object to your speaking in such a most inconsiderate manner."

"All right, aunt," said Kitty, good humouredly; "I'm sorry I vexed you – I'll be more careful another time. I didn't for a moment mean to imply that you aren't all you should be, you know."

But though she said this, I don't think it followed that she believed Mrs. Rollin's mind to be always in absolute conformity with its own standard of perfection. Anyhow, there was a twinkle in Kitty's eye, which made me doubtful on the subject.

Their toilettes being now completed, they descended to dinner, leaving me quite satisfied that Kitty had no secret grief oppressing her. It must be one of two things, then, I thought, as I watched her going downstairs: either my theory is wrong from beginning to end, or else she as yet knows nothing of this approaching marriage. However, it is very likely that she may not have had time to look at the papers yet, as they had only just come before she went out.

When next I saw her it was very different; and I no longer doubted that I had been right in thinking she cared for Captain Norroy. About an hour after dinner was over I was in her room arranging some clothes, when the door opened, and she entered. Her head was drooping, instead of being carried proudly thrown back as usual; her face was deadly pale, and wore an expression of misery. On seeing her like this, I felt sure that she must have just read the paragraph concerning him, and had rushed off to be alone, so that she might be relieved from the irksome restraint imposed by the presence of other people, and might let her features relax for a while into whatever expression of pain came natural to them.

In taking refuge in her own room she had evidently forgotten the possibility of anyone being there; for as soon as she saw me she started violently, and seemed to strive to replace the mask, and look the same as usual for a few moments longer.

"You can leave those things for the present, Jill," she said, controlling her voice with an effort; "I have come to lie down, as I have rather a bad headache."

I saw she longed to have me gone, and as I did not want to add to her troubles, I prepared to take myself off as quickly as possible. But I was bound to play my part of lady's-maid; and as I knew that it would be an unheard-of solecism for such an official not to profess sympathy – whether she really felt it or not – with her mistress' ailments, I was obliged to pause a moment before departing, that I might express concern for her headache, and ask if I should bring her a cup of tea or coffee, or if there was anything else I could do for her. My offer, however, was not accepted.

"All I want is to be left quiet," she said, rather impatiently; "if I want you I will ring."

I withdrew accordingly. She stayed in her room by herself during the remainder of the evening, saying that her headache was still bad. At bedtime she summoned me to assist her as usual, and I thought she looked perfectly wretched. She meant, however, to keep up appearances, for when her aunt came in to inquire how she was, and say good night, she exerted herself to seem as lively as usual. She declared that her headache was all the fault of those stays Jarrot had wanted her to have. The mere idea of such an enormity of tininess had so shocked her nerves, liver, lungs, brain, and organs in general, that they had felt bound to make some forcible demonstration of disgust; and the demonstration had taken the shape of a headache. A night's rest would put her all right, she said, if she did not dream about those horrid stays; but if she were to have a nightmare about wearing them, she really could not say *what* might be the consequences to her health. This nonsense was uttered with enough of her customary vivacity to deceive Mrs. Rollin, who went away, quite satisfied that there was nothing the matter except an ordinary headache. But *I* thought differently. I had seen Kitty's lips quivering while she spoke, and had seen unmistakable traces of tears in her eyes; I had felt that her head was burning hot, and the rest of her body like ice; and these things made me believe that there was something more amiss with her than a mere commonplace headache.

When I had performed my duties for the night, and gone to my own room, my heart *would* keep aching for her, in spite of my efforts to restore it to its habitual condition of sensible hardness. Our recent adventures in Corsica had taught me that she would face death and danger unflinchingly; and I knew her to be exceptionally proud, strong, and brave. Yet for all her strength, courage, and pride, she seemed to be almost broken down tonight. And it naturally moves one more to see such a person as that give way than to witness the upsetting of a weaker mortal.

Anxiety about her, as I pictured to myself her solitary suffering, and longed to be able to comfort her, kept me awake and restless. What if she were to have a brain fever, or a nervous fever, or some other kind of illness such as I had heard of being brought on by a sudden mental shock? Perhaps at that very moment she was ill, and in need of assistance. So uneasy did I become, that at last I could stay away from her no longer, but determined to relieve my mind by going at once to assure myself of her well-being.

I got up accordingly, put on a dressing-gown, and stole quietly to the door of her room, where I stood listening for a minute, and wondering whether she had had the good fortune to fall asleep. No; for I heard a deep sigh, followed by an inarticulate, moaning sound, which – though so low as to be hardly audible – had something about it that seemed to me unutterably sad and forlorn. An incontrollable impulse seized me to go to her and try if I could not find some way of being of use or comfort to her. But I could not enter the room unless she choose to admit me, for she always kept her door locked at night when in a hotel. I knocked gently, and she responded, *"Qui est-ce?"*

"It is Jill," I replied; "may I come in? I came to see if your head is still bad? and if so, if I shall bathe it with eau de cologne, or fetch you anything, or try and read you to sleep, or do anything else for you?"

"Oh no, thanks," she answered in a weary voice; "pray go to bed and leave me, for I am better to be quite alone. You know if I want anything I can ring."

Was the reminder of the bell intended as a gentle hint that it was officious to disturb her with an offer of services which she could command if she required them? That was the light in which I regarded it, at all events; and I left her door, feeling that I had been a fool for my pains, and richly deserved the snub I had received, I asked myself scornfully what had made me try to obtain admittance into the room? what good it could have been? and what I supposed I should have done had she opened the door to me? Should I have flung my arms around her, and told her that I knew all, and was come to comfort her, or behaved in some similarly gushing manner? Most certainly not! I knew better than to imagine that an absurd demonstration of that kind would gratify her from anyone, and, least of all, from a servant. Besides, when she was doing all she could to keep her trouble and its cause a profound secret, it would hardly have been a happy method of consolation to go and inform her that her efforts had failed, and that her secret was no secret at all. What, then, *should* I have done? I had not the remotest notion, and was forced to confess that my impulse to be with her had been simply a piece of senti-mental, impractical folly, which it was very lucky I had not been able to indulge. I could not possibly have done anything to help her, and it would clearly have been wiser and kinder of me to have left her in peace; and, laughing at myself bitterly, and feeling decidedly small and ridiculous in my own eyes, I retired to bed.

CHAPTER XXII

Notice to Quit

MY fears lest Kitty's health might be affected by what had happened proved unfounded. By next morning she had got herself once more in hand, and I did not again see the expression of utter abandonment to misery which had been visible on her face the previous night at the moment when she entered her room, and before she was aware of my presence there. If ever she allowed herself to look like that again, I expect it was not until she had made quite sure first that there was no human being within reach to see what her countenance might betray.

Some change in her, however, it was impossible that there should not be, after the great and sudden mental commotion which she had experienced. I observed that she was paler than her wont, and had black marks under her eyes, which, when commented on by her aunt, she accounted for as being the results of her violent headache. I saw, too, that when she was not laughing or talking, and her features were in repose, they settled into a hard stern expression which they had not worn before; and that there was in her eyes a new look of haughty defiance, as though they were challenging the whole world to penetrate one hair's-breadth further than she chose into the locked casket of her inner self. In other respects she was outwardly unaltered, and went about and conducted herself in much the same way as usual. The first shock of the blow had made her stagger for an instant, but she had never broken down altogether, and was now prepared to stand firm, and give no sign of pain. Natures like hers, endowed with strength, pluck, and indomitable pride, are generally more likely to be embittered than crushed when trouble and disappointment comes upon them.

Just at this period my studies of Kitty's character were cut short abruptly, and my own concerns forced themselves unpleasantly into the foreground, and demanded exclusive attention.

Whilst I had been abroad my mind had been fully occupied with the various incidents of our travels, and I had forgotten all about my quondam-admirer Perkins, Lord Mervyn's valet. Unluckily, however, he had not been equally oblivious of me; for, in rejecting his attentions and causing the loss of his cherished whiskers, I had inflicted an injury that he could neither forgive nor forget, and for which he had vowed vengeance. When, therefore, chance unkindly enabled him to discover an opportunity for doing me a bad turn, he lost no time in profiting by it; and the effect which his malice had upon my fortunes I was now to experience.

The day before we were to leave Paris and return to England, I was up in my room, beginning to pack my box, when a housemaid came to tell me to go to Kitty, who was in her bedroom, and wished to see me. I obeyed the summons immediately, without a suspicion of impending trouble; but my tranquillity vanished as soon as I reached her room, and caught sight of her face. She was sitting by the writing-table, and looked up at me, on my entrance, with an air of cold dignified displeasure, which showed me plainly there was something wrong, and that I was in her black books for some cause or other. What the dickens is the matter? I thought. I began hastily considering what recent actions of mine to which she was likely to object could have come to her ears; but I could not recollect any misdemeanour important enough to make her look so displeased. I wished I could guess what sort of accusation was going to be brought against me, so that I might know whether to prepare denial, excuse, or frank confession. For which of these three would be the best defence for me to offer must obviously depend upon what likelihood there was that the real truth would be ascertained.

"I have to speak to you, Jill," she said, "about a most disagreeable matter. A letter which I have just received from my mother tells me that she has seen Sir Bartholomew Brown, who has lately returned to London, and that when she questioned him about you he denied all knowledge of anyone of your name, or answering to your description; declared that no such person had ever been in his service; and that the character, purporting to have been written by him, which you produced in applying for our situation, was a forgery. What have you to say to this?"

That was just what I did not know myself; for I was completely dumbfounded by this sudden attack from a quarter where I had anticipated no danger. Why on earth could not Sir Bartholomew have stayed in the East, as he had been supposed to be going to do? In vain did I rack my brains for some way of extricating myself from this dilemma. Not a single idea would occur to me, so I simply remained silent – a course which had, at all events, the recommendation of not committing me one way or other.

Kitty waited for a little while; and then, perceiving that I did not intend to answer, she said:

"Am I to understand by your silence that you are unable to contradict the truth of what Sir Bartholomew said?"

"Oh, if you *choose* to understand it so, m'm, of course I can't help that," replied I, shrugging my shoulders, and still evading a direct admission of the charge which it was evidently useless for me to dispute.

"I do not choose it at all," she returned quickly; "on the contrary, I should greatly prefer to find that you are able to clear yourself. But I wish to have a definite answer from you, either yes or no, when I ask – Is the thing true?"

I hesitated for a moment. Then, seeing that I could gain nothing by denying, and that to tell a lie about it would only sink me yet lower in her eyes without doing me the least good, I replied desperately, "'Well – yes."

For a few minutes she did not speak, and sat with her head resting on her hand, and apparently reflecting about something. At last she said:

"I have been considering what to do. My mother thinks that you should at once be given in charge of the police; but that I do not feel inclined to do, after what we went through together in Corsica the other day, and the way in which you behaved then. Besides, I have had no cause of complaint since you have been with me, and I think you have served *me* well – whatever you may have done elsewhere. Therefore, though of course I dismiss you, yet I wish to treat you with no needless harshness. I propose, then, that you should continue to be my maid for a day longer, so as not to leave me till we arrive in London. Thus you will not be turned adrift in a foreign country, as would be the case if I discharged you here, on the spot; you will also have been brought back to whence you came, and be left in no worse position than you were before entering our service. As for your wages, I shall, of course, pay them to you fully. If you like this arrangement – which is, I think, as favourable a one as you can expect – I am quite willing to make it. I daresay some people would say I ought not to let you stay an hour longer in my service; and that all the thanks I shall get is to be laughed at, and perhaps robbed, by a person who has already shown herself to be a forger. But I would rather take my chance of that than have to reproach myself with having wronged you."

I did not like her to think worse of me than I deserved, and for a moment I felt very much inclined to tell her who I was, in order that she might see that circumstances had really *compelled* me to act as I had done. For if I had not forged a character to start with, how could I ever have obtained a chance of earning one honestly? I think I should inevitably have yielded to the inclination, and imparted my history to her there and then, if there had been anything in her manner to make me believe that I had won a footing, however low down, in her affection – that she cared about me just one little bit. But there was no such indication. She would not defraud me of one atom that might be due for the services I had rendered, because it would have wounded her own self-respect to do that. But I saw (or imagined myself to see) that the consideration she showed for me was dictated solely by a sense of justice, and not by any softer feeling; and the rising impulse to confide in her was frozen back by the cold, haughty severity of her demeanour towards one whom she regarded as a mere common cheat and forger. Consequently I only replied stiffly that I was much obliged for her offer, which I should be glad to accept; and that she might depend upon it I would not give her cause to repent of her kindness.

"Very well," she returned; "then we will consider the matter settled so, and you will leave me when we get to Charing Cross. By the by, I may as well let you know that I have not told my aunt of what I heard today, and that I shall not do so till after you have left. It would only fuss her needlessly."

Then I withdrew, feeling extremely provoked at the turn affairs had taken, and heartily anathematising Sir Bartholomew for having come back to England so inopportunely, instead of staying in the East, as he had been expected to do. How unlucky, too, that Lady Mervyn should have happened to meet him, and to have had nothing better to talk about than *me!* The more I thought about it, the more extraordinary did it seem that she should have ever troubled herself to mention me to him: for, from what I knew of her ladyship, I should have thought that a lady's-maid was far too insignificant to be honoured by being made a topic of her conversation with a stranger – that is to say, unless there had been some special reason for it; and I did not think any such reason was likely to have existed in this instance. Very likely the letter she had written to Kitty about me would contain some enlightenment on this point. If only I could get hold of that document, I would see; but the chances were that I should not be able to lay hands on it, as Kitty rarely left correspondence about – a carefulness which deprived her maids of a good deal of the amusement they might otherwise have had. On this occasion, however, fortune favoured my desires. When Kitty changed her dress that evening, in taking her handkerchief, purse, and other et-ceteras out of her pocket, she dropped a letter on the floor without noticing its fall; I, who was standing close by and helping her, instantly covered it with my dress, in hopes it might be the epistle I wanted to see; I managed to keep it under my feet and dress till she was looking in another direction, and then shoved it under the skirts of the toilette-table, where it was safely out of sight. She finished dressing, and went down to dinner, without having perceived the loss; and as soon as the coast was clear, I rushed to the table, and extracted the letter, which I had hidden there. On opening it, I found, to my delight, that it was the one from Lady Mervyn about me; the contents sufficiently explained why she should have condescended to discuss so humble an individual as myself with Sir Bartholomew, showing that it was all owing to the interference of Perkins, and that I had only him to thank for the misfortune by which I was now overtaken. After relating what I already had heard from Kitty, Lady Mervyn went on to say:

"It was only by the merest accident that we came to hear anything about the matter. Your father's valet, Perkins, is member of some club or other (fancy one's servants having clubs, like gentlemen! I can't think why parliament doesn't make them illegal), to which a man who used to be with Sir Bartholomew belongs also. With this man Perkins happened to make acquaintance, and, on hearing where he had been in service, asked him if he knew Lady Brown's last maid, Jill, who was now abroad with you."

Ah, thought I, when I had read so far, I can quite believe that that spiteful wretch Perkins, directly he thought he had met an old fellow-servant of mine, lost no time in going spying and sniffing about, and trying to rake up some ill-natured story against me! *I* know his tricks and his manners, as the doll's dressmaker in *Our Mutual Friend* used to say.

"When Perkins said that, however," continued the letter, "the man stared at him, and declared he was talking nonsense. Lady Brown's last maid, the man asserted, had been called Smith; had married a man named Roberts soon after her mistress's death; and had then gone with her husband to live at Liverpool, where she had been ever since, to his positive knowledge. This seemed very odd to Perkins, and made him suspect there was something amiss, so he, very properly, told me of what he had heard. As it happened that Sir Bartholomew had returned to England, I had no difficulty in learning the truth from the fountainhead; and now that I have just had an interview with him, I write at once to tell you the result. *Of course* you will not lose a moment about handing the odious woman over to the police as a forger and impostor. I shan't be a bit surprised to find that they want her already, and know lots of other things against her; goodness only knows what she is – thief, coiner, swindler, incendiary, or anything! It is so lucky that we should have found her out in time. Mind that you see all your things are quite right, and if they are not, have her boxes searched. Don't pay her anything, by the by. I should not think a person who gets a situation as she has done can claim wages – it would be getting money under false pretences, I fancy. At any rate, there's no need to hurry about paying until we find out whether we are legally bound to or not."

Having perused the letter I folded it up, and replaced it where Kitty had let it fall on the floor, so that she might find it there whenever she missed it, and went to search for it.

One thing, at all events, the letter proved clearly, and that was that Lady Mervyn's servants had spoken with perfect truth when they said she was mean; for how contemptibly mean and petty was her suggestion about withholding my wages! It seemed to me that as I had earned them honestly I was unquestionably entitled to them, whatever my character might be. And I might conclude that Kitty, who was not so little-minded as her mother, and whose pride made her incapable of an ignoble action, took the same view of the matter that I did; for I knew that if she had intended obeying her mother's instructions about dismissing me unpaid, she would certainly not have mentioned, as she had done, that I was to receive the full amount due to me. Honour and truth were integral parts of her character, and apparent in all her dealings; and though I was not myself sensitively particular about those things, yet I could not help admiring them in her all the same.

Well, I had not deserved badly of her, I thought; and in reviewing my past conduct it seemed to me that, on the whole, she had not much reason to complain of me. No doubt, my acquisition of her purse at the railway station had been somewhat questionable; but, after all, it had only been picked up – not stolen; and my subsequent retention of it had been caused chiefly by pique, because my feelings had been hurt for the moment, when I found that she had forgotten me. Since I had been her maid I had, I considered, served her faithfully enough; and so I would continue to do during the short remaining period of being in her service. This resolution, be it said, was prompted by no ulterior views of self-interest, as I was quite aware of the impossibility of my ever referring to her for a character. But she had declined to rob me of my wages and send me to prison, as her mother would have had her do, and had also troubled herself to soften the dismissal in some way, and I wished to show that I appreciated the consideration with which she had treated me, and was not ungrateful for it. Consequently I omitted nothing that it was in my power to do for her comfort on the journey back to England, and performed my duties as her maid up to the last moment of quitting her every bit as zealously as though I had hoped to gain some advantage by my attentions.

At Charing Cross Station we separated, to the intense astonishment of her aunt, who as yet knew nothing of what had taken place. They went one way and I went another; and thus I was cut off from the first person I had ever come across who possessed the gift of arousing the sluggish capacity for affection which lay dormant in my cold-blooded nature. Our being parted was entirely the doing of that abominable Perkins; and, as I looked after her with a sigh, I relegated him to the same place as my stepmother amongst my enemies, and regarded him with sentiments of similar detestation.

CHAPTER XXIII

A Doggy Place

WHEN first cut adrift from Kitty, I felt disgusted with service and had a great mind not to be a maid again, because I knew I should hate waiting on any other mistress. But people who have to earn their own living cannot afford to be fanciful, and reflection soon showed me the unwisdom of throwing up in a pet a profession in which I had now acquired some little experience; so, within a couple of days after my return to London, I was once more advertising for a place as travelling maid.

The next consideration was how I was to get myself a character, as I certainly could not apply to my late employers for one. Of course it was open to me to supply myself with it in the same way I had done before; but though I had then thought it a good joke and laughed at the deception I practised, yet somehow I did not find myself taking to the idea nearly as kindly now. I had been in the habit of making fools of people for the mere fun of the thing, and had regarded a falsehood much as the historian Green says that Queen Elizabeth did, *i.e.* as an intellectual means of meeting a difficulty. But my views seemed to have undergone an alteration of late, and I was conscious of a certain amount of repugnance for what was untrue, which perhaps showed that my intercourse with Kitty had had some effect in educating my conscience, and that I had imbibed something of her contempt for lies. Therefore I hesitated about writing a false character; and no doubt my scruples were all the more lively in consequence of my recent detection and narrow escape of prosecution for forgery; for I had a horror of going to prison.

Consider as I might, however, I could see no honest way out of the difficulty. A character I *must* have, as without one I had no chance of a situation, and without a situation I should starve. And as I had no one to give me a character, I was bound to give it myself. So – with a sigh for my own roguery – I took a pen and indited an epistle, highly recommending Caroline Jill, from a lady with whom she had lived two years and eight months, and who, before departing for the Cape (where she did not want to be accompanied by a maid) had written this character for the aforesaid Jill. I flatter myself it was an artistic composition, decidedly complimentary, and yet not ascribing to me such perfection as might arouse suspicion by its incompatibility with the frailty of human nature.

After waiting for two or three weeks without receiving a single answer to my advertisement, and searching the papers diligently during that time without discovering any place advertised of the kind that I wanted, I came to the conclusion that travelling-maids were at a discount just at present. Living in lodgings and earning nothing was too expensive a process to be continued long, so it seemed to me that I had better alter my plans, and try and be something which was *not* at a discount. Should I go in for being a shopwoman? But that was a monotonous existence, I thought, with not enough chance of variety and amusement to suit me. And then it struck me that I might let my talents as courier-maid lie idle for a while, and try for an ordinary lady's-maid's situation. I knew that my lack of dressmaking knowledge was much against that scheme; but still I *might* have the luck to meet with one of those ladies who always have their dresses made out. At any rate I determined to make the attempt.

As soon as possible next morning I procured one or two newspapers, copied the addresses of as many advertisers for ladies-maids as I should be able to go and see in the day, and set off to call upon these ladies. At every place, however, I found that dressmaking was an indispensable qualification, and I returned to my lodgings weary and unsuccessful. Next day I repeated the process with no better result; and on the third day also it was just the same story over again. Wherever I went there was a universal demand for dressmaking on the part of the maid; and I began to wonder if, in all England, there existed such a person as a struggling dressmaker; and if so, why she did not instantly take to lady's-maiding.

Though discouraged by these repeated failures, I thought I would still persevere a little longer before giving up, and accordingly started on a fourth day's round as before. In the course of them I came to the house of a Mrs. Torwood, who lived in Chester Square. My ring at her bell was not answered for several minutes, and I was thinking of repeating it when a noise something like a miniature steam-engine approaching from within the house made me pause to see what was coming. Directly afterwards the door was opened, and I perceived that the puffing and blowing I had heard proceeded from a fat, apoplectic-looking man-servant, to whom stairs were evidently antipathetic, and who was panting tremendously after his ascent from the inferior regions to the front door. Being too much out of breath to waste words, he only nodded affirmatively when I inquired whether his mistress was at home and disengaged.

"Then please will you go and tell her," I said, "that I have called about the maid's place, and ask if she can see me now?"

By this time he had recovered sufficiently to be able to speak.

"Why it's *hanother* of 'em! Is this hever going to hend?" he groaned in a melancholy voice, when he heard what my errand was. Then, some happy thought seemed to occur to him, for his face brightened, and he muttered to himself, "But why shouldn't she and me settle it? *I'll* soon see if its hany good her going further." And without stirring from the spot, or giving the slightest indication of any intention of taking my message, he addressed me thus:

"'Scuse me hasking, miss, but was your father, or hany near rela*tive* of yours, a 'untsman?"

"No," I answered; whereupon his countenance fell a little, and he resumed:

"Or a gamekeeper, p'raps?"

I repeated the negative, and he looked still more disappointed, but continued:

"No hoffence, miss, if I hasks one more question, and that is, 'ave you hever, in hany way, bin abitooally brought in con tack with kennels, or packs of 'ounds?"

I shook my head; feeling not a little astonished at all this questioning.

"Hah, then there's not a ghost of a chance as you'll take the place," he exclaimed regretfully, "and you may as well say good day, for I can't in conshence hadvise you to go a wasting of your vallyable time with seeing the missis! I'm sorry – very; for I'm quite sick of a hopening this old door to maids come about the sitooation, and I did 'ope as you might 'ave done, and put a hend to it. But it's no use; from what you've told me, I can see plainly as you won't do."

That the man was a character was evident; but as I was getting tired of standing talking to him, and did not at all wish to receive his confidences about his employers, I politely reiterated my former request that he would go and find out if his mistress would see me.

"Well; but 'aven't I just *told* you as it's no good?" he returned, looking at me with an air of aggrieved surprise. "When I tells you as I *knows* as you hain't the individooal for the place, can't you go hoff agin quietly, without a giving no more trouble? If you 'aven't no considerashin for yourself, you might 'ave some for *me,* and not give me all the wear and tear of toiling hup a lot of steps just for nothing."

The seriousness with which he seemed to expect that I should accept his opinion, and be satisfied to go away without having seen the lady of the house, was intensely ludicrous, and I had some difficulty in keeping my countenance.

"I am quite grieved to be so troublesome," I said, "but I have a strange fancy for always making sure for myself whether a place will suit me or not, and I'm afraid I really must ask you to be so good as to let the lady know I am here."

He did not at all resent this (to him, probably, incomprehensible) pertinacity on my part, but only put on a sort of resigned-martyr air, saying:

"Come halong then, since you hinsists hupon it. But you'll soon find as I was right, and p'raps that'll make you less hinkredulous of my words hanother time. If you honly knowed what a lot of maids I've a took hup these 'ere blessid stairs and down hagain, all for nothing! Putting a hunfair strain hupon a man's lungs, *I* considers it; but there! – people *are* so thoughtless."

He took care to reduce the strain upon his lungs to a minimum by making me accompany him as far as the first landing on the stairs, and wait there whilst he proceeded to the drawing-room. Thus, when he had ascertained that his mistress would see me, it was only necessary for him to lean over the bannisters and beckon, whereby he avoided having to descend any steps to fetch me, and could wait placidly till I joined him on the first floor to be ushered into Mrs. Torwood's presence.

There were dogs dispersed about the room in all directions, and my entrance was the signal for a sudden chorus of sharp barks, which gave me some clue to a comprehension of the butler's enigmatical allusions to a kennel. It would have been impossible to hear oneself speak had the clamour continued; but it subsided as quickly as it had arisen, and, with two exceptions, the dogs took no more notice of me. One exception was a terrier, who uttered subdued yaps at intervals, as if half-ashamed of it; and the other was a collie, who thought he would like my umbrella (which I held in my hand), and who kept sidling up with an innocent air, and giving unobtrusive tugs at the coveted object from time to time, apparently in hopes of getting possession of it at some unguarded moment when I might be too much engrossed in talking to his mistress to notice his proceedings. The rest of the dogs, however, evidently thought that they had done their duty conscientiously when they had pro-claimed my advent, and that there was no need to pursue the subject further. Very possibly they considered barking to be the proper canine equivalent to the human practice of announcing a visitor's name, which is only done on the visitor's entrance, and not repeated afterwards.

Mrs. Torwood looked to me pretty, elegantly dressed, and silly, and I guessed her age to be about thirty. She began by asking me my name; after I had told her that, I expected the usual queries as to qualifications would follow, and waited with dread for the mention of that abominable dressmaking which had so often been my rock ahead. But her next remark was quite unlike anything I had anticipated. She hesitated a moment, and then said:

"You see these dogs of mine? Well, I can assure you that they are the nicest, best-behaved darlings possible, and not a bit of trouble. Why anyone should mind doing anything for them, I can't conceive; but so many maids *do* object to it, for some unaccountable reason or other, that I had better tell you at once that I expect my maid to brush and comb these dogs every morning and take them out walking, besides washing them once a week. So if you would dislike that, of course it is no use my thinking of engaging you."

Certainly this was rather a variety on the ordinary ideas of what a lady's-maid's duties would be; but as I had always been fond of animals, I did not feel averse to the notion. Still, as Mrs. Torwood evidently thought it likely that I should make difficulties about undertaking the dogs, I would not be in too great a hurry to consent, and would appear to make rather a favour of it. So I paused to consider, and then asked: "How many dogs are there to look after, m-m?"

"There are six at present," she replied; "but of course, if I were to get any new ones, you would have them also."

It flashed upon me that here was an excellent opportunity for escaping the demand for dressmaking which had hitherto been my stumbling block at every place for which I had applied.

"I have never been expected to take care of any lower animals before," I said, speaking as like a dignified lady's-maid as I could; "still, I would not object to oblige you by doing so, provided no dressmaking is required."

"Why not?" she inquired, looking surprised. "Because I know I should not have time for it," I answered. "Oh, but the dogs won't take you the whole day," she returned. "I don't say you would have time for a great deal of dressmaking. But surely you might manage just a little – especially if you weren't hurried about it?"

"There will be you to wait upon, and your clothes to keep in order, m-m," said I, "and that, with washing, combing, and taking out six dogs, is quite as much as I could *think* of undertaking to get through in the day; because if I undertook anything more, I know I should only fail to give you satisfaction."

She hesitated. She had, however, met with so many maids who had from the first moment flatly refused to have to do with her pets, that one like me, who had no objection to them, seemed to her a *rara avis*. Besides, her present maid was just going away, and she was in a hurry to secure another. And therefore, after a little more opposition, my firmness carried the day, and the obnoxious dressmaking was conceded. Then we discussed other details, and I had to produce the character with which I was provided. This, and the account of myself which I gave, being deemed satisfactory, the interview terminated in my engagement as her maid – upon which office I was to enter in another three days. She rang the bell when I left the room, and in the hall I found the fat butler waiting to see that I left the premises without committing any depredations on the plate or other portable property.

"Well; so now you knows as I was right, I s'pose, and that you might as well 'ave gone away at once when I told you," he observed.

"Not exactly," I returned, "seeing that I have taken the situation."

"You don't say so!" he cried joyfully, elevating his eyebrows in extreme surprise. "Thank goodness for that; and I honly 'opes as you'll keep it, so as I shan't 'ave no more worrit with maids coming about the place! What haggeravated me, you see, was knowing all the time as they was *sure* not to take it, and that I was just a trotting hup and down them beastly old stairs, all for nothing. A man doesn't like to think as he's being sackerified in vain; and that there's no hobjeck in heggsershuns sitch as may land him in a consumpshun or a hastma."

"But you made sure once too often," I said, laughing; "you declared that it was no use showing *me* upstairs, and yet you were wrong, you see."

"Not a bit of it," he retorted severely; "no young 'ooman need think as she'll make me out wrong so heasy as all that. Did you never 'ear tell of the eggsepshun as proves the rule? Because that's what *you* are, let me tell you; and I doesn't form my judgement by eggsepshuns but by rules! Precious slow those eggsepshuns are in showing theirselves, too, sometimes. I've known one keep a man waiting till he's just wore out, instead of 'urrying to the fore sharp when 'twas wanted, as it *might* 'a done."

Having thus refuted the charge of error, and given me a pretty broad hint that I – by not making my appearance on the scene sooner – had incurred the responsibility of his numerous needless journeys up and downstairs on behalf of aspirant maids, he relaxed his severity, and bid me goodbye with a graciousness which showed he bore no malice for the injuries I had done him.

I returned his farewell civilly, little dreaming that this man would ever give me a means of annoying my hated step-mother; then I went straight to buy a dog-whistle, which seemed to me a most essential article for Mrs. Torwood's maid to possess.

It was on that same day, I remember, that the papers announced the engagement of the Hon. K. Mervyn to Lord Clement. I had not expected it to come quite so soon, but otherwise I was not at all surprised; for I had never doubted that the Earl's chance of winning her would go up as soon as Captain Norroy was out of the question.

CHAPTER XXIV

A Discovery

MRS. TORWOOD was lady-like, good-natured, indolent, rather foolish, easily-influenced, not difficult to get on with, and thinking more of her clothes, her appearance, and her dogs, than anything else. She spoilt these last terribly, and let them do whatever they pleased. But I liked them for all that; indeed, if it had not been for them, I doubt whether I should not have found myself too much bored in the situation to stay there, for their mistress was very uninteresting in my eyes, and did not move about enough to please me. Her pets, however, had considerably more individuality than she had, and afforded me sufficient amusement and occupation to keep me contented. As my ignorance of dressmaking had prevented me from getting other places that I had tried for, and as it was through the dogs that I had at last sur-mounted that obstacle, mere gratitude would have prompted me to do well by them, even if the work of looking after them had been distasteful to me. But this was not the case, thanks to my fondness for animals; and it was not long before they and I were on the best of terms together.

In some respects, however, they caused me a good deal of anxiety. The chief of these causes was the daily airing which it was my duty to give them; and I was always thankful to find myself safely at home again without either of my charges being lost or stolen, or having got into any mischief. I used to take them out singly and in a chain just at first; and as soon as our acquaintance was sufficiently advanced for me to discard the chain, I took them two at a time. But I did not venture to go beyond that number when in town, as all the dear creatures had some little characteristic peculiarity or other, which made it necessary to keep a sharp look-out upon each individual during the whole walk, if one did not want to lose them or get into a scrape. If I enumerate these little peculiarities, I think it will be evident that my precaution of not taking more than two together was not uncalled-for.

I will begin with Dart, a terrier whose mouth always watered after the calves of children's legs, though he only wanted to enjoy the feel of the flesh between his teeth, and had not the least wish to do any real harm. As soon as he saw a pair of these tempting objects anywhere near, he would go and join the owner, wagging his tail, smoothing back his ears, smiling, wriggling his body, and altogether looking sweet enough to inspire confidence in the breast of the most distrustful infant. Then, turning his head insidiously as he walked along, he would seize the nearest calf, give it a good squeeze, and depart hastily, leaving the victim more frightened than hurt, howling dismally, kicking, and struggling. Of course it was easy to prevent the catastrophe by recalling him the instant he assumed an expression of extra-amiability, and set off in the direction of a barelegged child; but, as barelegged children are plentiful in London, it was obviously well for whoever had charge of Dart to keep an eye upon him constantly.

Yarrow, again, was a collie who had a rooted conviction that his constitution required carriage exercise, and who never failed to do his best to give effect to that idea by trying to get into any carriage, cab, or 'bus whose door he saw open. This habit of his sometimes gave rise to laughable scenes, as, for instance, one day when he skipped up the steps of an extremely grand barouche, just as the gorgeously-apparelled footman was holding the door open for his mistress to get in, whilst a dignified butler, and a couple more men in gorgeous liveries were respectfully attending her to the door of the house she was leaving. The flunkey at the carriage nearly fell backwards with horror, but did not venture to interfere with the audacious intruder, so Yarrow settled himself in triumph on the front seat, and sat there at ease with his tongue hanging out, and shedding drops on the smart cushions which he was profaning. He looked blandly at the dismayed servants – not one of whom dared lay a finger on him – and at the lady standing laughing on the doorstep of the house; and how the scene would have terminated if I had not arrived to the rescue and dislodged him, I cannot imagine. He was complete master of the situation as far as the servants were concerned; but I suppose one of them would eventually have called a policeman if I had not intervened.

A third member of my pack was Royal, a fat King Charles, who always made me wish I had eyes in the back of my head. He was the veriest dawdle that ever existed, and was possessed with the idea that whoever took him out was walking too fast, and that it was his duty to protest against such haste; therefore, no matter how slowly one went, he was sure to lag far behind. His dilatoriness was especially provoking, because of his being so handsome and well-bred as to be unusually attractive to dog-stealers; and many a collision have I had with other street passengers in consequence of walking backwards so as not to lose sight of that precious animal.

I come next to Sue, a spaniel of inordinate appetite, who, like Royal, kept me in a continual state of alarm during her walks lest she should be stolen. As she *never* thought she had had enough to eat, she was sure to follow anyone who carried food, and would also constantly stop to sniff about in the gutter in search of something to satisfy her cravings; for she was not in the least dainty, and devoured everything edible with relish. She was a shocking thief, too; and now and then, before I could stop her, she would manage to whip a beefsteak or mutton-chop off some butcher's tray that had been left unguarded by the area-rails whilst the butcher was below enjoying a gossip with the cook. On these occasions I felt a little puzzled how to act. To let Sue carry off her prize quietly would be robbing the butcher, and I did not want to be dishonest if I could help it. Yet, if the man knew what had happened, he would probably make a bother and claim damages, and I did not want that either. So I adopted the middle course of running after Sue, taking the meat from her and restoring it to the tray, and getting clear off from the spot as quickly as possible before the return of the owner. This arrangement seemed to me fair to all parties, as it saved me from unpleasantness, and, at the same time, did no wrong to the butcher. No doubt his customers would not buy the meat if they knew it had been in the dog's mouth, and would declare it to be disgusting and uneatable; but then the idea is everything in matters of taste; and as the little accident with Sue would be unknown, the meat would be eaten without a qualm, and was therefore undeteriorated in value, I argued; for I was sure it was not *really* any the worse. Sue often aggravated me also in respect of poor working men eating an *al fresco* breakfast or dinner. As soon as ever she saw one of these men, off she would go, and sit up on her hind-legs in front of him, begging with glistening eyes, slobbering mouth, and an eagerness that might have made one think she was starving, if her sleek sides had not told a different tale. Her beseeching face and manner generally produced an effect, and I have seen many a man, who looked ill able to afford a morsel out of his scanty meal, throw her a scrap. I always interfered with this little game of hers, and prevented her from being given anything if I could get to the spot in time; for I felt quite ashamed to be in charge of an evidently well-fed dog like her, who went sponging upon poor people who probably had not enough for themselves – I almost wondered she had not too much self-respect to do it.

Chose was a light-hearted French poodle, with a strong taste for sport, which had, unluckily, never been developed in the right direction. Sheep appeared to him to be quite legitimate game, and he never could see them without trying to sneak off in their direction, with a drooping tail and general air of depression, which may have been caused by a consciousness of wrongdoing, or else by fear of being recalled before he was out of reach, and thus deprived of the *chasse* on which his heart was set. As for birds, he considered all to be fair game alike, and rushed madly after any feathered creature that was sitting or running on the ground, or flying low anywhere near him. Repeated failure did not discourage him; he evidently believed it to be his mission to catch birds, and dashed off accordingly in frantic pursuit of rooks, swallows, chaffinches, sparrows, and other birds on the wing, though he had no more chance of catching them than he had of jumping over the moon. This was all very well when he hunted wild birds that could flyaway; but it was a more serious matter when poultry were concerned, and the scrapes he got into with ducks and chickens in the course of his career would require a chapter to enumerate.

Finally, I come to Jumbo, a diminutive terrier, with a mania for digging, who was the abomination of all the gardeners in his neighbourhood. Soft, freshly-turned earth was an irresistible temptation to him; and if not watched carefully, he was sure to slip off to the nearest flower-bed in park, square, or garden, and there dig gigantic graves in a surprisingly short space of time. I expect he thought that, considering what a lot of moles, rabbits, rats, and mice had holes underground, he must infallibly light upon some one of these creatures at last, if he persevered in his researches long enough. He had also a weakness for flowers, and liked to pick them for himself; so, altogether, I don't wonder he was not loved by gardeners, one of whom once remarked to me indignantly;

"That 'ere dawg o' yourn is the werry wusstest little beast I ever see! I'd just like to take and give 'im to one o' them 'ere willysectin doctors, *that* I would!"

Well, those six dogs gave me a good bit of trouble in one way or other, no doubt; and all the more because their mistress spoilt them, and did not try to get them out of their bad ways, and they were not with me long enough for me to be able to undo the effect of her spoiling. But they amused me and I liked them, notwithstanding their troublesomeness; and when I went near them it pleased me to hear the thump thump of tails against the ground, which showed that I was welcome.

The Torwoods kept no indoor man-servant except the butler already mentioned, who rejoiced in the name of Eliezer Scroggins; and as he was a respectable, steady-going married man, I found, to my great satisfaction, that I was in no danger of suffering from persecutions like those of the detestable Perkins. I got on very well with Scroggins, and was often amused by his peculiarities; for he was (as I had guessed at first) somewhat of a character, though a very good sort of fellow, for all that. His prejudices were very strong, and he was sure to cling with pig-headed obstinacy to whatever idea he had taken into his head. I soon discovered that amongst his pet aversions were people who, in his opinion, gave themselves airs, and presumed to push their way up to a station above that in which they had been born. Such people he hated as he hated stairs – perhaps more; and no matter whether they moved in his mistress's sphere of life or his own, they irritated him as the proverbial red rag does the bull. Indeed, I rather suspect that he sometimes had premeditated accidents when any of these objects of his dislike were dining at the Torwoods, and that any visitor of theirs who was considered by him to be what he called a "parvenyoo" was not at all unlikely to receive a bath of soup, sauce, tea, coffee, or wine, or to suffer from some similar misadventure, caused by the intentional clumsiness of the butler.

His bitterness on the subject of people who had risen above their natural position was so great that I had little doubt of there being some particular reason for it; and idle curiosity moved me to try and find out what that reason was, though I never for an instant supposed that the history could be one in any way specially concerning *me.* However, he did not choose to confide his private family affairs to a complete stranger; and so, though he dropped occasional dark hints, whence I concluded that he had a step-sister whom he detested, yet it was not till I had been nearly a year in Mrs. Torwood's service that I at last was permitted to know the cause of his inveterate spite against the whole race of parvenus.

His mother, it appeared, had been twice married, and he was her child by the second marriage. Her first husband was a clerk named Brown, who had died before he was thirty, leaving only one child, a daughter named Mary. He had had rather exalted ideas about education, and had no opinion of home teaching, and consequently had sent his daughter to a cheap boarding-school as soon as ever she was old enough to leave home.

After Brown's death his young widow had married into a social position a shade below that of the clerk, and become the spouse of a grocer in the East End, named Joshua Scroggins, to whom in due time she presented my friend Eliezer, and sundry other children.

On the second marriage the grocer, a goodhearted conscientious man, had declared that it would be a shame for her daughter Mary not to have the same education as her own father would have given her, so he generously went on paying for her at the school where she had been already placed. Here the girl picked up a fair education, and also many ridiculous and fine ideas. She took to spell her name with an "e" at the end; would sooner have died than let her school-fellows know that she was connected with a small retail shopkeeper bearing a name so odiously vulgar as Scroggins; and brooded over the grievance of having so unpresentable a step-father, until she became convinced he had done her a mortal injury by marrying her mother, and got into the habit of disliking and despising him in spite of the kindness and liberality with which he always treated her. Now Scroggins was an honest hard-working man, who minded his shop in person, with the assistance of his wife and children; though he had managed to defray Mary's schooling, yet the expense had now and then pressed on him a little heavily, and he had not the least intention of keeping her as an idle fine lady when she left school for good and came to live at home, but expected her to take her turn in the shop, as the rest of the household did. Her disgust at this was intense, and she showed it by doing her work as badly as she dared, scolding and flouncing about the house, and losing no opportunity of making herself generally disagreeable.

The Scroggins family – consisting of father and mother, and four children, of whom my friend Eliezer

was the eldest – had hitherto lived in unbroken peace and
harmony, and now groaned sorely under the infliction of
the new-comer, with her airs and graces and tantrums.
The recollection of her being fatherless kept them from
resenting her nonsense as it deserved, and made them
more gentle and patient with her than they would perhaps
have been otherwise; but it was felt by all to be a blessed
relief when the disturbing element was removed by
marriage to a city gent. He was in business, but did not
keep a shop, and so she graciously condescended to
accept him as a means of escape from the intolerable
humiliation of serving behind her step-father's counter.
The city gent proved a good speculation. A few lucky
ventures gave him a rise in the world; and when, in the
course of years, he left her a widow, her social position
was very considerably better than it had been when she
first became his wife. By the time he died, all intercourse
between her and the Scrogginses had long been at an end.
Though she had not hesitated to receive a dowry from her
step-father, yet she had never evinced the smallest
gratitude for that, or any of the numerous other benefits
he had bestowed upon her. On the contrary, she took no
trouble to conceal her aversion to him; declared that
vulgarity was necessarily attached to such a name as
Scroggins; and, after her marriage, saw less and less of
the family, and rudely checked all friendly advances on
their part, till at last she succeeded in altogether cutting
the connection. Mrs. Scroggins – a peace-loving, kindly
soul, who could not bear to be mixed up in any kind of
dissension – was grieved by this, and by the separation
from her daughter, though it was no fault of hers, and she
could not possibly help it. But she bore no malice, and
when the news came of her son-in-law's death, she
thought only of her daughter's present distress, and forgot
the many slights and insults that had been cast upon her

and hers. Full of unaffected hearty sorrow and sympathy, she set off immediately to visit the bereaved Mary, hoping to be able to comfort her and be of use to her. What took place on the occasion of this visit Eliezer never exactly knew. But he knew well that the reception of his goodhearted and forgiving mother must have been both unseemly and unpleasant, when he saw her return home in tears, thoroughly upset, and saying that she could not have believed any woman would have behaved so rudely to her own mother; and that, unless she was sent for, she would *never* again try to see Mary. This had made a deep impression on Eliezer, who adored his mother; and the bitter enmity he had ever since cherished against the person who had treated her so badly, and whom he regarded as an upstart, had extended to the whole race of "parvenyoos."

"Do you know what has become of your stepsister?" I asked carelessly; "and do you ever see her?"

"See 'er!" he ejaculated wrathfully; "not if I knows it. I'm none so fond of raising my corruption by looking at what I 'ates! But I 'ears tell on 'er now and agin; she married some swell with a 'andle to 'is name some years back. Mary Grove's clever enough – you may trust 'er to do well for 'erself wherever she is."

In telling his tale he had not before mentioned the name of his step-sister's husband; but when he spoke of Mary Grove, I pricked up my ears with a sudden recollection that that had been the name of my step-mother. "Was Grove the name of the city gent?" I enquired eagerly.

Scroggins nodded.

"Had they any children?" I continued.

" A couple o' gals named Jane and Margret there was," he returned; "I don't know what they be like now, for I ain't seen 'em – not since they was little mites o' things."

Jane and Margaret! these had been the names of my step-sisters, and I felt almost sure that his step-sister and my step-mother must be one and the same person. One more question would make the matter absolutely certain, so I said: "What was the name of Mary Grove's second husband – do you know it?"

"Oh yes, I knows it; but I can't lay tongue to it at this moment. What hever is it now? Sir Hanthony something or other – I should know it if I was to 'ear it."

"Was it anything like—" I began, and then paused. Never once had my own name passed my lips since I left home, and somehow now, when I tried to say it, it seemed to stick in my throat. Overcoming this feeling, however, I completed my sentence – "like Trecastle?" It was strange how, in spite of my first hesitation about uttering the word, yet when once it was out, my tongue clung lovingly to it, and I should have liked to repeat it over and over again. I thought it sounded better than any other name I had ever heard, and felt a thrill of pride to think that it was mine by right.

"That's the very thing!" he exclaimed triumphantly; "Sir Hanthony Trecassel, and I wishes 'im joy of 'is bargain! 'Ow hever did you come to think of 'im?"

"Oh, I had heard of a Sir Anthony Trecastle before," I replied, "and so when you started me with the first name, the second suggested itself quite naturally."

Here our conversation was interrupted, and I retired to meditate complacently on the means of being revenged on my step-mother, which fortune had so kindly thrown in my way. There was nothing *really* to be ashamed of in such a connection as the Scrogginses, who were evidently highly respectable and excellent individuals. Yet few people in society would altogether enjoy having a mother named Scroggins, who sold soap and tallow candles in the East End; and, least of all, the former Mary Brown, who had striven so indefatigably and successfully to cut herself free from every trace of the grocer's shop. It would be gall and wormwood to her to have her secret revealed; and I chuckled with delight to think that it had fallen into my hands, and that the whole world would know it when I chose.

But I would not be in too great a hurry with my vengeance. I would take time about it – prolong her torment by keeping her in suspense, and letting her see the blow coming before it actually fell. Therefore I commenced operations by posting to her an anonymous letter in a feigned hand, stating that the writer was a benevolent individual to whom the spectacle of domestic discord was inexpressibly shocking, and who was much inclined to undertake the good work of endeavouring to bring about a public reconciliation between the Scrogginses and one of their family who had long been estranged from them.

This would suffice to alarm her and make her anxious as to what the writer's real intentions were. Perhaps she would think he meant only to extort money – from which idea her parsimonious soul would shrink with horror; or perhaps she would think that he meant to execute his threat, which she would regard as a still more terrible possibility. Either way she would be made miserable, and so my object would be gained.

After leaving some weeks for the digestion of this missive, I despatched another, stating that the writer considered it part of a wife's duty to introduce her husband to her parents; and that if any wife failed to perform that duty, it behoved someone else to do it in her place.

This I presently followed by a third and still more menacing letter, so as continually to increase her terrors, and keep her perpetually with a sword hanging over her head. At every epistle I sent off I gloated over the thought of the state of disquietude in which she must be; and as I remembered how uncomfortable she had once made me, I regretted that I could not be present when the letters arrived, so as to have the pleasure of seeing my shafts take effect and wound her. The execution of the threats should come soon, I thought. My intention was to play with her and keep her on tenterhooks for a while, and then to send anonymous letters containing information of her antecedents to my father, his family, the county people, and others with whom she had formerly been intimate. I should of course give the address of the Scroggins' shop, so that it would be easy for the recipients of the letters to verify my statement if they cared to do so; and there could be little doubt that all her bosom friends would give themselves that much trouble, even if mere chance acquaintances did not think it worthwhile. Therefore there was no danger of the history being hushed up and kept quiet, and of her being spared the humiliation she dreaded.

Before, however, I had brought my operations to a climax, they were interrupted by an unforeseen event, which must be related in the next chapter.

CHAPTER XXV

The Last of Perkins

I DARESAY my readers will take it for granted that I adopted a fresh name when I went into Mrs. Torwood's service. So I most certainly *ought* to have done after my previous forgery of a character having been detected. But sometimes one is astonishingly stupid; and the idea of making that very necessary alteration never entered my head. Caroline Jill I had dubbed myself when I dropped the secretly-venerated name of Trecastle, and Caroline Jill I – like an idiot – continued to be, without having the wits to see how foolish it was of me to stick to a name upon which I had brought discredit. I was now to feel the consequences of this imprudence, the penalty being brought about, indirectly, by three of the dogs under my care.

One morning when I went as usual to call Mrs. Torwood, she said she should stay in bed a little longer, as she had a headache, and that I was to leave her to sleep till half-past ten, when she meant to get up. It so happened that I was particularly desirous of getting through my work early on that day, and as by taking out the six dogs in two instead of three detachments, I should have just time to give the whole lot their daily airing before the hour when I was to return to my mistress, I determined to break my rule for once, and take them out three together, instead of in couples, as usual.

Behold me, then, sallying forth at about 9.30A.M., accompanied by the greedy Sue, the vivacious and sport-

255

loving Chose, and the dawdling Royal. Our progress was characteristic of my three companions. First went Chose, trotting ahead of us, and keeping a bright look-out for a chance of a *chasse*. Next came Sue and I – she making occasional foraging excursions into the gutter, and I continually walking backwards and wringing my neck, in order not to lose sight of Royal. Finally came Royal, lagging far behind, with his customary leisurely imperturbability. All went well till we came to where a footman had lounged out from his master's house, leaving the front door open behind him, and was standing a few yards off chatting with a friend. I and my pack had passed there before often enough for the footman to know us by sight; and I knew him in the same way, and knew also that his employers had a pet in the shape of a magnificent Persian cat. Now this cat had taken advantage of the open door to come out upon the pavement, where she was sunning herself tranquilly when Chose, who, as I have mentioned, headed our party, drew near to that spot. At sight of puss he stopped short with uplifted paw and quivering tail, and for a second or so the two animals stood motionless and gazing at each other. Then the cat, distrusting his appearance, whisked round, and flew like lightning up the doorsteps into the house. Had she stayed still, Chose might very likely have let her alone; but the instant he saw her run he became convinced she was game, and therefore to be hunted. I whistled and called to him in vain; without a moment's hesitation, and paying no attention to me, he dashed after her in hot pursuit across the hall and up the front staircase. Of course it would never do to have him hunting a pet cat all over its owner's house; so I said to the footman, who was looking on and laughing without seeming to think there was any need for him to interfere: "I'd better run in and fetch the dog back, hadn't I?"

"All right," answered he, knowing that I was not to be suspected of designs on the spoons; and in I went without more ado.

The family to whom the house belonged would doubtless have been considerably astonished to see a stranger invading their premises in this unceremonious manner; but luckily they were still in their bedrooms, and I met with none of them as I rushed after my truant. I followed him upstairs, through the drawing-room, and into a little boudoir on the first floor. Here I found him standing on his hind legs upon a light-blue satin sofa (which bore marks of his dirty feet), and vainly endeavouring to get to the top of a high cabinet where puss had taken refuge. She, feeling herself in security, was indulging in a candid and emphatic expression of opinion respecting her pursuer by growling, spitting, arching her back, swelling out her tail to three or four times its usual size, and now and then striking viciously in his direction with her paw. I imagine this last action was merely meant to relieve her feelings in the same way that fist-shaking relieves those of human beings, for she must have been perfectly well aware that the poodle was quite out of reach from her perch.

Chose was one of those dogs who are always completely subdued directly they find themselves captured, so I had no more trouble with him now that I had come to close quarters; he followed me downstairs unresistingly, feebly wagging the very tip of his tail, and looking a touching picture of apologetic meekness and penitence.

That smell-feast of a Sue meanwhile had profited by the commotion to get into a little mischief on her own account. Having accompanied me as far as the hall, she had then immediately sniffed out the dining-room, and turned in there in preference to going on with me upstairs, and I, having my head full of Chose, did not attend to her proceedings. In the dining-room there were preparations for breakfast, and Sue's nose guided her unerringly to a side-table whereon some cold meat had been set out. By help of a conveniently placed chair she speedily mounted on to this table, took up a cold chicken of which she thought she could fancy a morsel, jumped down again to the floor, and made off for some safer place where she might hope to enjoy her fowl peacefully.

The footman, thinking it time to go and see what was taking place indoors, bade adieu to his friend, and entered the house just as Sue was in the act of issuing from the dining-room door with the bird in her mouth. He immediately armed himself with a riding whip that lay in the hall, barred her exit from the house, and tried to make her give up what she had stolen. In this, however, he was unsuccessful; for though he hit her smartly enough to make her squeak, yet she still clung resolutely to her booty. Consequently, when I came downstairs with the recently-disobedient but now abjectly-submissive Chose at my heels, congratulating myself on being out of this bother, the first thing I saw was Sue, carrying a chicken, scrimmaging from side to side of the hall, and endeavouring to avoid the footman's whip and dodge past him in the street. Very much disgusted at her having thus got into mischief the instant my attention was taken off, I swooped down upon her from the rear; and as she was only thinking of the foe in front and did not notice my approach, I was easily able to catch hold of her, and enforce the surrender of the bird.

Provoked as I felt with these two dogs for their bad behaviour, I could not stop to scold them much at that moment; for I was disturbed by the possibility that Royal, too, might have taken it into his head to get into a scrape on this unlucky morning, and I wanted to have him safe under my wing again as soon as possible. Hastily telling the footman that I hoped the chicken was not much the worse, and that I was sorry the dogs had been so troublesome, I hurried off to look for the King Charles. Even such a slow-coach as Royal had had plenty of time to overtake us by now, and it would not be at all like him to exert himself needlessly by going an inch along the road in advance of the person who had taken him out. Therefore, as he had not made his appearance in the house, I made sure that he must be waiting for me outside.

To my dismay, however, he was nowhere to be seen; look which way I would, not a hair of the precious animal was visible. "Did ever anyone see such a handful as these dogs are?" ejaculated I mentally; "and oh, what a fool I was to take out more than two of them at a time!"

I had not the slightest idea in which direction to look for Royal, and was wondering what I had better do, when a ragged little girl whom I had not before observed, ran up and said:

"Please, 'as yer losted suthin?"

"Yes; a little dog," I returned; "can you tell me where it is?"

"I seed a man pick'n hup and put'n in a bastik, and I thought it warn't hisn, neither," she exclaimed, pointing down the street; "he'm jest gone 'long the fust turn to the right there. Run quick and you'll ketch 'im p'raps."

I delayed not a moment, but set off at full speed; and the two dogs ran with me, greatly excited at my sudden haste, and mystified as to the cause of it. As for Chose, he forgot all about his penitence, was immediately in the highest spirits, and bounded along with an up-in-the-air, elastic, springing action which implied an unlimited stock of suppressed energy ready to display itself the instant he should succeed in discovering what game I was in pursuit of, and he was to go for.

On reaching the turning indicated, I saw a respectably dressed man with a basket on his arm at some little distance off. When first I saw him he was walking fast in the same direction as I was; at the sound of my footsteps he looked round, and then began to run. Close to the other end of the street was a crowded thoroughfare where it would be easy enough for him to give me the slip; so I strained every nerve to come up with him before he could get out of the street in which we then were. But it was not an equal race between us; for he had a start and was quite fresh, whilst I was already a little bit out of breath with running; and I soon perceived that he would escape unless I could procure assistance.

Thinking Chose might be useful, I tried to incite him to rush on and tackle the man. But he only responded by barking, springing higher than ever in the air, and looking wildly about to find out what he was being set at. Evidently it never entered his head that he could be meant to hunt a human being. Two or three times I called out "Stop thief!" But that was mere waste of breath; for the street was empty, and though the cry attracted some of the inhabitants to their doors and windows to see what was going on, no one made any attempt to come to my aid. I suppose they wanted to know the rights of the matter first – and I had not time to stop and explain it just then.

The man had almost gained the end of the street, and I was giving up all hopes of success, when, in the very nick of time, a policeman came in sight just in front of him. My shouts and gesticulations made the policeman comprehend that I wanted the runner stopped. The latter tried to bolt past the official, but was foiled; and, to my joy, I beheld the fugitive captured and held fast. When I came up, I found him expostulating with his captor with an assumption of much virtuous indignation, declaring that he was hurrying to catch a train, that it would be ruin to him to miss it, and that he should hold anyone who stopped him responsible for whatever loss he had to suffer in consequence.

"Please look in his basket," I panted to the policeman, "and see if there isn't a King Charles spaniel in it that he has just stolen."

"In *corse* there's a dawg," exclaimed the fugitive with an air of injured innocence, whilst the policeman lifted up the lid of the basket, and discovered Royal ensconced underneath, "and why not? It's my own dawg as I'm a takin' with me, and 'as I'm 'bliged to carry when I'm in a 'urry cos he can't go fast enough to keep up. Does the good lady think as no vun 'as a right to 'ave a dawg besides 'erself?"

"Certainly not," replied I, "but that dog is not yours for all that, as you know well enough. He belongs," I continued, addressing the policeman, "to a lady living in Chester Square, whose maid I am. Come there with me, and you will soon see whether this man's story is true or not."

"Oh, hof corse you sez that," grumbled the thief, "when I've jest a told you as I can't hafford to miss my train, not on no consideration! But there! What's the lost of a dawg to the lost of a fortin? Take 'im, then, since you hinsists! Do hanythink you pleases, honly don't keep me 'ere no longer."

But the policeman was not to be gammoned. He said we must both go along with him to Chester Square to find out if my story was true; and added with gentle satire, that as the man claimed the dog and was so unwilling to be parted from it, he might have the pleasure of continuing to carry it in the basket till the real ownership should be proved. And so we all set out together for the Torwood's house, notwithstanding the prisoner's fluent remonstrances and protestations.

As I rather prided myself on being habitually wide-awake and capable of performing whatever I undertook to do, I should have felt it was a disgrace to me to lose one of the dogs; and therefore I was sincerely thankful to the little girl by whose means I had been saved from incurring such a slur. I saw her loitering at the end of the street, watching the result of my chase; and as we passed back that way, I went up to thank her for her timely information. So grateful did I feel, that I was pulling out my purse to express my sentiments in a substantial form, when, to my surprise, she stopped me by saying:

"Don't do that! I 'on't take nothin' for tellin' what you wanted to know, cos I was honly payin' a debt as I've owed you this long time."

Seeing my look of astonishment, she continued:

"'Twas you as bought flowers off o' me so as I could get brexhus, one mornin' two years back and more, when I was that 'ungry I didn't know what to do; and I've hoften thought as I'd like to pay you back for it, and wondered if I should hever get a chance. When I seen the chap grab the dawg I didn't mean to say nothin' 'bout it at fust – for I doesn't never care to go gettin' coves into trouble; but then I see you come out o' the 'ouse, look in' like as you'd losted suthin; and I 'membered your face all of a suddint, and I thought if the dawg was yours, I'd tell you where 'twas gone, to pay back what you done for me afore."

I recollected the girl now, and saw she was the same whose breakfastless condition had excited my compassion one day long ago, just after I had run away from home and come to London. Certainly she more than repaid what I had done for her then. Value for value, I should have had very much the best of the bargain if the dog had – as she supposed – belonged to me; for I knew that £30 had been offered and refused for Royal, whereas the amount that I had given her was only a shilling. "I should like to be able to invest all my shillings at that rate of interest!" thought I, as I nodded goodbye to her, and hurried to join the policeman and his prisoner.

Mrs. Torwood regarded dog-stealers with much the same antipathy that some sporting squires seem to feel towards poachers – deeming them natural enemies to the common weal, who might advantageously be extirpated, root and branch. She had, therefore, no idea of letting slip the excellent opportunity which now presented itself for the punishment of one of these abominated miscreants, and the prosecution of Royal's thief was a matter of course. When the trial came on, naturally I was a principal witness; and thus the police reports in the paper contained the name of "Caroline Jill, lady's-maid to Mrs. Torwood, of – Chester Square," as having given evidence in a dog-stealing case.

As luck would have it, this caught the eye of my old enemy Perkins, and set him wondering whether the person referred to could be the same individual who had once presumed to reject his advances so rudely. Though he had already been the means of turning me out of one place, yet still his spite was not satisfied; so (as I suppose) he hung about Chester Square till he had seen me pass, and ascertained my identity; then he came to our house, and had an interview with Mrs. Torwood.

It happened that I was looking out of the window when he left the house. I was extremely astonished to see him, and still more astonished at the state he was in, for he looked deadly pale, and all wild and frightened, and was shaking visibly. The sight of him made me uneasy; for though I had no notion of the object of his visit, still I was sure that his appearance in my vicinity was not likely to bode any good to me.

I took the first opportunity of trying to find out from

my friend Eliezer, what the man's business with our mistress had been. But Eliezer could tell me nothing about it; all he knew was that the party had asked to speak to her, saying that he had something important to say, and that he had left her again after a not very long interview.

"She must have frightened him pretty well, whatever it may have been about," said I; "he looked worse than if he'd seen a ghost, when he went away."

"Ah, he did that," returned Eliezer, chuckling at the remembrance, "but it was, so to say, hisself as he was 'feared on. I never see sitch a coward in hall my born days, 'afore."

This naturally excited my curiosity; and I made Eliezer tell me what had taken place to give Perkins a fright, which, I need scarcely say, was not an unpleasant hearing to one who owed him a grudge, as I did.

The collie Yarrow, it appeared, had been lying on a mat in the hall when the visitor departed; and the latter, not seeing the dog, had inadvertently trodden heavily on his toe. Now Yarrow's temper was, like that of many collies, a little uncertain; and as, furthermore, he had always a particular objection to have his toes walked upon or hurt, he lost not an instant in retaliating by biting his injurer in the leg. Perkins, startled at first to find himself stumbling over a dog which he had not seen, seemed completely overcome by terror when the stumble was followed promptly by a severe bite; he staggered back against the wall, turning as pale as ashes, and hardly able to speak. When he had recovered himself a little, Eliezer discovered that the cause of this great fright was that Perkins had a sort of craze about hydrophobia, and held it in such intense horror that he was really not capable of being reasonable where it was concerned.

Eliezer, being the only person handy at the moment, was besieged by Perkins with flurried questions. Wasn't it as bad to be bitten by an animal that was angry as by one that was mad? How long was it before madness showed in a person who had been bitten by a mad dog? Was it a *certain* cure to have the place burnt out? Was there any other less painful remedy? It would be so horrid to have one's flesh burnt but still – hydrophobia would be worse. Whatever should he do?

These and similar questions were poured into the ears of Eliezer as though he had been an authority upon madness, because Perkins was in that state of absurd panic which made him long to hear a word of comfort from anyone no matter who. But he did not get any consolation from Eliezer, who had a hearty contempt for cowards, and rarely lost a chance of tormenting them by playing upon their weakness. Therefore the butler carefully abstained from saying anything reassuring, shook his head and sighed, and affected to think the bite an extremely serious matter. Finally, the victim departed in a state of the utmost disquietude, divided between anxiety to try and put himself in safety by undergoing cauterisation, and fear of the pain which it would cause him.

Whichever way he settled it, he was sure to make himself miserable lest he was going mad for a very long while to come, Eliezer opined, laughing contemptuously at the idea of a man's torturing himself gratuitously in that ridiculous fashion. And my anxiety as to what had brought Perkins there did not prevent my joining in the laugh at his absurd terror and folly.

A day or so elapsed, during which I heard nothing unpleasant from Mrs. Torwood, and I began to hope that, after all, the visit that had alarmed me might have had nothing to do with my affairs. This, however, was not the case. Perkins had told her that I was an impostor, who had been dismissed from my last place because the character with which I obtained it was a forgery. But she was reluctant to have to part with a maid who suited her and got on with the dogs as well as I did, and was not inclined to credit so startling an accusation brought against me by a man whom she had never seen before and knew nothing of. When her husband came home, however, she told him what she had heard, and was advised by him to wait, and say nothing about the matter, till Lady Mervyn had been communicated with to find out whether the story was true or not. That lady, of course, confirmed it entirely; and as the date of my being sent away by her was only a few weeks before I had entered the service of my present mistress, it was very evident to the Torwoods that my second character was as unreliable as my first one, and that the lady who had recommended Caroline Jill before going to the Cape had had no existence save in my own imagination.

Thereupon my fancied security was scattered rudely to the winds. Mrs. Torwood at once informed me of what she had discovered, and said it was impossible that she should allow me to remain in the house a day longer. Her husband, she added, had thought she ought to prosecute me; but she refused to do that, because during the whole time I had been with her (over a year) I had given her no cause of complaint, and had always taken excellent care of the dogs. Therefore she should content herself with insisting on my immediate departure.

It was hopeless for me to deny the misdeeds with which I was charged, so there was nothing for it but to pack up my things and take myself off as soon as might be.

Really, I thought, as I made the requisite preparations, it is very provoking that my employers will not be satisfied to judge me by their own personal knowledge! First there was Kitty, and now there's Mrs. Torwood. I am sure they both of them were well-disposed in my favour, and believed that I served them satisfactorily. Yet they let their own experience go for nothing, and are afraid to keep me in their service, just because I am not provided with the proper conventional, often quite unreliable, certificate of somebody else's opinion of me! I call it very silly of people to have so little confidence in their own judgment.

As for Eliezer, he was aghast at my sudden flitting, and began ruefully anticipating the many futile journeys up and down stairs that would probably be inflicted upon his cherished lungs before a satisfactory successor to me would be found.

I confess I thought his anticipations very likely to be realised; for though the place suited *me* well enough, it was not one that many maids would care to take. The general run of abigails study dressmaking as an art, are ambitious of displaying their skill in that line, and naturally turn up their noses at the idea of throwing away their talents by spending the best part of their time in attending to dogs. Whereas I, who had neither taste nor capacity for any form of millinery, regarded the animals as far the most congenial and interesting occupation of the two.

As I reflected indignantly on the behaviour of the mean, spiteful, meddlesome, cowardly Perkins, who had thus a second time been the means of turning me adrift, I rejoiced to think that dear Yarrow had avenged me to *some* extent at all events, though not perhaps as completely as l could have wished. The pain of a bite was not much of a set-off against the harm he had done me, to be sure; but then I might add to his sufferings an unknown amount of terror, because of his being such an abject coward as he was; and there was the chance too of his having thought it necessary to have the bitten place cauterised. Altogether, I thought Yarrow was a most discriminating dog, and my last act before leaving the house was to caress him and give him one of his favourite biscuits.

It proved, however, that he had avenged me more thoroughly than I had imagined, and that Perkins' interference was to cost him his life. His horror of hydrophobia made him take a hot poker and try to burn the bite on his leg; but his dread of pain made him timid and clumsy, and, letting the poker slip accidentally, he inflicted a really very severe burn upon himself. Being in a bad state of blood at the time, the wound would not heal; and after a good deal of festering and inflammation, blood poisoning set in, and finally caused his death.

I learnt these particulars from the newspapers, which reported the inquest that was held upon him; and as this was not till some time after I was dismissed by Mrs. Torwood, I am anticipating the proper course of events by introducing it here. But I do so because I think that this is the best place to relate what eventually became of him, and in the next chapter I will return to an account of my proceedings in due chronological order.

CHAPTER XXVI

An Accident

EVIDENTLY the first thing to be done when I was turned out of the Torwood's house was to find a habitation for myself somewhere else; and the search for a suitable lodging occupied me till late in the evening. When at last I had succeeded, I told the landlady that my name was Charlotte Jackson; for I had learnt wisdom by experience, and, having now perceived the folly of continuing to call myself Caroline Jill, I substituted for it the first name that occurred to me whose initials would correspond to the C. J. with which my linen was marked.

By the time I had taken possession of my new quarters I felt quite ready for supper, and betook myself, therefore, to a neighbouring coffee-tavern, where, for the sum of twopence, I procured a satisfying and not extravagant meal, consisting of a large hunch of good bread and a basin of thick pea-soup, which – though perhaps somewhat coarsely flavoured – was undeniably savoury and nourishing. Then I returned to my lodging and composed another of the anonymous letters with which I was harassing my stepmother. I took especial pains to make it as unpleasant and likely to alarm her as I could, because it was the last that I intended sending her. I meant to let about a week more elapse, and then to put my threats into execution and proceed to the final act of vengeance, by making known to her husband and friends the whole history of her Scroggins connection.

Having written this letter and directed it all ready to post next day, I proceeded to consider my present situation, and what my next effort for a livelihood should be. But I suppose the pea-soup must have been indigestible, for I was out of sorts somehow, took a gloomy view of things in general, and was unwontedly dispirited about my prospects. My mind seemed to have no elasticity or variety, and would keep reverting to the difficulty of getting a place without a character, and the impossibility of getting a character without forging it. The pitcher that goes often to the well gets broken at last, thought I; and though, hitherto, the detection of my forgeries has brought no worse consequences than dismissal from my situations, yet I cannot reckon on always escaping so easily. If I do not mind what I am about, I may find myself in prison some fine day; and to *that* I should object most strongly. It would be too horribly disgraceful; I should never be able to hold up my head again afterwards!

I could arrive at no settled determination whatever, and finally went to bed in a very bad humour with myself for being so irresolute and inclined to be disheartened.

When I woke next morning I was more cheerfully disposed, and thought I would get a newspaper and give a look at the advertisements. There could be no reason why I should not do that, at all events, as reading them did not by any means necessarily involve answering them. Accordingly I procured a newspaper and proceeded to study it. Here a temptation to recklessness at once presented itself in the shape of a notice setting forth that excellent situations for courier-maids were to be heard of on application to Mrs. Asterisk's registry office. The idea of going abroad again made my mouth water; and, putting aside the character difficulty for future consideration, I proceeded immediately to Mrs. Asterisk's, paid the preliminary fee without which her lips were sealed, received in return the addresses of a couple of ladies in want of travelling-maids, and set off to call at one of these addresses.

The way to this place took me near the chief approach to a large railway station, whence a train was shortly about to start; and I had to pause before crossing the road in order to let a string of luggage-laden cabs and carriages go past. In the line of vehicles coming towards where I stood, there was a brougham which exhibited signs of wealth combined with perfect taste, which made me notice it particularly, and wonder who the fortunate owners could be. The colouring, liveries, etc., were as quiet as possible, and there was nothing showy about the turn-out except the splendid pair of high-stepping horses by which it was drawn. But, though not showy, none the less was every detail of its appointments faultless, and I lingered to see if the occupants were as well worth looking at as their equipage was. As the fiery horses came slowly abreast of me, tossing their heads, snorting, and champing their bits with impatience at being delayed, I saw that there was an earl's coronet on the harness, and that a lady and gentleman were in the carriage. In a moment more it was near enough for me to recognise who they were, and then I saw that they were Lord and Lady Clement.

I had not before set eyes on Kitty since I parted from her at Charing Cross; but I had often and often thought of her, and wondered whether her marriage had brought her happiness; and now I gazed at her eagerly, trying to guess this from her countenance. Impossible, however, to read the secrets of a face as impenetrable as hers! All I could tell was that she looked handsomer than ever, and just a trifle more stern; and I had an idea, too, that the haughty immovable expression which had been always somewhat characteristic of her had become intensified. Her husband addressed some remark to her, and she answered him promptly with a gracious pleasant smile, that showed them to be on thoroughly good terms together. Yet I fancied it was a smile of conventionality rather than of affection; it seemed only to come from the lips – the eyes and rest of the face had nothing to do with it; and I hardly thought it was such a smile as a young wife would be likely to bestow upon a husband who possessed her heart. Yet after all, what did I know of the matter? It would be absurd for me to think I could form any opinion as to her happiness from a mere glimpse of her like this.

It was strange how the old charm which she had always had for me reasserted itself the instant I beheld her again. In her I seemed to recognise the sole human being in the world whose affection I would have taken trouble to obtain; and as I looked wistfully after her, thinking that I might possibly have had a chance of it, if it had not been for my stepmother and Perkins, I felt a fresh access of resentment towards them. My stepmother, by making home intolerable, had exiled me from the sphere of life where I could, perhaps, have made friends with Kitty as an equal; and Perkins, by spitefully driving me out of her service, had deprived me of the opportunities I might have had of winning her regard as an inferior. How curious it was that, notwithstanding what untoward circumstances had done to separate us, there yet existed between her and me the sort of half-bond which is involved in the possession of a mutual secret. For had not I discovered the love for Captain Norroy which she had striven zealously to conceal? And did not I know that about her which she believed herself to have kept secret from the whole world?

The carriage went on into the station, and I continued my course without dreaming that the trivial incident of waiting to see Kitty Clement drive by had affected my destiny materially. Such, however, was in truth the case; and the way in which it happened was this:

The sight of Kitty had, as I have just said, reminded me of my stepmother; and that made me think of the letter I had written on the previous night. I had put it in my pocket when I came out, and afterwards forgotten all about it till the present moment. Now, however, that I had remembered it, I thought I would post it at once so as to make sure of not forgetting it again, and accordingly looked about for a post-office. At the corner of a small side street was a pillar-box, which was only a few steps out of my way, so I walked up to it and posted the letter there.

Near by a groom was capering and careering about on an obstreperous horse; and just as I turned away from the box, the steed sprang on to the pavement in spite of all the rider's efforts to restrain him. There he set to plunging and kicking so close to me, that I was obliged to jump hastily into the road in order to get out of reach of his hoofs. Thinking only of the danger from the animal prancing on the pavement, I did not observe a hansom that was dashing up the side street. It came shaving round the corner at full speed, and in another instant I was knocked down, run over, and stunned.

Then comes a confused recollection of acute pain which made me groan; of being moved; of wishing to know what was happening to me, and feeling absolutely incapable of rousing myself sufficiently to find out. And then I must have lost consciousness altogether; for the next thing I remember is, becoming gradually aware that I was in bed. That one fact was as much as my mind was equal to take in at first; I was not altogether sure of my own identity, and recollected nothing whatever of the accident. After lying thus inert for a short time, I opened my eyes and looked at as much as was to be seen without moving my head, which I felt far too languid to do. The result of my observations was, that there were other beds near me, and that I was in a large airy room; I perceived also a prevailing odour of carbolic acid in the place. Had I been in my ordinary condition of energy, I should have been wild to know where I was, and how I came there; but, as it was, I was too limp both in body and mind to be curious or astonished at anything. Therefore I reclosed my eyes with a vague impression that there was something a little odd about my situation; but that as long as I could lie still and do nothing I had all that I desired.

This transient dream of consciousness was succeeded by an interval during which I can only recollect nightmarish visions and miseries. The next thing that my memory recalls definitely is a short conversation between two people whose voices sounded to me as though coming from some remote distance, though in reality, as I knew afterwards, they were close to my bedside.

"What is this case?" said the first voice.

"It's a woman who was run over by a cab," replied the second; "her leg is broken, and she has other injuries also. She was brought in yesterday morning, and hasn't recovered her senses properly yet."

"Indeed!" returned the former speaker. "How did you find out her name, then? I see you've got it stuck up over the bed."

"Oh, there was an envelope in her pocket addressed to Caroline Jill, *No. –* Chester Square," was the answer. "We sent to the address to ask if she was known there, and to say she had been brought to the hospital. It appeared that she had been lady's-maid at the house, and been dismissed the day before, and they knew nothing of who her belongings were, or where she lived, or anything about her."

As I heard no more, I conclude that here the speakers moved away from my bed. The few words they had said, however, had sufficed to enlighten my cloudy state of mind. At first I had listened without having an idea that *I* could be the person referred to; but when the name of Caroline Jill was spoken I remembered all about myself, knew clearly who I was, and realised what had occurred to me. Yes; I had gone to a pillar-box to post the letter to my stepmother, and there had been an unmanageable horse to be avoided. Then there had come suddenly a rattle, a violent concussion, confusion, pain, and utter blank; and I comprehended that I had been run over and brought to the accident ward of a hospital. I recollected, too, my prudent design of dropping the name of Jill; and as I realised that that intention was frustrated for the present, I felt a faint trace of amusement at the persistency with which the old childish name had stuck to me.

Was it true that my leg was broken, as those two people had just said? Very likely. Anyhow I would take their word for it, for I certainly did not feel inclined to stir hand or foot to verify the statement. And as my head ached, and I was quite exhausted with the effort of so much consecutive thought, I speedily relapsed into my former comatose condition.

When next I recovered my senses, my head was clear; I remembered directly how I came to be in a hospital, and looked around me. It was night, and by the dim light of a shaded lamp I could see the nurse in charge of the ward sitting in an upright-backed wooden chair, where she had fallen fast asleep notwithstanding the hardness and discomfort of her seat. I could see, too, a glass containing lemonade standing on a table near the head of my bed, and, as I was parching with thirst, I managed slowly, and with difficulty, to draw one hand out from under the bedclothes, and stretch it out towards the tempting drink. Alas! the glass was out of my reach. The sight of the delicious liquid made my thirst grow worse and worse, till it seemed quite unendurable, and I was impelled to try and wake the nurse, to ask her to give it to me. Accordingly I called out to her as loudly as I could. But my utmost efforts produced only a wheezing feeble sound, which was powerless to produce any impression on her slumbers. The amount of fatigue which it cost me to uplift my voice was quite disproportionate to the insignificance of the result, and I was so tired with the attempt to make myself heard, and the exertion of getting my hand out of bed and reaching after the glass of lemonade, that I realised it was useless to think of waking the nurse, and that I must resign myself to bear the thirst as best I could, till she should wake of herself. Mortification at my helplessness, and profound pity for my poor dear self, caused tears to rise to my eyes and moisten my cheeks. I lay still and watched her so anxiously that one might almost have thought the mere ardour of my gaze ought to have disturbed her repose. Still she slumbered on blissfully. Oh, why would not she wake when I was so very very thirsty!

Suddenly I heard a door open at the other end of the room, and, on looking round, saw a woman enter whose dress showed her to belong to some Sisterhood. I had never thought well of Sisters in my life. They always had seemed to me to be useless, so eccentric as to be well-nigh mad, and – though otherwise harmless – yet objectionable on the ground that their mere existence conveyed a continual tacit reproach and assumption of superiority to more self-indulgent mortals, who shrank from the strictness and hardness which the Sisters imposed upon themselves voluntarily. Hence the fact of the new-comer's wearing a Sister's habit sufficed to prejudice me against her; and on an ordinary occasion I should not have spoken to – far less asked a favour of – her.

But the present was *not* an ordinary occasion. All I cared for was to have the thirst that tormented me relieved with the least possible delay; and no sooner did I see her than I made a frantic effort to call out loud enough for her to hear. The cry, feeble as it was, reached her ears; and as she was not sure from which bed it proceeded, she advanced slowly up the room, saying, in a low voice, "Who called me?"

I held up my hand to show it was I who had summoned her; she came straight to the bedside and asked what I wanted. "Drink!" I gasped, with some difficulty; for my throat was so dry that I could scarcely articulate the word intelligibly.

With one hand she took up the coveted draught, and, putting the other arm under my pillow, raised me to exactly the right height at which I could drink comfortably, and then held the glass to my lips. Never was nectar more delicious and refreshing than that lemonade tasted to me! When I had drained the last drop I begged eagerly for more, and she quickly replenished the tumbler from a jug on the table, and again gave me the liquid for which I craved. At last my burning thirst was quenched, and when she had gently restored me to my former position in the bed, I could not help feeling beholden to her, notwithstanding that it was a shock to my previous notions to think a Sister could be useful, and notwithstanding, also, that one never altogether relishes the upsetting of any of one's preconceived cherished ideas.

I could speak better now, so I said: "Thank you. I am sorry to have troubled you, but I was so dreadfully thirsty, and the glass was out of my reach."

"No trouble," she replied kindly; "the only object of my being here is to help people if I can. But why didn't you call to the nurse in charge of this ward? She would have attended to you at once."

"I did call to her more than half an hour ago by the clock," I replied, "but I couldn't call loud enough to wake her."

In consequence of my having drawn the Sister's attention to myself directly she entered the room, she had not yet noticed that the nurse was asleep. Now, however, she perceived it. A look of displeasure came over her face, and she at once proceeded to wake the sleeper, who was evidently much disconcerted at having been caught napping, and started up with a great pretence of liveliness when she saw the Sister standing by her.

"This is against all rules, Nurse Mary, as you know very well," said the Sister; "it is a serious offence for a nurse to sleep when on duty, and I shall have to report you."

"I knew it was very wrong, Sister, and I'm quite shocked that I should have been so careless," replied the culprit. "But indeed you mustn't think as there's any harm done. It was only five minutes back as I was going about, and seeing as everyone was all right; and then I sat down and dropped off into a bit of a doze somehow. I wasn't reg'larly asleep – only dozing so light that I should have heard d'rectly if anyone made a sound."

"Don't make your fault worse by falsehood," said the Sister severely; "I found the woman over there," pointing to me, "in great want of something to drink; and she told me she had been thirsty for a long time, and unable to wake you when she tried. You must attend to your duty better than this. If I find you asleep again when I visit your ward, you must expect to be dismissed."

The Sister continued her rounds through the hospital to

see that everything was right; and as soon as she was gone the nurse came towards me. I regarded her approach with awe. I saw by her face that she did not feel particularly amiable towards the individual who had been the means – however innocent – of procuring her a wigging; and as a nurse has it in her power to make a patient very miserable if she chooses, I was naturally dismayed at having been so unlucky as to get into her black books. The desire which I felt at that moment to ingratiate myself with her, if possible, was quite degrading; and when she rebuked me sharply for having got part of one arm uncovered, and told me not to do so again, I promised obedience with the most servile meekness, though I was quite sure that there was no real harm whatever in what I had done. My bed-clothes were as tidy as need be; but she pretended to think they wanted straightening, and twitched them about in a vigorous and jerky manner which was not comfortable, and kept me alarmed all the time lest I should be hurt. When she had completed this unnecessary process, she left me alone, to my great relief, and nothing short of the extremest necessity would have induced me to recall her to my bed. I felt frightened, helpless, and in the power of a person who had taken a dislike to me; and the only comfort I had was to think that the Sister's protecting influence would perhaps save me from anything more serious than petty annoyances. But even petty annoyances are bad enough in all conscience when one is as sick, weak, and miserable as I was then.

CHAPTER XXVII

In Hospital

CERTAINLY nursing is very far superior, now-a-days, to what it was in the *régime* of the untrained Sairey Gamp confraternity; but while gladly recognising that fact, I am inclined to think that there is still some room for improvement. For one thing, I doubt whether any particular care is taken to impress upon nurses the important fact that no two human beings are exactly the same; and that people's characteristic peculiarities are never in greater need of being studied and humoured, than when pain and sickness have weakened the will and rendered the nerves unwontedly sensitive and irritable. If this were insisted upon as it might be in the training of nurses, I do not imagine it would be as common as it is to find them performing their duties mechanically, and apparently regarding patients as machines to be wound up, regulated, and treated according to fixed principles applying to all alike, instead of as living men and women, possessing widely-differing peculiarities of both mind and body. I think that one or two of my own experiences whilst at the hospital will show that there is some reason for this criticism.

The prolonged thirst from which I had suffered, and the exertion involved in my endeavour to relieve it, fatigued me greatly in my enfeebled condition. Then came the mental wear and tear of terror which I underwent during Nurse Mary's alarmingly vigorous bedclothes-straightening process; and thus, what with one thing and another, by the time she left me to myself again I felt completely worn out, and anxious for nothing so much as sleep. In vain, however, did I try to compose myself to slumber. I was feverish; I ached all over; and, turn which way I would, I could get no ease. Each new position that I tried seemed more uncomfortable than the last; and though the cradle in which my broken leg was fixed prevented me from moving far, yet within the narrow space to which I was thus restricted, I kept shifting my place, and twisting to and fro incessantly.

Of course this restlessness was by no means conducive to my welfare; and when the doctor visited me in the morning he pronounced me to be in a very exhausted state, and said I was to have nourishment and stimulants every two hours.

I cannot say that I took kindly to the idea of being stuffed like this; for I was so far from being hungry that my gorge rose at the mere thought of food. And when the nurse who had succeeded Nurse Mary in charge of the ward came up to me with a cup of broth in her hand, I had about the same amount of inclination for it that fair Rosamond may be supposed to have had for the potion presented to her by Queen Eleanor.

But I had fully made up my mind to get well as soon as possible, and had the sense to know that I certainly could not recover without eating, so I struggled to overcome the internal rising of which I was conscious. Perhaps, too, the broth would tempt my appetite, so that after I had got down a mouthful or so, I should find the aversion to food pass away, and be able to go on eating easily. And thus resolved to do my best to obey the doctor's orders, I took a sip out of the cup.

But the first taste was a shock to me. It was not in the least like what I expected, somehow, though I was not just then clear-headed enough to discover immediately what was wrong with it. I did not believe it was broth at all; at all events, if it was, it was the nastiest that I had ever tasted in my life. I could hardly swallow even the small quantity I had taken; and as for getting down any more of it – pah! The thing was impossible. My loathing for food became more violent than ever, and I pushed away the cup feebly, saying: "Take the nasty stuff away! I *can't* eat it; and it'll only make me sick to try."

"Nasty indeed!" replied the nurse; "why, what better would you have than beautiful chicking-broth like this? You can drink it well enough if you like; it's only your fancy as you can't."

"I don't think it beautiful at all," replied I; "indeed, indeed, it's nasty. Do pray let me alone; perhaps I shall be hungrier by and by."

"Rubbish!" she answered, again advancing the cup towards me; "it's the doctor's orders for you to be fed, and fed you shall be – even if I have to drench you. Come now; down with it!"

At this moment, when I was ruefully contemplating the broth and wondering if it would be anyhow possible for me to gulp it down, the Sister whom I had seen in the night came into the room. She was general superintendent of the nursing all through the hospital, and had a keen eye for anything amiss. My unhappy look at once attracted her attention, and she came to us and asked the nurse what she was giving me.

"Chicking broth, with a tablespoon of whisky in it, Sister," responded the woman; "that's what the doctor ordered for her. But she's making as much fuss as if it was – I don't know what, and declaring as it'll make her sick."

"I can quite understand your objecting to eat," said the Sister, addressing me gently; "people so often do when they're ill. But it's the beginning is the great difficulty with them, and after that they generally get on much better; I dare say you'll find it so if you try. Or is broth a thing to which you have any special dislike? And do you think you would fancy some other kind of food more?"

"No; I like broth well enough in general," answered I, "and I *have* tried to eat what the nurse brought me. But I couldn't, indeed – it is too nasty."

"Well, suppose I see if *I* can find anything the matter with it," she said, taking the cup from the nurse. "Why! Did you ask to have it cold?"

"No," replied I.

"Did the doctor say it was to be given cold?" she inquired, turning to the nurse.

"He didn't say nothing one way or other," answered the latter; "and as I had a jugful cold, ready by me, I just took and poured some into the cup to give as it was – not thinking as it mattered."

"Oh, but it does matter, very much," returned the Sister; "broth is far nicer hot than cold. Go and warm this, and then see if the patient doesn't find it easier to get down. And don't forget in future that broth should always be given hot, unless there are special orders to the contrary."

Now surely the woman might have known that of herself, if she had taken the trouble to think for a moment, and might have perceived that cold chicken broth, with whisky in it, was a thing that no ordinary human palate could be expected to relish. But no; the doctor had not specified it was to be hot; she had some cold to hand; the question of trying to make it palatable never entered her head; and therefore, though the warming would have been but very little trouble, she just brought it me as it was. In that condition I doubt whether I could possibly have eaten it; when warmed, however, I was able to get through the requisite portion – though even then not without considerable difficulty, in consequence of my aversion to food of any kind.

Thus a second time was the conviction forced upon me that the existence in the world of Sisters might perhaps not be so altogether devoid of utility as I had previously imagined.

I daresay the food did me good; but yet it did not procure me the rest for which I craved, and I had to endure hours more of miserable tossing about before my weary body at last hit upon the posture which would best accommodate its numerous aches and bruises. With a sigh of satisfaction I gave myself up to repose, intending not to stir hand or foot as long as I remained comfortable, lest, if I once lost the position which had been so hard to find, I might not again succeed in discovering it. Soon a delicious sense of drowsiness stole over me, and I was on the point of falling sound asleep, when I was aroused by the voice of a nurse, telling me it was time to feed again. If my repugnance to eating had made all the previous feeding-times during the day objectionable to me, it may be imagined that the present summons was doubly odious, coming at the very moment when I could not bear the idea of stirring so much as a hair's-breadth from where I lay, and would have given the world to be left in peace. Dismayed at the prospect of immediate movement, and loath to be parted from the long-sought rest which I had at length attained, I appealed for a reprieve – however brief. I was so *very* tired of being uncomfortable, I said. I had had such a weary tossing about all night and all day till now. And now that I had at last found some comfort, might not I stay as I was for just five minutes more?

But the nurse would not hear of such a thing. The doctor's orders, she said, were for me to have food every two hours. The last time had been at 1.25 – there it was marked on the slate by the bed – and now it was 3.25. Her business was to obey the doctor's orders exactly; and I must just take what she had brought me that instant, and make no more fuss about it.

So my appeal was disregarded, and I was, then and there, ruthlessly routed up to be fed. And as my nervous system was by no means robust enough at that moment to bear the shock of any abrupt disturbance, I immediately afterwards relapsed into the same state of miserable, feverish restlessness as before.

Now, though it seems unreasonable to blame anyone for strict obedience to orders, yet I think in a case like this the woman might well have departed from them so far as to grant the five minutes delay for which I pleaded. It would have softened the blow to have time to make up my mind gradually to the moving which I dreaded; and I think her own sense might have told her that

I was in a condition when rest was essential, and when everything unpleasant should be smoothed over to me as much as possible. But though she was not wilfully harsh or unkind, yet the advisability of making small concessions to an invalid's weakness – fancifulness, as *she* called it – never entered her head. All she thought of was that she was there to carry out the doctor's orders, and that provided they were obeyed to the letter, come what might, she would have nothing to reproach herself with. As for the idea of there being any special necessity for a nurse to be quick in reading, understanding, and making allowances for the fancies, infirmities, and idiosyncrasies of human nature, because she is professionally brought into constant contact with it when in its greatest need of sympathy – why, I do not suppose such a notion had ever occurred to her. But might it not have formed a part of her professional education?

I hope that my criticisms will not be misunderstood. If I venture to point out defects which seem to me remediable, it does not therefore follow that I fail to do justice to the enormous benefits which we derive from trained nurses. On the contrary, when I look back upon my sojourn at the hospital, I feel grateful for and astonished at the punctilious care and attention which was shown towards a mere friendless, helpless, unknown nobody such as I was, from whom no return could be expected. It may be that I have known nurses act hastily under provocation; that I think them apt to be hard, because too mechanical; and that I doubt whether they always bring their brains to bear as much as might be on the performance of their duty. But none the less do I believe that they are, as a body, a thoroughly conscientious, well-meaning, and valuable set of women; and that a nurse who behaves with deliberate cruelty, or wantonly neglects a patient, is hardly ever to be met with.

In speaking well, however, of the hospital attendants and the treatment I received from them, I must except Nurse Mary. She was a careless, good-for-nothing nurse, unfit for her post, constantly asleep on duty, bad tempered to the patients, and quite regardless of truth in what she said. I was unfortunate enough to be an especial object of her animosity, because she had been reprimanded and fined for her neglect of me and false excuses on the night when I had first become acquainted with her. As it had been on account of me that she had got into hot water, she took a dislike to me then and there, and took advantage of our relative positions to make me feel her displeasure. A nurse has plenty of opportunities for thwarting, bullying, and inflicting small miseries on a patient; and Nurse Mary always availed herself of these opportunities as freely as she dared. Whatever she had to do for me was sure to be done as roughly and disagreeably as possible, and I looked forward with dread to the periods when the ward I inhabited was under her charge.

Unluckily for me, it was on one of these occasions that it fell to my lot to have to take a dose of castor oil. Now, that is a physic to which I have always had an intense antipathy. The mere smell of it makes me feel qualmy, even at the best of times; and it stood to reason that I should dislike it ten times more when my stomach was in an unusually squeamish condition, so that I found it difficult to eat even food that I liked. Hence I looked forward to the impending dose with much trepidation, and reflected anxiously on the probability of my being unable to keep down the nauseous stuff, even when swallowed. It would evidently be a help to avoid having the nasty smell beforehand if possible, as I knew that would make me feel poorly to start with; so I asked Nurse Mary if she would mind pouring out the oil at some distance off, and not bringing it to my bedside till all ready to be taken.

She refused roughly, saying she had no time to be bothered with all kinds of fads and whims like that; and, instead of trying to spare me any preliminary unpleasantness, she measured out the dose quite close to my nose, so as to give me a full benefit of the odour. It seemed to me, too, that she was purposely slow in her proceedings, and kept the bottle uncorked for a most needless length of time – but that may possibly have only been my excited fancy.

The oil having been poured into a glass with water in it, I was sat up in bed, the glass was put into my hands, and I raised it towards my mouth. Being already qualmy from the effect of the smell, and very nervous lest I should be actually sick, I was altogether in an unsteady condition; and just before the glass had touched my lips, an involuntary convulsive shiver of disgust that came over me made me for the moment unable to control my muscles. My shaky hand lost its grasp of the glass, which toppled over, and spilled all the contents over me and the bed.

The nurse was as indignant at this catastrophe as if I had done it on purpose. She had not the least pity for the horrible plight I was in, nor did it seem to occur to her how improbable it was for any human being to bring him or herself into such a state willingly.

"Troublesome, mischievous, awkward, careless, stupid," were the kindest and least offensive words she uttered whilst preparing a fresh jorum of oil. As for me, I simply endured existence in silent misery as best I could whilst the second dose was being got ready. All I wanted was to take that, and get it over as quickly as possible, so that everything which the filthy oil had contaminated might be removed, and I might be washed, and made sweet, dry, and comfortable again.

When the draught was presented to me, I made a heroic effort, flung it down my throat, and returned the empty glass, murmuring faintly: "Oh please, *do* make haste to rid me of all this mess!" But what was my dismay to find that she had no intention of doing anything of the kind! Since I had chosen to spill the oil, she said, I might just stop in it and see how I liked it; and perhaps that would teach me not to play tricks of that kind again. What? fetch a clean nightdress and sheet, and a sponge to wipe my face and chest! Not she, indeed! She had plenty of other work to do without extras of that kind; and she had not time to stop worritting with me any longer – I had delayed her quite long enough, as it was. So saying, she coolly walked away, and left me helpless in a sort of castor-oil purgatory.

My misery may be imagined. The cold, clammy, wet linen chilled me; every movement risked bringing me in fresh contact with the loathsome stuff, which I could not touch without a shudder; and the surrounding air was impregnated with its abominable smell. I would have done anything to escape; and if my leg had not been fixed in the cradle, I believe I should have rolled out of bed on to the floor, and as far away as I could go from the hateful spot. But I was powerless to do that, or to lessen my wretchedness by any other means; for I was not strong enough even to pull off my nightdress unaided, nor yet to fold back the wet part of the sheet, and shove it away to the far end of the bed.

Nor was this all I had to suffer; for the smell made my qualminess increase every minute, and I foresaw with dismay that being sick would probably involve a repetition of the dose.

Oh, why could not I escape from this abominable odour? And could I anyhow manage to avoid the consequences with which it threatened me? I remembered having heard it said that sickness may sometimes be checked by a strong effort of will. Let me see if mine would help me in this emergency. I told myself resolutely that the unpleasant sensations which I felt were purely imaginary, and that I need not give way to them unless I chose. And then I tried to turn my mind to various agreeable and interesting subjects, such as Kitty; Mrs. Torwood's dogs; my plan for being revenged on my stepmother, and how I would complete it as soon as I was well again; anything under the sun to take my thoughts off from this beastly oil! But it was no use. The qualmy sensation forced itself to the front in spite of all I could do; I felt that the dreaded climax was a mere matter of time, and lay awaiting it in terror with my eyes shut. Suddenly I heard someone say: "What a smell of castor oil! Where does it come from?"

The speaker's nose naturally answered this question, and on opening my eyes I saw the good Sister approaching me. This sight gave me a ray of hope that I might still be saved, and she seemed to me to be a very guardian angel. Never would I have believed that the quaint dress which I had often laughed at and considered ugly, obtrusive, and absurd, could have appeared to my eyes so lovely and acceptable as it did at that moment!

She perceived at a glance that the case was urgent, and went to work to relieve me without an instant's delay. Instead of stopping to ask questions (which would have been a needless prolongation of my sufferings) as to how I came to be in such an oily plight, she immediately despatched the nurse to fetch clean things, and herself brought some strong aromatic vinegar and held it to my nose. This neutralised the smell of the oil, revived me, and enabled me to conquer the feeling of nausea. Her timely aid averted the catastrophe I had been dreading, and in a wonderfully short space I enjoyed the felicity of feeling myself purified, and restored to a dry, sweet, and comfortable condition. Not till this had been accomplished did she seem to think of anything else. But then she proceeded to inquire how I had come to be in the state in which she had found me, and to take the nurse to task for having left me so.

The delinquent tried to excuse herself by saying that she had been so exceedingly busy that she had had no choice about leaving me to go and attend to someone else. Besides that, she added spitefully, the accident had been all my own doing, for I had deliberately upset the glass out of mischief.

I was commencing an indignant denial of this falsehood when the Sister interrupted me. She said it was quite immaterial whether the glass had been overturned by accident or not, as there were *no* circumstances which could justify a nurse for letting a patient remain an instant longer than could be helped in such a state as I had been in – all in a mess, and in wet things that might cause a chill. The alleged press of business was no excuse either; for all the nurses knew perfectly well that they were to ask for assistance if they had too much to do, but were on no account to neglect a patient. She was extremely displeased at Nurse Mary's conduct, and proceeded to rebuke her sharply.

Considering the barbarity with which that nurse had just been behaving to me, it will not be wondered at that to hear her being scolded gave me a sensation of acute satisfaction.

But my gratification was speedily diminished as I recollected that she would probably object to me more than ever, now that I had again been the unlucky means of getting her into a scrape. I was filled with alarm at the idea. If she had bullied me hitherto, what was she likely to do in the future? And what chance had I of defending myself from her malice? I would confide my troubles to the Sister who had already befriended me so often, and ask her to take care of me, I thought. Only I must mind not to let the nurse suspect that I was complaining of her, or she would be still angrier than before with me. I would wait till her turn of duty was over, and some other nurse had taken her place.

After the next change of nurses, therefore, I watched anxiously for the Sister to appear in our ward. At last she arrived there, and I made signs to her to come to my bedside. Then, whispering in a very low voice, so that no one else should hear and report what I said to my enemy, I begged her to protect me from Nurse Mary, who hated me, and treated me so badly that I was afraid of her.

"In what way, and on what occasions, have you been treated badly?" asked the Sister.

It was a most natural question to ask, but it was one that I was puzzled to answer satisfactorily. Though perfectly convinced that I needed to be defended, yet when I began recalling to mind (in order to tell the Sister) the numerous trifling persecutions to which I had been subjected, I found it was by no means easy to discover any grievance that seemed important and tangible enough to take hold of and bring forward in support of my assertions, except the recent castor oil affair, and that she knew of already. I could not recollect anything else that seemed worth erecting into a formal accusation, so I only answered that I could not think of any particular case to mention just then, but that indeed what I had said was true, that the nurse was unkind to me always, and that I was afraid to see her come near me.

"Oh, if that is all," replied the Sister kindly, "I should hope your fears have no real foundation; probably you have taken into your head one of those prejudices that people are very apt to have when they are ill; you must try and get over it, instead of indulging it. But, in any case, you may be sure that I am looking after you, and will see that no one hurts you, so don't alarm yourself about it."

Though she spoke cheerfully and pleasantly, yet still I did not consider my complaint had met with a very encouraging reception; and I was desperately afraid that what I had said would be altogether forgotten, and I should be no better off than before. But she was a person who never turned a deaf ear to any cry for help; and I soon saw that my appeal had not passed unheeded, and that – whether she believed me to be mistaken or not – from that time forth her protecting wing overshadowed me with especial closeness (yet not so ostensibly as to make the fact generally conspicuous) when my enemy was in command of the ward. Not only did the Sister take to coming in and out with extra frequency at these times, but I could perceive also that I was then sure to receive a larger share of her attention than I did on other occasions. And as this kindly, unobtrusive, vigilance made it impossible for me to be made to suffer seriously without her discovering it, my peace of mind was gradually restored.

Thus, thanks to the restraining presence of the Sister, Nurse Mary could not make me as miserable as she would evidently have liked to do; but I know very well that I should have been sadly at her mercy if the Sister had *not* been there to look after me, for to appeal to the doctor would almost certainly have been worse than useless. I have known people rash enough to do that when they were dissatisfied with their nurses, and the result of their appeals was invariably the same. That is to say, the patient was pooh-poohed with more or less politeness, according to the disposition of the doctor; no attempt was made to investigate the truth of the complaint, and things went on exactly as before, except that the nurses certainly did not increase in amiability towards the individuals who had presumed to find fault with them.

I must say, I think it would be in the interests of the sick, if, in both private and public cases, the doctors would beware of the blind confidence which they, as a rule, are inclined to repose in nurses. My experience is, that if a patient complains of his nurse to the doctor for neglect, roughness, or any other fault, she is apt either to relate what took place so as make it appear that she could not possibly have acted otherwise than she did; or else to deny the charge absolutely; or else to say, with affected compassion, that the poor fellow sometimes wanders in his mind and does not know things rightly, so that it is useless to think of attending to all he says. And the doctor invariably accepts her version as the true one, and takes it for granted that she is all right, and there is no necessity for his interference.

That a doctor should trust much to a nurse is only natural, seeing that there are cases in illness where as much depends upon her as upon him – perhaps even more. But her importance does not make her infallible; and though it is all very well to have confidence in her, yet it is carrying confidence to excess to make it a rule *always* to think her word better than that of her patient. If a sick person's account of his symptoms differed materially from that given by the nurse, I suppose the doctor would hardly think it wise totally to ignore what had been told him by the former, and to act solely upon the information received from the latter. And ought not the same rule to apply to other statements also?

CHAPTER XXVIII

Sister Helena

MY PROGRESS towards restored health was but slow; and poor I – an individual who had always regarded with mortal aversion confinement and monotony in every shape was forced to undergo the tedium of a protracted illness and convalescence. Terribly weary did I get of the long days and nights as they dragged on without bringing anything to amuse me, and to enliven the dullness of existence. Other patients had friends and acquaintances who came to see them on visiting days, but I had not even that mild excitement to look forward to, for I was utterly solitary and unknown. Unluckily, too, the literary resources of the place were but limited. For though there was a so-called library yet its stock of books was lamentably small, and, as it seemed to me, uninteresting. And though odd numbers of old magazines and newspapers would drop in upon us at intervals, yet their appearance was nothing like as regular and frequent as I should have liked, or as I think it would have been if benevolently disposed people had realised what a boon it is to many hospital patients to know something of what goes on in the outside world from which they are excluded.

My mind, then, having but few distractions, was all the more ready to occupy itself with whatever person or thing happened to come prominently before it. And thus I found myself continually engaged in studying and thinking about the Sister, who, for the time being, filled a position of conspicuous importance in my life, as a sort of guardian angel in whom I felt a serene confidence that she would see I was never seriously wronged or ill-used in any way.

She was the first Sister with whom I had ever come in contact, and, by my acquaintance with her, the prejudice I had previously entertained against all sisters was speedily swept away. Sister Helena, as she was called, must, I think, have been between thirty and thirty-five years old, and was tall and graceful in figure. She had handsome features; a high broad forehead; a keen eye that seemed to notice everything within its range; a square chin, and a firm mouth; and no one who saw her could doubt that she possessed both power and intelligence above the average. Her face was pale, and her expression – except when she smiled – grave to the verge of austerity. But it was the gravity of thoughtfulness, not of gloom and sadness; and whatever tendency to austerity she may have had was reserved exclusively for herself. Most certainly it was never visible in her behaviour to the sick; for she always showed them the kindliest sympathy and tenderness, devoting herself to them absolutely, and treating them with a loving gentleness and tenderness that was enough to make one suppose they were her dearest friends.

As she was general superintendent of the hospital-nursing and arrangements for the relief of the sick, she had usually too much to do with looking after her subordinates and seeing that they did their duty, to be able to officiate in person as nurse. But she was thoroughly capable of doing so in case of need, and whenever circumstances happened to make it necessary for her to bandage, sew up, or dress wounds, or perform any other services of the kind for patients, she was sure to do whatever was required as gently, skilfully, and efficiently as anyone – or indeed more so.

One very marked distinction between her and the ordinary professional nurses was, that she was unmistakably a lady by birth, and possessed naturally – without effort or thinking about it – the subtle charm of refinement. I – who had fondly imagined myself to be superior to the influence of any sentimental vanity of that kind – was astonished and disappointed to find how quickly I detected this in her, and how attractive it was to me. I could not disguise from myself that I was highly susceptible to the charm to which I had believed I was indifferent; and that it was infinitely preferable to me to have to do with the person in whom I instinctively recognised an equal than with those who were inferiors. Refined associates were more congenial to me than vulgar ones, in spite of all my knocking about; and even though provoked at my own folly, I sometimes could not repress a sigh to think that I had left my own rank of life in favour of a lower one.

Well; the more I observed and thought about Sister Helena, the more did I wonder what her previous history could have been. Here was a woman, evidently well born and bred, good-looking, below middle age, clever, amiable, sensible, capable, and in every way qualified to make her mark and be popular in society. Why on earth, then, should she be spending her existence in hard work amongst the painful sights and scenes of a hospital, instead of enjoying herself in the sphere to which she belonged naturally? For the fact that she *was* at the hospital I was profoundly thankful, because I was myself a gainer by it; but none the less was it an inexplicable mystery to me, and one which I was constantly endeavouring to find plausible theories to account for.

As, therefore, I was intensely curious about her, admired, liked, and was grateful to her, and through her could enjoy the, to me, pleasant feeling of association with a cultivated and refined lady, it followed naturally that I sought eagerly for opportunities of having to do with her, and never failed to profit by any excuse for making her occupy herself about me. The pleasure her company gave me was too evident to escape her quick observation, and when she perceived it her kindness of heart prompted her to gratify my wishes as far as might be; for she was one of those to whom nobody ever held out their hands in vain. Therefore, though her multifarious avocations made it impossible, as a rule, for her to bestow much individual attention on any particular person whose case was not so critical and special as to give it precedence over ordinary business, yet she would always – unless in a very great hurry – stop and say a kind word to me in passing through the ward; and sometimes, on the rare occasions when she had a few minutes to spare, she would even come in on purpose to chat with me. I do not know whether or not she had the same intuitive consciousness that I had of our both belonging to the same social order; but, at all events, there sprung up between us by degrees an intimacy beyond that which is ordinarily produced by the relations of nurse and patient.

As it was not in her nature to see any kind of suffering without trying to relieve it, she tried to hit upon some means of varying the unchanging sameness of life by which she perceived me to be oppressed. It was not possible to do much for me in this way whilst I was tied by the leg in bed, but when at last I was able to get up and crawl about a little with the help of sticks, she asked me if I thought I could get as far as her room, which was on the same floor as the ward, and only a short distance from it. On my replying in the affirmative, she filled me with delight by inviting me to go and have tea there with her that afternoon. Oh how impatiently I counted the minutes till tea-time came! And how welcome and refreshing was the change to her room from the dreary old ward of which I was so tired!

From that date our intimacy advanced much more rapidly than before; for, as she saw how I enjoyed the visit to her room, hardly a day passed on which I was not invited there at some time or other. It was not often that she was able to be with me all the time, for she was almost always called off elsewhere on business. But when this happened she did not expect me to go back to the ward unless I chose, and if I preferred – as I invariably did – to stay where I was, and amuse myself with books, work, or my own thoughts whilst awaiting her return, I was at liberty to do so. Indeed, if she had not been willing to trust me in her room without her, it would generally not have been worthwhile my going there at all; for the demands upon her time were perpetual, and she hardly ever had any leisure. It was Sister here and Sister there from morning till night; and, as far as I could see, she had not a single minute in the day which she could call her own, and reckon on as secure from interruption.

I have already said that one object which I had had for desiring to know her was that I wanted to learn her past history, wherein I believed must lie some mysterious reason which had caused her to adopt her present hard, untempting, self-denying life. But as our acquaintance progressed and I came to know her more and more, I perceived with surprise that there was no hidden mystery at all about the matter, and that instead of any thrilling romance or tragedy such as I had imagined, the reason for her life was simply the love of God, and desire to serve Him in the best way she could. That was the sole motive for every deed, word, and thought of hers – the one compass by which her course was steered.

The reason why this discovery amazed me as it did was, that I had never dreamt of its being possible for anyone with respectable mental abilities to take religion thus *au grand sérieux*. I cannot say I had ever troubled my head much about religion at all; but still I had a vague idea of it as a thing which people of weak intellect sometimes made a fuss about, but which the wiser part of the world treated as a mere unreal conventionality – a sort of outer garment which was assumed and respected solely out of deference to Mrs. Grundy.

It was startling to me, therefore, to meet with such a living contradiction of this idea as Sister Helena. She was no fool, as I knew, but very much the reverse; and in her management of the hospital she gave daily proofs of good sense, shrewdness, and sound judgment, which made it impossible to think she would be led away by visionary notions, or act lightly and without due consideration. Nor was she a person who ever bestowed a thought upon Mrs. Grundy, or who could be suspected of any taint of humbug and unreality in either word or deed. Yet to this sensible, intelligent, absolutely honest woman, religion was a fact of such vital importance as to be the mainspring of her life – the one thing to be put before everything else! So extraordinary did it seem to me, that I should certainly have refused to believe in the phenomenon at all if I had not beheld it with my own eyes.

It appeared evident to me that it must need a very powerful engine to be the motive force of such steady, self-sacrificing, practical goodness as hers, and I thought I should like to understand somewhat of the nature of that engine. With this object in view I directed constant questions towards the subject that interested me, and thus it came about that religion was the theme upon which we conversed more frequently than any other. I do not recapitulate our conversations, because I consider they would be out of place in a book of this kind; but this much

I will say, that they made a strong impression on me, and caused me to think of religion very differently from what I had done hitherto. She was the first person I had ever met whose deeds really harmonised with her professions, and all that she said had weight with me, because her life was an unmistakable proof that she honestly and fully did believe the things she professed to believe. I began to contemplate the possibility of there being a real meaning in the creeds and prayers which I had often heard and joined in when at church without attaching any sense at all to them. I began, too, to have an idea that perhaps church membership might be something more than a mere empty form, and that there might be some real advantage in belonging to that church of which I had been a member all my life as a matter of course, and without ever supposing it could make the slightest difference to me, one way or other. And, more than all, in proportion as I became inclined to believe in the truth and reality of religion, so also did the conviction grow upon me that I myself was not exactly altogether what I should be, and that it behoved me to set about reforming.

I really did want to amend what was amiss, and to become better than I was; but still I did not want to be *too* good. Such goodness as Sister Helena's, for instance, was, I knew, far beyond my powers; and besides that, my hearty admiration for it in her did not lead me to desire it for myself, because I was quite sure that even if it were possible for me to attain to such a pitch of self-denying excellence, I should not enjoy it, as I was a deal too fond of worldly comforts and joys ever to be happy without them.

Certainly it was very singular that there should be so wide a difference between one person's sense of duty and another's. When first this difference struck me, I was inclined to be somewhat uneasy at the comparatively diminutive proportions of my own virtue; but then there occurred to me a very comfortable and reassuring way of accounting for it. People's bodies were predisposed towards measles, whooping cough, and other illnesses in varying degrees, and had them lightly or severely according to the extent of that predisposition; and some people even never had these illnesses at all – being apparently endowed with some constitutional peculiarity which acted as an antidote to the poison of disease. And from this I argued that probably people's minds varied in a similar fashion in regard to virtue – some being more, and some less receptive of it. I supposed that a person could only be affected by religion and goodness according to the degree of his mental predisposition towards such things, and that some people could never be influenced by them at all. I thought this supposition a perfectly reasonable one, and highly satisfactory also. For in that case it was obviously absurd to expect much goodness from a person whose mind was so constituted as to be antagonistic to virtuous influences; and of course no one could be blamed for what was merely a natural defect.

I propounded my theory triumphantly to Sister Helena one day when she was insisting upon the necessity of some virtue or other which I thought ordinary mortals need not trouble themselves about. But she refused absolutely to agree with me; declared that goodness was equally attainable by all who chose; and laughed at the idea of people having a natural liability towards or against it, like they might have towards or against a fever.

"All very well for you to talk," answered I; "but I should like to know how else it's to be accounted for that some people should be so much better than others as to become sisters, monks, and nuns, and all that sort of thing. I'm sure it must need a very special and uncommon predisposition towards goodness to make anyone give up every mortal thing that can make them happy as they do!"

"Not at all," she replied quickly; "you'll find good and earnest people in the world, just as much as in convents. It's a question of vocation not of superior goodness. Some people have such a natural inclination for a conventual life that they are happier there than they would be in the world; and some people, on the other hand, are happier in the world. Each set seeks happiness in its own way. And for anyone to join a religious community without having a real vocation for it is a very great mistake, and not a good or desirable thing at all."

"Well, then," said I, "you believe that people are born monks and nuns, just as they are born poets, painters, musicians, or sculptors. *Nascitur non fit.* After all, I don't see that that's so very unlike my predisposition theory."

"Why, there's this great difference," she said smiling; "according to *you,* some people would have no chance of goodness at all; and *I* maintain, on the contrary, that everyone has an equal chance. Goodness certainly *manifests* itself differently in different individuals; but you can't argue from that that it *exists* in them in different degrees. Remember that it is no great hardship for a person who doesn't care for society to give it up; and that you mustn't judge the merit of an action by its effects, but by how much it costs the doer."

And then a knock at the door, and an urgent request for the Sister to go and see after something or other immediately, terminated our conversation abruptly as usual; and I remained alone, musing on the fresh proof I had just received of the erroneousness of my original ideas regarding Sisters. Never for an instant had I doubted that they enjoyed – whether legitimately or not – a profound sense of superiority to the general run of humanity; and now that my old prejudice against them was overcome, I had arrived at the conclusion that, as they really *were* immeasurably better than the rest of the world (judging by Sister Helena), they had a perfect right to pique themselves thereon. Yet, instead of that, Sister Helena had not only refused to acquiesce in my ascription of honour and glory to them, but had argued with evident sincerity to prove that there was no special merit whatever in being a Sister! If *I* had been one, I should not have thought anything of the sort, I knew very well.

As the spark latent in flint needs a blow to bring it out, so, I suppose, whatever capacity I possessed for faith and virtue must have lain dormant in me till quickened to life by Sister Helena. They are elements which cannot possibly begin to mix actively in anyone's existence without producing a commotion in that person's previous ways of going on, and so I soon found myself sorely troubled in mind respecting my uncompleted project for being revenged upon my step-mother. Up to the present time I had only disquieted her with threatening letters, and had not yet arrived at the finishing touch of making known her humble origin to her husband and her friends. That had necessarily been deferred by my being laid up in hospital; but I had not given it up for a moment, and had meant that the execution of my threats against her should be one of the first things I would do when I should be able to get about again. In my opinion she richly deserved punishment for the undutifulness to her mother, ingratitude to her step-father, absurd vanity, and bad behaviour in general, of which she had been guilty. And as my own personal enmity for her gave me an especial willingness to be the instrument whereby justice was to overtake her, I looked forward with extreme satisfaction to the completion of my scheme, and regarded it as a most righteous and proper proceeding.

All of a sudden, however, this pleasant prospect was

disturbed by my newly awakened conscience insisting on taking a very different view of the matter, and declaring that as forgiveness was a duty and revenge was wrong, therefore I ought to give up the intention that I was cherishing. I opposed this conviction, struggled, argued, and tried to evade the conclusion that was so distasteful to me. But it was no use; conscience was too strong, and stuck firmly to its point, till I was forced, at last, reluctantly to abandon my beloved scheme.

So far, therefore, virtue was victorious; but its power did not extend far enough to prevent my regretting bitterly that I had not fully accomplished my designs against Lady Trecastle before any new ideas had come to interfere. Since conscience declared positively that I ought to overcome the old grudge which I bore her, I should have to do so; but it would now be a hard matter to accomplish, whereas I was sure that I could have done it sweetly and with hardly any effort at all, if only I had had the satisfaction of feeling that my plan of revenge had been carried out fully. For forgiveness is a duty whose performance is marvellously facilitated by the knowledge that the offender has had to suffer in some way or other for his wrongdoing.

I was quite in earnest about desiring to be true to such light as I had arrived at, and therefore did not exactly wish to return to my previous unenlightened condition. Yet I sighed as it dawned upon my mind that these new ideas might involve new restraints, and that perhaps henceforth I should be less my own mistress than before.

It would be so much easier to take to religion if it did not seem likely to deprive me of freedom, thought I, ruefully.

CHAPTER XXIX

A Catastrophe

AT last I was pronounced fit to be discharged from the hospital, and on the morrow I was to depart. I was still far from strong enough to think of undertaking any employment involving hard work and exertion; and how to keep from starving when once more turned adrift to earn my own livelihood was a problem which I should have been puzzled to solve if left to myself. Sister Helena, however, had come to my aid, and procured me a light place as assistant to the owner of a small newspaper-shop, who, on account of advancing years, wanted extra help and was willing to engage me on her recommendation. Thus was added another to the many benefits for which I was already indebted to that excellent woman, whose life was one long series of acts of kindness done, without thought of return, for whoever was in need. No wonder that I had learnt to admire, love, trust, and look up to her as though she had belonged to some higher order of beings! For she was certainly immeasurably superior to any other of the human race with whom I had ever been acquainted.

My last day, then, in hospital had arrived. The desire to have a farewell talk with the Sister in peace and comfort had made me ask her if she could not manage that we should have a quiet half-hour together for once, without any of the tiresome interruptions by which our conversations were usually cut short. She had said it was impossible for her to promise such a thing certainly, as it must depend on what work had to be done; but that she would do her best to arrange matters as I wished, and if successful would come and fetch me to her room when she was at leisure. All day, therefore, did I hope for the expected summons, and was greatly disappointed as hour after hour passed without my seeing or hearing anything of her. At last, quite late in the evening, she entered the ward looking unusually fagged, and came and sat down by me.

"I've been so sorry not to be able to come for you as I'd hoped," she said kindly, "but you know business *must* have precedence of everything else, and I was kept so unexpectedly long with one case that all my arrangements were upset. It was a man who was brought in yesterday with a couple of slight scalp wounds that had to be sewn up, and who didn't seem to have much the matter with him. But twice to-day he got so odd that there was a doubt whether he was not going out of his mind; and I stayed with him to see whether he was or not. If he had been, and if he had become violent, it would have been an awkward job to manage him, for he's immensely powerful. I never saw anyone so extraordinarily sensitive to loud sounds and commotion of any kind as he seems to be. There was an unusually loud noise going on both times when his oddness came on, and as the noise diminished so did he calm down again. I'm sure he has a highly irritable nervous system, which is excited to an almost ungovernable pitch by any fuss, and can then only be pacified by perfect tranquillity."

"Is he all right now?" I asked.

"Yes, I hope so. The unfavourable symptoms didn't return, and the doctor thought him going on quite satisfactorily. But I stayed with the man a long time, because it was so important for him to be watched attentively whilst we were uncertain about his sanity, that I did not like to leave the responsibility to anyone else. Then, when I could trust him to a nurse alone, I had such an accumulation of work to get through that I've been hard at it ever since, and not had a moment to myself till now; so you see I had no choice about giving up the quiet talk with you that we had proposed having. I'm on my way back to him now, as I want to hear the nurse's account of him during my absence."

"Humph!" grunted I, feeling that I need not fear saying what I thought, now that I was on the verge of quitting the hospital; "you won't be much the wiser for that, if it's Nurse Mary that's looking after him. If you knew her as well as I do, and knew how sleepy she is, how constantly she neglects her business, and what a wonderful facility she has for inventing false excuses when she's blamed, you'd never believe a word she tells you."

"It wasn't her I left him with, but one of the others," replied the Sister. "To tell you the truth, I should not have trusted such a case as that in her hands alone. For though I don't think quite so badly of her as you do, yet still I am by no means satisfied with her. You are not the only patient who has, either directly or indirectly, intimated she is not what she should be; and I have myself noticed things tending to confirm these complaints."

"Why don't you get rid of her, then, when you yourself allow that you've no confidence in her?" asked I.

The Sister hesitated a moment, and then answered: "Had the matter rested solely with me, I believe I should very likely have done so. But when I told the authorities what I thought of her, the doctor took her part so strongly that nothing came of it. He declared that he saw no reason whatever to be dissatisfied with her; and that sick people were always so fanciful, exacting, and peevish, that it was ridiculous to take any notice of their imaginary grievances. And as he was quite positive of being right, whilst I spoke more from suspicion than actual knowledge of the woman's behaviour, he carried the day. Perhaps it's as well so after all. To dismiss her would very possibly have ruined her professional prospects; and I should never forgive myself if I thought I had been the means of inflicting so severe a penalty on anyone without sufficient cause."

"Oh Sister!" exclaimed I, abruptly; "is that the man you were talking of?"

In order to enable my readers to understand what ensued, I must delay my narrative for a moment to explain how we were all placed.

Sister Helena and I were sitting at a table about the middle of a very long room, having a door at each end, and beds ranged down both sides. In the bed nearest to us was a poor woman who had been badly burnt in an explosion; and by her side stood the nurse of the ward, employed in changing the dressings of the burns. I was the only patient who was still up and dressed; the rest were in bed, and one or two of them already asleep. They were all women who had been injured severely in some way or other; and as I, though well enough to be discharged from the hospital, was still extremely weak after my long illness, it will be seen that Sister Helena and the nurse were the only two able-bodied individuals in the ward.

The cause of the exclamation I had uttered was this. I – who was facing one of the doors towards which the Sister had her back – suddenly saw that door pushed partially open, and a man's head poked in as though for the purpose of reconnoitring. After a hasty survey the owner followed his head quickly into the room, closed the door cautiously behind him, executed a fantastic pirouette, advanced a yard or so in a kind of polka-step, came to a standstill by a chair near the door, and commenced bowing and smiling with extravagant gestures. On his shoulder he carried an implement used for breaking and piercing ice, which was rather like a hammer, with a sharp, triangular, steel spike at one end of the head. He was big, broad-shouldered, and muscular; his head was bound up in bandages; and he was clad in shirt, trousers, and socks. In consequence of having no shoes on, his movements were noiseless; and this noiselessness considerably enhanced the uncanny and startling effect produced by the sudden appearance amongst us of so strange a figure, demeaning itself in so eccentric a manner.

Sister Helena looked round at my exclamation, and a momentary expression of horror crossed her face, and showed me that my conjecture had been right, and that our visitor was the man of whom she had been speaking. But that one transient look of horror was the only sign of nervousness she gave, and she did not lose her self-possession and composure for an instant. "Yes," she answered me quietly, turning towards the nurse who, as I have said, was employed not far from us. "Nurse!" she said, softly. The woman looked up from her occupation and saw the intruder, whom she at once recognised as the patient whose sanity had been considered doubtful. His present appearance left very little doubt about the matter, and she was naturally filled with consternation at the sight of an armed madman like him in the midst of a lot of helpless women. Dropping the dressings she had in her hand, she started violently, and was about to break forth into exclamations, when the Sister checked her by continuing in the same low, steady voice: "Hush! Make no fuss or he'll get worse. Go for help. As long as you're in the ward, walk quietly, as if nothing was the matter; and as soon as you're outside, run as fast as you can. I'll stay here, and try to prevent his doing any harm till help comes."

"Indeed, 'tisn't safe for you to stay, Sister," whispered the frightened nurse; "he's raving mad by the looks of him, and goodness only knows what he mayn't do!"

"All the more reason someone should stay and take care of the sick," returned the other. "Off with you! Mind not to hurry till you're out of the ward; and then, the faster you go the better."

Judging by the nurse's appearance, I should say it was fortunate for her character for obedience that she was not told to remain in the ward instead of to leave it; for I am inclined to doubt whether any power on earth would have induced her voluntarily to stay in so unsafe a neighbourhood. As it was, however, her orders exactly corresponded to her inclinations, and she promptly set out towards the door opposite to that near which the man had taken up his position. He had left off bowing and smiling by this time, and was seated in the chair, leaning forward meditatively and scratching the floor with the point of his weapon, and apparently unconscious of the presence of anyone else.

"If he'll stay like that till help comes, we shall do," whispered the Sister to me. "I'm sure he's a man for whom quiet is *everything;* what I dread is any fuss or noise to irritate him. It's lucky all the patients are in bed, so that he doesn't see people moving about."

This was all very well; but then there was no *certainty* of his continuing to stay quiet. And supposing he were to become mischievous, what chance had any of us in the ward of defending ourselves against a powerful, armed madman? So strongly was this borne in upon me that I felt an ignominious desire to get up and follow the retreating nurse, and was only prevented from doing so by my affection for Sister Helena. For some inexplicable reason or other I did not like to go away and leave her in danger, even though I was perfectly aware that I was too feeble to have a chance of being of any assistance if the man *did* become violent. Besides that, I saw how anxious she was to keep everything as quiet as possible; and perceived also that as the departure of two people would necessarily create more disturbance than that of one, therefore my going away must certainly be contrary to her wishes. On no account would I cause her one atom of additional worry and annoyance; I could sit still, at least, though there was no other way in which I could help her. So, notwithstanding my state of inward trepidation, I stayed where I was, and hoped that the nurse might be fortunate in meeting with succour speedily.

Unluckily I was not the only person on whom the preservation of tranquillity in the ward depended. The other patients, having heard nothing of the possibility of the presence of a lunatic in the building, had at first had no suspicion of the real state of affairs when they beheld the stranger's entrance. Still, they were uneasy, because what was taking place was evidently altogether unusual; and what is out of the common is, for that reason alone, presumed to be alarming by the majority of mankind. And they found confirmation for their apprehensions in the ominous haste with which the nurse went out of the ward; for, in spite of the caution she had received, she made her exit in a manner that was decidedly suggestive of flight.

From one bed after another issued whimperings, timid cries, or eager demands to know what was the matter; and the murmurs and outcries were rising swiftly to an uproar when they were repressed by the Sister. Speaking loud enough to be heard by all, she said that she would take care of every one there, but that she insisted on strict silence. That sufficed to quell the gathering storm; for there was not a soul in the place but had confidence in Sister Helena.

The noise made, however, had already taken effect on the maniac, and aroused him from his previous meditative condition. Springing up and flourishing the ice-hammer in the air wildly, he mounted upon the seat of the chair in which he had been sitting, and began to speak.

Sister Helena had been hitherto standing quiet in pursuance of her policy of keeping everything as absolutely still as possible. But on seeing his increased excitement, she began to advance gently towards him – moving slowly and apparently carelessly, but getting steadily nearer to him. Forgetting my uselessness and my fear of the man, I rose instinctively to accompany her when she set out; but she motioned me back, saying quickly:

"No; stay quiet. It's *my* business to protect the patients – not *yours*." All this takes time to write down; but in actual fact it occupied very few seconds, and it was still too soon to look for succour to arrive, unless the nurse's search for it should have been unexpectedly fortunate.

The idea which had seized the madman appeared to be, that he was in the middle of delivering a lecture on anatomy or some subject of that kind; and he seemed most intent upon the theme which he imagined himself to be pursuing, as he shouted out:

"And now, ladies and gents, I come to that wonderful horgin – the brain. Wait one moment, whilst I get one to show you; for hillustrations is hindispensible to the lecterer!"

With these words, he jumped off the chair, brandishing his weapon, and approached the nearest bed, wherein lay a woman whose leg and ribs had been broken, and whose injured limb was fixed in a cradle. She – perceiving that he had sinister designs upon her – began to scream dismally, and to make unavailing efforts to extricate herself from the bed and try to escape. Her screams were echoed by many of the other patients, who, convinced they were all going to be murdered, and filled with dismay on their own account as well as hers, either forgot or ignored the command which had been given for silence. Sister Helena, rushing forward to the rescue, reached the bedside just in time to interpose herself between the shrieking, struggling, fear-distraught woman calling piteously for help, and the man who was on the point of attacking her.

"Get out of the way there!" exclaimed he fiercely to the Sister, "or I'll take your brain instead. I'm bound to have one for my lecter!"

"Oh no!" she replied calmly; "the lecture is put off till tomorrow, so you won't want a brain till then."

The tranquillity of her looks and manner seemed to produce an impression on him; for he lowered his weapon, and looked perplexed, and as if doubting whether to believe her or not. If only the other inmates of the ward had obeyed her instructions and kept quiet, I think that even then she would have been able to restrain him. But the clamour they made served to excite him afresh and add fuel to his frenzy.

"Nonsense!" he shouted; "I'm wanted to go hon with the lecter at once. Don't you hear 'em calling me back? If you hinder me, I'll kill you!"

Pushing her aside so roughly that she staggered and nearly fell, he returned to his original victim, whom he caught hold of with one hand, while with the other he raised the hammer to strike. The blow was about to fall when it was arrested by Sister Helena, who recovered her equilibrium in time to spring back and seize his uplifted arm. Shaking her off as if she had been a feather, he turned upon her with a savage cry, and raised his weapon once more. In another moment it descended, and was buried with all his force in the centre of her forehead. She sunk to the ground with one shuddering groan at the very instant that the nearest door was burst open, and two or three men rushed in. Flinging themselves upon the maniac before he had well realised their presence, they succeeded – after a short furious struggle – in overpowering him and carrying him off. But they were too late, alas, to save the life of the best and noblest human being I have ever known; for the sharp spike of the ice-hammer had penetrated to her brain, and killed her instantaneously. And so ended the life of one who died as she had lived, that is to say, devoting herself voluntarily and unreservedly to the good of others. Characteristic of her, also, was the manner of disposal of her body, which was burnt in a crematorium, in accordance with her own frequently expressed wishes on the subject. For it was horrible to her to think that her material part might possibly, after death, be the means of bringing death and sorrow to the fellow-creatures whom she loved so well, by poisoning the air they breathed or the water they drank; and, therefore, she had always been a steady up-holder of cremation.

When the history of the catastrophe which had caused her untimely end was investigated, it came out that the person in charge of the man when he made his escape had been Nurse Mary after all, and that what had happened was owing to her negligence. The way of it was this: The nurse with whom he had been left, being taken ill suddenly, and thinking that an hour's quiet would put her right again, had had recourse to one of her fellows to replace her whilst she went to lie down, and that other individual had happened to be Nurse Mary. Before going away the nurse who was ill had not neglected to caution her substitute of the special reason that existed for watching the patient carefully, and Nurse Mary had assured her she might be quite easy on that score – which assurance, however, had in no wise prevented her who gave it from acting in her usual manner, and going to sleep when so inclined. Thus, when the man's insanity returned, there was no one to hinder his roaming off wherever the fancy took him. And this was how he came to arrive at our ward, armed with the ice-hammer, which he had happened to see and pick up on the way.

Had Nurse Mary had her deserts and been dismissed from the hospital long before, Sister Helena's life would not have been cut short by the madman. But she was sacrificed, in my opinion, partly to the nurse's inefficiency, and partly to the folly of the doctor, who had refused to believe it possible for patients to have any real cause of complaint against a nurse, and had not hesitated to condemn their assertions as unfounded without inquiry, and had therefore opposed the dismissal of the nurse they had complained of.

Brief as was my acquaintance with Sister Helena, it sufficed to make an indelible impression on my life; and it is owing to her influence, and to the seed she sowed, that I am no longer the unprincipled, heathen, scampish individual that I was before I knew her – a woman whose life was more in harmony with the Saviour's precept than that of anyone else whom I have ever known, "A new commandment I give unto you, That ye love one another."

CHAPTER XXX

A Change of Fortune

ON leaving the hospital I straightway entered the situation as assistant newspaper-seller which Sister Helena had procured for me. I did not contemplate staying there long, because, as the work was light, the pay was proportionately small; so as soon as my health should be thoroughly re-established, I meant to give up vending papers, and look out for some more remunerative employment; providing always that it was one which I could obtain honestly, for I was quite determined not to have recourse to any more false testimonials in future. But an undreamt of surprise was in store for me, and all my schemes were destined to be completely altered before I had been many weeks at my new post.

When, as sometimes happened, business was slack, I had nothing to do but to wait idly for customers to appear; and on these occasions I usually beguiled the time by studying some of the papers which composed our stock in trade. One day whilst thus engaged I was astonished to come across an advertisement commencing thus: "Gilbertina, daughter of the late Sir Anthony Trecastle of Castle Manor—" Having read so far, I put down the paper. The *late* Sir Anthony! Then my father must have died whilst I was in the hospital, for I had heard of him as alive and well shortly before that. He and I had never cared for one another, but notwithstanding this mutual indifference, it gave me a shock to learn thus suddenly that he was dead. So many thoughts and recollections of old days rushed into my mind, that it was some little time before I remembered that I had not yet finished reading the advertisement, and that as it began with my name, I had probably better see what it was all about.

This was how the whole ran: "Gilbertina, daughter of the late Sir Anthony Trecastle of Castle Manor, is requested to communicate with Messrs. Fox and Snail, Lincoln's Inn Fields, from whom she will hear of something greatly to her advantage."

What could Messrs. Fox and Snail, who had been, as I knew, my father's solicitors, have to tell me, I wondered? And should I answer this advertisement of theirs or not? If I did, I must evidently surrender the "incog." which I had hitherto preserved so successfully, and in that case I saw that I could not reckon certainly on being able to resume it again. Therefore the question which I put before myself to be decided upon was this: Am I inclined to take a step which may involve my leaving the independent career on which I am launched, and going back to my original station of life?

Well! I had by this time discovered that people who were by birth and education my equals were, as a rule, more congenial associates to me than my inferiors; I knew, too, that I had an innate and ineradicable prejudice in favour of the name of Trecastle, which would make it pleasant to me once more to call myself by it openly; for even though I had voluntarily discarded it, yet I had always felt a secret pride in thinking that it was mine, and that I had the right to bear it if I chose. Besides this, my experiences had taught me to appreciate better than formerly the comfort of having my bread and butter found for me, instead of being obliged to find it for myself, and I had learnt that there are sometimes drawbacks attendant upon earning one's own livelihood, notwithstanding the halo of adventure and enterprise surrounding that process, which constituted its principal attraction in my eyes. Furthermore, Messrs. Fox and Snail promised to tell me of what would be greatly to my advantage, and it is not in human nature to feel averse to hearing of anything that answers to that description, or to learn that such information is to be had, without being curious to know exactly what it may be. Altogether, therefore, there was clearly a good deal to be said in favour of my complying with the request in the advertisement, and consenting to become Gilbertina Trecastle once more.

But then, on the other hand, it seemed to me that however desirable this course might be in some ways, its advantages would be more than counterbalanced if it involved anything derogatory to my dignity. Upon no account whatever would I condescend to take any step which could be construed into a confession of failure and defeat, or be considered equivalent to taking cap in hand, and suing humbly for reinstatement. No, indeed – I had supported myself by my own exertions ever since I had left home, and saw no reason to doubt my being able to continue to do so. Therefore I had neither failed nor been defeated, and it was not likely that I was going to do anything to give rise to a contrary supposition.

After careful consideration of the advertisement, however, I came to the conclusion that there was nothing to compromise dignity in responding to such an invitation as it contained, and that I could do so without any fear of injuring my self-respect, or appearing to humiliate myself either in my own eyes, or in those of other people. And, my pride being thus satisfied, I went next day to the office in Lincolns Inn Fields, announced who I was, and inquired what Messrs. Fox and Snail had to tell me.

The information I received in reply was this. Before

my father left England, immediately after my mother's death, he made a will and deposited it with his solicitors. He seems to have thought of altering it after his second marriage, for he observed to them casually once, that he should not wonder if he were to make a fresh will some day or other when he had not anything else to do, and happened to be in the humour for it. But whatever his intentions on the subject may have been, that day was still to come when he died suddenly. The only will he left was the one already mentioned, and as in that he bequeathed everything he had to me, it was now only necessary that I should prove my identity in order to enter into possession of my inheritance without further obstacle. I had but little difficulty in establishing satisfactorily that I really was Gilbertina Trecastle, and as soon as that had been done, my fortunes changed for the better as suddenly as though a benevolent magician had waved his wand over them. Instead of being an ill-paid shop assistant at the beck and call of an employer, I found myself raised all at once to a position of ease and independence, with ample means, and no one to dictate to or interfere with me. And this latter condition was, as may be imagined, decidedly preferable to the former one.

Considering the manner of my departure from home, and the antipathy that had always existed between my step-mother and me, I certainly anticipated that she would now disapprove of me more strongly than ever, and avoid having to do with me as much as possible. But it seemed that the transformation of my circumstances had worked an equally marvellous transformation in her opinion of me; for the tone she adopted towards me was totally different from what it had been in the days of my insignificance, when I could be snubbed and bullied to any extent with impunity. Then she had been all verjuice, gall, and vinegar: now she was all honey, oil, and butter.

Then she had pronounced me ignorant, stupid, evil-disposed, tiresome, all that was objectionable, and utterly unfit to be admitted into society: now she sang my praises unweariedly whenever she had an opportunity, and declared me to be clever, amusing, witty, agreeable, and in every way charming and delightful. How she can have thought it likely for anyone of ordinary intelligence to be taken in by such palpable and unblushing humbug, I cannot imagine. Certainly the chief effect it had upon me was to make me feel more disgusted with her than ever, and wonder whether there was *any* limit to her capacity for toadying and cringing when she thought it suited her game to do so.

Of course I knew very well that she would not be thus anxious to curry favour with me for nothing; and that there was sure to be some secret motive for all the lying compliments and fulsome flattery with which she sought to impress me favourably, and to make me forget her former conduct. Very soon this motive became apparent; for the hints she gave showed plainly that, as she found Castle Manor an extremely comfortable abode, she did not at all want to leave it, and was in hopes of being able to establish herself there permanently.

I really must not be offended at her frankness, she said; but I had such a place in her affection and esteem, and she was so anxious for my welfare, that she could not resist giving me a word of advice, even at the risk of being thought interfering. In her opinion I was too young and inexperienced to live alone, and I should find the management of property a great tie and worry. She did hope, therefore, that I would get some older person to live with me, whom I could regard as a friend; who would set me free to amuse myself by relieving me of business cares when I liked; and who would be always at hand to be consulted in case of need. There would certainly be plenty of candidates for the post of companion to an individual so attractive and popular as I was, to associate with whom would be a constant pleasure and privilege; so I might reckon on a wide field to choose from, as soon as I should make known what I wanted. Till then, was there any way in which *she* could be useful? Would I not like her to stay for a while and help me to settle down comfortably? I had only to say the word, and she would be most happy to fall in with any arrangement of the kind that I might propose.

I, however, had not the slightest wish to have her as an inmate of my house on any terms at all. To forgive her was one thing; to live with her was another. Having learnt that it was a duty to forgive her, I had made up my mind to do so, and had therefore renounced all intention of revealing her early history and plebeian connections, or making any other attempt to pay her off for past injuries. But beyond that point, it seemed to me I was not bound to go; and I saw no kind of necessity for inviting her to live with me. She could not be in want of money, as she still possessed whatever she had had when she married my father. And if she disliked solitude, she could go and domicile herself with one of her own daughters – both of whom had got married during my absence from home. Evidently, therefore, there was no possible reason for me to think that I ought to inflict her company upon myself; and I might, with a clear conscience, turn a deaf ear to her overtures. So, instead of responding as she hoped, I took the liberty of giving her plainly to understand that the sooner she cleared out of Castle Manor the better, as I was in a hurry to occupy my house, and only waited for her departure in order to do so.

I really did try hard not to do anything needlessly harsh by her. But she would *not* go till I put my foot down firmly and unmistakably; and it was scarcely to be expected that I should, of my own free will and without any feeling of obligation in the matter, ever choose to live in the same house with her again. So I do not know that I could well have acted otherwise than I did.

Finding that I stuck firmly to my point, she took herself off at last; whereupon I went straight home, and have lived there the greater part of the time since – endeavouring to the best of my ability to perform the duties of my new position as a lady squire. What with looking after the interests – both physical and moral – of my tenants and poorer neighbours, and managing my house and estate, I have plenty of occupation to keep my brain active and to interest me; and, consequently, I have taken to this quiet country existence much more kindly than I should have imagined possible in the days when I had not become acquainted, by personal experience, with the feelings of a landowner. But that does not prevent me from contemplating another foreign trip before long; for my natural spirit of restlessness and adventure is too vigorous to rest satisfied without an occasional indulgence.

My present age is just twenty-four; but I often find it hard to realise that I am not a great deal older than that, when I come in contact with other young ladies of the same age. I seem to have knocked about the world and seen so much more of it than they have, as a rule, that I can hardly fancy it possible for the length of their lives and mine to be identical – unless they have wasted their opportunities sadly!

As Kitty Clement has played a somewhat prominent part in these pages, it may be well that I should tell all I know of her career up to this time. Since my restoration I have seen her several times at parties in London, and have, on these occasions, studied her only from a distance; because, as I am not anxious to be recognised as her former maid, Jill, I do not intend to claim kindred, renew the old acquaintance begun at Lugano, or do anything else that would direct her attention to me. But the strange charm which she always had for me is not yet wholly dead; and I still cannot help observing her course with an interest which I do not feel in that of anyone else. Her great object evidently is, to make her husband a conspicuous figure in the political world. She has persuaded the Premier to appoint him to some government office of minor importance; receives at her parties hosts of members of parliament, fashionables, and lions, once a week regularly; and does all she can to increase the influence and popularity of his name in every way possible. If he had anything like her ability, strength, and wits, and were as much above the common run of men as she is above that of women, her help would certainly make him Prime Minister before long. But, unluckily for her schemes, his talents are in no respect above the average; and though he discharges the duties of his office in a most painstaking and praiseworthy manner, yet devotion to work alone will never enable a man to rank as a great leader. Even, however, if her ambition should not be fully gratified, she may at all events congratulate herself on being an extremely great lady, and enjoying a position that many women would deem the acme of felicity. She interchanges dinners with royalties; her parties are thronged; and as I frequently see her goings and comings chronicled in the newspapers, I imagine that she has attained sufficient celebrity for the general public to wish to be informed of her movements. And what more than that does the heart of an ordinary woman desire?

She has presented her husband with an heir to the title, and other children also; she is spoken of as an exemplary wife and mother; no breath of slander has ever touched her; and she is – to all appearance – as perfectly contented with her lot as she certainly has cause to be. As for the feeling she once had for Captain Norroy, I have no doubt it has been crushed to nothing, and that when he and his wife are amongst her guests, she behaves to them exactly as she does to everyone else – that is to say, with a stately graciousness and *aplomb* which seem as though beyond the power of human beings or events to ruffle.

Yet the expression of her face strikes me as being strangely hard and cold for a person so admired and popular as she is, and who is so successful in making herself generally agreeable. It is not the look of a woman who has all she wants, but of one who has incased herself in impervious armour, which she never lays aside, and which no soft emotion can penetrate either from within or from without. And notwithstanding all her prosperity and appearance of contentment, I cannot help doubting whether she is really and in her secret soul happy. Does ambition fill and satisfy her life entirely? Or is there room for any lurking regret for the dream of love that came to her once – the romance that might have been, which is now buried far out of sight, and can never come to life again?

And sometimes, too, I wonder, whether her nature was always as stony as it is now (for even to her husband and children she is rather kind than loving), whether her softness towards Captain Norroy was only the exception that proved the rule, and whether she ever has felt or could feel genuine, warm affection for other people. She seems incapable of tenderness now; but I am not sure whether before her marriage she may not have had a capacity for loving which she has now lost – perhaps killed deliberately for fear of its proving troublesome to her. And if so, and if in those days she and I had been thrown together (as might very likely have happened, had it not been for my step-mother) as equals instead of as mistress and maid, should we have become friends, I wonder? Who can say! Now, as always, she is an enigma hard to read.

Welsh Women's Classics

Series Editor: *Jane Aaron*

Bringing back into print neglected and virtually forgotten literary texts by Welsh women from the past, for a new generation of readers.

"*[The Honno Classics series is] possibly the Press' most important achievement, helping to combat the absence of women's literature in the Welsh canon.*" (*Mslexia*)

Titles published in this series:

Clasuron Honno

Honno also publish an equivalent series, *Clasuron Honno*, in Welsh.

Formerly known as the *Honno Classics* Series
Published with the support of the Welsh Books Council

ABOUT HONNO

Honno Welsh Women's Press was set up in 1986 by a group of women who felt strongly that women in Wales needed wider opportunities to see their writing in print and to become involved in the publishing process. Our aim is to develop the writing talents of women in Wales, give them new and exciting opportunities to see their work published and often to give them their first 'break' as a writer.

Honno is registered as a community co-operative. Any profit that Honno makes is invested in the publishing programme. Women from Wales and around the world have expressed their support for Honno. Each supporter has a vote at the Annual General Meeting.

For more information and to buy our publications, please write to Honno at the address below, or visit our website:

www.honno.co.uk

Honno
Unit 14, Creative Units
Aberystwyth Arts Centre
Aberystwyth
Ceredigion
SY23 3GL

Honno Friends
We are very grateful for the support of the Honno Friends: Gwyneth Tyson Roberts, Jenny Sabine, Beryl Thomas.

For more information on how you can become a Honno Friend, see: http://www.honno.co.uk/friends.php